**Praise for *New York Times* bestselling author
RaeAnne Thayne**

"RaeAnne Thayne is quickly becoming one of
my favorite authors…. Once you start reading, you
aren't going to be able to stop."

—*Fresh Fiction*

"Thayne is a master at creating richly dimensional
and kind characters from different generations who
find themselves facing difficult challenges."

—*Booklist* on *The Path to Sunshine Cove*

"Thayne knows how to write the perfect romance."

—*Frolic*

**Praise for *USA TODAY* bestselling author
Michelle Major**

"Striking the perfect balance of romance, heat,
and drama, this optimistic love story is a sweet
start to a promising series, perfect for fans of
Debbie Macomber."

—*Publishers Weekly*, starred review,
on *The Magnolia Sisters*

"Major's characters and small-town romance
worldbuilding are unique, engaging, and emotionally
compelling… A dynamic start to a series with a
refreshingly original premise."

—*Kirkus Reviews*
on *The Magnolia Sisters*

RaeAnne Thayne finds inspiration in the beautiful northern Utah mountains, where the *New York Times* and *USA TODAY* bestselling author lives with her husband and three children. Her books have won numerous honors, including RITA® Award nominations from Romance Writers of America and a Career Achievement Award from *RT Book Reviews*. RaeAnne loves to hear from readers and can be contacted through her website, www.raeannethayne.com.

Michelle Major grew up in Ohio but dreamed of living in the mountains. Soon after graduating with a degree in journalism, she pointed her car west and settled in Colorado. Her life and house are filled with one great husband, two beautiful kids, a few furry pets and several well-behaved reptiles. She's grateful to have found her passion writing stories with happy endings. Michelle loves to hear from her readers at www.michellemajor.com.

New York Times **Bestselling Author**

RaeAnne
THAYNE

DANCING IN THE
MOONLIGHT

**HARLEQUIN
BESTSELLING
AUTHOR
COLLECTION**

HARLEQUIN®
BESTSELLING
AUTHOR
COLLECTION

Recycling programs
for this product may
not exist in your area.

ISBN-13: 978-1-335-40626-2

Dancing in the Moonlight
First published in 2006. This edition published in 2022.
Copyright © 2006 by RaeAnne Thayne

Always the Best Man
First published in 2016. This edition published in 2022.
Copyright © 2016 by Michelle Major

This edition published by arrangement with Harlequin Books S.A.

For questions and comments about the quality of this book, please contact
us at CustomerService@Harlequin.com.

Harlequin Enterprises ULC
22 Adelaide St. West, 41st Floor
Toronto, Ontario M5H 4E3, Canada
www.Harlequin.com

Printed and bound in Barcelona, Spain by CPI Black Print

CONTENTS

Also by RaeAnne Thayne

HQN

The Cliff House
The Sea Glass Cottage
Christmas at Holiday House
The Path to Sunshine Cove
Sleigh Bells Ring

Harlequin Special Edition

The Cowboys of Cold Creek

Starstruck
Light the Stars
Dancing in the Moonlight
Dalton's Undoing
The Cowboy's Christmas Miracle
A Cold Creek Homecoming
A Cold Creek Holiday
A Cold Creek Secret
A Cold Creek Baby
Christmas in Cold Creek
A Cold Creek Reunion
A Cold Creek Noel
A Cold Creek Christmas Surprise
The Christmas Ranch
A Cold Creek Christmas Story
The Holiday Gift
The Rancher's Christmas Song

Visit her Author Profile page at Harlequin.com,
or raeannethayne.com, for more titles!

DANCING IN THE MOONLIGHT

RaeAnne Thayne

To all men and women who have made sacrifices
for freedom. You have my deepest gratitude.

Chapter 1

For a doctor dedicated to healing the human body, he certainly knew how to punish his own. Jake Dalton rotated his shoulders and tried to ignore the aches and pains of the adrenaline crash that always hit him once the thrill of delivering a baby passed.

He had been running at full speed for twenty-two hours straight. As he drove the last few miles toward home at 2:00 a.m., he was grimly aware that he had a very narrow window of about four hours to try to sleep, if he wanted to drive back to the hospital in Idaho Falls to check on his brand-new patient and the newborn baby girl's mother and make it back here to Pine Gulch before his clinic opened.

The joys of being a rural doctor. He sometimes felt as if he spent more time behind the wheel of his Durango on the forty-minute drive between his hometown and the nearest hospital than he did with patients.

He'd driven this road so many times in the past two

years since finishing his internship and opening his own practice, he figured his SUV probably knew the way without him. It didn't make for very exciting driving. To keep himself awake, he drove with the window cracked and the Red Hot Chili Peppers blaring at full blast.

Cool, moist air washed in as he reached the outskirts of town, and his headlights gleamed off wet asphalt. The rain had stopped sometime before but the air still smelled sweet, fresh, alive with that seductive scent of springtime in the Rockies.

It was his favorite kind of night, a night best suited to sitting by the woodstove with a good book and Miles Davis on the stereo. Or better yet, curled up between silk sheets with a soft, warm woman while the rain hissed and seethed against the window.

Now *there* was a particular pleasure he'd been too damn long without. He sighed, driving past the half-dozen darkened shops that comprised the town's bustling downtown.

The crazy life that came from being the only doctor in a thirty-mile radius didn't leave him much time for a social life. Most of the time he didn't let it bother him, but sometimes the solitude of his life struck him with depressing force.

No, not solitude. He was around people all day long, from his patients to his nurses to his office staff.

But at the end of the day, he returned alone to the empty three-bedroom log home he'd bought when he'd moved back to Pine Gulch and taken over the family medicine clinic from Doc Whitaker.

On nights like this he wondered what it would be like to have someone to welcome him home, someone sweet and soft and loving. It was a tantalizing thought, a bittersweet one, but he refused to dwell on it for long.

He had no right to complain. How many men had the chance to live their dreams? Being a family physician in his hometown had been his aspiration forever, from those days he'd worked the ranch beside his father and brothers when he was a kid.

Besides, after helping Jenny Cochran through sixteen hours of back labor, even if he had a woman in his life, right now he wouldn't be good for anything but a PB and J sandwich and the few hours of sleep he could snatch before he would have to climb out of his bed before daybreak and make this drive to Idaho Falls again.

He was only a quarter mile from that elusive warm bed when he spotted emergency flashers from a disabled vehicle lighting up the night ahead. He swore under his breath, tempted for half a second to drive on past.

Even as the completely selfish urge whispered through his brain, he hit the brakes of his Durango and pulled off the road, his tires spitting mud and gravel on the narrow shoulder.

He had to stop. This was Pine Gulch and people just didn't look the other way when someone was in trouble. Besides, this was a quiet ranch road in a box canyon that dead-ended six miles further on—at the gates of the Cold Creek Land & Cattle Company, his family's ranch.

The only reason for someone to be on this road was if they'd taken a wrong turn somewhere or they were heading to one of the eight or nine houses and ranchettes between his place at the mouth of the canyon and the Cold Creek.

Since he knew every single person who lived in those houses, he couldn't drive on past one of his neighbors who might be having trouble.

The little silver Subaru didn't look familiar. Arizona plates, he noted as he pulled in behind it.

His headlights illuminated why the car was pulled over on the side of the road, at any rate. The rear passenger-side tire was flat as a pancake and he could make out someone—a woman, he thought—trying to work a jack in the damp night while holding a flashlight in her mouth.

He bade a fond farewell to the dream he had so briefly entertained of sinking into his warm bed anytime soon. No way could he leave a woman in distress alone on a quiet ranch road.

Anyway, it was only a flat tire. He could have it changed and send the lost tourist on her way in ten, fifteen minutes and be in that elusive bed ten minutes after that.

He climbed out and was grateful for his jacket when the wind whistled down the canyon, rattling his car door. Here on the backside of the Tetons, April could still sink through the skin like a thousand needles.

"Hey, there," he called as he approached. "Need a hand?"

The woman shaded her eyes, probably unable to see who was approaching in the glare from his headlights.

"I'm almost done," she responded. "Thanks for stopping, though. Your headlights will be a big help."

At her first words, his heart gave a sharp little kick and he froze, unable to work his mind around his shock. He instantly forgot all about how tired he was.

He knew that voice. Knew her.

Suddenly he understood the reason for the Arizona plates and why the Subaru wagon was heading up this quiet road very few had any reason to travel.

Magdalena Cruz had come home.

She was the last person he would have expected to encounter on one of his regular hospital runs, especially not at 2:00 a.m. on a rainy April Tuesday night, but that didn't make the sight of her any less welcome.

A hundred questions jostled through his mind, and he drank in her features—what he could see in the glow from his vehicle's headlights anyway.

The thick hair he knew was dark and glossy was pulled back in a ponytail, yanked through the back of the baseball-style cap she wore. Beneath the cap, he knew her features would be fragile and delicate, as hauntingly beautiful as always, except for the stubborn set of her chin.

Though he didn't want to, he couldn't prevent his gaze from drifting down.

She wore a pair of jeans and scarred boots—for all appearances everything looked completely normal. But he knew it wasn't and he wanted more than anything to fold her into his arms and hold on tight.

He couldn't, of course. She'd probably whack him with that tire iron if he tried.

Even before she had come to hate him and the rest of his family, they'd never had the kind of relationship that would have been conducive to that sort of thing.

The cold reality of all those years of impossible dreams—and the ache in his chest they sparked—sharpened his tone. "Your mama know you're driving in so late?"

She sent him a quick, searching look and he saw her hands tremble a little on the tool she suddenly held as a weapon as she tried to figure out his identity.

She aimed the flashlight at him and, with an inward sigh, he obliged by giving her a straight-on look at him, even though he knew full well what her reaction would be.

Sure enough, he saw the moment she recognized him. She stiffened and her fingers tightened on the tire iron. He could only be grateful he was out of range.

"I guess I don't need help after all." That low voice, normally as smoothly sexy as fine-aged scotch, sounded as cold and hard as the Tetons in January.

Help from *him,* she meant. He didn't need her to spell it out.

He decided not to let it affect him. He also decided the hour was too damn late for diplomacy. "Tough. Whether you need help or not, you're getting it. Hand over the tire iron."

"I'm fine."

"Maggie, just give me the damn thing."

"Go home, Dalton. I've got everything under control here."

She crouched again, though it was actually more a half crouch, with her left leg extended at her side. That position must be agony for her, he thought, and had to keep his hands curled into fists at his side to keep from hauling her up and giving her a good shake before pulling her into his arms.

She must be as tired as he was. More, probably. The woman had spent the past five months at Walter Reed Army Hospital. From what he knew secondhand from her mother, Viviana—his mother's best friend—she'd had numerous painful surgeries and had endured months of physical therapy and rehabilitation.

He seriously doubted she was strong enough—or stable enough on her prosthesis—to be driving at all, forget about rolling around in the mud changing a tire. Yet she would rather endure what must be incredible pain than accept help from one of the hated Daltons.

With a weary sigh, he ended the matter by reaching out and yanking the tire iron out of her hand. "I see the years haven't made you any less stubborn," he muttered.

"Or you less of an arrogant jackass," she retorted through clenched teeth as she straightened.

"Yeah, we jackasses love driving around at 2:00 a.m. looking for people with car trouble so we can stop and harass them. Wait in my car where you can be warm and dry."

She was still holding the flashlight, and she looked like she desperately wanted to bean him with it but she restrained herself. So the Army had taught her a little self-discipline, he thought with amusement, then watched her carefully as she leaned against the trunk of a nearby tree, aiming the beam in his direction.

He was a doctor with plenty of experience in observing the signs of someone hurting, and Magdalena Cruz's whole posture screamed pain. He thought of a million more questions for her as he quickly put on her spare tire—what medication was she on? What kind of physical therapy had her doctors at Walter Reed ordered? Was she experiencing any phantom pain?—but he knew she wouldn't answer any of them so he kept his mouth shut.

Questions would only piss her off. Not that *that* would be any big change—Maggie Cruz had been angry with him for nearly two decades. Well, not him specifically, he supposed. Anybody with the surname Dalton would find himself on the receiving end of her wrath.

Knowing her animosity wasn't something she reserved just for him didn't temper the sting of it.

"Your mom know you're coming?" Tightening the lugs on the spare, he repeated the question he'd asked earlier.

She hesitated for just a heartbeat. "No. I wanted to surprise her."

"You'll do that, all right." He pictured Viviana's reaction when she woke up and found her daughter home. She would be stunned first, then joyful, he knew, and would smother Maggie with kisses and concern.

He didn't know a mother in town more proud of her

offspring than Viviana Cruz was of First Lieutenant Magdalena Cruz.

As well she should be.

The whole town was proud of her, first for doing her duty as an Army nurse in Afghanistan when her reserve unit was called up, then for the act of heroism that had cost her so dearly.

He finished the job, then stowed the flat tire and the jack and lug wrench in the cargo area of the Subaru, though he had to squeeze to find room amid the boxes and suitcases crammed in the small space.

Was she home to stay, then? he wondered, but knew she likely would tell him it wasn't any of his business if he asked. He'd find out soon enough, anyway. The grapevine in Pine Gulch would be buzzing with this juicy bit of information.

He had no doubt that by the time he returned from Idaho Falls in the morning, his office staff would know all the details and would be more than eager to share them.

"There you go." He closed the hatch. "You don't want to run for long on that spare. Make sure you have Mo Sullivan in town fix your flat in the morning and swap it back out."

"I will." She stood, and in the headlights he could see exhaustion stamped on her lovely features.

"Your help wasn't necessary but…thank you, anyway." She said the words like they were choking her, and he almost smiled when he saw the effort they took. He stopped himself at the last minute. Accepting his help was tough enough on her, he wouldn't make things worse by gloating about it.

"Anytime. Welcome home, Lieutenant Cruz."

He doubted she heard him, since by then she had already

climbed back into her Subaru and started the engine. He shook his head, used to the familiar chill from her.

He watched her drive away, then wiped his greasy, muddy hands on his already grimy scrubs and hurried to his Durango, pulling out behind her.

As he passed his own driveway a moment later, he thought with longing of his warm bed and the sandwich calling his name, but he drove on, following those red tail-lights another five miles until she reached the entrance to the Rancho de la Luna—Moon Ranch.

When she drove her little Subaru through the gates without further mishap, he flashed his brights, then turned around to drive back toward his house. Somehow he wasn't a bit surprised when she made no gesture of acknowledgment at his presence or his small effort to make sure she reached home safely.

Maggie had been doing her best to ignore him for a long time—just as he'd been trying equally hard to make her notice him as someone other than one of the despised Daltons.

Despite the exhaustion that had cranked up a notch now that he was alone once more, he doubted he would be able to sleep anytime soon. He drove through the dark, quiet night, his thoughts chaotic and wild.

After a dozen years Magdalena Cruz was home.

He had a sudden foreboding that his heart would never be the same.

Jake Dalton.

What kind of bad omen made him the first person she encountered on her return?

As she headed up the curving drive toward the square farmhouse her father had built with his own hands, Maggie watched in her rearview mirror as Dalton turned his shiny silver SUV around and headed back down Cold Creek Road.

Why would he be driving back to town instead of toward his family's ranch, just past the Luna? she wondered, then caught herself. She didn't care where the man went. What Jake Dalton did or did not do was none of her concern.

Still, she hated that he, of all people, had come to her aid. She would rather have bitten her tongue in half than ask him for help, not that he'd given her a chance. He was just like the rest of his family, arrogant, unbending and ready to bulldoze over anybody who got in their way.

She let out a breath. Of course, he had to be gorgeous.

Like the other Dalton boys, Jake had always been handsome, with dark wavy hair, intense blue eyes and the sculpted features they inherited from their mother.

The years had been extremely kind to him, she had to admit. Though it had been dark out on that wet road, his headlights had provided enough light for her to see him clearly enough.

To her chagrin, she had discovered that the boy with the dreamy good looks who used to set all the other girls in school to giggling had matured over the years into a dramatically attractive man.

Why couldn't he have a potbelly and a receding hairline? No, he had to have compelling features, thick, lush hair and powerful muscles. She hadn't missed how effortlessly he had changed her flat, how he had worked the car jack it had taken all her strength to muscle, as if it took no more energy than reading the newspaper.

She shouldn't have noticed. Even if he hadn't been Jake Dalton—the last man on the planet she would let herself be attracted to—she had no business feeling that little hitch in her stomach at the sight of a strong, good-looking man doing a little physical exertion.

Heaven knows, she didn't *want* to feel that hitch. That part of her life was over now.

Had he been staring? She couldn't be sure, it had been too dark, but she didn't doubt it.

Step right up. Come look at the freak.

She was probably in for a lot of that in the coming weeks as she went about town. People in Pine Gulch weren't known for their reticence or their tact. She might as well get used to being on display.

She shook away the bitter self-pity and thoughts of Jake Dalton as she pulled up in front of the two-story frame farmhouse. She had more important things to worry about right now.

The lights were off in the house and the ranch was quiet—but what had she expected when she didn't tell her mother she was coming? It was after 2:00 and the only thing awake at this time of the night besides wandering physicians were the barn cats prowling the dark.

She should have found a hotel room for the night in Idaho Falls and waited until morning to come home. If she had, right now she would have been stretched out on some impersonal bed with what was left of her leg propped on a pillow, instead of throbbing as if she'd just rolled around in a thousand shards of glass.

She had come so close to stopping, she even started signaling to take one of the freeway exits into the city. At the last minute she had turned off her signal and veered back onto the highway, unwilling to admit defeat by giving in so close to her destination.

Maybe she hadn't fully considered the implications of her stubbornness, though. It was thoughtless to show up in the middle of the night. She was going to scare Viviana half to death, barging in like this.

She knew her mother always kept a spare key on the porch somewhere. Maybe she could slip in quietly without waking her and just deal with everything in the morning.

She grabbed her duffel off the passenger seat and began the complicated maneuver for climbing out of the car they taught her at Walter Reed, sliding sideways in the seat so she could put the bulk of her weight on her right leg and not the prosthesis.

Bracing herself, she took a step, and those imaginary shards of glass dug deeper. The pain made her vaguely queasy but she fought it back and took another step, then another until she reached the steps to the small front porch.

Once, she would have bounded up these half-dozen steps, taking them two or three at a time. Now it was all she could do to pull herself up, inch by painful inch, grabbing hold of the railing so hard her fingers ached.

The spare key wasn't under the cushion of either of the rockers that had graced this porch as long as she could remember, but she lifted one of the ceramic planters and found it there.

As quietly as possible she unlocked the door and closed it behind her with only a tiny snick.

Inside, the house smelled of cinnamon coffee and corn tortillas and the faint scent of Viviana's favorite Windsong perfume. Once upon a time that Windsong would have been joined by Abel's Old Spice but the last trace of her father had faded years ago.

Still, as she drew the essence of home into her lungs, she felt as if she was eleven years old again, rushing inside after school with a dozen stories to tell. She was awash in emotions at being home, in the relief and security that seemed to wrap around her here, a sweet and desperately needed comfort even with the slightly bitter edge that seemed to underlie everything in her life right now.

She stood there for several moments, eyes closed and a hundred childhood memories washing through her like spring runoff, until she felt herself sway with exhaustion and had to reach for the handrail of the staircase that rose up from the entryway.

She had to get off her feet. Or her foot, anyway. The prosthesis on the other leg was rubbing and grinding against her wound—she hated the word stump, though that's what it was.

Whatever she called it, she hadn't yet developed sufficient calluses to completely protect the still-raw tissue.

The stairs to her bedroom suddenly looked insurmountable, but she shouldered her bag and gripped the railing. She had only made it two or three steps before the entry was flooded with light and she heard an exclamation of shock behind her.

She twisted around and found her mother standing in the entryway wearing the pink robe Maggie had given her for Mother's Day a few years earlier.

"Lena? *Madre de Dios!*"

An instant later her mother rushed up the stairs and wrapped her arms around Maggie, holding her so tightly Maggie had to drop the duffel and hold on just to keep her balance.

At only a little over five feet tall, Viviana was six inches shorter than Maggie but she made up for her lack of size by the sheer force of her personality. Just now the vibrant, funny woman she adored was crying and mumbling a rapid-fire mix of Spanish and English that Maggie could barely decipher.

It didn't matter. She was just so glad to be here. She had needed this, she thought as she rested her chin on Viviana's slightly graying hair. She hadn't been willing to admit it but she had desperately needed the comfort of her mother's arms.

Viviana had come to Walter Reed when Maggie first returned from Afghanistan and had stayed for those first hellish two weeks after her injury while she had tried to come to terms with what had been taken from her in a moment. Her mother had been there for the first of the long series of surgeries to shape the scar tissue of her stump and had wanted to stay longer during her intensive rehab and the many weeks of physical therapy that came later.

But Maggie's pride had insisted she convince her mother to return to Pine Gulch, to Rancho de la Luna.

She was thirty years old, for heaven's sake. She should be strong enough to face her future without her mama by her side.

"What is this about?" Viviana finally said through her tears. "I think I hear a car outside and come to see who is here and who do I find but my beautiful child? You want to put your mother in an early grave, *niña,* sneaking around in the middle of the night?"

"I'm sorry. I should have called to make sure it was all right."

Viviana frowned and flicked a hand in one of her broad, dismissive gestures. "This is your home. You don't need to call ahead like…like I run some kind of hotel! You are always welcome, you know that. But why are you here? I thought you were to go to Phoenix when you left the hospital in Washington."

"It was a spur-of-the-moment thing. I stayed long enough to pick up my car and pack up my apartment, then I decided to come home. There's nothing for me in Phoenix anymore."

There had been once. She had a good life there before her reserve unit had been called up eighteen months ago and sent to Afghanistan. She had a job she loved, as a nurse practitioner in a busy Phoenix E.R., she had a wide circle of friends, she had a fiancé she thought adored her.

Everything had changed in a heartbeat, in one terrible, decimating instant.

Viviana's expression darkened but suddenly she slapped the palm of her hand against her head. "What am I doing, *niña*, to make you stand like this? Come. Sit. I will fix you something to eat."

"I'm not hungry, Mama. I just need sleep."

"*Sí. Sí.* We can talk about all this tomorrow." Viviana's hands were cool as she pushed a lock of hair away from Maggie's eyes in a tender gesture that nearly brought her to tears. "Come. You will take my room downstairs."

Oh, how she was tempted by that offer. Climbing the rest of these stairs right now seemed as insurmountable to her as scaling the Grand Teton without ropes.

She couldn't give in, though. She had surrendered too much already.

"No. It's fine. I'll use my old room."

"Lena—"

"Mama, I'm fine. I'm not kicking you out of your bed."

"It's no trouble for me. Do you not think it would be best?"

If Viviana had the strength, Maggie had no doubt her mother would have picked her up and carried her the short way off the stairs and down the hall to her bedroom.

This was one of the reasons she hadn't wanted her mother in Washington, D.C., through her painful recovery, through the various surgeries and the hours of physical therapy.

It was also one of her biggest worries about coming home.

Viviana would want to coddle. It was who she was, what she did. And though part of Maggie wanted to lean into that comforting embrace, to soak it up, she knew she would find it too easy to surrender to it, to let that tender care surround her, smother her.

She couldn't. She had to be tough if she was going to figure out how to go on with the rest of her life.

Climbing these steps was a small thing, but it suddenly seemed of vital importance.

"No, Mama. I'm sleeping upstairs."

Viviana shook her head at her stubborn tone. "You are your father's daughter, *niña*."

She smiled, though she could feel how strained her mouth felt around the edges.

"I will take your things up," Viviana said, her firm tone attesting to the fact that Maggie's stubbornness didn't come only from Abel Cruz.

Maggie decided she was too tired to argue, even if she had the tiniest possibility of winning that particular battle. She turned and started the long, torturous climb.

By the time she reached the last of the sixteen steps, she was shaking and out of breath and felt like those shards of glass she'd imagined earlier were now tipped with hot acid, eating away at her skin.

But she had made it, she thought as she opened the door to her childhood bedroom, all lavender and cream and dearly familiar.

She was here, she was home, and she would take the rest of her life just like that—one step at a time.

Chapter 2

She woke from dreams of screaming, dark-eyed children and exploding streets and bone-numbing terror to soothing lavender walls and the comforting scent of home.

Sunshine streamed in through the lace curtains, creating delicate filigree patterns on the floor, and she watched them shift and slide for several moments while the worst of the dreams and her morning pain both faded to a dull roar.

Doctors at Walter Reed used to ask if her pain seemed worse first thing in the morning or right before bed. She couldn't tell much difference. It was always there, a constant miserable presence dogging her like a grim black shadow.

She wanted to think it had started to fade a little in the five months since her injury, but she had a sneaking suspicion she was being overly optimistic.

She sighed, willing away the self-pity. Just once she'd

like to wake up and enjoy the morning instead of wallowing in the muck of her screwed-up psyche.

Her shower chair was still down in the Subaru and she wasn't quite up to running down the stairs and then back up for it—or worse, having to ask her mother to retrieve it for her. She hadn't been fitted for a shower prosthesis yet, and since she couldn't very well balance on one foot for the length of time needed, she opted for a bath.

It did the job of keeping her clean but was nowhere near as satisfying as the hot pulse of a shower for chasing away the cobwebs. Climbing out of the tub was always a little tricky, but she managed and dressed quickly, adjusted her prosthesis then headed for the stairs to find her mother.

When she finally made her painstaking way to the ground floor, she found the kitchen empty, but Viviana had left thick, gooey sweet rolls and a note in her precise English. "I must work outside this morning. I will see you at lunch."

She frowned at the note, surprised. She would have expected her mother to stick close to the house the first day after her arrival, though she felt a little narcissistic for the assumption.

Viviana was probably out in her garden, she thought, tearing off a sticky chunk of cinnamon roll and popping it in her mouth.

Savoring the rich, sweet flavor, she poured a cup of coffee and walked outside with the awkward rolling gait she hadn't been able to conquer when wearing her prosthesis.

The morning air was sweet and clear, rich with new growth, and she paused for a moment on the front porch to savor it.

Nothing compared to a Rocky Mountain morning in springtime. She had come to love the wild primitiveness of the desert around Phoenix in the dozen years she'd lived there, but this was a different kind of beauty.

The Tetons were still covered with snow—some of it would be year-round—but here at lower elevations everything was green and lush. Her mother's fruit trees were covered in white blossoms that sent their sweet, seductive scent into the air and the flower beds bloomed with color—masses of spring blossoms in reds and yellows and pinks.

The Luna in spring was the most beautiful place on earth. Why had she forgotten that over the years? She stood for a long time watching birds flit around the gardens and the breeze rustle the new, pale-green leaves of the cottonwood trees along the creek.

Feeling a tentative peace that had been missing inside her for months, she limped down the stairs in search of her mother.

There was no sign of Viviana on the side of the house or in the back where the vegetable beds were tilled and ready for planting.

Maggie frowned. So much for being coddled. She didn't want her mother to feel like she had to babysit her, but she couldn't help feeling a little abandoned. Couldn't Viviana have stuck around at least the first day so they could have had a visit over breakfast?

No matter. She didn't need entertaining. She would welcome a quiet moment of solitude and reflection, she decided, and headed for the glider rocker on the brick patio.

She settled down with her coffee, determined to enjoy the morning on her own here in the sunshine, surrounded by blossoms.

The ranch wasn't big, only eight hundred acres. From her spot on the patio she could see the pasture where her mother's half-dozen horses grazed and the much-larger acreage where two hundred Murray Grey cattle milled around, their unique-colored hides looking soft and silvery in the morning sun.

She shifted her gaze toward the creek 150 yards away that gave this canyon and the Dalton's ranch their names. This time of year the Cold Creek ran full and high, swollen with spring runoff. Instead of a quiet, peaceful ribbon of water, it churned and boiled.

The rains the night before hadn't helped matters, and she could see the creek was nearly full to the banks. She whispered a prayer that it wouldn't reach flood stage, though the ranch had been designed to sustain minimal damage for those high-water years.

The only building that could be in jeopardy if the creek flooded was the open-air bowery she and her father had built for her mother the summer she was ten.

She looked at the Spanish-tiled roof that gleamed a vibrant red in the sunlight and the brightly colored windsocks flapping in the breeze and smiled at the vibrant colors.

A little slice of Mexico, that's what she and Abel had tried to create for her mother. A place Viviana could escape to when she was homesick for her family in Mexico City.

After the car accident that claimed her father's life, she and Viviana used to wander often down to the bowery, both alone and separately. She had always been able to feel her father's presence most strongly there, in the haven he had created for his beloved wife.

Did her mother go there still? she wondered.

Thoughts of Abel and the events leading to his death when she was sixteen inevitably turned her thoughts to the Daltons and the Cold Creek Land & Cattle Company, just across the creek bed.

From here she could see the graying logs of the ranch

house, the neat fencelines, a small number of the ranch's huge herd of cattle grazing on the rich grasses by the creek.

In those days after her father's death, she would split her time here at the bowery between grieving for him and feeding the coals of her deep anger toward that family across the creek.

The Daltons were the reason her father had spent most of her adolescence working himself into an early grave, spending days hanging on to his dreams of making the Luna profitable and nights slogging through a factory job in Idaho Falls.

Bitter anger filled her again at the memories. Abel would never have found himself compelled to work so hard if not for Hank Dalton, that lying, thieving bastard.

Dalton should have gone to jail for the way he'd taken advantage of her father's naiveté and his imperfect command of English. Thinking he was taking a big step toward expanding the Luna, Abel had paid the Cold Creek thousands of dollars for water rights that had turned out to be virtually useless. Abel should have taken the bastard to court—or at least stopped paying each month for nothing.

But he had insisted on remitting every last penny he owed to Hank Dalton and, after a few years with poor ranch returns, had been forced to take on two jobs to cover the debt.

She barely saw him from the age of eleven until his death five years later. One night after Abel had spent all day on the tractor baling hay then turned around and driven to Idaho Falls to work the graveyard shift at his factory job, he'd been returning to the Luna when he had fallen asleep at the wheel of his old Dodge pickup.

The truck rolled six times and ended up in a ditch, and her kind, generous father was killed instantly.

She knew exactly who should shoulder the blame. The Daltons had killed her father just as surely as if they'd crashed into him in one of the shiny new pickups they always drove.

She sipped her coffee and shifted her leg as the constant pins-and-needles phantom pains became uncomfortable.

Was there room in her life right now for old bitterness? she wondered. She had plenty of new troubles to brood about without wallowing around in the mud and muck of ancient history.

Now that she'd come home, she saw no reason she and the Daltons couldn't just stay out of each other's way.

Unbidden, an image of Jake Dalton flitted across her mind, all lean strength and rumpled sexiness and she sighed. Jake should be at the top of the list of Daltons to avoid, she decided. He had always been the hardest for her to read and the one she had most in common with, as they had both chosen careers in medicine.

For various reasons, there had always been an odd bond between them, fragile and tenuous but still there. She would just have to do her best while she was home to ignore it.

A tractor suddenly rumbled into view, and she was grateful for the distraction from thoughts of entirely too-sexy doctors.

She craned her neck, expecting to see her *tío* Guillermo, her father's bachelor brother who had run the ranch for Viviana since Abel's death. Instead, she was stunned to find her mother looking tiny and fragile atop the rumbling John Deere.

Ranch wives were bred tough in the West, and Viviana was no different—tougher than some, even. Still, the sight of her atop the big tractor was unexpected.

Viviana waved with cheerful enthusiasm when she spied

Maggie in the garden. The tractor shuddered to a stop and a moment later her mother hopped down with a spryness that disguised her fifty-five years and hurried toward her.

"Lena! How are you feeling this morning?"

"Better."

"You should be resting after your long drive. I did not expect you to be up so early. You should go back to bed!"

Here was the coddling she had expected and she decided to accept it with grace. "It was a long drive and I may have overdone things a little. But I promise, I'm feeling better this morning."

"Good. Good. The clean air of the Luna will cleanse your blood. You will see."

Maggie smiled, then gestured to the tractor. "Mama, why are you doing the planting? Where's Tío Guillermo?"

An odd expression flickered across her mother's lovely features, but she quickly turned away. "Do not my flowers look beautiful this year? We will have many blooms with the rains we've had. I thought many of them would die in the hard freeze of last week but I covered them with blankets and they have survived. They are strong, like my daughter."

With Viviana smiling at her with such love, Maggie almost let herself be deterred, but she yanked her attention back. "Don't change the subject, Mama. Why are you planting instead of Guillermo? Is he sick?"

Viviana shrugged. "This I cannot say. I have not seen him for some days."

"Why not?"

Her mother didn't answer and suddenly seemed wholly focused on deadheading some of the tulips that had bloomed past their prime.

"Mama!" she said more firmly, and her mother sighed.

"He does not work here anymore. I told him to go and not return."

Maggie stared. "You what?"

"I fired him, *sí?* Even though he said he was quitting anyway, that I could not pay him enough to keep working here. I said the words first. I fired him."

"Why? Guillermo loves this place! He has poured his heart into the Luna. It belongs to him as much as us. He owns part of the ranch, for heaven's sake. You can't fire him!"

"So you think I'm a crazy woman, too?"

"I didn't say that. Did Guillermo call you crazy?"

Her mother and her father's brother had always seemed to get along just fine. Guillermo had been a rock of support to both of them after Abel's death and had stepped up immediately to run the ranch his brother had loved. She couldn't imagine what he might have done to anger her mother so drastically that she would feel compelled to fire him—or what she would have said to make him quit.

"This makes no sense, Mama! What's going on?"

"I have my reasons and they are between your *tío* and me. That is all I will say about this to you."

Her mother had a note of finality in her voice but Maggie couldn't let the subject rest.

"But Mama, you can't take care of things here by yourself! It's too much."

"I will be fine. I am putting an ad in the newspaper. I will find someone to help me. You are not to worry."

"How can I not worry? What if I talk to Guillermo and try to smoothe things over?"

"No! You are to stay out of this. You cannot smooth this over. Sometimes there are too many wrinkles between people. I will hire someone to help me but for now I am fine."

"Mama..."

"No, Magdalena." Her mother stuck her chin up, looking at once fierce and determined. "That is all I will say about this."

This time she couldn't ignore Viviana's firmness. But Maggie could be every bit as stubborn as her mother. "Fine." She pulled herself up to stand. "Between the two of us, we should be able to manage until you're able to hire someone."

Her mother gaped, her flashing dark eyes now slightly aghast. "Not the two of us!"

She reverted to Spanish, as she always did in times of high emotion, and proceeded to loudly and vociferously tell Maggie all the reasons she would not allow her to overexert herself on the Rancho de la Luna.

Maggie listened to her mother's arguments calmly, hands in her sweater pockets, until Viviana wound down.

"Don't argue. Please, Mama," she finally said, her voice low and firm. "You need help and I need something to keep me busy. Working with you will be the perfect solution."

Her mother opened her mouth to renew her objection but Maggie stopped her with an upraised hand. "Please, Mama. The doctors say I must stay active to strengthen my leg and I hate feeling so useless. I want to help you."

"You should rest. I thought that is why you have come home."

Maggie had her own reasons for coming home but she didn't want to burden her mother with them, especially as she was suddenly aware of a deep, powerful need to prove to herself she wasn't completely helpless.

"I will be careful, Mama, I promise. But I'm going to help you."

Viviana studied her for a long moment while honeybees

buzzed through the flowers and the breeze ruffled the pale new leaves on the trees, then she sighed.

"You are so much like your father," she said in Spanish, shaking her head. "I never could win an argument with him, either."

Maggie wasn't sure why she was suddenly filled with elation at the idea of hard, physical labor. She should be consumed with fear, with trepidation that she wouldn't be able to handle the work. Instead, anticipation coursed through her.

She meant her words to her mother—she needed something to do, and pitting herself against the relentless work always waiting to be tackled on a small ranch like the Luna seemed just the thing to drag her off her self-pitying butt.

"No wonder the kid's not sleeping." Jake finished his quick exam and let his three-year-old nephew off the breakfast bar of the sunny, cheerful Cold Creek kitchen. Glad to be done, Cody raced off without even waiting for a lollipop from his uncle.

"What's the verdict?" his sister-in-law, Caroline, asked, her lovely, normally serene features worried.

"Ear infection. Looks like a mild one but still probably enough to cause discomfort in the night. I'll write you a prescription for amoxicillin and that should take care of it."

"Thank you for coming out to the ranch on such short notice, especially after a long day. We probably could have waited a day or two but Wade wouldn't hear of it. He seems to think you have nothing better to do than spend your free time making house calls to his kids."

"He's right. I can't think of anything I'd rather do." Jake smiled at her but Caroline made a face.

"If that's true, it's about the saddest thing I've ever heard."

"Why?" he asked. "Because I love the chance to see my niece and nephews?"

"Because you need something besides work, even when that work involves family! I'm not going to lecture you. But if you were my client, we would definitely have to work on finding you some hobbies."

Caroline was an author and life coach who had moved her practice to the Cold Creek after she married his oldest brother eighteen months earlier and willingly took on the challenge of Wade's three young kids.

In that time, she had wrought amazing changes at the ranch. Though the house was still cluttered and noisy and chaotic, it was filled with love and laughter now. He enjoyed coming out here, though seeing his brother's happiness only seemed to accentuate the solitude of his own life.

"I don't have time for a hobby," he answered as he returned his otoscope to his bag.

"My point exactly. You need to make time or you're going to burn out. Trust me on this."

"Yeah, yeah."

"I've been right where you are, Jake," she said. "You might scoff now but you won't a few years in the future when you wake up one morning and suddenly find yourself unable to bear the idea of treating even one more patient."

"I love being a doctor. I promise, that's not going to change anytime soon."

"I know you love it and you're wonderful at it. But you need other things in your life, too."

Her eyes suddenly sharpened with a calculating gleam that left him extremely nervous. "You at least need a woman. When was the last time you went on a date?"

He gave a mock groan. "I get enough of this from Marjorie. I don't need my sister-in-law starting in on me, too."

"How about your stepsister then?"

"You can tell her to keep her pretty nose out of my business, too."

She grinned. "I'll try, but you know how she is."

They both laughed, as technically Caroline filled both roles in his life, sister-in-law and stepsister. Not only was she married to his brother but her father, Quinn, was married to his mother, Marjorie. The happy couple now lived in Marjorie's little house in Pine Gulch.

"I heard through the grapevine our local hero has returned," Caroline said with a look so sly he had to wonder what he possibly might have let slip about his barely acknowledged feelings toward their neighbor. "Maybe you ought to ask Magdalena Cruz on a date."

A snort sounded in the kitchen and he looked over to find his youngest brother, Seth, lounging in the doorway. "Maggie? Never. She'd probably laugh in his face if he dared ask."

Seth sauntered into the kitchen and planted himself on one of the bar stools.

Caroline bristled. "What do you mean? Why on earth wouldn't she go out with Jake? Every woman in the county adores him."

Though he was touched by her defense of him, he flushed. "Not true. Seth's the Romeo in the family. All you have to do is walk outside to see the swath of broken hearts he's left across the valley."

"Does that swath include Magdalena Cruz's heart, by any chance?" Caroline asked.

Seth snorted again. "Not by a long shot. Maggie hates everything Dalton. Always has."

"Not always," Jake corrected quietly.

Caroline frowned at this bit of information. "Why would she hate you? Oh, I'll agree you can be an annoying lot on the whole, but as individuals you're basically harmless."

"You never knew dear old Dad."

Seth's words were matter-of-fact but they didn't completely hide the bitterness Jake and his brothers all carried toward their father.

"I don't know all the details," Jake said. "I don't know if even their widows do—but Hank cheated Viviana Cruz's husband Abel in some deal the two had together. He lost a lot of money and had to work two jobs to make ends meet. Maggie blamed us for it, especially after her father died in a car accident coming home from his second job one night."

"Oh, the poor thing." Caroline's eyes melted with compassion.

"Maggie left town for college a few years after her dad died. She studied to become a nurse and along the way she joined the Army National Guard," Jake went on. "The few times she's been back over the years, she usually tries to avoid anything having to do with the Cold Creek like a bad case of halitosis."

Unless one of the Daltons happens to stumble on her in the middle of the night, he thought.

"Hate to break it to you, Carrie, but you might as well take her right off your matchmaking radar." Seth grinned around a cookie he'd filched from the jar on the counter.

Caroline looked disappointed, though still thoughtful. "Too bad. From all her mother says, Lieutenant Cruz sounds like quite a woman."

Oh, she was that, Jake thought a short time later as he drove away from the ranch. Their conversation seemed to have opened a door in his mind and now he couldn't stop thinking about Maggie.

He was quite certain she had no idea her impact in his life had been so profound.

If not for her, he wasn't sure he would even have become a doctor. Though sometimes it seemed his decision to pursue medicine had been blooming inside him all his life, he could pinpoint three incidences that had cemented it.

Oddly enough, all three of them involved Maggie in some way.

Though the Rancho de la Luna was next door, he hadn't noticed Maggie much through most of his youth. Why should he? She was three years younger, the same age as Seth, and a girl to boot. A double whammy against her, as far as he'd been concerned.

Oh, he saw her every day, since she and the Dalton boys rode the same school bus and even shared a bus stop, a little covered shack out on the side of the road between their houses to protect them in inclement weather.

Her father constructed it, of course. It never would have occurred to Hank Dalton his sons might be cold waiting outside for the bus in the middle of a January blizzard.

Even if he thought of it, he probably wouldn't have troubled himself to make things easier on his sons. Jake could almost hear him. *A little snow never hurt anybody. What are you, a bunch of girls?*

But Abel Cruz had been a far different kind of father. Kind and loving and crazy about his little girl. Jake could clearly remember feeling a tight knot of envy in his chest whenever he saw them together, at their easy, laughing relationship.

Maggie had been a constant presence in his life but one

that didn't make much of an impact on him until one cold day when he was probably eleven or twelve.

That morning Seth had been a little wheezy as they walked down the driveway to the bus. Jake hadn't thought much about it, but while they were waiting for the bus, his wheezing had suddenly developed into a full-fledged asthma attack, a bad one.

Wade, the oldest, hadn't been at the stop to take control of the situation that day since he'd been in the hospital in Idaho Falls having his appendix out, and Marjorie had stayed overnight with him.

Jake knew there was no one at the Cold Creek, and that he and Maggie would have to take care of Seth alone.

Looking back, he was ashamed when he remembered how frozen with helplessness and fear he'd felt for a few precious seconds. Maggie, no more than eight herself, took charge. She grabbed Seth's inhaler from his backpack and set the medicine into the chamber.

"I'm going to get my mama. You stay and keep him calm," he could remember her ordering in that bossy little voice. Her words jerked him out of his panic, and while she raced toward her house, he was able to focus on calming Seth down.

Seth had suffered asthma attacks since he was small, and Jake had seen plenty of them but he'd never been the one in charge before.

He remembered thinking as they sat there in the pale, early-morning sunlight how miraculous medicine could be. In front of his eyes, the inhaler did its work and his brother's panicky gasps slowly changed to more regulated breathing.

A moment later, Viviana Cruz had come roaring down the driveway to their rescue in her big old station wagon and piled them all in to drive to Doc Whitaker's clinic in town.

That had sparked the first fledgling fire inside him about becoming a doctor.

The second experience had been a year or so later. Maggie and Seth had still been friends of sorts, and the two of them had been tossing a baseball back and forth while they waited for the bus. Jake had been caught up in a book, as usual, and hadn't been paying attention, but somehow Maggie had dived to catch it and landed wrong on her hand.

Her wrist was obviously broken, but she hadn't cried, had only looked at Jake with trusting eyes while he tried to comfort her in a slow, soothing voice and carried her up the long driveway to the Luna ranch house, again to her mother.

The third incident was more difficult to think about, but he forced his mind to travel that uncomfortable road.

He had been fifteen, so Maggie and Seth would have been twelve. By then, Maggie had come to despise everything about the Daltons. They would wait for the bus at their shared stop in a tense, uncomfortable silence and she did her best to ignore them on the rides to and from Pine Gulch and school.

That afternoon seemed no different. He remembered the three of them climbing off the bus together and heading toward their respective driveways. He and Seth had only walked a short way up the gravel drive when he spotted a tractor in one of the fields still running and a figure crumpled on the ground beside it.

Seth must have hollered to Maggie, because the three of them managed to reach the tractor at about the same moment. Somehow Jake knew before he reached it who he would find there—the father he loved and hated with equal parts.

He could still remember the grim horror of finding Hank on the ground not moving or breathing, his harsh face frozen in a contortion of pain and his clawed fingers still curled against his chest.

This time, Jake quickly took charge. He sent Seth to the house to call for an ambulance, then he rapidly did an assessment with the limited knowledge of first aid he'd picked up in Boy Scouts.

"I know CPR," he remembered Maggie offering quietly, her dark eyes huge and frightened. "I learned it for a babysitting class."

For the next fifteen minutes the two of them worked feverishly together, Jake doing chest compressions and Maggie doing mouth-to-mouth. Only later did he have time to wonder about what kind of character strength it must have taken a young girl to work so frantically to save the life of a man she despised.

Those long moments before the volunteer ambulance crew arrived at the ranch would live forever in his memory. After the paramedics took over, he had stood back, shaky and exhausted.

He had known somehow, even as the paramedics continued compressions on his father while they loaded him into the ambulance, that Hank wouldn't make it.

He remembered standing there feeling numb, drained, as they watched, when he felt a slight touch and looked down to find Maggie had slipped her small, soft hand in his. Despite her own shock, despite her fury at his father and her anger at his family, despite *everything,* she had reached out to comfort him when he needed it.

He had found it profoundly moving at the time.

He still did.

Maybe that was the moment he lost a little of his heart to her. For all the good it would ever do him. She wanted nothing more to do with him or his family, and he couldn't really blame her.

He sighed as he hit the main road and headed down toward town. Near the western boundary of the Luna, he spotted a saddled horse standing out in a field, reins trailing. Maybe because he'd been thinking of his father's heart attack, the sight left him wary, and he slowed his Durango and pulled over.

What would a saddled horse be doing out here alone? He wondered, then he looked closer and realized it wasn't alone—Maggie sat on a fallen log near the creek, her left leg outstretched.

Even from the road he could see the pain in her posture. It took him half a second to cut his engine, climb out and head out across the field.

Chapter 3

He had always considered himself the most even-tempered of men. He didn't get overly excited at sporting events, he had never struck another creature in anger, he could handle even the most dramatic medical emergencies that walked or were carried through his clinic doors with calm control.

But as Jake raced across the rutted, uneven ground toward Magdalena Cruz and her horse, he could feel the hot spike of his temper.

As he neared her, he caught an even better view of her. He ground his teeth with frustration mingled with a deep and poignant sadness for what she had endured.

She had her prosthesis off and the leg of her jeans rolled up, and even from a dozen feet away he could see her amputation site was a raw, mottled red.

As he neared, he saw her shoulders go back, her chin lift, as if she were bracing herself for battle. Good. He wasn't about to disappoint her.

"Didn't the Army teach you anything about common sense?" he snapped.

She glared at him, and he thought for sure his heart would crack apart as he watched her try to quickly yank the leg of her jeans down to cover her injury.

"You're trespassing, Dalton. Last I checked this was still Rancho de la Luna land."

"And last I checked, someone just a few days out of extensive rehab ought to have the good sense not to overdo things."

She grabbed her prosthesis as if she wanted to shove it on again—or at least fling it in his face—but he grabbed hold of it before she could try either of those things.

"Stop. You're only going to aggravate the site again."

Every instinct itched to reach and take a look at her leg but he knew he had to respect her boundaries, just as he knew she wouldn't welcome his efforts to look out for her.

"How long have you had this prosthesis?" he asked.

She clamped her teeth together as if she wasn't going to answer him, but she finally looked away and mumbled. "A few weeks."

"Didn't your prosthetist warn you it would take longer than that to adjust to it?" he asked. "You can't run a damn marathon the day after you stick it on."

"I wasn't trying to run a marathon," she retorted hotly. "I was only checking the fence line. We had a couple cows get out last night and we're trying to figure out where they made a break for it."

"Two days back in town and you think you have to take over! Tell me why Guillermo couldn't handle this job."

She slanted him a dark look. "Tell me again why it's any of your business."

"Maggie."

She sighed. "Guillermo can't check the fence because he no longer works for the Luna."

He blinked at this completely unexpected piece of information. "Since when?"

"Since he and my mother apparently had a falling out. Whether she fired him or he quit, I'm not exactly sure. Maybe both."

Jake knew Guillermo Cruz had taken over running his brother's ranch for Viviana after Abel's death. As far as he could tell, the man was hardworking and devoted to the ranch. He knew Wade had nothing but respect for him and his older brother didn't give his approval lightly.

"Anyway, he doesn't work here now. It's just Mama and me until she hires someone."

He couldn't take any more. Despite knowing the reaction he would get, he reached out and put a hand on the prosthesis she was trying to jam onto her obviously irritated residual leg, unable to bear watching her torture herself further.

"You don't have to try to hide anything from me."

"I wasn't!" she exclaimed, though color crept up her high cheekbones.

"I'm a physician, remember? Will you please let me take a look to see what's going on with your leg?"

"It's just a little irritated," she said firmly. "Nothing for you to be concerned about."

He folded his arms across his chest. "Here are your choices. You either let me look at it or I'm packing you over my shoulder and driving you to the E.R. in Idaho Falls so someone there can examine you."

She glared at him, her stance fully combative. "Try it, Dalton. I dare you."

This bickering wasn't accomplishing anything. He moderated his tone and tried for a conciliatory approach. "Don't you think it's foolish to put yourself through this kind of pain if you don't have to? How quickly do you think you can get in to see a specialist at the VA? A week? Two? I'm here right now, offering to check things out. No appointment necessary."

Her glare sharpened to a razor point, but just when he thought she would impale him on the sharp points of her temper, she drew a deep breath, her gaze focused somewhere far away from him, then slowly pulled the prosthesis away.

Despite his assurance that she didn't have to hide anything from him, he found himself filled with an odd trepidation as he turned for his first real look at her amputation.

Despite the obvious irritation, her stump looked as if it had been formed well at Walter Reed, with a nice rounded shape that would make fitting a prosthesis much easier. Scar tissue from various surgeries puckered in spots but overall he was impressed with the work that had been done at the Army's premier amputee care center.

She gave him possibly ninety seconds to examine her before she jerked away and pulled her jeans down again.

"Are you happy now?"

Despite her dusky skin, her cheeks burned with color and she looked as if she wished him to perdition.

"No," he said bluntly. "If you were my patient, I'd recommend you put your leg up, rent a bunch of DVDs with your mother and just take it easy for a few days enjoying some time with Viv."

"Too bad for you, I'm *not* your patient."

He stood again. "And you won't take my advice?"

She was silent for a moment and he had maybe five seconds to hope she might actually overcome her stubbornness and consider his suggestion, then she shook her head.

"I can't. My mother needs help. She can't run Rancho de la Luna by herself."

"Didn't you say she was looking to hire help?"

"Sure. And I'm certain whole hordes of competent stockmen are just sitting around down at the feedlot shooting the breeze and waiting for somebody to come along and hire them."

In the late-afternoon sunlight, she looked slight and fragile, with the pale, vaguely washed-out look of someone who had been inside too long.

All of his healer urges were crying out for him to scoop her off that log and take her home so he could care for her.

"Someone out there has to be available. What about some college kid looking for a summer job?"

"Maybe. But it's going to take time to find someone. What do you suggest we do in the meantime? Just let the work pile up? I don't know how things work at the Cold Creek, but Mama hasn't quite figured out how to make the Luna run itself."

His mind raced through possibilities—everything from seeing if Wade would loan one of the Cold Creek ranch hands to going down to the feed store himself to see if he might be able to shake any potential ranch managers out of the woodwork.

He knew she wouldn't be crazy about either of those options but he had to do something. He couldn't bear the idea of her working herself into the ground so soon after leaving the hospital.

"I can help you."

While the creek rumbled over the rocks behind her and the wind danced in her hair, she stared at him for a full thirty seconds before she burst out laughing.

He decided it was worth being the butt of her amusement for the sheer wonder of watching her face lose the grim lines it usually wore.

"Why is that so funny?"

She laughed harder. "If you can't figure it out, I'm not about to tell you. Here's a suggestion for you, though, Dr. Dalton. Maybe you ought to take five seconds to think through your grand charitable gestures before you make them."

"I don't need to think it through. I want to help you."

"And leave the good people of Pine Gulch to drive to Jackson or Idaho Falls for their medical care so you can diddle around planting our spring crop of alfalfa? That should go over well in town."

"I have evenings and weekends mostly free and an afternoon or two here and there. I can help you when I'm not working at the clinic, at least with the major manual labor around here."

She stopped laughing long enough to look at him more closely. Something in his expression must have convinced her he was serious because she gave him a baffled look.

"Surely you have something better to do with your free time."

"Can't think of a thing," he said cheerfully, though Caroline's lecture still rang in his ears.

Maggie shook her head. "That's just sad, Doctor. But you'll have to find something else to entertain you, because my answer is still no."

"Just like that?"

He didn't want to think about the disappointment settling in his gut—or the depressing realization that he was desperate for any excuse to spend more time with her.

If she had any idea his attraction for her had any part in

his motive behind offering to help her and Viv, she would be chasing him off the Luna with a shotgun.

"Right. Just like that. Now if you'll excuse me, I need to get back to work."

She moved to put her prosthesis back on but he reached a hand to stop her, his mind racing to come up with a compromise she might consider. "What if we made a deal? Would that make accepting my help a little easier to swallow?"

She slid back against the log with a suspicious frown. "What kind of deal?"

"A day for a day. I'll give you my Saturday to help with the manual labor."

"And what do you want in exchange?"

"A fair trade. You give me a day in return."

Why wouldn't the man just *leave?*

Maggie drew a breath, trying to figure out this latest angle. What did he want from her? Hadn't he humiliated her enough by insisting on looking at her ugly, raw-looking stump? The man seemed determined to push her as far as he could.

"Give you a day for what?" she asked warily.

"I'm in dire need of a translator. I open my clinic on Wednesdays for farm workers and their families. A fair number of them don't have much English and my Spanish is limited at best. I've been looking for someone with a medical background to translate for me."

"No."

"Come on, Maggie. Who would be more perfect than a bilingual nurse practitioner?"

"Former nurse practitioner. I'm retired."

His pupils widened. "Retired? Why would you want to do that, for heaven's sake?"

She had a million reasons but the biggest was right there in front of her. Who the hell wanted a one-legged nurse? One who couldn't stand for long periods of time, who was constantly haunted by phantom pain, who had lost all of her wonder and much of her respect for the medical establishment over the last five months?

No, she had put that world behind her.

In civilian life, she had loved being a nurse practitioner in a busy Scottsdale pediatric practice. She had admired the physicians she worked with, had loved the challenge and delight of treating children and even had many parents who preferred to have her, rather than the pediatricians, see and treat their children.

How could she go back to that world? She just didn't have what it took anymore, physically or emotionally. It was part of her past, one more loss she was trying to accept.

She certainly didn't need Jake's accusatory tone laying a guilt trip on her for her choices. "I don't recall making you my best friend here, Dalton," she snapped. "My reasons are my own."

More than anything, she wanted him to leave her alone, but she had no idea how to do that, other than riding off in a grand huff, something she wasn't quite capable of right now.

"Whatever they are, one day translating for me is not going to bring you out of permanent retirement. These people need somebody like you who can translate the medical terminology into words they can understand. I do my best, but there are many times I know both me and my patients walk out of the exam room with more questions than answers."

"I'm not interested," she repeated firmly.

He opened his mouth, gearing up for more arguments, no doubt. After a moment he shrugged. "Your call, then."

She stared at him, waiting for the other punch. Dalton men weren't known for giving up a good fight and they rarely took pity on their opponents, either.

Jake only stood, brushing leaves and pine needles off the knees of his tan Dockers. "I'm sure you know the risks of wearing your prosthesis too long at a stretch if it's causing that kind of irritation. If I were your doctor—which, as you said, too bad for me I'm not—I would advise you to leave it off for the rest of the day."

"I can't ride a horse without it."

Exasperation flickered in his blue eyes. "I can give you a ride back to the ranch. We can walk the horse behind my Durango."

She hated herself for the little flickers of temptation inside her urging her to accept his offer. The pain—or more accurately, the powerful need to find something to ease it—sometimes overwhelmed every ounce of common sense inside her.

She wanted so much to accept his offer of a ride rather than face that torturous horseback ride back to the ranch, but the very strength of her desire was also the reason she had to refuse.

"Thanks, but I think I'll just wear it back to the house and then rest for a while after that."

He studied her for a moment, then shook his head. "You could teach stubborn to a whole herd of mules, Lieutenant Cruz. Will you at least let me help you mount?"

She had no choice, really. At the barn she had used Viviana's mounting block to climb into the saddle.

Even with the block, mounting had been a challenge, accomplished best in the privacy of her own barnyard where she didn't have an audience to watch her clumsy efforts.

Here, she had nothing to help her—unless she could

convince the horse to come to this fallen log and stand still out of the goodness of her heart while Maggie maneuvered into the saddle.

He reached a hand out. "Come on. It won't kill you to say yes."

To him, it might. She swallowed. "Yes. Okay. Thank you. Just a moment. I have to put the prosthesis back on or I won't be able to dismount."

"I can help you with that, too. I'll just drive around to the barn and meet you there."

Just leave, for heaven's sake! "No. I'll be fine."

Ignoring the sharp stabs of pain, she pulled her stump sock back on, then the prosthesis over that. With no small amount of pride in the minor accomplishment, she forced herself to move casually toward the sweet little bay mare she liked to ride whenever she was home.

Jake met her at the horse's side. Instead of simply giving her a boost into the saddle as she expected, he lifted her into his arms with what appeared to be no effort.

For just a moment he held her close. He smelled incredible, a strangely compelling mixture of fabric softener, clean male and some kind of ruggedly sexy aftershave that reminded her of standing in a high mountain forest after a summer storm.

She couldn't believe how secure she felt to have strong male arms around her, even for a moment—even though those arms belonged to Jake Dalton.

Her heart pounded so hard she thought he must certainly be able to hear it, and she needed every iota of concentration to keep her features and her body language coolly composed so he wouldn't sense her reaction was anything but casual.

He lifted her into the saddle and set her up, careful not to jostle her leg, then he stepped away.

"Thank you," she murmured.

"No problem. I'll meet you at the barn to help you dismount."

"That's not necessary," she assured him firmly. "My dad built a mounting block for my mother to help compensate for her lack of height. It works well for us cripples, too."

His mouth tightened but before he could say anything, she dug her heels into the mare's side and headed across the field without another word.

Her mother would have been furious at her for her rudeness. But Viviana wasn't there—and anyway, her mother had always had a blind spot about the Daltons.

Because Marjorie was her best friend, she didn't think the arrogant, manipulative males of the family could do any wrong.

Ten minutes later Maggie reached the barn. She wasn't really surprised to find the most manipulative of those males standing by the mounting block, waiting to help her down.

He wore sunglasses against the late-afternoon sun, and they shielded his expression, but she didn't need to see his eyes to be fairly sure he was annoyed that she'd ridden away from him so abruptly.

Too bad. She was annoyed with him, too.

"I told you I didn't need help," she muttered as she guided the mare alongside it.

"Just thought you might need a spotter."

"I don't. Go away, Dalton." She hated the idea of him witnessing her clumsy, ungainly efforts, hated that he had seen her stump, hated his very presence.

To her immense frustration, he ignored the order and leaned a hip against the block, arms crossed over his chest as if he had nothing better to do with his time.

She wanted to get down just so she could smack that damn smile off his face.

She swung her right leg over so she was sitting side-saddle, then she gripped the horn, preparing herself for the pain of impact and angling so most of her weight would land on her good leg and not the prosthesis. Before she could make that final small jump to the mounting block, he leaped up to catch her.

She had no idea how he moved so fast, but there he was steadying her. Her body slid down his as he helped her to the block. Everywhere they touched, she could feel the heat of him, and she was ashamed of the small part of her that wanted to curl against him and soak it up like a cat in a warm windowsill.

He didn't let go completely until he'd helped her from the mounting block to solid ground. With as much alacrity as she could muster without falling over and making an even bigger fool of herself, she stepped away from him.

"Consider this your Boy Scout good deed of the day. I can take it from here."

He studied her for a moment, then shook his head. "I should offer to unsaddle the horse for you, Lieutenant, but I think the black eye you'd give me if I tried might be tough to explain to my patients tomorrow."

"Smart man."

"Put your leg up when you're done here. Promise?"

"Yeah, yeah." She turned away from him to uncinch the saddle. She felt his gaze for a long time before she heard his SUV start up a few moments later and he drove away.

Only when the engine sounds started to fade did she trust herself to turn her head to watch him go, her cheek resting on the mare's twitching side.

She hated all those things she'd thought of earlier—that

he'd seen her stump, that she'd been so vulnerable, that he wouldn't take no for an answer, like the rest of his family.

Most of all, she hated that he left her so churned up inside.

How could she possibly be attracted to him? Her stomach still trembled thinking about those strong arms holding her.

She knew better, for heaven's sake. He was a Dalton, one of those slime-sucking bastards who had destroyed her father.

Even if they hadn't had such ugly history between them, she would be foolish to let herself respond to him. That part of her life was over. She'd been taught that lesson well by her ex-fiancé.

Though she tried not to think of it very often, she forced herself now to relive that horrible time at Walter Reed five months ago when Clay had finally been able to leave his busy surgery schedule in Phoenix to come to the army hospital.

Of all the people in her life, she thought he would be able to accept her amputation the easiest. He was a surgeon, after all, and had performed similar surgeries himself. He understood the medical side of things, the stump-shaping process, the rehab, the early prosthesis prototypes.

She had needed his support and encouragement desperately in those early days. But the three days he spent in D.C. had been a nightmare. She didn't think he had met her gaze once that entire visit—and he certainly hadn't been able to bring himself to look at her stump.

One time he happened to walk in when the nurses were changing her dressing and she would never forget the raw burst of revulsion in his eyes before he had quickly veiled it.

She had given him back his ring at the end of his visit,

and he had accepted it with an obvious relief that demoralized and humiliated her.

She couldn't put herself through that again. She had been devastated by his reaction.

If a man who supposedly cared about her—who had emailed her daily while she was on active duty, had sent care packages, had uttered vows of undying love, and who was a surgeon—found her new state as an amputee so abhorrent, how could she ever let down her guard enough to allow someone new past her careful defenses?

She couldn't. The idea terrified her. Like her career as a nurse practitioner, sex was another part of her life she decided she would have to give up.

No big whoop, she decided. Lots of people lived without it and managed just fine.

She hadn't even had so much as an itch of desire since her accident, and she thought—hoped even—that perhaps those needs had died. It would be better if they had.

If she wasn't ever tempted, she wouldn't have to exercise any self-control in the matter.

To find herself responding on a physical level to any man would have been depressing, proof that now she would have to sublimate those normal desires for the rest of her life or face the humiliation of having a man turn away from her in disgust.

To find the man she was attracted to was none other than Jake Dalton was horrifying.

The best thing—the only thing—would be to stay as far away as possible from him. She had enough to deal with, thanks. She didn't need the bitter reminder that she was a living, breathing, functioning woman who could still respond to a gorgeous man.

Chapter 4

The sneaky, conniving son of a bitch went over her head.

Maggie stood with her mother at the window of the Luna kitchen. From here, she had a perfect view of the ranch—the placidly grazing Murray Greys, the warm, weathered planks of the barn, the creek glinting silver in the sunlight.

And that scheming snake Jake Dalton unloading the hay that had just been delivered.

His muscles barely moved under a thin International Harvester T-shirt, she couldn't help notice. He was far more buff than she would have guessed. Tight and hard and gorgeous.

She indulged herself by watching that play of muscles under cotton for only a moment before wrenching her eyes away and forcing her hormones under control.

"I cannot believe you did this, Mama!"

Her mother raised an eyebrow at her accusatory tone. "Tell me what did I do that is so terrible, hmm?"

"You let Jake Dalton sucker you into letting him come to the ranch and help us!"

Viviana laughed. "Oh, yes. I am such a fool to accept the help of a strong, hardworking man when it is offered. Yes. I can see how he—what is the word you used?—*suckered* me. I am a crazy old woman who allows this man to take terrible advantage of me by hauling my hay bales and mending my fences."

Maggie ground her teeth. "Mama! He's a Dalton!"

"He's a good boy, Lena," her mother said, her voice stern. "A good boy and a good neighbor. He says he will help us when he has the time, and I can see no reason to say no."

She could come up with at least a hundred reasons, including the dreams she'd had the night before. Those steamy, torrid dreams of strong muscles and hard chests and sexy smiles.

While she had to admit, she had experienced a tiny moment of gratitude to be caught up in dreams that didn't involve explosions and terror for a change, she had hated waking up alone and aching and vaguely embarrassed at her unwilling attraction to him.

She shifted away from the window, hoping her mother wouldn't notice her suddenly heightened color. "Just what did you have to offer him in return?"

Viviana met her gaze briefly then looked away. "Nothing."

Her sweet, churchgoing, butter-wouldn't-melt-in-my-mouth mother was lying through her teeth. Maggie had absolutely no doubt.

"Mama!"

Viviana's shoulders lifted in a casual shrug. "Nothing you need to worry about right now, anyway."

Maggie said nothing, only continued glaring. After a moment Viviana sighed heavily.

"Okay, okay. I told him I would see that you help him at the clinic on the days he opens to the Latinos."

She added *manipulative, underhanded* and *duplicitous* to the list of unflattering adjectives now preceding Jake Dalton's name in her mind. She had told him no. But with typical Dalton arrogance, he'd found a way around her.

"How could you promise that without talking to me?"

"I thought you would be happy to help him."

"I'm not!"

"But why?" Viviana looked genuinely bewildered. "I thought it would be a good chance for you to stay involved in medicine until you are ready to return to being a nurse."

"I'm not going back, Mama. I told you that."

As usual, her mother heard only what she wanted to hear. "You say that now but who knows what you might want to do a few months from now? This way you are, how do you say, covering your bases."

"I don't want to cover anything! Mama, this is my decision. I don't know what I'm going to do yet but I'm not going back to nursing."

How could she? She had been a good nurse, dedicated and passionate about her patients. But nursing could be physically demanding work and she couldn't even stand up for longer than a few moments at a time. She couldn't see any way that she could spend a whole shift on her feet. Or on one foot and one stump, to be more precise. It wouldn't be fair to her patients.

In her mother's eyes she saw the one thing she hated above all other maternal manipulative tactics—disappointment.

"I gave Jacob my word that he would have a translator, Lena. If you refuse to do this, I will."

Maggie pinched the bridge of her nose. Did anyone on earth know how to lay on the guilt better than her mother?

More than anything, she would have liked to tell her to go right ahead. Translate for the sneaky bastard. But Viviana's English could be dicey sometimes and she had absolutely no background to translate difficult medical concepts.

While it would serve Jake right if she sent her mother to his clinic in her place, she knew she couldn't put Viviana through something that would be so difficult for her.

"You would be much more help to the people than I, of course," Viviana said guilelessly, "but I will do my best."

She watched Jake again, who was looking suspiciously cheerful as he pulled another bale of hay off the truck.

If he'd been within arm's reach, she would have been hard-pressed not to slug him.

He had very neatly boxed her into a corner, and she couldn't see any way to climb out without hurting her mother.

"Fine," she growled. "I'll do it."

Viviana's smile reminded her of a cat with a mouthful of canary feathers. "Oh, good. Jacob will be so pleased."

"Yippee," she muttered, wondering how she could have so completely reverted to her childhood after being home less than a week. Her mother could play her as well now as she could when Maggie was ten.

Viviana stepped away from the window, and for the first time, Maggie registered her clothes. Her pale-green sweater, slacks and bright, cheerful silk scarf weren't exactly appropriate for ranch work and Maggie's stomach gave an ominous twist.

Her mother's words confirmed her sudden suspicion. "I must go to Idaho Falls today for a meeting of the Cattleman's Association. I told Jacob you would be here to show him what to do."

"Me?"

"Is that a problem?"

I don't want to, she almost said. But since she had taken a solemn antiwhine pledge to herself at Walter Reed, she just shrugged and went on the offensive. "What about Tío Guillermo?"

Her mother's shoulders stiffened. "What about him?"

"When are you going to stop this silliness and hire him back to do his job?"

"I hear he has a new job now. He works for the Blue Sage. Lucy Warren told me when I went to the feed store yesterday."

She digested this and tried to imagine her uncle working anywhere but the Luna, especially for a Hollywood actor and wannabe rancher like Justin Hartford.

"Even if that's true, you know he would come back in a minute if you said the word. He loves the ranch."

"Not this time." For just a moment, Maggie thought she heard something deeper behind her mother's brisk tone, but before she could analyze it, Viviana turned away. "I will be late if I do not leave. You are to be nice to Jacob while I am gone."

Hmmph. When those cows out there started singing "Kumbaya."

After her mother left to finish preparing for her meeting, Maggie shifted her weight, trying to ignore the ache in her leg from standing in one position. Though she knew it was cowardly, she couldn't seem to bring herself to walk out there.

She dreaded facing him again, especially knowing she would have to spend an entire day with him, after all.

No, more than one, since her mother had committed her to helping him as a translator.

So much for staying away from him. She sighed, despising her cowardice. She could do this. He was only a man.

Only a man she couldn't stand, a man she wanted absolutely nothing to do with.

A man who had played the starring role of some pretty feverish dreams. And played it quite flawlessly.

She turned on the faucet, ran the water as cold as it would go, then took a bracing drink. She could handle this. She had survived eight months in Afghanistan, a terrorist attack and having a third of her leg chopped off, for heaven's sake.

She could surely face one man.

Chin high, she headed outside, where she found him spreading some of the new hay in the horse pasture.

He stopped working as soon as she approached, folding his arms on top of the pitchfork to watch her progress. It took every bit of concentration but she forced herself to walk slowly and confidently, with no trace of limp.

"You must think you're so clever," she said when she reached him.

He shrugged. "When I have to be."

"You Daltons don't know the meaning of the word no, do you?"

"Oh, we know the meaning of all kinds of words. Like *stubborn,* for instance. Or *obstinate. Thick-headed* is another phrase in our vocabulary, though I think we'd all agree you've got us beat on that one."

For one moment, she was tempted to swing her prosthesis out and sweep that pitchfork he leaned on right out from under him. That would probably be childish, not to mention would likely hurt her like the devil.

"I don't know what you're hoping to achieve by all this, but I'm not about to make it easy for you. You offered to work so, believe me, I'm going to make you work. I only hope your whole doctor gig hasn't turned you into a pansy."

She sounded like a serious bitch, she realized, but he didn't seem offended. He laughed and gave a mock salute.

"Private Pansy reporting for duty, Lieutenant. Put me to work. I'll let you know when it's time for my afternoon nap."

Her insides twirled at the sight of that smile. How in the world was she going to get through this?

She wiped her hands on her jeans and frowned. "Why are you standing around, then?"

"I'm about done here," he said. "I was thinking about heading back along the fence line you were riding yesterday, if that's okay with you. I brought my own horse down from the Cold Creek and thought I'd see how far I could get around the perimeter of the ranch."

"That's as good a place to start as any, I suppose." She gave him a determined look. "I'm coming with you."

She saw arguments brimming in his blue eyes, but after a moment he sighed. "I suppose there's no way you'll let me talk you out of that idea so you can rest."

"You could try. But you wouldn't win."

He studied her a moment longer, those blue eyes probing. "And I guess you're going to climb up my grill if I ask how your prosthesis feels today."

"It doesn't have feelings. It's a fake leg, Doc. That's kind of the point."

"Ha-ha. Seriously, how's the leg?"

He seemed genuinely concerned so she dropped the attitude for a moment and gave him the truth. "A little better. I made sure to put it up last night, just as the doctor ordered."

"Good. You can do more harm than good if you push yourself too hard. Adjusting to a prosthesis can be a complicated process. You can make it worse if your stump becomes too irritated to wear the thing for the long stretches of time needed to become accustomed to it."

"Yeah, that's what they tell me."

She wasn't in the mood to take medical advice from a man in a tractor T-shirt, so she quickly changed the subject. "I'll go get my horse while you finish things here. Oh, and I don't know how you did things on the Cold Creek but we've learned pitchforks work better if you actually lift them out of the dirt instead of just leaning on them."

His low, amused laughter sent shivers rippling down her spine, and she forced herself to turn away and head for the horse pasture as fast as her fake leg would take her.

Jake watched her hurry for the horse pasture. She stumbled a little on a rough patch of grass and he had to fight every impulse to race ahead of her and smooth her path.

She wouldn't appreciate it, he knew, but he couldn't stand watching her struggle, especially when he could see she wasn't telling the complete truth about her pain level.

She was hurting worse than she let on. Whether that was phantom pain or continuing adjustment irritation from the prosthesis, he didn't know. It didn't matter, anyway. She wouldn't want his help, even if he had the magic potion to fix either problem.

She had to make her own way. While the doctor in him might want to do his best to take away her pain, he knew she was trying her best to play the wild card she'd been dealt the way she saw fit, and he had to respect her determination.

Of course, there was a fine line between determination and outright stubbornness.

He was leading his own horse out of the trailer when she rode around the corner of the barn on the same mare she'd ridden the day before. She led another horse loaded with coiled wire.

She looked beautiful on horseback, natural and relaxed and graceful. No one watching her ride with such confidence would ever guess what she'd been through the last five months.

Her glossy dark braid swung behind her, and she lifted her face to the sun as if she couldn't soak in enough.

Jake's stomach tightened, and he could feel blood rush to his groin. He cursed himself for the inappropriate reaction and slammed the horse trailer closed with a little more force than strictly necessary.

"Come on, Doc," she called. "I don't have all day to wait for you."

"Aw, hold your horses."

She rolled her eyes at his lame attempt at a joke. "I hope you don't slow me down like this all day."

"I'll do my best to keep up," he promised.

Keeping up with her wasn't the problem, he discovered by lunchtime. Coming up with subtle, creative ways to slow her down and keep her from overdoing things was another story.

"You need to stop *again?*" Halfway around the perimeter of the ranch, she stared at him, her eyes dark with suspicion. "That's three times in four hours. You *are* a pansy, Dalton."

"I'm hungry, okay? I'm not used to all this physical labor. It works up a heck of an appetite. I packed two sandwiches and a couple colas. You want lunch?"

Since fixing fence was a two-person job, he knew she

couldn't insist on going ahead by herself. Just as he intended, after a moment she shrugged and made her way to the small grassy hill where he'd settled. Though she tried to act tough as nails, he could see the lines of pain around her mouth and the cautious steps she took across the uneven ground.

Stubborn woman. He wanted to toss her over the back of her little mare and haul her back to the house where she could spend the afternoon with her leg up. The next best thing was manufacturing these little excuses to stop as often as he could so she could rest.

"Ham and cheese or PB and J?" he asked when she settled against a tree, her leg extended in front of her.

"Whichever."

He handed over the ham and one of the colas he'd had the foresight to stick in the icy river when they stopped at this section of fence a half hour before.

She popped the top and took a healthy swallow, her eyes closed with obvious appreciation, and he had to focus on his lunch to keep from jumping her right there.

"Oh, that's good. Spring runoff gives the water just the perfect temperature for maximum chill. That water's running fast. How'd you keep the cans from floating downstream?"

"Old cowboy trick one of the ranch hands taught me when I was a kid. Tie fishing line around the plastic rings and lash that to a tree on the bank. I always keep some in my saddle bag for emergencies."

"Just in case you're ever stranded in the middle of nowhere on horseback with a warm soda. I can see where that would come in handy."

"What can I say? I appreciate the finer things in life."

She made a snort that might have been a laugh, but he wouldn't let himself get his hopes up.

She took another sip. "Since you can't seem to get through a half hour of work without taking a break, explain to me how a wimp like you ever survived the eighteen-hour shifts of a resident."

"Black coffee and plenty of No-Doze. But then, I didn't have a harsh taskmaster of an Army Lieutenant riding my butt at the University of Utah."

She shifted her leg, and he didn't miss her wince, even though she quickly took another sip of soda to hide it. "I forgot that's where you went to medical school," she said after she'd swallowed.

"Yeah. The Running Utes."

"Good medical school. So why didn't they throw you out for sheer laziness?"

He thought of the summa cum laude hanging in his office and how he'd worked his tail off to earn it. "Must have been a fluke. I guess I can fake it when necessary. You know how it works, look busy when the attending is around."

Her shoulders had relaxed, he saw, and she had lost some of those pain lines around her mouth. Good. He wondered what chance he had of keeping her right here insulting him for the next couple of hours. He supposed he'd have to be happy with a few minutes.

"So, why does a moderately intelligent medical student with a talent for fakery choose general medicine as a specialty instead of something more lucrative like plastic surgery or urology?"

"I guess because I like treating the whole patient, not just bits and pieces."

"Okay, so you still could have broadened your horizons a little and opened a general medicine practice somewhere more interesting than Pine Gulch, Idaho. So why come home?"

He had many answers to that particular question, some

easier to verbalize than others, but he did his best to put his reasons into words.

"Old Doc Whitaker gave me my first taste of medicine, literally and figuratively. He probably did the same for you, right?"

She nodded with a small smile for the robust man who had treated everyone in the county for nearly fifty years.

"He brought all three of us boys into the world, treated us when we had the chicken pox, helped Seth through the worst years of his asthma," Jake went on. "In high school, I worked at the clinic on Saturdays and a few afternoons a week. I grew to admire that old coot for his dedication, for the connection he had to his patients. He knew them all. Their kids, their parents, their sisters and brothers."

He was quiet for a moment, remembering the man who had been such a steady influence in his life. "When I was finishing my residency, I tried to picture myself working in some impersonal HMO somewhere treating thirty patients a day. I just couldn't do it. Around that time, Doc called me, said he wanted to retire and was I interested in buying his practice. Coming home seemed right."

"Any regrets?" she asked. "Does fame and fortune ever come calling your name?"

"Not that I've heard. But maybe I had my cell phone turned off and missed it."

A smile almost broke free but she sternly forced her mouth back into a straight line before it could escape. "I forget. You're one of the Daltons of Cold Creek. With your share of the ranch, you probably don't have to worry about money at all, do you? I guess that makes you just another dilettante."

He swallowed a sigh. What would he have to do to get past her anger at his family?

"*Dilettante.* Now there's a big word for an Idaho cowgirl."

"Must have read it on a cereal box somewhere."

"If I were one of those dili-thingies just out for a good time, I'm pretty sure the amusement quotient would have disappeared once I actually started treating patients. We GPs see some pretty nasty stuff. Anything from impacted colons to uncontrolled vomiting to gangrenous sores."

"Try being a nurse, wussy-boy. You doctors get to waltz in, make your godlike proclamations and waltz out again, leaving us hardworking nurses to do the dirty work."

"I don't ever waltz," he protested, then grinned. "I prefer to sashay."

She did smile at that and he couldn't help feeling he'd just won a major victory. Their gazes held for a long moment and then her smile slid off her face as if she just realized it was there.

She jerked her gaze away and drank the last of her cola, her expression suddenly fierce. "Okay, party time's over. If I've only got a day to make use of your puny muscles, I don't want to waste it sitting around shooting the breeze."

He almost told her she could make use of his puny muscles—or anything else of his that might interest her—any time she wanted, she only had to say the word.

But while he wasn't exactly the lazy wimp she seemed to enjoy taunting him about, he wasn't an idiot, either, so he decided to keep the thought to himself.

By the time they finished checking and repairing every fenceline on the Rancho de la Luna and headed back for the house, he was beginning to question either his intelligence or his sanity.

Why was he torturing himself like this? Maggie hadn't let up all afternoon about not wanting or needing his help.

If anything, she seemed to ride him even harder as the afternoon wore on.

He had to wonder if she was trying to see just how far she had to push to drive him away.

If she were any other woman—and if not for those lines of pain around her mouth or the stiff way she sat in the saddle—he would have acknowledged defeat hours ago and let her run him off.

But he hadn't been about to leave her to all this work by herself. What she needed was a rest. The quicker they finished up and put the horses away, the quicker she could put her leg up.

She didn't seem to want to talk, and he didn't push her, as the horses made their way along the creek back to the house, the afternoon sun warm on their shoulders and the water churning beside them.

At the barn he slid down quickly from his horse and looped the reins around the fence, then crossed to the mounting block so he could help her off her horse.

She'd been stubborn about it all day but he could tell climbing down from the horse was a movement that bothered her. He'd insisted on helping her mount and dismount throughout the day, if only for the chance to touch her, and he intended to this time but she glared at him.

"Go away, Dalton," she snapped when he approached. "That's why we have a mounting block here, so you can stop babysitting me."

He just smiled blandly and stood beside the wooden block, just in case she needed him.

She seemed determined not to, though her teeth clamped together and she couldn't hide a wince as she swung her prosthetic over the saddle and slid down.

Before Maggie was completely ready to take her own

weight, the mare shifted, just enough to leave her off balance. She stumbled on the block, but before she could fall, he leaped up and caught her, absorbing her weight, and she steadied herself against his chest.

All day she had tried to act tough as rawhide as she rode alongside him, but now she felt small and fragile in his arms.

He reacted like any other normal, red-blooded man who suddenly found his arms wrapped around the beautiful woman who had been his secret fantasy for years—the same woman who had tormented him all day just by her presence.

He kissed her.

She made a small gasping sound of surprise when his mouth drifted across hers, and then she seemed to freeze in his arms.

He could feel the soft sough of her breath in his mouth, feel the tremble of her fingers against his chest, and wondered if she could hear his heart hammering against his ribs.

That smart mouth of hers was surprisingly soft, like apple blossoms, and she tasted like cola and spearmint gum.

He might have expected her to shove him off the mounting block or give him a judo chop to the head. When she didn't, when her lips seemed to soften in welcome, he took that as enough encouragement to deepen the kiss.

Chapter 5

She couldn't seem to make her brain work, other than one stunned moment of disbelief that he would have the audacity to kiss her out of the blue without any kind of advance warning.

Wasn't that like a Dalton, to just take what he wanted without asking permission?

Before she could manage to work through her shock enough to actually do something about it—like jerk away or, better yet, give him a swift knee to the privates, her initial astonishment began to give way to something else, something terribly dangerous.

A slow, sultry ache fluttered to life inside her, and before she fully realized what she was doing, her hands slid into the thin fabric of his T-shirt, holding him fast.

He made a low sound and deepened the kiss, his mouth firm and purposeful on hers, and she forgot about the pain below her knee, forgot about the frustration she had been fighting the entire day over her own limitations, forgot the man who held her was Jake Dalton, son of the bastard who had destroyed her father.

For one glorious moment he was only a man—a strong, gorgeous male who smelled of leather and horses and a few lingering traces of that sexy aftershave he used; a solid, strong wall of muscle against her, around her.

The man was one incredible kisser, she had to admit. She shivered as his mouth explored hers, caressed it. He used exactly the right pressure for maximum impact—not too hard, not too soft. Just right to turn her bones to liquid, her insides to mush.

Oh, it felt good to be in a man's arms. For one brief, self-ish moment she allowed herself to enjoy it, to savor the sensation of being held and cherished and protected, her blood surging through her, her nerve endings buzzing with desire.

She wasn't sure at exactly what moment she shifted from passive recipient to ardent participant. Maybe at the first slight exploring brush of his tongue along the seam of her lips.

The next thing she knew, her arms had somehow found their way around his neck, she found herself pressing against him tightly, and she was returning his kiss with an enthusiasm that took her completely by surprise.

She jerked her eyes open and saw him gazing back at her, an unreadable expression in the pure, stunning blue of his eyes.

The sight of those Dalton eyes looking back at her seemed to shock her back to her senses as if she'd just fallen into the creek.

What in heaven's name was she doing?

She jerked away, nearly stumbling in her haste to put

space between them. He steadied her so she wouldn't fall off the mounting block, then dropped his hand.

She stared at him, horribly aware of how hard her lungs had to work to draw air, of the tremble of her stomach and how she had to fist her hands together to keep from reaching for him again.

How mortifying that she would react to his uninvited touch with such eagerness, even a subtle hint of desperation she hoped he couldn't taste. This was Jake Dalton, the last man on earth she should want to tangle tongues with.

But she did. Oh, did she!

Emotions raged through her, and she wanted to yell and curse and rip into him. At the very least, she wanted to ask him what the hell he thought he was doing.

She took a deep, steadying breath. She refused to let him know how much he affected her.

"Was that really necessary?" she asked coolly. "A helping hand would have been sufficient."

A muscle quirked in his cheek as if he was amused, though she could see his chest rise and fall rapidly as he tried to catch his breath.

"I don't know about you, but I certainly needed it."

What kind of game was he playing? she wondered. A pity kiss for poor Stump Girl?

"Next time I'll dismount on my own if you're going to paw me," she snapped.

"Is that what you'd call what just happened?"

She didn't know *what* to call it. She only knew she couldn't get away from him fast enough.

"Don't let it happen again," she ordered.

He studied her for a long moment.

"What if it does?" His low-timbred voice sent shivers cascading down her spine.

She drew in a sharp breath and decided to ignore him. Instead she gripped the hand railing and made her way down the three steps of the mounting block.

"Running away, Maggie? I would have thought you had more spine than that."

She bristled. "I'm not running away. I have things to do—unlike some people, who apparently can spend all day mending fence and accosting unsuspecting women."

"I hope those things involve stretching out and taking the weight off your prosthesis."

"Eventually. I need to put my horse away first and make some notes in the ranch logs."

"I'll take care of your horse. Go make your notes so you can take it easy."

She would have argued with him—on principle if nothing else—if she wasn't so desperate to get away from him.

"Thank you," she muttered, though the words tasted bitter as a bad cucumber.

While she was gnawing on it, she might as well devour the whole thing. "Thank you also for your help today. It would have taken me a week if I'd been on my own."

If she expected him to gloat or give her a bad time, she was doomed to disappointment. He only nodded. "You're welcome. I'm glad we got the fence line checked."

She nodded, wanting only for this day to be over. Aware of his gaze following her, she turned and made her way toward the ranch office in the barn.

She had to hope he couldn't see the wobble in her knees—both of them, not just the overworked left one.

When she turned the corner of the barn and was certain he could no longer see her, she let out a long, slow breath and leaned a hand against the weathered wood planks.

What was the point of that little demonstration? For the

life of her, she couldn't figure out what he was trying to prove. If he wanted to show she had questionable taste in men, he'd certainly made his point.

Dalton or not, the man certainly knew how to kiss. She still couldn't seem to catch her breath.

She pressed two fingers to her lips as if she could still taste the imprint of his mouth there, then shook her head at her own ridiculous reaction, far out of proportion to what had happened.

Still, it *had* been an incredible kiss. She supposed if she'd ever given it much thought, she might have expected it of Seth Dalton. The youngest of the three brothers was the ladies' man of the family, the one who left every woman in the county sighing and giddy.

Whoever would have thought the quiet, studious doctor would have such hidden depths?

Not that she would ever allow herself the opportunity to plumb those depths. That was the first and only kiss she would ever share with Jake Dalton, no matter how proficient at it he might be.

Even if he wasn't Hank Dalton's son, she couldn't let this happen again.

Like it was some kind of grim lodestone, she rubbed the spot just below her knee where flesh met metal.

It had been difficult to remember his surname all morning. He was a good companion and a hard worker, when he wasn't manufacturing excuses for her to take a break.

She saw right through his efforts. On the one hand, she had to admit she had been grateful to him for his sensitivity to the frustrations and the challenges she faced in doing things that had always been second nature to her six months ago.

On the other hand, each time he had made up some silly

reason to take a break had been another painful reminder that she couldn't keep up with him, that her life had changed dramatically.

Different was not the same thing as *over,* she reminded herself as she opened the barn door and walked inside. The barn smelled sweet and musty, a combination that instantly transported her back to her childhood.

Dust motes floated like gold flakes in the sunbeams shining down from the rafters, and the air smelled of horses and new hay and life.

She paused for a moment to enjoy the memories that rushed back, of chasing mischievous kittens through the barn, of learning to saddle a horse for the first time in one of the stalls that lined the wall, of the stomach-twirling excitement of swinging on the rope Abel hung from the crossbeams, to land in piles of soft hay below.

She spied the rope, still there but looped over the rafters, and she could vividly picture her father standing about where she was, watching with delight as she would swing down from the loft, shrieking all the way until she let go and landed in the welcoming piles of hay.

It was a good memory, one she hadn't thought of in years. She wondered if, before her accident, she ever would have taken time to notice something as quietly lovely as a barn in springtime, to remember that long-ago moment with her father.

She would have been in too much of a hurry to get somewhere important.

A person learning to walk all over again moved at a slower pace by necessity. Sometimes that wasn't always such a bad thing.

She made her way through the barn to the ranch office. The small room was cluttered with tack and coiled rope and other odds and ends. She pulled out the log book Guillermo had always maintained religiously in his neat, precise English.

Under the day's date, she wrote, "Rode entire perimeter of ranch checking fence. Significant repairs performed on southwest corner and near road."

Kissed Jake Dalton until I couldn't think straight. Knees still wobbly.

She set down her pencil when she realized where her mind carried her again. At least she'd only *thought* that last bit, not written it down. It might be a little tough to explain to her mother.

Nothing like that would happen again, she thought sternly. She couldn't allow it.

Right now she needed to focus on the job at hand. There would be time later to worry about the good doctor—and what he might be after.

She turned back to the log, which inevitably drew her thoughts to her uncle. He should be here making this notation. He should have been out there today checking the fenceline. Perhaps it was time she paid him a visit and begged him to come to his senses.

Anything to keep Jake Dalton from showing up to torment her again.

She found time the next evening after dinner. Viviana had phone calls to make, she said, so Maggie told her she wanted to drive into town to pick up a few things at the small market.

Guillermo's house, a mile toward town on Cold Creek Road, hadn't changed in all the years she'd known him— still just as small and square, with clapboard siding that received a new coat of white paint every other year whether it needed it or not.

It was too early for the extravagant display of roses he tended so carefully to burst along the fence, but cheerful spring flowers neatly lined the sidewalk and an American flag hung proudly on a flagpole in the front yard. A large yellow ribbon dangled just below it, and she felt emotion well up in her throat, knowing it was for her.

Chickens ran for cover when she pulled into the driveway and as soon as she turned off the engine, a couple of border collies hurried out of the shade to investigate the visitor.

When he wasn't raising Murray Grey cattle for her mother, Guillermo bred and trained the smart cattle dogs. The two who came out didn't bark, they just waited politely for attention.

She patted them both in turn and was just preparing to head off in search of her uncle when he rounded the corner of the garage, a shovel in his hand.

His brown eyes widened when he saw her, then they filled with raw emotion.

In one quick move he dropped the shovel to the concrete driveway with a thud and rushed to her side and reached for her. "Lena! Oh Lena, it is good you are home."

Guillermo spoke Spanish, though she knew he was comfortable in English, also.

"It is wonderful to see you, as well," she responded in the same language. It was, she thought.

Though only a few inches taller than she was, she had always considered Guillermo one of her heroes. He was quiet and sturdy, a steady source of strength throughout her life, even before her father's death.

Abel and Guillermo had been brothers and best friends,

had come together from Argentina to ranch together. After Abel's death, Guillermo had taken over as ranch manager and had also stepped up to assume a more active fatherly role in her life.

After she enlisted, she could still remember how he sat her down for a heart-to-heart talk before she left for basic training.

"To serve your country is a good thing you are doing," he told her. "You make me proud. Hold your head high and serve with honor and courage. Never be ashamed of what you have done and always do your best to stand for what is right."

More than once throughout her years of service, his quiet advice rang in her ears, saving her from what could have been major career mistakes.

"How about a Pepsi?" he asked now, and she couldn't help her smile. Like the flag out front and his neat, ordered flower beds, some things never changed. He'd been giving her cola since she was old enough to drink from a straw. "Sure."

"Come. Sit."

She followed him onto the porch and took one of the two comfortable rockers that had been there as long as she could remember. She could vividly remember playing on the little postage-stamp front yard while her uncle and father sat on this front porch drinking beer and shooting the breeze.

Guillermo joined her in a moment and set a tray with a couple of Pepsis and some pretzels on a little table between the rockers.

She sipped at her drink, enjoying the unobstructed view of the mountains he enjoyed here.

Her uncle didn't seem in any hurry to determine the reason for her visit, though surely he must have his suspicions. Instead, they made small talk about her drive up from Arizona, about how her car was running, about the litter of puppies he was just about ready to wean.

Finally she gathered her nerve and blurted out the topic she knew had to be on both their minds.

"Guillermo, what's going on? Why aren't you at the Luna?"

He scratched his cheek, where the day's salt-and-pepper stubble already showed. "Did your mother send you?"

"No," she confessed. "She told me not to come."

"When will you learn to listen to your mama, little girl?"

"I can't believe that whatever happened between you two can't be mended. Think of the history you share! You've been running the Luna for years. You have a financial and emotional stake in it. It's as much yours as Mama's and you both know it."

He said nothing, just sipped his cola and watched a car drive past, and she wanted to scream with frustration.

For two mature adults, both her mother and her uncle were acting like children having a playground brawl, and for the life of her, she couldn't understand it.

"*Tío!* What is this about? Tell me that much at least. Mama won't say anything. She just said you fought and she fired you."

His dark gaze narrowed over the rim of his soda. "She did not fire me. I quit."

"What difference does it make who did what? She's still over her head trying to run the ranch by herself."

A frown flitted across his weathered, handsome features. "She did not find someone to help her yet?"

Just me, she wanted to say. *Me and a sexy, interfering doctor who should mind his own blasted business.*

Instead she only shook her head. "She hasn't hired anybody yet. She's got an ad in the paper and a couple of ag job websites, but she hasn't had any takers."

"She will find someone. The Luna is a good operation."

"It's a good operation because you built it into one! You're the one who brought in the Murray Grey's, who watched the market enough to know when the time would be right for their marbled beef. We all know that. Mama's just being stubborn."

"She is good at that, no?" Though his words were hard, Maggie thought she saw something odd flicker in his eyes at the mention of her mother.

"I'd say the two of you are about even in that department. Isn't there anything I can say to change your mind?"

"Not on this," he said firmly. "I am not welcome at the Luna now even if I wanted to return, and that is as it should be."

"*Tio!*"

"No, Lena. I have taken a new job now."

"So I hear. I can't believe it, though. You said you'd never work for one of the Hollywood invaders who are taking over all the good ranch land."

"Things change. Mr. Hartford at least wants to raise cattle and not bison."

She opened her mouth to argue again, but he held up a hand. "Enough, Lena. Your mother has made her choice. And I have made mine."

Choice about what? she wondered, but before she could ask, her uncle quickly changed the subject, asking about her time in Afghanistan before her injury, how her leg was doing, what her plans were now that she'd returned to Pine Gulch.

Though she tried several times to draw the conversation back to the Luna and her mother, each time Guillermo neatly sidestepped her question until she finally threw up her hands.

"Okay, I've had it with both of you. You both want to throw away a good team, years of history, go right ahead."

Her words seemed to distress her uncle, but he didn't argue with her.

She stayed for another half hour then took her leave.

Guillermo hugged her tightly after he had walked her to her car. "You are a good girl, Lena. Take care of your mother and yourself. But don't forget your old *tío*."

"I won't," she assured him.

"What is between your mother and myself, that is one thing. But you are always welcome on my porch."

She smiled, kissed his leathery cheek, then climbed carefully into her Subaru and drove away.

He had to admit, he had thought she would bail on him.

Four days later Jake stood at the reception area of his clinic and watched Maggie's little Subaru SUV pull into the parking lot. The afternoon sunlight shone silver when she swung out a pair of forearm crutches, then leveraged herself onto them and started making her painstaking way toward the door.

A thick knot of emotions churned through him as he watched her slow approach—awe and respect and a distinctive kind of pride he knew he had no right to feel.

She wore tan slacks and a crisp white shirt that would have looked severe if not for the turquois-and-silver choker and matching earrings she wore with it.

She had pulled her thick hair back in a headband, and she looked springy and bright and so beautiful he decided he would have been content to spend the rest of the afternoon just gazing at her.

Though she wore her prosthesis, she wasn't putting weight on it, and his mind started racing through all the possible reasons for that. Had she reinjured herself? Was there a problem with the fit?

He wanted to rush out to help her as she made her cautious way across the parking lot to the clinic, but he managed to restrain himself, though it was just about the toughest thing he'd ever had to do.

If he made any kind of scene, he had no doubt she would turn around, head back to her car and take off. She didn't seem to welcome any effort on his part to help her, no matter how well intentioned, so he forced himself to remain at the door.

At last she reached him.

"You're here. I didn't expect to see you."

She frowned. "I may not have been involved in making this stupid deal, but I refuse to be the one to break it, either. My mother gave you her word, and the Cruz family honors its promises."

Her implication that his family couldn't say the same was obvious, but he decided to overlook it for now.

"Come in. We don't open for another ten minutes or so. That should give you a few moments to look around."

She made a face but moved through the doorway, her shoulder brushing his chest as she hobbled past.

She smelled divine, like the lavender in his mother's garden, and he tried to disguise his deep inhalation as a regular breath.

She paused for a moment, looking around the waiting area of the clinic, and he tried to read her reaction to the changes he'd made since taking over from Doc Whitaker.

Beyond the obvious cosmetic changes—the new row of windows looking over the mountains, the comfortable furniture with its clean lines—the entire clinic was designed to soothe frayed nerves and help patients feel more comfortable.

A few things hadn't changed from Doc Whitaker's time, and one of those was coming around the receptionist counter with a smile.

"Magdalena, you remember Carol Bass? She's been the receptionist and dragon at the gate for going on thirty years now."

Maggie smiled with delight, and Jake wondered what he would have to do to become the recipient of one of those looks.

"Of course," she exclaimed. "I still remember all those cherry lollipops you used to dole out if we didn't cry during shots."

Carol gave Maggie a hearty hug. "I still give them to the kids. Amazing how a litle sugar will take away the worst sting."

"I figured that out with my patients in Phoenix. Even the grown kids handle shots better with a little chocolate."

Carol returned her smile before her expression grew solemn and she squeezed Maggie's hand. "I'm so sorry about what happened to you over there, honey. I hope you know how much your service means to all of us here in Pine Gulch."

Maggie's shoulders stiffened and she looked uncomfortable at the sudden direction of the conversation, but she merely smiled. "Thank you. And you should know how much I appreciated the card and flowers you and Dale sent me after I returned stateside. They were so lovely. All the nurses at Walter Reed raved about them. I was very touched that you thought of me."

He had sent her flowers, too. Most likely she tossed them when she'd seen his name on the card.

He caught the bitterness in his thoughts and chided himself. She could do what she wanted with his flowers. He hadn't sent them to earn her undying appreciation.

"Of course we thought of you," Carol answered firmly. "This whole town prayed for you after you were hurt over there. We're still praying for you, honey."

Maggie looked overwhelmed suddenly by Carol's solicitude, fragile as antique glass, and he gave in to his fierce need to protect her.

"Why don't I give you a quick tour before the clinic opens again so you know your way around when the patients start showing up?"

"Yes. All right." It might have been his imagination but he thought for a moment, there, she actually looked grateful.

She followed him through the security door to the inner hallway between exam rooms. He opened the first door and gestured for Maggie to go inside, then he closed the door to the exam room behind them so they were out of Carol's earshot.

He wanted to kiss her again. The need to touch her once more, to taste her, burned inside him.

He forced himself to push it aside. She hadn't been thrilled the first time he did it. If he tried it again, she'd probably stab him with the nearest surgical instrument.

"Okay, what's the story with the cruches?" he asked.

Her pretty mouth tightened. "In case it slipped your attention, I'm missing half my leg. Crutches are sometimes a necessary evil."

He ignored her sarcasm. "You're having problems with the prosthesis, aren't you?"

"Nothing a good trash compactor couldn't take care of for me."

"What's going on?"

He thought for a moment she wouldn't answer, but after a moment she sighed. "I'm having a little continuing irritation. After a conference call between my prosthetist and one in Idaho Falls, I've been strongly encouraged to go back to wearing it without weight bearing for a while."

His sorrow for what she had to deal with was a physical ache in his chest. He wanted so much to take this struggle away from her, and he hated his helplessness. What was the point of twelve years of medical training if he couldn't ease this burden for her?

Some of his emotions must have shown in his expression because her eyes suddenly turned cool. She didn't want anything from him, apparently, especially not sympathy.

"Let's get on with it. Since I'm being blackmailed to be here, you might as well give me the tour."

She was pushing him away, and he knew he could do nothing about that, either.

"This is one of six exam rooms." He opened the door and walked down the hall, measuring his steps so she could keep up with him on her crutches. "We have one trauma room that can double as an operating room for minor emergency procedures. Just as under Doc Whitaker, we're part first-aid station, part triage center and part family medicine practice."

"And your free clinic?"

"We started doing it once a month on what is supposed to be my half day off, to try meeting some of the medical needs of the underserved populations. It's open to anyone without insurance but we especially encourage agriculture workers and their families. Examinations are free, and lab work is available at reduced cost through a foundation we set up here at the clinic."

"Very philanthropic of you."

"But shortsighted. We quickly learned we'd underesti-mated demand and a monthly clinic just wasn't enough. We're doing it bimonthly now, and even that is always full."

"What kinds of patient care do you typically give?"

"A little of everything. Prenatal care, diabetes manage-ment, well-child visits. A wide gamut."

Carol called down the hall, interrupting him. "It's show-time. Three cars just pulled up in the parking lot. You ready to go?"

"Where's Jan?"

His nurse popped her head out of the reception area. "Right here. Sorry, I was late getting back from lunch. The diner was packed. Let's rock and roll."

"Jan, this is Maggie Cruz. She's going to translate for us today."

"Cool. Nice to meet you."

Tall and rangy, with short-cropped blond hair, Jan Sun-vale was a transplant to Pine Gulch from Boston. She was an avid hiker and climber who had moved West looking for room to breathe. He considered her one of the clinic's biggest assets and praised the day she decided to make a pit stop in Pine Gulch and ended up staying.

He turned back to Maggie. "I don't want you to overdo it today. If you need to rest or you've had enough altogether, let me know. None of this foolish-pride crap, okay?"

Her eyes flashed. "I've already got a mother, Dalton. I don't need another one."

He raised an eyebrow. "Believe me, the last thing in the world I want to be is your mother."

She blinked a little at his low words, but before she could respond, the reception area began to fill with patients.

Chapter 6

Ten patients later Jake finished his exam of a young girl of about six and pulled his stethoscope out of his ears, smiling broadly.

"Tell Señora Ayala that Raquel's lungs are perfect, with no more sign of the pneumonia. I can't hear any crackles, and the X-rays look as clean as a new toothbrush."

She made a face at him and translated his message—without the last metaphor—to the girl's worried-looking mother. The mother beamed and hugged first the little girl and then Jake, who gave a surprised laugh but returned the embrace.

"*¡Gracias! ¡Gracias por todo!*" She appeared overcome with gratitude but Jake simply smiled.

"De nada," he answered. "Tell Señora Ayala she is the one who did all the work and deserves all the credit. She took wonderful care of her daughter. I wish all my patients' parents were so diligent about giving meds and following advice."

Maggie dutifully translated his words to Celia Ayala, whose dark eyes filled with tears as she hugged her daughter again.

"Raquel had to spend a few nights in the hospital," Jake informed Maggie. "But she's been home for two weeks now and is doing great, aren't you, sweetie?"

The little girl apparently spoke much more fluent English than her mother. She nodded at Jake's words and smiled at him. "You made the bad cooties go away."

"I didn't do that, your body fixed itself. Remember, I just helped all those good cootie-fighters you already had with a little medicine to make them stronger."

"It tasted icky but Mami made me take it, anyway."

"That's just what she was supposed to do. And now you're all better. You can go back to school and play with your friends and all the things you did before you got sick."

The little girl appeared to have mixed feelings about this. "Does that mean I will not come to see you anymore?"

"Of course not." He grinned. "Anytime you want to have a shot, I can probably find one for you. You just come talk to me."

Raquel giggled. "No. No more shots!"

"Are you sure?" he teased. "I can give you one now if you think you need one."

She shook her head vigorously, then slanted him a look under long eyelashes. "I colored a picture for you."

Tongue between her teeth, she reached into the backpack she had lugged into the exam room with her and pulled out a paper.

Maggie wasn't an expert at interpreting children's artwork but even she could figure out this one. A stick figure of a girl with dark hair and braids lay on a bed. Beside her, another stick figure in a white coat wore what was either a snake or a stethoscope around his neck and held a bunch of brightly colored balloons in one hand. A red-crayon heart encircled the whole picture.

"This is you." Raquel pointed to the doctor figure. "When you came to see me in the hospital."

Jake studied it as closely as an art critic preparing to write a review. "I love it! You know what I'm going to do? When we're done here, I'm going to hang it in my office, right where I can see it."

"Why do you not hang it now?"

"Now, that is a great idea. Maggie, do you think you'll be okay for a moment here?"

Since he was already halfway out the door, she didn't know what else to do but nod. He hurried out, leaving her alone with the little girl and her mother, who was looking confused at their exchange.

Maggie apologized for her lapse in translator duties and quickly explained to the woman where Jake was headed.

The little girl listened to their exchange, swinging her legs on the exam table and studying Maggie curiously.

"Are you married to Dr. Jake?" she asked after a moment, switching to Spanish.

"No! Absolutely not!"

"Good. Because I want to marry him."

Maggie had to smile at the determination in the girl's voice, the almost belligerent way she crossed her arms and gave Maggie a look that dared her to contradict.

"I'm sure he'll be thrilled to hear that, but I'm afraid you might have to wait a little while. Don't you think you need to finish kindergarten first?"

"Do I have to?"

"Yes," her mother answered firmly.

Raquel looked so disappointed by this that Celia and Maggie shared a smile.

"She loves Dr. Jake," Celia said in her mellifluous Spanish. "He was so kind while she was sick and drove to the hospital in Idaho Falls every morning and evening to check on her. I caught a cold while she was in the hospital and one night I was too sick to stay with her and my husband had to work. We could not find anyone else. When Dr. Jake heard, he insisted on staying all night at the hospital so she would not wake up and be afraid."

For one silly moment Maggie wanted to shove her hands over her ears and start blabbering to block out the woman's words.

She didn't want to hear all this, didn't want to know anything that contradicted the cold, heartless picture she had created in her mind of him and the rest of his family.

"Everyone in the Latino community loves him," Celia Ayala went on, her expression suddenly sly. "Especially the *señoritas. ¿Sí?*"

To her dismay, Maggie suddenly couldn't think about anything else but that sizzling kiss they'd shared. She could feel heat creep over her cheekbones and had to hope Señora Ayala didn't notice.

If the *señoritas* knew how the man kissed, they would be camping out on his doorstep.

"I wouldn't know about that," she said, her voice brisk. "I'm just helping out today."

Before the other woman could respond, Jake returned to the exam room. Maggie could feel her face heat up another notch, though she knew there was no possible way he could know they'd been talking about them.

Jake smiled at the trio of females, and Maggie thought

for one insane moment that something deep and tender flickered in his gaze when her looked at her, though it was gone so quickly she was certain she must have been mistaken.

"I found a place of honor for your picture," he told the little girl. "You need to come see it."

Raquel jumped from the exam table eagerly. "Please, Mami? Dr. Jake wants me to see the picture."

Celia nodded, and the girl slipped her hand into his.

"We'll be back in a minute," Jake promised.

After they left the room, Señora Ayala turned to Maggie. "He likes you, I can tell."

Maggie stared at the woman. "That's crazy. He does not!"

The other woman shrugged, an unmistakable matchmaking light in her dark eyes. "You can say that but I always sense these things. And you like him too, no?"

"No," she said firmly. "Our families are neighbors but that's all. I'm only helping him today because my mother volunteered me. I'm absolutely not interested in Jake Dalton that way."

The other woman studied her for a moment, then shrugged. "Too bad. He's a good man. My husband works hard but his job does not pay for doctors. Without Dr. Jake, we would have nowhere to take our children when they are sick."

Again she wanted to tell the woman she wasn't interested in a Jake Dalton testimonial, but she had no idea how to make her stop.

She didn't want to know any of this. She preferred to picture him as the arrogant rich boy playing at doctor, not as the caring, compassionate physician she had witnessed the past two hours.

She was finding it very difficult to nurture her anger against the Daltons since she'd returned to Pine Gulch. How could she continue to detest the lot of them when at least one member of the family had done nothing but confound her expectations since she'd been back?

She didn't like it. Things had been easier, cleaner, when she could lump the whole family in with their arrogant SOB of a patriarch.

Jake wasn't very much like his father. He never had been, she acknowledged. Hank had been brash and forceful, the kind of person who sucked all the oxygen from a room wherever he went.

Even in the years before he had double-crossed her father, Jake's father had always made her uncomfortable. His voice was loud, his hands were as huge and hard as anvils, and he had always seemed so different from her own smiling, gentle papa.

The three Dalton boys had been a part of her life as long as she could remember. She didn't remember much about Jake's older brother, Wade, simply because the age difference between them was wide—six years. But Seth had been her age and they'd shared classes together from kindergarten on.

Jake, on the other hand, had only been three years older than her and Seth but he had always seemed closer to Wade's age than theirs.

She remembered him as quiet, studious, never without a book open in front of him.

While they waited for the bus at the little enclosed bus stop her father constructed at the end of their driveways, she and Seth would sometimes play tag or catch. Jake rarely joined in, though she knew he was athletic enough. He had been an all-state baseball player and she knew he worked just as hard as the other brothers on the Cold Creek ranch.

He had been a quiet, serious boy who had grown into a dedicated physician with quite a fan club.

She sighed and shifted her leg to a more comfortable position. She could sense her feelings about him were subtly changing and she wasn't very thrilled about it.

It had been much easier to dislike him on principle than to face the grim truth that a man like Jake Dalton would never be interested in her now. Before her accident, maybe. She knew she wasn't ugly, and she used to be funny and smart and interesting before her world fell apart.

The bombing in Kabul had changed everything. She was no longer that woman, the kind of woman who could interest a man like Jake Dalton.

He had kissed her, though.

If he wasn't interested in her, why had he kissed her, that puzzling, intense kiss she couldn't get out of her head?

In the four days since their heated embrace, the memory of kissing him seemed to whisper into her mind a hundred times a day. The scent of him, the taste of him, the strength and comfort in those arms holding her close.

She couldn't seem to get her brain around it. She had tried to analyze it from every possible angle and she still couldn't figure out what might have compelled him to kiss her like that.

"If you like him," Celia said, yanking her from that sunny afternoon and back into Jake Dalton's comfortable exam room, "you should do something about it before some other lucky *chica* comes along."

Some other *chica* with two feet, no doubt, and a healthy, well-adjusted psyche.

She was saved from having to respond by the return of Jake and Raquel to the room.

As she translated his final instructions for the girl's follow-up care, Maggie determined again that she had to figure out a way to put a stop to this ridiculous arrangement her mother had suckered her into.

She wasn't sure what was worse—dealing with him at the ranch, in his faded jeans and thin cotton tractor T-shirts, or watching him interact with his patients, and the consideration and compassion that seemed an inherent part of him.

Right now both situations seemed intolerable.

He shouldn't have manipulated her into this.

Jake studied Maggie out of the corner of his eye as he finished examining Hector Manuel, a sixty-year-old potato factory worker with a bleeding ulcer. After three hours of clinic—and with an hour's worth of patients still sitting in the waiting room—he couldn't for the life of him figure out how to tell Maggie he didn't want her there anymore.

She had been an incredible help, he had to admit. This week's clinic had run more smoothly than any he'd done yet. With the improved communication, he'd been able to see more patients and he felt as though the advice he'd been able to give had been better understood and would be better followed.

She had translated in at least two-thirds of his cases today, and he couldn't figure out how they had ever gotten by without her. Her fluency with both Spanish and the medical jargon had been a killer combination, enormously helpful.

At what cost, though? he wondered.

Although she was doing her best to hide it, she looked beat: her eyes had smudges under them that hadn't been there when she walked in; her shoulders stiffened tighter with each passing hour; and every few moments she shifted restlessly on her chair trying to find a better position, though he was sure she had no idea she was doing it.

Even if he told her in no uncertain terms to go home, somehow he knew she wouldn't quit until every last patient was treated.

He could almost hear her argue that she was sticking it out as long as necessary, if only to avoid giving him the satisfaction of watching her throw in the towel.

She was stubborn and contrary and combative. And he was crazy about her.

With a barely veiled wince, she shifted her prosthesis again, and he frowned as he listened to Hector's heart. She should be home taking it easy, not sitting in his cramped exam room. He should never have come up with this ridiculous plan.

On the other hand, if she wasn't here, where else would she be? Probably riding a horse or driving the tractor at Rancho de la Luna. At least here he could keep an eye on her.

With a sigh, he turned back to Hector. "I'm going to prescribe some pills that should help but like I told you last month, you're going to have to lay off the jalapeños for a while until things settle down a little."

Maggie dutifully translated his words into Spanish. He listened to her, pleased that he could understand most of what she said.

Listening to her fluid words was a guilty kind of pleasure. How pathetic was he that he could be turned on listening to talk about ulcer advice in Spanish?

Somehow the words seemed lush and romantic when she spoke them in her low, melodic voice.

Hector asked him a question too rapidly for him to catch it all. He looked toward Maggie for help.

"He wants to know if he should continue his current dose of acid reflux medicine."

"I'd like to increase the dose to twice a day. Call me next week to see how that works. Oh, and if you don't take ten minutes to put your leg up in my office I'm going to carry you in there myself."

Maggie started to translate his words to Hector, but stopped and glared when the last phrase registered.

"Try it, Dalton, and you'll find out every dirty trick they taught me in the Army."

Hector snickered, apparently understanding more English than he let on. Jake spared the man only a quick glance, then turned his attention back to her. "Take a rest, Maggie. I'll be okay for a while on my own, I promise. If I need it, I can muddle through with my high school Spanish for my next few patients."

"I'm fine."

"Please, Maggie. I don't want you to wear yourself out."

"You better do what he says," Hector said to her in Spanish. "The man knows what he's talking about."

"Gracias," Jake said, earning a grin from Hector.

It was killing her not to rip into him in front of a patient. He could see thunderclouds gather in her dark eyes and her slim hands clench in her lap. After a charged, frustrated moment, she let out a breath and grabbed her forearm crutches.

"You know how to find my office?"

"I'll look for the Obnoxious Know-It-All sign above the door."

He grinned. "That's one way to find it. It's also the last room on the right."

"Just so you know, Dalton, I'm growing very tired of you ordering me around," she muttered at the door. "I don't remember asking you to babysit me."

"Somebody has to. If you would take care of yourself, I wouldn't have to do it for you."

She apparently decided not to dignify that with a response. With another fulminating glare that included the hapless Hector Manuel, she swung out of the exam room on her crutches and headed down the hall, still managing to convey anger even with her back to them.

"Man, are you in trouble." Hector shook his head in sympathy.

He didn't know the half of it. Jake sighed as he wrapped things up and moved on to his next patient. How would he ever get through the barricades she seemed determined to erect between them? Was it even possible?

What if his last name wasn't Dalton? Would she still be so confrontational?

It seemed like the height of irony that she should hate him for his father's sins.

Maybe he would look at things differently if he'd had a glowing relationship with Hank Dalton, if he considered his father someone who deserved love and respect. He had lived with the man. He knew what a bastard he could be.

He'd resolved early in life that when he grew up, he would be nothing like his father. He thought he had succeeded fairly well, until Magdalena Cruz came home.

What could he do to make her see him as a man, not just Hank Dalton's son?

He was still wondering that precisely ten minutes later when he finished with his next patient, eighty-year-old Millicent Hall, who suffered from rheumatoid arthritis and who brought him her famous angel food cake every time she came to the clinic. He was in the hallway making notes in her chart when Maggie rejoined him.

Her eyes seemed a little less shadowed but she still looked tired, he thought.

He set the chart on the counter. "You didn't have to take me so literally about that ten minutes. You can have longer if you need."

"I don't," she assured him coolly, her flashing eyes daring him to contradict her.

"Fine. I'll have Jan send in the next patient. Exam room three is open. Go ahead and wait for us."

She turned and headed down the hall, conveying her stubbornness in every proud line of her body.

Chapter 7

Maggie belonged in this world.

As he listened to her translate final instructions to his last patient of the day—Carmela Sanchez, twenty-one years old and at thirty-five weeks gestation with her first baby—Jake didn't miss the way Maggie's eyes softened as she looked at Carmela, how her exhaustion and pain seemed to slip away while she helped someone else.

He had seen Carmela several times for prenatal visits over the past three months, but in those other visits she had always only listened solemnly as he mentioned a few things that would be going on with her pregnancy.

She had never asked him a single question, had always seemed eager simply to take whatever printed information he had about her stage of pregnancy and leave.

But she and Maggie had been jabbering nonstop. He picked up only about half of it.

"I wish I could speak better English," he thought she

might have said at one point. "I'm afraid I will not understand the doctors and nurses when I am in labor."

"You will be fine," Maggie assured her. "What about
the baby's father? Does he know English?"

Carmela looked nervous suddenly and slanted a cautious
look to Jake. "He won't be there."

She said something else too fast for him to understand
but he thought he picked out the word *deporte* and deduced
that the baby's father was in the country illegally and either
had been deported or was in danger of it.

Maggie squeezed her hand, sympathy in her dark eyes.
"Well, do you have a friend who could go with you? A
mother or a sister?"

Carmela shook her head. *"Ninguna."* No one.

She looked down at the floor, then back at Maggie. "I
am frightened," she whispered. "So frightened. Would you
come with me? The doctor could tell you when I am delivering and you could help me so I'm not alone."

Jake listened to the fear in her voice and wanted to kick
himself. He should have thought to ask Carmela if she had
someone to help her during labor and delivery.

It was a basic question he asked all his pregnant patients, but he had always been so busy trying to get past
the language barrier with Carmela—to get her to even *talk*
to him, it had never occurred to him she was heading into
all this alone.

"Please," Carmela begged. "I am afraid I will not know
what to do and I will hurt my baby."

"You won't. You'll be just fine. The hospital in Idaho
Falls should have translators available."

"They do," Jake interjected. "I promise, I will make sure
we have someone there to translate."

Maggie conveyed his words to Carmela, but the girl

still looked distressed, as if she would burst into tears at any moment. "I will not know those people. They will be strangers to me. I will not know anyone but Dr. Jake. Please say you will help me."

Maggie studied her for a long moment, then sighed heavily. "Yes. All right. Dr. Dalton can contact me when you begin to go into labor and I will try to come. I can't make any promises that I'll definitely be there, but I will do my best."

The young woman beamed, her shoulders slumping as if a huge weight had just been lifted from them. She rushed to Maggie, nearly knocking her off balance as she embraced her and kissed her cheeks with effusive, genuine gratitude.

Maggie returned the embrace, he noted, but she didn't look at all thrilled by the prospect of participating in a labor and delivery. He wondered at it but didn't have time to give it more than a passing thought as, to his deep surprise, Carmela turned her gratitude in his direction. She even went so far as to hug him. She stopped after only a few seconds and pulled away, obviously flustered.

"I'll call her when you go into labor," he promised. "This close to the end of your pregnancy, I'd like to see you every week. Can you come back next Wednesday?"

Maggie translated his words to Carmela. The young woman frowned and said something back to Maggie that he missed.

"She thought you only had the clinic every two weeks," Maggie translated.

"Tell her we're having it every week for a while."

"Are you?" Maggie asked under her breath.

"As far as she knows, yes. Just tell her."

Maggie related the information, and Carmela smiled

shyly at him, looking much more relaxed as she left than she had when he first came into the examination room.

"Poor thing, to have her husband deported this close to the end of her pregnancy," Maggie said after Carmela left. "I can't imagine many things more terrifying than having your first baby all alone in a strange country where you don't speak the language."

"You were kind to ease her fears by agreeing to help when she's in labor. The remaining few weeks of her pregnancy will go far more smoothly without that added stress."

Maggie shrugged. "What choice did I have? I certainly wasn't about to let a Dalton outshine me when it comes to helping out my fellow creatures on earth."

He laughed and couldn't help himself from covering her hand with his—both out of gratitude and simply because he had spent all day without touching her and couldn't go another minute.

Her fingers quivered under his and he thought she would jerk away, but they stilled after a moment. His heart gave a little leap, though he knew it was likely a foolish hope. Maybe he was making progress.

"You were wonderful today," he murmured. "I can't tell you how much you expedited the process. Having someone with a medical background along to translate was invaluable."

"With the growing Latino population in this area, maybe you need to have someone bilingual on staff."

"What about you?"

Her fingers twitched and she finally did slide them away. "What *about* me?"

"If you decide you're coming home to stay you've always got a place here at the clinic. The patient load is more than I can handle and I would love to have an experienced nurse practitioner—especially a bilingual one—on board in the practice."

"You'll have to look somewhere else for that."

He frowned at her dismissive tone. She wouldn't even consider it? Stubborn little thing. "Come on, Maggie. We worked well together today, and I don't see any reason we couldn't continue the same way. Can't we be done with this whole Hatfield and McCoy thing?"

"It's not that. Well, not completely that. I'm looking for a different career path now."

He blinked. "You what?"

"I told you this the other day. I'm leaving nursing.'"

"You told me, but I suppose I didn't really believe it. Today just showed me what a terrible mistake that would be. You were incredible today! Even though you were only translating, your compassion came through loud and clear. All the patients responded to it. Everything I know about you and everything I saw today proves to me you're too good to just throw it all away on a whim."

"A whim? A *whim?*" Her spine stiffened. "Is that what you call having half your leg blown out from under you?"

He wouldn't let her do this, give up a successful, re-warding career out of self-pity or martyrdom or whatever excuse she used in her mind for denying herself something she so obviously loved.

"Your foot might be gone but your brain is still there. Or at least it's supposed to be. There's no possible medical reason you couldn't continue as a nurse practitioner. I went through med school with a paraplegic, for heaven's sake. He was one of the finest doctors I've ever met. If anything, your own experience as a patient will no doubt make you even more compassionate and caring."

"That's all fine in theory. But practice is something else entirely."

"Don't do this to yourself, Maggie. Please. Don't rush into a major life change until you give yourself a little more time to adjust to what's happened to you."

"How much time would you recommend, Dalton? At what point can I have my life back the way it was? Six months postamputation? A year? I'd really like to know what the magic formula is."

The raw edge to her voice finally managed to break through his anger and frustration, and with effort he choked down the arguments brewing inside him.

He could see the exhaustion shadowing her eyes and wanted to kick himself for bullying her when she didn't have the physical or emotional reserves to fight back fairly.

What he really wanted to do was pull her into his lap and hold her close until the pain went away, but he had a feeling she'd clock him upside the head with one of her crutches if he tried.

"Mind your own business, Jake," she finally said, her voice low and her expression closed.

"I'm sorry," he murmured. "I just hate to see you waste your training and your abilities."

"My training, my abilities, my choice."

"All right," he said after a moment. "I won't say anything more about about it today."

"Or how about ever?"

He gave a rueful smile. "Afraid I can't promise that but I'll let it go for now."

"I guess I need to take what I can get."

She moved as if to rise and he quickly stepped forward and handed her the crutches, then stood by ready to stabilize her if necessary.

"Thanks. I guess that means we're done here, then."

He wasn't even *close* to being done with her, but he didn't think she would appreciate that information. This was another thing he'd probably better keep to himself for now.

"Thanks again for your help. I'll walk you out. And for once in your life, please don't argue."

She clamped her lips together and started making her way out of the exam room.

Outside, the early-evening sky was alive with soft pastels—ribbons of pink and lavender and yellow across the pale blue. This was just the kind of evening he loved best, and another reason he'd chosen to set up shop in Pine Gulch.

Maggie drew a deep breath into her lungs, then made her way quickly across the parking lot. He followed, not missing the wince she tried to hide when she slid into the driver's seat.

"You're having a rough day painwise, aren't you? Is it just the prosthetic?"

He saw the denial form in her eyes but after a moment she shrugged. "The phantom pain has been a little hairy for the last few days."

"What are you on for it?"

She gave him her prescription combination and he immediately thought of some alternatives. "I can tweak that for you if you want to try a different dosage or something else entirely."

"Maybe. I'll give it another day or two and call you if things don't improve."

"Right. I'm sure you will. And you can bet, I'll just be waiting by the phone."

She actually smiled at his dry tone before she pulled the door to her car closed and started the engine.

It wasn't much of a smile, but he still wanted to freeze the moment in his mind forever.

Someone was following her.

She picked up the tail in her rearview mirror five minutes after she left the clinic, just as she turned onto Cold Creek Road and headed home.

She slowed down a little to give him time to catch up so she could verify who her pursuer might be. Sure enough, she saw Jake's silver SUV in her rearview mirror.

She sighed heavily, torn between giving a little scream of frustration or bursting into hot, noisy tears. Why wouldn't the man just give it a rest, for heaven's sake?

She wanted to convince herself he was simply heading to his family's ranch beyond the Rancho de la Luna, but she knew better. He was following her to make sure she arrived home safely.

How was she supposed to respond to him? On the one hand she found it highly annoying that he didn't seem to have any faith in her ability—or willingness—to take care of herself.

On the other hand, though she didn't want to admit it, she found the gesture kind of sweet. Chauvinistic and presumptuous, certainly, but still a little flattering that he cared enough to worry about her.

She *must* be tired if she could find anything positive about Jake Dalton's obstinacy.

A moment later she turned into the Luna's gravel driveway and stopped her Subaru, prepared to wave him past. To her surprise, he followed her, pulling his vehicle right behind her.

Okay, there was a fine line between protective and annoying.

She grimaced and threw her car in gear. How had she suddenly become his pet project? she wondered. He was a busy doctor. Surely he had more important things to do than harass her.

He followed her up to the house and pulled directly behind her again. Almost before she had the keys out of the ignition, he was at her door, pulling it open for her.

She swung the crutches out and pulled herself up. "I thought we established I'm a little old for a babysitter."

His bland smile didn't fool her for a second. "I was heading out here anyway."

She was too blasted tired to fight it out with him again, so she decided not to call him a rotten liar.

"Anyway, while I'm here, I figured I could help you get the prosthesis off and see how everything looks."

"Oh, can you?"

He seemed impervious to her sarcasm and simply smiled. "I should have suggested it at the clinic but you seemed in a hurry to get home. I thought you might be more comfortable here."

She shook her head. "You are a piece of work, Dalton. It's a wonder you ever have time to eat and sleep if this is the kind of obsessively diligent care you give all your patients."

He lifted a shoulder in a half shrug. "Except, you're not my patient, remember?"

She rolled her eyes at having her own words thrown back in her face. Nothing she said ever seemed to discourage him, so she decided not to waste her remaining energy reserves in arguing with him this time.

She told herself it was exhaustion that led to her giving in, not the lingering warmth settling on her shoulders like a thick blanket at his concern.

She wouldn't go so far as to actually issue an invitation to him, but she didn't protest when he followed her to the house and up the steps of the porch.

The door was locked, the house dark, but she called for her mother out of habit when she unlocked it and walked inside.

On the table in the entryway, she found a note from Viviana:

Lena, I have a library board meeting tonight but dinner is in the oven. Your favorite fajita casserole. Don't wait up for me.
P.S. I hope you enjoyed your day at the clinic. Did I not tell you Jacob was a good doctor?

She shook her head at this and shoved the note into her pocket.

"Mama's gone to a meeting of the library board."

"That's right. I forgot they met tonight. You know, Guillermo's on that board, too. Maybe they'll have a chance to talk and start settling their differences."

"Maybe." She didn't expect it, though, especially after she'd met with him and seen he was as intractable on this as Viviana.

Her mother didn't seem in any kind of mood to make things right with Guillermo. Whenever Maggie brought up his name, Viviana either clammed up or turned prickly and cool. Her visit with her uncle had accomplished nothing. But at least she had tried.

"I'm sure you're anxious to take off your prosthesis. Why don't you sit down and let's have a look?"

She made a face but led the way into the living room, with its Mission furniture and bright, colorful textiles.

She hated being so nervous about all this. He'd seen her leg already so he knew all her ugly secrets. Still, some trace of lingering edginess made her flippant.

"If you keep asking to see my stump," she said as she sat down in a leather and oak armchair and started to pull up her pant leg, "I'm going to think you're one of those weir-does with an amputee obsession."

Instead of responding in the same flippant tone, he sent her a look she couldn't quite identify. "What if I just have a Maggie Cruz obsession?" he murmured.

Her stomach quivered at his words and the intensity be-hind them. She didn't believe him. Not for a second. He was teasing her, that was all. Still, her hands trembled a little as she pulled off the prosthesis and the thick stump sock covering her.

The relief of having it off—the sudden absence of irri-tation and pressure—always left her a little light-headed.

That was the reason her stomach fluttered as he touched her leg just above the amputation and studied it.

"Still a little red, but that might be a result of having just removed the device. Other than that, it looks good."

"I suppose that's a matter of opinion."

"You don't think it looks better?"

"Better than what? Frankly, I preferred it when it still had a foot attached."

He gave her a quick, sharp look, and she flushed at her unruly tongue. She hadn't meant to let that smudge of bit-terness slip through. Not to Jake, anyway.

Embarrassed at herself for revealing some of her inner angst, she tugged the leg of her slacks back down. "Okay, you've seen enough," she snapped.

After a moment, he rose. "Keep weight off it as much as you can for a few more days. I called Wade on the way over here, and he's sending one of his workers over tomorrow to help your mother with anything that needs to be done until you can move around on it a little better."

"We don't need your arrogant Cold Creek charity."

"It's not arrogance to watch out for a patient and make sure she doesn't overdo things. And before you tell me again that you're not my patient, how about watching out for a friend? Am I allowed to do that?"

She opened her mouth to tell him she absolutely wasn't his friend, either, and had no desire to be but the words clogged in her throat. They sounded sulky and rude and also didn't ring true.

Since her return to Pine Gulch, in a strange, twisted way, he *had* become a friend of sorts.

Friends with a Dalton? The concept shook her but she couldn't dismiss it completely. Friends had been in short supply these last few months. She had a few loyal ones from the Army who visited her at Walter Reed to keep her spirits up during rehab, and a couple other amputees she'd become friendly with during treatment.

She had kept most others at arm's length, unable to bear their pity. After Clay's defection, it had become second nature to shut people out.

Jake didn't make that easy. And, Dalton or not, in his overbearing way he had been kind to her since she returned to Pine Gulch. She had repaid his kindness with sarcasm and meanness at every turn.

Maybe it was the exhaustion or the natural outcome of spending all day in his company, but she was tired of being bitchy with him. More than anything, she suddenly craved an evening of quiet conversation and companionship. A few moments where she could forget her pain for a while in the company of someone else.

"Would you like to stay for dinner?"

The words escaped before she really thought them through, and for one horrible moment as she saw the surprise register on his rugged, handsome features, she wanted desperately to retrieve them.

Why would he want to spend any more time with her when she had been nothing but bad-tempered and grouchy? Heavens, most days she didn't even want to spend time with herself!

"Forget it. Of course you wouldn't."

"Who says? I'd love it." His smile appeared genuinely pleased. "I'm starving, and those smells coming from the kitchen are starting to make me feel like I haven't eaten in days."

Maggie hadn't socialized much since her injury, but she remembered enough of conventional etiquette to know it would be considered terribly bad form to rescind an invitation seconds after it had been made, no matter how much she might want to.

She was stuck.

Heart pounding, she picked up her crutches and led the way to the kitchen, hoping she hadn't just made a terrible mistake.

Chapter 8

He decided he would never understand women.

Ten minutes later, in the warm Luna kitchen with its bright sunny walls and crisp white curtains, he leaned against the counter trying to make sense of Maggie's impetuous invitation.

He didn't know what to make of her. One moment she was prickly and confrontational and didn't seem to want him anywhere near her, the next she was asking him to share a meal.

The sheer unexpectedness of it left him wary and alert. If her strategy was to confuse and befuddle the opposition, she was definitely succeeding.

Still, who was he to argue when the capricious hand of fate reached down to help him out? Spending more time with Maggie exactly matched his own agenda, so it seemed foolish and self-defeating for him to question the invitation.

Even on the forearm crutches, she moved through the

kitchen with the ease of someone who had spent much time in one. Another surprise. For some reason, he would have expected her to be of the fast-food and takeout persuasion, though with Viviana Cruz for a mother, he supposed that supposition was shortsighted.

Maggie seemed completely at home here despite the challenge of moving through the kitchen on her sticks. She stirred something on the stove, tasted something else, then reached down to open the oven.

The sight of her trying to lift a foil-covered casserole out while balancing on the crutches compelled him to step forward, guilty and embarrassed that he had wasted precious moments watching her when he could have been helping out.

"Here, I can do that."

She raised an eyebrow. "So can I. Sit down. You're a guest."

"Let me at least set the table."

She appeared torn, then pulled some dishes out of a cupboard to the right of the sink and handed them to him. "Silverware is the top drawer on your right."

"Glasses?"

"Left of the sink."

For a moment they worked in a companionable silence and the domestication of it made him smile. Who would have thought a week ago that he would be preparing to share a meal with the woman who had haunted him for so long?

He arranged the place settings at right angles on the rectangular table. When he finished he tried to help her with the rest of the meal, but she waved him off.

"I've got this. Sit down," she insisted.

Though it pained him like a bad abscess to watch her

work while he did nothing, he obeyed, settling into the sturdy oak chair. He watched, uncomfortably helpless as she bustled around the warm kitchen.

She carried the casserole to the table with care, using only one crutch and carrying the dish in her other hand, and he had to admit he let out a sigh of relief when she set it carefully on the table. He didn't feel like treating any burns tonight.

"I know you think I've got some kind of chip on my shoulder about having to do everything without help but it's important for me to do things on my own," she said on her way back to the table with a tossed salad. "Mama wants to do everything for me, too, and every day I have to tell her to back off."

"That's just a mother thing, isn't it? Mine still thinks I should be dropping off my laundry at her house."

She smiled and he thought his heart would burst with delight.

"I tell her that it might take me longer to figure out how to do things now," she said. "But just because things might take a little longer, that doesn't mean I can't do it."

"That's certainly true."

"I'm going to be confronting challenges the rest of my life. Bumpy sidewalks, prostheses that don't fit right, the inevitable stares and questions from strangers. I know I have to be tough enough on my own to face whatever comes along."

"Accepting help once in a while doesn't make you weak, Maggie. Only human."

"You know, I'm getting a little tired of being human. Where are some superhero powers when I need them?"

Before he could respond, she carried a bottle of wine to the table. "That's it. I think everything is ready."

He stood until she was settled in her chair, then he slid it to the table for her. Something close to amusement sparked in her dark eyes but she said nothing.

Jake sat down, determined to enjoy every moment of the meal. Viviana Cruz was a fabulous cook and he knew he was in for a treat—even beyond the obvious pleasure of sharing Maggie's company.

From the first bite of moist, spicy chicken in a molé sauce, he knew he was right.

Perhaps because of the food or perhaps because she had put in such a long day, Maggie seemed to have sheathed her prickly quills. She was in a mellow mood and seemed content with quiet conversation.

"So tell me what it's like being the only doctor in Pine Gulch," she asked after a moment.

He swallowed a bite of chicken. "Busy. I don't have time for home-cooked meals like this one very often. It's usually TV dinners or takeout."

"Poor baby." Again she seemed amused at him. "Maybe you need to hire a housekeeper to cook for you. Or a wife."

"I believe I'll continue to muddle through."

"So why don't you have one?"

"A wife or a housekeeper?"

She took a sip of wine. "A wife. You're probably prime meat on the Pine Gulch dating scene. I mean, the Dalton good-looks gene obviously didn't pass you by. And judging by the way you kiss, at least, you're quite comfortable with your heterosexuality. You're wealthy, successful and a doctor, for heaven's sake. You should have women out the eyeballs. So what the heck is wrong with you?"

He laughed out loud. "Do you practice being insulting or does it just come naturally when you're with me?"

"It's a gift. So why aren't you attached, Dr. Dalton?"

"Maybe I'm too picky."

And maybe the one woman he compared all others to was a heartbreakingly beautiful wounded soldier who wanted nothing to do with him.

"Any near misses?"

"In the relationship department? A few. I was engaged a few years ago, right after I finished my residency."

"What happened? She dump you?"

"It was a mutual decision, if you must know. Sad, really. Our lives were heading on different tracks, and neither of us seemed willing to shift direction to accommodate the other. Carla was a lawyer and she couldn't bear the idea of moving to Podunk, Idaho, and I couldn't imagine practicing anywhere else. It was a mistake from the beginning, I guess."

"Knowing that doesn't make it hurt less, does it?"

He thought about the sense of guilt and failure he'd lived with for some time after they called it off. Eventually that had given way to relief when he realized how miserable they would have made each other.

"What about you?" he asked. "Any—what was the phrase you used—'near misses' for you?"

She took a healthy swallow of wine, and he wondered if she'd eaten any of her chicken or just pushed it around her plate.

"So near I can still feel the wind whistling past my ears," she said with a smile that didn't seem at all amused.

"That close?"

"I was engaged until just a few months ago, actually. Dr. Clay Sanders, brilliant young surgeon at Phoenix General. Which, by the way, I think he had printed on his business cards. But I digress."

"What happened?"

She tried for a nonchalant shrug, but he could clearly see it was forced. "A similar story to yours. We dated for a year or so, then he asked me to marry him before my reserve unit headed for Afghanistan. When I returned, the intervening months had changed us both too much and we both decided we no longer suited."

She said the words with a studied casualness that told him far more than he was sure she intended and he could feel a slow, simmering fury spark to life.

"Because of your injury?"

"Not officially." She turned her attention to her plate, though she was still mostly moving her food around.

"Did you break it off or did he?" Some wild need inside him compelled him to ask.

"Do you really need to hear all the gory details?"

Hell, yes, if only so he could go find the bastard and pound his smarmy face in.

"I broke it off." Her smile seemed forced, wooden. "I decided I would rather not spend the rest of my life with a man who couldn't hide his pity and revulsion when he looked at me."

How was he supposed to respond to that? His first reaction was fury at any bastard who would hurt her, especially at such a vulnerable time in her life. But he also had to wonder if she might have been exaggerating her ex's reactions, looking for reasons to end the relationship.

He chose his words carefully. "Are you sure it was pity and not just concern for what you were going through?"

"Maybe. I don't know, those first few months were a weird time for me. But I can say without question we were both more relieved than crushed when I gave him back his ring."

"Well, the man was an idiot, then. Want me to go beat the hell out of him?"

Her laugh seemed much more natural this time, and he thought he saw some of the darkness lift from her eyes. "And deprive your patients of your special brand of above-the-call-of-duty care while you're gone? I couldn't do that to the good people of Pine Gulch. But thanks for the offer—I'll keep it in mind."

He thought about changing the subject but he wasn't quite ready to leave Dr. Clay Sanders behind. "So was your heart broken?" he asked, trying for a casual tone.

Her brow furrowed as she appeared to give the question serious thought. "I don't know. That's the sad thing, I guess. I've had quite a bit of time to analyze it. Amazing how much time you have to think when you can't go anywhere. To be honest, I think I would have ended things with him when I finished my tour, explosion or not. My time in Afghanistan changed me in some significant ways. Just like you and your lawyer, I don't think we were on the same page anymore."

"Such as?"

"Well, Clay loved the wealth and privilege from being a successful doctor, unlike certain people at this table."

"I've got to tell you, I'm disliking the guy more and more with every word."

"No, he wasn't a jerk. I wouldn't have agreed to marry him in the first place if he had been. Maybe I missed the signs that he was a little superficial. He just grew up in a large, poor family where there was never enough to go around and he liked having money and being able to spend it on himself. But after serving in Afghanistan and seeing the conditions there, I had a hard time imagining a life devoted to caring about which country club to join and how to improve my tennis swing. That wasn't what I wanted anymore."

"What do you want now?" The question exposed his raw heart but he doubted she even noticed.

"Nothing. I've sworn off relationships."

He hadn't meant to tip his hand this early, but he couldn't let such a misguided blanket statement pass unchallenged. Maybe it was time to let her know where he stood. He reached for her fingers and leaned across the table until his face was only inches from hers.

"What would a man have to do to change your mind?" he asked, his voice low.

For a charged moment, their gazes held and he couldn't breathe as he watched awareness blooming to life in those dark and seductive eyes that suddenly looked huge in her slender face.

He watched her throat move as she swallowed and felt a delicate tremor in her fingers. He might have been able to release her fingers and let his question lie there on the table between them. But then her gaze shifted to his mouth and something hot and sultry sparked between them and he knew he was doomed.

With a muffled groan, he leaned forward and touched his mouth to hers, heedless of the plates and glasses and serving dishes between them.

She tasted sweet and heady like the wine, and it took every ounce of strength he had to keep the kiss gentle, easy, when he wanted to slake his ravaging thirst, then come back for more.

With the table between them, only their mouths and fingers touched yet that slim connection was enough to send heat pouring through him. More than enough. He wanted to throw her onto the remains of their dishes and devour her.

Still he held himself in check, not pushing her at all, letting her become accustomed to the taste and feel of him. After what felt like a blissful eternity he felt her lips part slightly and the soft, erotic slide of her tongue against the corner of his mouth.

He deepened the kiss, nibbling and tasting until his breathing was harsh and ragged and his blood pumped through his veins like liquid fire.

He ached to touch her, to caress and explore, but some dark corner of his mind urged caution. A kiss was one thing, but he knew she wasn't ready for anything else.

It was harder than the time he'd had to deliver a baby who was in too much of a hurry to wait for the hospital in the back seat of a VW Bug. But with arduous effort, he drew away from her and had the minor satisfaction of seeing her sway slightly, her eyes unfocused, aroused.

"Don't cloister yourself off from life, Maggie," he murmured, and couldn't resist caressing her soft cheek with his fingers. "You lost part of a leg, something that genuinely sucks. But you don't have to give up the rest of yourself because of it."

She blinked as if he'd reached across the table and poured the rest of their wine over her head. The soft, hazy desire in her eyes vanished with jarring abruptness, and she let out a long, heavy breath. She said nothing for several moments as if she didn't quite trust herself to speak. When she did, her voice was cool.

"What are you doing here, Jake?"

He shrugged and sipped his wine. "Sharing dinner and a very sexy kiss with a beautiful woman. And doing my best to remember how exhausted that woman is and keep things at only a kiss, when I want far more."

She narrowed her eyes. "You don't have to lie to me, Dalton, or pretend something you don't feel."

His laugh sounded ragged, even to him. "Here's a little tip about men, Maggie. There are certain things I just can't fake. I could prove exactly what I'm feeling if I stood up right now, but at this point I think that would only embarrass us both, don't you agree?"

Maggie could feel her face heat, and her own flustered reaction made her even more angry. He had no right to do this to her—to come to her house and kiss her and say such things and leave her so stirred up.

What kind of cruel game was he playing? Did he have any idea how painful she found this, how much she hated the blunt reminder that her body could still burn with the same desires and needs she had before her world shattered?

She didn't want this, the sweet surge of blood through her veins, the tremble of anticipation in her stomach, the heady, seductive taste of him still on her lips.

Damn him.

Damn him for filling her senses with needs and wants she had tried so hard to forget about since her injury. She suddenly ached to be held and kissed and adored, even though she knew it was impossible. He had no right to do this—to leave her restless and aroused and *needy*.

"Why are you so scared?"

She bristled. "Scared of what?"

"I'm not like your fiancé, Maggie. I haven't turned away from you, have I?"

His words seemed to resonate in her chest. He was right. He hadn't turned away. He had been in her face since the moment she came back to town, pushing her, riding her. Every time she turned around, there he was with that damn smile and those killer eyes and his blasted insidious charm that somehow made her forget all the reasons why she didn't want anything to do with him.

She hadn't asked him to take her on as his pet project, she reminded herself. Maybe it would have been better if he *had* turned away; then she wouldn't be left here aching and hungry.

"I told you I'm not interested in any kind of relationship," she said curtly.

"Like it or not, we have a relationship, Maggie."

"Only because you won't leave me alone!"

"So you can sit around feeling sorry for yourself? Or worse, pretend you're the same person you were six months ago and can do everything you did before, without blinking an eye?"

"Listen carefully here, Dalton. It's none of your business what I do. If I wake up in the morning and decide I want to scale the Grand Teton, you have absolutely nothing to say about it!"

"You're right." He stood up and started clearing the dishes and she had to keep her eyes firmly fixed forward so she didn't give in to the urge to see if he was telling the truth about being aroused.

"I can clear those," she snapped.

"So can I."

His voice was so calm, so rational as he carried the stack of dishes to the sink and started to rinse them that Maggie, conversely, felt a slick, hot ball of rage lodge in her throat.

She wasn't helpless, damn it, and she was so tired of everyone treating her like some kind of chipped and fragile porcelain figurine.

Her stump throbbed as she shoved herself onto the crutches, but she ignored it and swung herself to the sink.

All her anger and frustration of the past five months seemed to simmer up to the surface of her psyche like viscous acid.

She burned with anger on a dozen different levels, furious with Jake for his obstinance but also livid at the world, at her own bleak future, at the relentless pain she couldn't seem to beat into submission, no matter how hard she tried.

All of it coalesced suddenly into one big spurt of fury and all she could focus on was Jake.

"I said I can clear them," she snapped, and reached for the stack of plates in his hand.

She jerked them away, but they were wet and slick and she was balancing by her forearms on two narrow pieces of metal. With a horrified sense of inevitability she felt them slip through her fingers and then the whole stack crashed to the floor, shattering into hundreds of pieces.

She stared at the china on the floor, jagged and broken and rendered forever useless by one single moment.

The rage inside her dissolved as suddenly as it had struck. Instead she was filled with a deep, compelling sorrow. Who would ever want these dishes now? They were nothing. Less than nothing.

She gazed down at the floor, vaguely aware of the hot sting of tears in her eyes, trailing down her cheeks.

Jake studied her for all of three seconds, then she thought she heard him murmur a low endearment before he scooped her into his arms, letting her crutches fall to the ground.

"I pushed you too hard with the clinic today and everything. I'm so sorry, sweetheart."

His words—his kindness—only made her cry harder, and she buried her face in his shirt, mortified but unable to stanch the flow. She couldn't even say for sure why she was crying—a jumbled mix of exhaustion and pain and fear for the terrifying future.

Through it all, she was only vaguely aware of him carrying her to the living room and lowering himself to the sofa. He smelled so good, spicy and male, and his arms were a solid, comforting sanctuary.

She knew when she came back to her senses she would eventually be mortified that she had let him this close. But for now she was helpless to do anything but let him hold her while she gave in to the thunderburst of emotion inside her.

She didn't know how long she cried out her rage and pain and grief against him.

Eventually, like the tide receding, she felt the wild storm seep out of her, leaving only exhaustion in its wake.

Chapter 9

She was beautiful in sleep and seemed ethereal, delicate.

Despite her emotional outburst before she fell asleep, he knew Magdalena Cruz was far from weak. She had to be tough as nails to survive what she'd been through, both before her injury and after. What she was still going through.

But in sleep, with her dark lashes fanning her cheeks and her dusky features still and lovely, she seemed as soft and fragile as a rare, extraordinary wildflower.

Her tears had stunned him to the core. Even now, an hour after she fell asleep as he continued to hold her in the dimly lit living room, he couldn't believe she had let down her barriers enough to let him glimpse the vulnerable, bruised woman inside the hard shell.

This opportunity to enfold her in his arms like this was a precious gift, one he knew she would never have allowed if she hadn't been at such a low emotional ebb.

He supposed it was probably unprincipled of him to take

advantage of the situation, but he didn't care. How many other chances would he have to feel the soft rise and fall of her lungs with each breath, the stir of air against his skin as she exhaled?

He held her as long as he could, long after his arms both fell asleep. Even then, he would have been content to hold her longer—through the night if he had his way—but she began to shift restlessly in his arms. A few times she whimpered, her brow furrowing then smoothing again.

He had watched enough of his postsurgery patients sleeping in the hospital to recognize the signs of someone in discomfort. She needed a change in position, he sensed, and with regret he shifted so he could lower her to the couch.

She stirred a little but didn't wake when he pulled a quilt in rich, dark colors from the back of a chair and covered her with it.

When he was certain she would continue to sleep, he left her long enough to return to the kitchen and clean up the broken china and the rest of their dinner dishes from the table and load them into the dishwasher, then he returned to sit in the armchair across from her.

A soft spring rain pattered against the window and watery moonlight filtered across her face.

He couldn't seem to look away.

The depth of tenderness washing through him took his breath away. He had never been able to classify this thing he had for her. He wouldn't go so far as to call it an obsession; before she came back to town, he could often spend weeks without thinking about her. But then he would bump into Guillermo or Viviana and she would somehow sneak to the forefront of his mind for several days.

But now as his gaze ranged over her—as he sat in the darkened room, content to watch her sleep—the truth seemed so obvious he couldn't believe he'd so stupidly missed it.

He was in love with her.

He wasn't sure how or when it happened. Maybe that terrible day his father died when she had reached out past her hatred and anger to comfort him. Maybe slowly over the years as he'd talked to her mother about what she was doing and learned of the strong, courageous woman she had become. Maybe that moment he had pulled up behind her on Cold Creek Road and found her crouched in the gravel changing a tire.

Maybe like that rare wildflower he had compared her to earlier, his love for her had been growing inside him his entire life, so quietly he'd never realized it was there until it burst forth in full, spectacular bloom.

Spectacular to him, maybe. But he had a feeling she would see it as a pesky weed that needed to be plucked out at all costs.

He sighed. In love with Magdalena Cruz. Now there was a recipe for disaster. He couldn't see any positive outcome for his poor heart. The woman was prickly and argumentative, hated anything to do with his family and was coping with a major life adjustment and the physical and emotional pain that went along with it.

She had told him in no uncertain terms that she wasn't at all interested in a relationship. And if she were, he knew he likely wouldn't even make the list of possible contenders.

He could change her mind. She wasn't immune to him— her response to his kiss had been real and unfeigned. But a physical reaction was one thing; a softening of her heart against him and his parentage was something else entirely.

She had asked him several times to leave her alone. The decent thing, the honorable road, would be to respect her words and wishes—to back off and give her time to deal with her new disability and the challenges she faced now, before he worked any harder at overcoming those barriers she had constructed between them.

He rubbed a hand across his chest, though he couldn't massage away the ache there at the thought of distancing himself from her. In a very short time, he had become addicted to her presence—to her sharp wit and her courage and those rare, incredible smiles.

Too addicted. He couldn't stay away from her, he realized, even though he had a grim feeling he was only setting himself up for deeper heartache.

She had no idea how long she slept on the sofa, but when she woke, the house was dark and there was no sign of Jake. In the moonlight filtering through the blinds she could make out her mother's slight form in the armchair next to the couch, her eyes closed and her breathing regular as she dozed.

Memories of the evening and her own behavior rushed back, and Maggie wanted to bury her face into the sofa and stay there forever. How would she ever face him again?

Sharing a kiss had been one thing. She wasn't thrilled about it but it was at least a memory she could live with. What came after—that raw explosion of emotion—was something else entirely.

How could she have broken down like that? She had worked so hard to keep herself under control around everyone, but it seemed especially important around Jake.

She hated that he had seen her in such a weak, vulnerable moment. She should never have invited him to dinner. It was an insane impulse in the first place and had brought her nothing but trouble.

She still wasn't sure what had sparked her tears. One moment she'd been angry and determined to show him she could handle anything. The next, she had completely fallen apart.

In this quiet room, listening to her mother's soft breathing and the rain wash against the window, she had no good explanation, other than exhaustion and the pain that still rode her like a PRCA broncbuster.

She shifted to ease the tingling, pins-and-needles ache in her leg, but her movement must have disturbed Viviana. Her mother's eyes opened and she straightened in the chair.

"Go back to sleep, *niña*," her mother said. "You need your rest."

"What time is it?"

Viviana sat up straighter and gave a sleepy shrug. "Midnight. Maybe later. I returned after nine and you were sound asleep. Jacob, he was sitting in this chair reading a book. I told him to go home."

Heat scorched her cheeks. Something else to keep her up at night—that he had sat here and watched her sleeping.

She supposed she should take some small comfort that he was a physician and had probably sat at the bedside of many sleeping patients. She was just one more in a long line. But somehow that didn't provide much solace to her turmoil.

She shifted her gaze back to her mother and found Viviana studying her closely, a hundred questions in her eyes. She could just imagine her mother's surprise at the scene she had walked in on. Finding Jake Dalton camped out comfortably in her living room must have been quite a shock, as Viviana plainly knew Maggie's negative feelings for Jake.

Or at least the negative feelings Maggie was fiercely trying to remind herself she should be having.

She reached over and turned on the lamp next to the

couch and decided to quickly change the subject, ignoring those implied questions. "How was your meeting? Jake told me Tío Guillermo is on the library board. Did you have a chance to talk to him?"

To her surprise, her usually unflappable mother blushed. "I talked to him," she said, then called him a string of words in Spanish so unflattering Maggie's eyes widened.

She couldn't figure out the sudden animosity between the two and she would have given anything to be able to get to the bottom of it. What on earth had happened to destroy their good working relationship? she wondered yet again.

"Did you convince him to come back to work?"

"No," Viviana said shortly.

"Why not? Did you tell him how much we need his help?"

Her mother rose, not quite five feet of stiff dignity. "I do not wish to discuss Guillermo with you. I have told you before. You will mind your own business, thank you."

She blinked at her mother's sharp tone. Ooo-kay. That was certainly plain enough.

The subject apparently exhausted in her mind, Viviana sat back down, her features relaxing. "So tell me of your day. How was the clinic? Is not Jacob a wonderful doctor?"

She thought back to the afternoon she had spent observing as he cared for his patients, most of whom could pay him nothing. Though it pained her, she had to agree. He *was* a good doctor.

She nodded slowly, and Viviana beamed as if she had trained him herself.

"And how did you do? The work, it was not too much for you?"

"I was only translating, Mama. I was sitting most of the afternoon. Jake made sure of that."

If anything, the afternoon had only illustrated that she

was right in her decision to find another career. She hadn't done anything strenuous, hadn't tried to give anyone a bath or change a dressing or administer meds. Yet she was still left exhausted and aching.

How could she ever hope to work a full shift, to give her patients the care they needed?

If you're tough enough for ranch work, why can't you still work in medicine?

The thought whispered in her mind and she frowned. She couldn't dismiss the logic of that. Ranch work was even more physically demanding than being a nurse.

While she had struggled with some of the things on the Luna she'd done since her return, she had found nothing impossible.

How much of her exhaustion now could she attribute to her afternoon at the clinic and how much was from the past few sleepless nights?

Definitely something she would have to devote more thought to.

"When I tried to fix Jake something to eat, he told me he ate with you." Viviana beamed. "This I was pleased to hear, that my daughter still has some good manners."

Maggie flushed. She wasn't sure she considered it good manners to kiss a dinner guest with wild passion one moment, then blubber all over him the next. She hated wondering what he must think of her—and she hated worse that she even cared.

"He followed me home like a stray dog. I didn't have much choice but to give him some dinner."

"His mother says he is so busy he doesn't eat very much of good food. He needs a wife, Marjorie says."

Maggie definitely didn't like the sudden calculating light in her mother's eyes, and she wondered if she ought to warn Jake. Viviana and Marjorie were best friends, something she had never really been able to understand, given the bitter history between their families. The two of them were likely to get all kinds of strange ideas in their heads if they put their minds to it and she, for one, didn't want to be in the middle of it.

The thought that she and Jake might find themselves caught in the matchmaking crosshairs of two such formidable adversaries as their respective mothers was enough to strike cold fear in her heart.

"I'm not sure Jake would agree that he needs a wife."

Her mother made a dismissive gesture, as if what Jake had to say on the subject was of little importance. "Men. They do not know what they want. Have you not learned that lesson? We have to show them what will be best for them."

She had to smile, amused despite her sudden foreboding. "Good luck with that, then, but I'm going up to bed."

She pulled the blanket away and she saw Viviana's gaze sharpen on her empty pant leg. Concern flicked in her mother's dark eyes, probably because she had rarely seen Maggie without the prosthesis.

"Sleep here tonight, Lena. You don't need to climb the stairs tonight if you are tired. I will bring you a nightgown and your own pillow."

"I'm fine," she lied and pulled herself up from the couch onto the crutches. "I'll see you in the morning."

She moved to her mother and kissed her on the cheek, then headed for the personal Armageddon she faced every night.

The next half hour was focused on the physical challenge of climbing the stairs, her nightly med regimen and preparing herself for bed, all on the despised crutches.

At last she slid under the cool and welcoming lavender quilt in her bedroom, everything aching.

Despite her physical exhaustion, sleep seemed far away as she lay in her narrow childhood bed gazing at the soft-pastel walls and listening to the rain outside the window.

She couldn't seem to force her mind away from Jake and the afternoon and evening in his company.

How would she ever face him again? Bad enough she'd responded to his kiss again with an eagerness that mortified her. She then compounded the humiliation by blubbering all over him.

And as if all that wasn't enough, she'd fallen asleep on the man. Literally. She must have fallen asleep in his arms. She could remember him holding her during her storm of tears, and then everything seemed a vast blank until she woke and found her mother there.

Well, it had taken the most embarrassing evening of her life, but maybe she'd finally accomplished her goal of keeping him away from her. She couldn't imagine he would want anything more to do with her after tonight's turbulent mood swings.

What sane man would?

She was relieved, she told herself. If he left on his own, she wouldn't have to keep trying to bolster her sagging determination to push him away. Heaven knows, she certainly wasn't succeeding very well in that department on her own. When she was with him, she couldn't seem to remember all the reasons she should stay away.

She had wanted him to kiss her again. She pressed a hand to her stomach, remembering the slow heat churning through her veins when he had looked at her out of those hot and hungry blue eyes. She had wanted his kiss, and as the kiss deepened, she had wanted far more.

How could she be foolish enough to let herself crave the impossible?

She reached for the bedside light again, then pulled the blankets away and tugged her nightgown up to her thighs. For a long moment she actually looked at her legs, something she tried to avoid as much as possible.

Her aversion was ridiculous, she knew. She was a nurse practitioner and had served in hospitals in a war zone, for heaven's sake. She had seen far worse than a stump of a limb that ended just below the knee. It was only skin and bone and nerve endings, not the essence of her entire psyche.

So why did it feel like she was nothing more than this now?

Intellectually, she knew losing part of her leg wasn't really the end of the world.

Just the end of the world as she knew it.

She sighed, despising herself for the melodramatic thought. If she'd been her own patient, she would have told herself to grow up, to put on her big-girl panties and just deal with what had been handed her.

She wanted to. At times she thought she did a pretty damn good job of coping.

At others, like now, she couldn't seem to move past this deep feeling of sorrow at what she had lost, at all the things she wouldn't be able to do in the future—or at least the things she would no longer be able to do easily.

As she looked at her stump, she tried to picture a man— okay, Jake—in a romantic situation, undressing her and encountering this lump of flesh instead of a whole, healthy woman. The idea was so painful she couldn't even stand imagining it.

She closed her eyes tightly. But while she could shut out

the sight of her residual limb, she couldn't block from her mind the image of his handsome features looking at her with disgust and revulsion.

Perhaps she wasn't being being fair to Jake. He had looked at her stump several times now and she had never witnessed the kind of reaction from him that she'd seen in her fiancé's eyes.

He wasn't Clay. She had to remind herself of that. But Clay had supposedly loved her and still he couldn't bear to look at her. Why should Jake respond any differently?

She blew out a breath and drew the quilt back over her legs. Torturing herself like this was silly, anyway. She wouldn't ever be in a situation where Jake Dalton would see her in a state of undress. After her hysterical behavior tonight, she was certain the man wouldn't be at all eager to spend any more time with a nutcase like her.

Not that she wanted to jump into that kind of relationship with him. Did she?

Enough doubt flickered through her to make her wonder. She wasn't sure how it happened, but suddenly the idea of a relationship with him didn't seem as completely irrational as it would have a week ago. Somehow her feelings for him were changing, helped along significantly by watching him with his patients that day.

She stared out the window at the shifting patterns of moonlight through the rain.

How could she actually be thinking of sex and Jake Dalton in the same moment? How could she even contemplate making love to the son of the man who had destroyed her father's dreams and ultimately cost him his life?

Somehow the old hatred seemed far away tonight as she thought of the heat of his kiss and his strong, tender arms around her while she wept.

* * *

As she expected, she saw and heard nothing of Jake for several days. By the time Saturday rolled around, she convinced herself she'd been right, that he wanted nothing more to do with her after her irrational outburst.

She was relieved, she told herself, though neither her body nor her subconscious were a hundred percent convinced. She had dreamed of him every night, more of those soft, erotic kisses, and had awakened trembling and achy.

At least she wasn't dreaming of explosions and screams and fear. She supposed she should be grateful to Jake for distracting her from her usual nightmares for a while.

Not that she intended to track him down to thank him for it, even if she'd had the time.

The Pine Gulch Founder's Day celebration was just a few weeks away, and Viviana, always heavily involved in community activities, was suddenly up to her ears planning the Cattlewoman's Association hamburger fry.

Every time Maggie walked into the kitchen, she would find her mother on the phone, and Viviana had been gone every evening on committee business.

As a result Maggie had more than enough work to do on the ranch, though, to her dismay, Wade Dalton sent over a ranch hand from the Cold Creek to help with the spring planting. Despite her best efforts, she couldn't talk her mother out of accepting their help.

Saturday morning found her loading alfalfa bales onto a pickup truck to take out to some of the cow-calf pairs in one of the far pastures. She was about halfway loaded and went inside the barn for another bale when she heard a vehicle pull up outside.

"In here," she called out, assuming it was Drifty Halloran, the Cold Creek cowboy. She hadn't been expecting him today, as she knew they were branding over at the Cold Creek, but maybe Wade had been feeling magnanimous and sent him anyway.

The barn was dim and dusty, and all she could make out at first was the hazy outline of someone standing in the doorway, silhouetted by the bright sunshine outside.

Not Drifty.

Jake.

She recognized him after only a few seconds, and to her dismay, her heart gave a sharp little leap of joy.

She hadn't seen him since that night and she had missed him, she realized suddenly, but the embarrassment that followed doused her initial reaction.

Heat soaked her cheeks, and she was grateful for the dim barn. She had a sudden vivid memory of bursting into tears, and for one panicked moment she wanted to dive behind the hay bales and hide until he left again.

Too late. He'd seen her. He gave a heavy, frustrated sigh and stepped into the barn. "What are you doing, Maggie?"

Stuffing her embarrassment back down inside her, she hefted the bale into her arms and headed out past him. "Embroidering pillows. What does it look like?"

He followed her into the sunshine. "I thought I signed on to do the heavy lifting. I'd say this certainly qualifies. Why didn't you wait for me to take care of this?"

She didn't answer as she lifted the bale onto the truck, but when she turned around to head back into the barn, he planted himself in front of her so she couldn't move around him without looking foolish.

"You didn't think I was coming today, did you? It's Saturday and we had a deal. A day for a day, remember? Did you think I was backing out?"

She had hoped. She wasn't ready to face him again; she wasn't completely sure she ever would be.

"It was a stupid deal and neither of us should be held to it. You don't have to give up your Saturday, Jake. I've got things under control here."

She stepped around him and walked into the barn.

Just as she expected, he followed her.

Chapter 10

The woman was making him crazy.

He wanted to shake her, to yell at her. To kiss her. He settled for yanking the alfalfa bale out of her arms. "I'm not going anywhere, Maggie, except out to the truck to load this."

She glared at him and reached for another one. With a sigh he took that bale from her with his other hand.

"Hey! I was carrying that."

"You think I'm going to stand here and watch you torture yourself?"

"So go home!" she snapped, reaching for another bale.

"I'm not going anywhere. Now put that down, go take the weight off your leg and let me finish this."

She gave him one of the more colorful phrases she probably learned in the Army but he only grinned.

"Nice try, Lieutenant. You can either put it down on your

own and go wait for me in the truck or I'll haul you in there and tie you to the steering wheel."

She lifted her chin, and he braced himself for the blast of her temper. Instead after a moment she gave him a look as cold as a dead snake, turned on her heel and walked stiffly outside.

He followed with the alfalfa bales and watched her climb awkwardly into the cab. She didn't look very happy about it, but she went, which was, he supposed, all he could ask.

In only a few moments he stacked the truck bed as high as he could with hay bales, then joined her in the cab, wondering as he took off his leather gloves whether he might need them to defend himself from the jagged emotion he could feel rippling off her.

Again he braced himself for anger, but she only gazed at him, an unreadable expression in those dark, lovely eyes.

"I'm not a child, Jake," she finally said, her voice low. "I'm a grown woman with a mind of my own. I've survived a war and having two of my closest friends blown to pieces beside me while I could do nothing to help them. I've seen horrible things. For that matter, I've *done* horrible things. I'm not fragile or weak or stupid and I'm not some infant who needs to be pampered and coddled."

He heard her words through a haze of great shame. She was exactly right—that's how he had treated her, like a child who couldn't be trusted to know her own limits. She deserved better.

"I know everyone worries about me overdoing it," she went on before he could respond. "And while I do appreciate that concern and know it's well meant, I'm suffocating here. Staying busy—doing as much as I can for myself—is the only thing keeping me sane right now. It's important to me. Even if it means a little pain in the short term, it's far better than the alternative, drowning myself in self-pity like I did the other night. Can you understand that?"

What had it cost her to say all this? She was not a woman who shared pieces of herself easily. She could have ranted and raved and put more of those barriers up between them, but she had trusted him enough to let him catch this rare glimpse into her psyche, and he found he was unbelievably touched.

"I'm sorry," he murmured.

His arms ached to hold her but he sensed she wouldn't welcome his touch right now, for a variety of reasons.

"You're absolutely right. I've built my life around healing and comfort, around trying to ease my patients' pain whenever I can. It's impossible for me to watch you hurt and not want to do everything possible to ease your way when I can. I tend to forget that you might have your reasons for taking the rougher road."

"You have to trust me to recognize my own limits, Jake. Please."

"Do you mind if I still worry about you?"

A small, wry smile tilted the corner of her mouth. "Any chance I could stop you?"

"Probably not," he admitted.

Her smile widened, became full-blown. "Go ahead, then. Just keep it to yourself."

They lapsed into a silence he didn't find at all uncomfortable. She didn't seem in a hurry to put the truck in gear and head to wherever she intended on taking the alfalfa. Instead she seemed as if she had something else on her mind, almost as if she were gathering her courage.

The impression was confirmed when she spoke. "While I'm getting everything out into the open here, I believe I owe you an apology."

He frowned, trying to figure out where she was headed with this. "For?"

"The other night." She cleared her throat, suddenly focused on something out the windshield. "I'm afraid I was having one of those pity parties and forced you to be an unwilling guest. I'm sorry I reacted that way and bawled all over you. I don't know what happened. I just...once I started, I couldn't stop."

She looked miserable, her features tight and embarrassed, and he hated being the source of it.

"Don't. You have nothing to apologize about."

"I suppose your patients are always unloading on you."

"You're not my patient, as you continually remind me."

He meant his words as a joke, something to lighten the mood a little, but somehow she looked even more embarrassed by them.

"Right. You're right."

He had to touch her. It had been four days and he had restrained himself as long as he possibly could. He covered her fingers flexing on the steering wheel. "Maggie. You're more than a medical case to me. I hope you understand that."

She blinked at him, her dark eyes wide and confused and still so miserable he couldn't help himself. He leaned across the cab of the pickup and found her mouth with his.

He tried his best to keep it light, casual. But her lush mouth tasted of coffee and cinnamon, and her fingers trembled under his on the steering wheel and she made a soft sound in her throat.

After only a tiny moment later, she pulled her hand from the steering wheel and shifted to face him on the bench seat, wrapping her arms around him and pulling him close as her mouth softened and welcomed him.

He had thought of nothing else these last few days but having her in his arms. Somehow the fantasies didn't come close to comparing to the reality of her small, compact frame snuggled against him, of her arms holding him and her mouth responding eagerly to his kiss.

He was hot and aroused in an instant, consumed by the fiery need to touch her, to taste her. His hand slid under the cotton edge of her T-shirt just above the waistband of her jeans, and her abdominal muscles contracted sharply as he touched skin.

He paused. "Sorry. Are my fingers cold?"

Her laugh was throaty and low. "Are you kidding?"

What else could he do but take that as permission to explore further? He curved a hand over her hip bone and leaned closer, until their bodies were tangled together.

For long moments he was lost, aware only that he was holding the woman he loved and that by some miracle she seemed caught up in the heat and wonder, too.

His hands slid from her waist higher, across the warm skin of her abdomen. He might have stopped there but her stomach muscles contracted and she made one of those soft, sexy little sounds and he explored further, stopping just below the curve of her breast.

She moaned and arched against him as if inviting more, then she suddenly seemed to freeze, making a sound more of pain than arousal.

He jerked back, feeling as if one of those alfalfa bales had just fallen on his head as awareness flooded through him.

What the hell was he doing, making out with her in the cab of a pickup in broad daylight, in cramped quarters that couldn't be comfortable for her, where anyone could come across them? Her mother, Wade's ranch hand. Wade himself, for crying out loud.

He let out a breath, disgusted with himself for losing control so completely. "I'm sorry. I wasn't thinking. See what you do to me?"

Her breathing was ragged and her eyes looked huge, the pupils so dark and wide they seemed to take over the irises. "What…what I do?"

He brought her hand to his mouth and kissed her knuckles. "I can't think straight when I'm around you. I should know better than to start something I know we can't finish right now, no matter how badly I might want it."

He wouldn't have expected it, but his tough lieutenant seemed flustered. She took several seconds to catch her breath and sent him one quick, wary look. "I… We'd better take this hay out to the pasture," she said.

She started the pickup, but before she could shift the transmission, he covered her fingers on the steering wheel with his hand again.

"I'd like to take you out tomorrow."

"Why?"

He almost laughed at her abrupt question. How could she ask it, after the wild heat they had just shared?

Because I'm crazy about you. Because you're like pure adrenaline in my bloodstream and I can't get enough.

"Will you come with me?"

She studied him across the width of the cab, and he saw the wheels turn in her head. When she spoke, her voice was smug, self-satisfied. "If you agree not to nag me for the rest of the day that I'm overdoing things, I'll promise to think about it."

"I have to keep my mouth shut all day and you're only going to *think* about it? That hardly seems fair."

She gave a short laugh, but it was enough for him to tumble a little deeper. She was stunning when she laughed, bright and vibrant and intoxicating.

"That's the deal. Take it or leave it. If you can actually zip your bossy, meddling lips while we're working together today, I'll go wherever you want tomorrow night."

"Done," he said quickly.

She shook her head. "You'll have to forgive me if I don't hold my breath, Dalton."

"Just watch me. You won't even know I'm here all day, I swear it."

She had allowed herself to be boxed into a corner again and she had no one to blame but herself.

As the sun started its long, slow slide behind the mountains, Maggie was exhausted, achy and beginning to realize she was in deep trouble.

All day she had worked alongside Jake on the ranch. She hadn't found it easy to ignore her awareness of him. It simmered under her skin, hot and tight, and she caught herself several times watching him work simply because she enjoyed the sight. He was a man comfortable with his body, every movement easy and fluid.

She knew it was dangerous and self-destructive. Simply watching his muscles ripple as he unloaded hay from the pickup out in the pasture shouldn't leave her stomach twirling, her mouth dry. And she certainly shouldn't go breathless at the sight of him leaning down to pat one of the cow dogs, a smile on his tanned, handsome features.

It was easier when she could stir up a good mad toward him, but he had been nothing but quietly helpful all day. Though she had spent the day right alongside him as they fed and watered and moved cattle from pasture to pasture, he had honored his promise and hadn't uttered so much as a single chastising word.

She had to admit, she'd even pushed the envelope, extending herself probably further than she should to see if she could goad him into breaking his vow.

A few times she thought he would bite through his tongue with the effort it must have taken him not to say anything, especially earlier when she went into the pasture with one of their prize bulls to check the water trough pressure.

The bull, though usually docile, had come over to investigate, head lowered, and Maggie had decided to play it safe and scramble back over the fence. Moving so fast had been painful and tough but worth it when the bull hammered against the fence a few times to show her who was boss.

Through every risky thing she did all day, Jake refrained from nagging her about it. She wasn't sure how he did it, but now it looked as if she was going to have to keep her end of the bargain, much to her burgeoning dismay.

Working alongside him on the ranch was one thing. Dealing with him on the much more dangerous terrain of a social situation was something else entirely.

She couldn't figure a way out of it, and the idea of an actual date filled her with panic.

Okay, the idea of a date with *Jake* filled her with panic.

She didn't know what to do about him, about the soft flutters inside her whenever he looked at her out of those blue eyes or the apparent interest she couldn't quite understand.

The whole idea of it made her more nervous than a dozen half-ton bulls on the warpath.

She pushed her panic away and focused again on the sprinkler pipe that had cracked during the winter. Jake was beside her, working probably twice as fast as she could, a fact she wasn't thrilled about.

Apparently he hadn't always had his head in a book growing up over at the Cold Creek. He certainly knew his ranch work.

He worked hard, he knew what he was doing and today, at least, he kept his mouth shut. He would have been the perfect employee—if only she could keep from noticing how well he filled out those blasted Wranglers!

She glanced at the sky, then wiped her face with the bandanna from her pocket.

"We're losing daylight. I can work on this Monday when Drifty comes back."

He settled back on his haunches, the last rays of sunlight shooting strands of gold through his dark hair.

"You dismissing me for the day, boss?"

She shoved her gloves in her pocket and stood, hoping he didn't notice she had to leverage herself up using the line wheel.

"Yeah. I think we're both beat." She paused. "Uh, thank you for your help today. We got a lot done."

He stood, looking pleased at her words. "You're welcome."

He studied her intently in the fading sunlight, and she could feel herself flush under his scrutiny.

"So would you agree I have kept our bargain all day? No nagging, no harassing, no badgering you to take it easy, right?"

She made a face. "I suppose, though a few times there it looked like your head was going to explode with the effort it was taking to keep your mouth shut."

"But I did, didn't I? I didn't say a word, so that means you agree to let me take you somewhere tomorrow night. I believe your exact words were, *I'll go wherever you want.* Am I right?"

She clenched her jaw, wondering if this is what a field mouse felt like just before an owl swooped. "You know you are," she muttered.

"So we have a deal, then. You're not going to back out on me, find some hidden loophole or something?"

"Jeez, Dalton. Do you need me to sign a frigging contract? It's just a date!"

"I'm only making sure we're clear."

"I said I would go and I'll go."

"Great. I'll pick you up at six-thirty, then. Wear something comfortable."

She rolled her eyes, hating that he could talk so casually about something that filled her with dread.

She opened her mouth to try answering in the same vein, but before she could get the words out, he scooped her into his arms and headed toward the house.

"Hey!" she exclaimed. "Put me down!"

"Forget it. I've kept my mouth shut all day just like you asked. And now you're damn well going to sit down and take off the prosthesis that's been killing you since noon."

"No fair. This is a deal breaker, Dalton! You promised."

"Too late. You already said you'd go with me. A soldier's word is her bond, right?"

She had two choices, as she saw it. She could throw a fit and force the issue. Or she could try to salvage a little dignity and wait until he set her down before ripping into him.

She decided on the second choice and contented herself with fuming the rest of the way, trying hard not to focus on how warm and comforting and solid his arms felt around her.

She was growing entirely too used to this, to him and

his concern for her, and it scared her senseless. What would she do when this phase of his passed—as she had no doubt it would—and he grew tired of dealing with her assorted physical and emotional problems?

He would break her heart into jagged shards. Didn't she have enough broken pieces right now?

"Okay, you've made your point. Put me down," she grumbled, even as she fought her body's instinctive urge to snuggle into his warmth and solid strength.

"Almost there," he said. She couldn't figure out how he didn't even sound breathless.

Just as they approached the house, she heard a car engine. Her mother's car pulled to a stop in front of the house and an instant later Viviana rushed out, her eyes panicky and her features tight with worry.

Too late, she realized how it must look to Viviana to find Jake carrying her.

"What is it? What has happened to her?"

"Nothing, Viv," Jake answered calmly. "Everything's just fine. I'm only making sure your daughter takes a rest."

His patients probably found comfort from those soothing tones, but they seemed to have the opposite effect on her. She curled her fists to keep from slugging him.

It worked well enough for her mother, though. Viviana let out a sigh of relief. "I thought perhaps she fell again."

He raised an eyebrow at the last word and gave Maggie a hard look but said nothing, to her vast relief. She didn't want to have to explain about the balance issues that still plagued her when she was tired.

"You can put me down anytime now," she snapped.

"Now why would I want to do that?" he asked, sounding genuinely puzzled, though she didn't miss the amusement in his gaze.

"You have any idea how many ways the Army teaches you to emasculate a man?" she asked idly.

He laughed. "A fair few, I'd guess."

He didn't seem threatened in the least as he carried her up the porch steps and into the house. In the living room, he lowered her to the couch, then stepped back, leaving her oddly, irrationally bereft.

Viviana had followed them and she stood in the doorway, watching their interaction with eyes still dark with worry.

"I'd ask you to let me take a look at your leg," Jake said, "but I don't want to risk you calling me a pervert again in front of your mother."

She felt color soak her cheeks as Viviana's worry changed to surprised laughter.

"Shut up, Dalton," Maggie snapped.

"Lena, your manners! Jacob, will you stay for dinner? I will have it fixed in only a moment."

"Can't tonight. Sorry. But Maggie and I are going out tomorrow. I told her six-thirty."

As she watched, a strange look passed between them, and Viviana nodded. "Good. Good. I will be sure she at least washes her face and brushes her hair before you are to come for her."

Feeling dusty and disheveled and about eight years old, she wanted to storm out in a huff and leave them to their jolly friendliness but she wasn't quite certain she trusted her leg to hold her.

She had to be content with folding her arms across her chest and glaring at both of them.

She was further dismayed when Jake smiled at her with a strange, almost tender expression.

"Good night, then. See you tomorrow. Six-thirty sharp."

Before she knew what he intended, he stepped forward

and planted a hard, fierce kiss on her mouth, right there in front of her mother.

Just when she was beginning to feel light-headed, he stepped back, shoved on his Stetson and sauntered out of the room. She could swear as he walked out of the house she could hear him whistling, the bastard.

She shifted her gaze to her mother and found Viviana beaming at her. Damn. Just what she needed, for Viviana to take that kiss as permission to fill her mind with all kinds of unreasonable things.

"He is taken with you." Viviana's eyes sparkled.

"He's only hanging around out of pity." She voiced out loud what her heart had been telling her all along.

Viviana frowned, planting hands on her petite hips. "Stop it! This is not true."

"Why else would he develop this sudden interest?"

"Not sudden. You just never see it before."

She paused in the middle of rolling up her pant leg so she could get rid of the prosthesis. "See what?"

"Jacob. He has always had the interest." Her mother's voice was brisk. "Always he asks of you. How you are, what you are doing. Every time he would see me, he would ask of you."

What was she supposed to think of that? She let out a breath as she worked to doff her prosthesis. Though she preferred taking it off in the privacy of her bedroom, the long day and strenuous activities she'd engaged in had lowered her pain threshold and she couldn't wait.

Nothing. His questions meant nothing. He was a polite person, probably only looking for some topic of conversation with her mother.

"I'm an interesting medical case. That's all."

Her expression solemn, Viviana watched her remove

the prosthesis. After she set it aside with an almost painful rush of relief, Viviana sat beside her on the couch and touched her hand.

"When your commander from the Army called to tell me about the attack and that you were very hurt, we did not know your condition or even if you would live. Marjorie came to be with me that night while we waited to hear, and Jacob came with his mother. Lena, never have I seen a man so upset. Marjorie and I cried and cried, we were so worried for you. Jacob was strong for us, but his eyes! They were shocked and sad and…and lost."

Viviana paused and she touched Maggie's hand again. "Then they called again to tell me you would lose part of your leg and we cried more. But Jacob, he made us ashamed. He told us to stop being sad for you. He sat in that chair there and said, 'A foot is only a foot. She will survive now. She will live, and that is the only thing that matters.'"

She barely had time for that to sink in when Viviana pressed her warm, soft cheek to hers. "He was only part right, *niña*. You survive. But you do not live. My heart, still it worries for you."

"I'm fine, Mama."

Her mother didn't look convinced, but she let the subject drop. "I will fix you something to eat and then you will rest." Viviana bustled from the room before Maggie could tell her she wasn't hungry.

After she left, Maggie leaned her head against the high-backed sofa and tried not to think about Jake, but it proved an impossible task, like trying not to think about a tooth that ached. He filled her mind, her senses, and she couldn't seem to think about anything else.

Chapter 11

At twenty-five minutes past six, Jake drove under the archway over the drive to Rancho de la Luna, his shoulders tight with exhaustion and his mood dark and dismal as a January storm.

Under other circumstances he would have called things off with Maggie tonight and rescheduled for a better day when he felt more in the mood. But events were out of his hands and he knew he had no choice.

The day had started out badly, with an early-morning call from one of his patients' wives that her husband was having a hard time breathing. By the time he arrived at their house five minutes later, just ahead of the ambulance crew, Wilford Cranwinkle had stopped breathing altogether and his wife, Bertie, had been frantic.

Heart attack, he'd quickly determined. A bad one, much worse than the one Wilford had suffered two years earlier that had led to behavior and diet changes.

Jake had ridden the ambulance with Wilford to the hospital in Idaho Falls, trying everything he and the paramedics could to save the man's life, to no avail.

By the time Bertie arrived, the task of telling her that her husband of forty-two years had not survived fell to Jake.

It had been a bitter day, the kind of terrible loss that made him question whether he could have done more—and even if he ever should have become a physician in the first place.

He also couldn't help but remember that fall day more than nineteen years earlier when he and Maggie had tried and failed to save another heart attack victim.

Some days it seemed the ghost of Hank Dalton followed him around everywhere, whispering in his ear what a poor excuse for a doctor he was, how he was a miserable excuse for a son, how he would never amount to any kind of stockman if he couldn't yank his nose out of a damn book.

As he'd been showering and changing to prepare to pick up Maggie, he also couldn't help thinking how his efforts to pierce her hard, prickly shell reminded him painfully of his youth and adolescence spent trying so hard to win his father's approval.

She pushed him away at every turn, blocking his every attempt to reach through her defenses to the woman inside.

Tonight, for instance, he half expected her to back out and refuse to go with him. The mood he was in, he almost wanted her to, just so he could vent some of the raging emotions inside him by the physical act of hauling her to his SUV.

He turned off his engine and sat for a moment trying to let the soft beauty of the Luna seep through his turmoil to calm him. The ranch was lovely in the gathering twilight, with its breathtaking view of the Tetons' west edge, the stately row of cottonwoods lining the creek, those unique silver-gray cattle quietly grazing in the fields.

It was a perfect evening for what was in store, he thought as he climbed out, unseasonably mild for late April with the lush smell of growth and life in the air.

Hoping his exhaustion didn't show in his eyes, he climbed the stairs and rang the doorbell. He could hear her slow steps approaching the door, and a moment later it swung open.

In an instant the breath seemed to leave his chest in a rush. She wore a loose, flowing pair of pants and a gauzy white shirt that made her dusky skin look sultry and exotic.

Her hair was a mass of soft curls that instantly made him want to bury his face in them, and she wore several bangle bracelets and long, dangly earrings.

It was the first time in recent memory he'd seen her dressed as a girly-girl. She looked as lovely and intoxicating as the spring evening, and with a little start of surprise, he realized all the dark memories of the day had started to recede. They were still there but they seemed suddenly as distant as the moon that gave her ranch its name.

When he said nothing, only continued to stare, Maggie squirmed. "You said wear something comfortable. This is comfortable."

Her belligerent tone finally pierced his daze. Beneath her truculence, she seemed apprehensive, and he wondered at it.

"You look perfect," he murmured, then couldn't seem to help himself. He twisted her fingers in his, leaned forward and kissed her cheek.

She smelled divine, some kind of perfume that reminded him of standing in his sister-in-law's flower garden, and he wanted to dip his face into her neck and inhale.

He forced himself to refrain, and as he stepped back he

had the satisfaction of seeing she looked even more adorably flustered.

"Is your mother around?" he asked, knowing perfectly well she wasn't.

Maggie frowned and tried to withdraw her hand. He held firm. "No. She left a few hours ago. She said she was visiting a friend, though she wouldn't tell me who. I wondered if it was Guillermo, but she wouldn't say. She's been acting very strange today. All week, really."

It took a great effort to keep his expression blandly innocent. "Really?"

"Taking phone calls at all hours of the day and night, running off on mysterious errands she won't explain, accepting package deliveries she won't let me see."

"Maybe she has a boyfriend."

Her jaw went slack as she processed that possibility. "Why on earth would you say that? Do you know something I don't?"

He thought of his own suspicions about Viviana but decided Maggie wasn't quite ready for them. "Sorry. Forget I said anything. Are you ready, then?"

She looked distracted, and he knew she was still dwelling on the possibility of Viviana entering the dating scene.

"I... Yes. I just need a jacket."

"What about your sticks?" He gestured to her forearm crutches, propped against a chair.

She made a face. "Am I going to need them?"

"You never know. Doesn't hurt to be prepared, does it?"

With a sigh she grabbed them. "I've really come to hate these things. Someday I'm going to invent a comfortable pair of crutches."

He took them from her and offered his other arm to her. After a moment's hesitation she slipped her arm through his, and he wanted to tuck her against him and hang on forever.

"So where are we going?" she asked on their slow way down the porch steps.

"Sorry. Can't tell you that."

"Why on earth not?"

"You'll see. Just be patient."

She didn't look very thrilled with his answer, just as he had an uncomfortable suspicion she wouldn't be very thrilled about their ultimate destination.

He couldn't worry about that. It was out of his hands, he reminded himself again as he helped her into the Durango, impressed by her technique of sitting first then twisting her legs around so she didn't have to put weight on her foot.

After he slipped the crutches in the back, he climbed in and then headed down the driveway.

They were almost to the road when she reached a hand out and touched his arm. The spontaneous gesture surprised him enough that he almost didn't stop in time to miss a minivan heading up the road to the Cold Creek. The traffic was much heavier than normal in that direction, and he could only hope she didn't notice.

"Is something wrong?"

He stared. "Why do you ask?"

She shrugged. "Your eyes. They seem distracted and you're not your usual annoyingly cheerful self."

He thought of the terrible task of telling Bertie her husband was gone, of the sense of failure that sat cold and bitter in his gut. Not wanting to put a damper on the evening, he opened his mouth to offer some polite lie but the words tangled in his throat.

The urge to confide in her was too overwhelming to resist. "I lost a patient today. Will Cranwinkle. Heart attack."

She touched his arm again. "Oh, Jake. I'm so sorry."

"I rode the ambulance to Idaho Falls with him, trying to shock him but we could never get a rhythm."

Her eyes were dark with compassion and he wanted to drown in them. "The last thing you probably feel like doing is socializing tonight. I don't mind if you take me home. We can do this another time."

He shook his head. "You're not getting out of this that easily. We're going. This is exactly where I need to be."

"What about where you *want* to be?"

"That, too. I promise, I wouldn't be anywhere else tonight."

He turned east, heading up the box canyon instead of down toward town. She made a sound of surprise. The only thing in this direction was the Cold Creek.

"I need to make a quick stop. Do you mind?"

A muscle flexed in her jaw, and he could tell she *did* mind but she only shrugged again. "You're driving."

She didn't look very thrilled about it but she said nothing more, though her features looked increasingly baffled as they reached the ranch entrance. Cars were parked along both sides of the road, and one whole pasture was filled with more parked cars.

"What's happening? Are we crashing some kind of party?"

Despite the lingering ache in his chest over the day's events, he had to smile. "You could say that."

They drove under the arch, decorated in red, white and blue bunting. She still looked baffled until they approached the ranch house, where a huge banner Bud Watkins down at the sign shop in town had made up read in giant letters "Welcome Home Lt. Cruz. Pine Gulch Salutes You."

Under it stood just about everyone in town—men, women, children—smiling and waving at them.

She stared at the crowd, her eyes wide. "Did you do this?"

He searched her features but he couldn't tell whether that tremor in her voice stemmed from shock or from anger. "I can't take much credit, I have to admit. Or blame, if it comes to that. Your mother and mine were behind the whole thing. I was only charged with delivering you here at the appointed hour."

He pulled up in the parking space set aside for her and walked around the SUV to help her out. When he saw the jumbled mix of emotions in her eyes, he paused in the open door of the Durango and shifted to block her from the crowd's view.

"I don't want this, Jake." The distress in her voice matched her eyes, "I'm not some kind of hero. I can't go out there and pretend otherwise. I'm a mess. You know I am. Physically, emotionally, all of it."

He grabbed her hands and held them tight. "You don't see yourself as we all do, sweetheart. This town is bursting with pride for you."

"For what? I returned a cripple! Everyone can see that. I can't even take a damn shower without it turning into a major production!"

"Maggie—"

"I didn't come home to be embraced and applauded by my hometown. I came to Pine Gulch to hide away from life, because I didn't have anywhere else to go."

Her eyes glittered, and he hoped like hell she didn't start to cry. He knew she would hate that more than anything, to break down in front of the whole town.

A heavy weight of responsibility settled on his shoulders. He knew whatever he said was of vital importance, and he tried to choose his words with the utmost care.

"You can say what you want, but I don't believe you came home because you had nowhere else," he said quietly.

"You came home because you knew this was where you belonged, a place where you knew you would be loved and supported while you try to adjust to the changes in your life. People in this town want to celebrate what you did over there and the fact that you've returned. Your *mother* wants to celebrate your return. Don't break her heart, Maggie."

She shifted her gaze past him to where Viviana stood, her hands clasped together at her chest and worry in her dark eyes. He held his breath, watching indecision flicker across her features for just an instant. She let out a long sigh, then nodded slowly, her eyes resolute.

She pasted on a smile—a little frayed around the edges but a smile nevertheless—and gripped the doorjamb to pull herself out, her shoulders stiff and determined.

If he hadn't already been hopelessly in love with her, he knew as he watched her face her fears that he would have tumbled headlong and hard at that moment.

She had never felt less like celebrating. But for the next hour Maggie forced herself to smile and make small talk and to ignore the stubborn pains in her leg as she moved from group to group.

It was a lovely night for a party, she had to admit, the twilight sweetly scented and just cool enough to be refreshing. The Daltons had strung lights in the trees, and more bunting hung from every horizontal space. Everything looked warm and welcoming.

She hadn't been to the Cold Creek in years, and she'd forgotten how beautiful the gardens were. Marjorie and her mother had that in common, she remembered, their love of growing things. Perhaps that had been one of the things they'd built their friendship on.

She knew Jake's mother didn't live on the ranch anymore, she owned a house in town where she lived with her second husband, so perhaps Wade Dalton's new wife was the gardener in the family. Whoever created it and maintained it, the gardens were lovely and peaceful.

On a makeshift wooden floor under the swaying branches of a weeping willow, locals danced to the music of a country music band that included Mr. Benson, the high school choir director, Myron Potter, who owned the hardware store, and a pretty girl with a dulcet voice Maggie could vaguely recall babysitting eons ago.

Not that she heard much of the band, introduced as Sagebrush Serenade. She didn't have much chance, too busy talking to everyone in town. She had been hugged more times tonight than she had in the entire dozen years since she left Pine Gulch, and she thought she had been greeted by every single person she went to school with.

She couldn't believe all the people who turned out—people she never would have expected. Mrs. Hall—her tenth-grade English teacher, whose favorite phrase on grade sheets had been "You're not working up to your potential"—looked as if she hadn't so much as changed a wrinkle in twenty years.

Pat Conners, her first date, was there with his wife and two young children.

Even Jesse Johnson, the bus driver who had picked her and the Dalton boys up as long as she could remember, was out on the dance floor, and he had to be pushing eighty by now.

More surprising was the sight of Carmela, the young pregnant woman she'd met at Jake's clinic. When she'd seen her in the crowd, Maggie had kept an eye on her. Carmela had started out sticking with others in the Latino community; now she was talking with two Anglo women, one of whom also looked pregnant.

Maggie probably would have found it all heartwarming, a reaffirmation of small-town values, if she hadn't been the guest of honor.

"We couldn't be more proud of you, young lady. You're a credit to the whole town."

She turned back to Charlie Bannister, the mail carrier who had been mayor of Pine Gulch as long as she could remember. She didn't think his years of service to the town had anything to do with a particular craving for power, more that no one else wanted the job.

She smiled politely. "Thank you, sir. I appreciate that."

"Purple Heart, I understand."

"Yes sir."

"A great honor. Yes, indeed. I'm only sorry you had to make such a sacrifice to earn it. But looks like you're learning to adjust. Good for you. Good for you."

She didn't know what to do except nod and smile as the mayor went on at length about how his cousin had to have a leg amputated—"the diabetes, don't you know"—and how he never walked again.

"You're getting around well. I wouldn't even know your leg was a fake if I didn't know your story," the mayor said.

As the mayor went on and on, Maggie spied Jake moving among the guests. Though she tried to catch his eye to send him a subliminal message to rescue her, he seemed to be as much in demand as she was.

He was the only doctor in town, she reminded herself. He probably couldn't even walk into the little grocery store in town without being assaulted for medical advice.

"Excuse me, won't you?" the mayor suddenly said, much to her relief. "The boss is trying to get my attention."

She followed his gaze and found Dellarae, his dumpling-plump wife, gesturing to him.

"Of course," she said with barely concealed relief. "It wouldn't do to keep the boss waiting."

The mayor gave her a grateful smile and a fatherly pat on the arm. "Knew you'd understand. You always were a sensible girl."

Since when? she wondered. If she were sensible, she wouldn't be here. She would have climbed back into Jake's SUV and driven away the moment she caught sight of the row of cars out front.

No, if she were sensible, she wouldn't have been in Jake's SUV in the first place. A woman with common sense certainly would know better than to spend time with a man who turned her knees to mush just by looking at her out of those stunning blue eyes of his.

Would her mother ever forgive her if she ditched the party and found a ride back to the Luna? Probably not.

But then, where was her mother? she wondered. She'd seen her that first moment when they pulled up, but since then she seemed to have disappeared. Probably in the kitchen. That was usually Viviana's favorite locale.

She spied the Elwood sisters heading in her direction, their lined faces set in matching expressions of pity and avid interest, and decided now would be a good time to check on her mother.

Shifting around so quickly she almost lost her balance, she turned and headed for the house. She discovered the back door opened into the Cold Creek kitchen, which at first glance wasn't at all what she expected. It was large and open, painted a sunny, welcoming yellow.

Her mother wasn't in sight—the only occupant was a

young woman in a white apron who looked to be arranging food on a platter.

"Sorry," Maggie murmured, guilt washing through her as she watched the woman work. This was all for her, she realized. Everyone throwing this party had been so kind, and all she could do was feel sorry for herself and wish she were anywhere else on earth.

"I was looking for my mother, Viviana Cruz."

The woman's smile was as warm as the room. "You must be the guest of honor, aren't you? I'm Caroline, Wade Dalton's wife. What a pleasure to meet you! I tried to talk to you earlier but you were surrounded by well-wishers. I'm so pleased to have a chance to say hello and welcome you back to town."

Maggie blinked, unsure how to respond to this woman. She tried to drum up her usual antipathy toward anyone related to the Daltons, but this woman seemed so nice and genuinely friendly, it was hard to feel anything but warmth.

"Um, thank you," she finally said. "Thank you for opening your home. I'm sure it wasn't easy throwing a party for a stranger."

"You're only a stranger to me, not the rest of the family. When Marjorie and Viv came up with the idea for a party, we knew the Cold Creek was the ideal place for it. We've got the room here for parking and for dancing, so when Jake suggested it, it just made sense. Wade insisted."

Wade? Jake's older brother barely knew her. Why would he want all these people wandering through his house, their vehicles ripping up a perfectly good pasture?

"Still, I'm sorry you had to go to so much bother."

"It was no trouble, I promise. Your mother and Marjorie did most of the work, with a little help from Quinn."

"Quinn?"

"My father. Marjorie's husband. He loves a good party."

"Right. I'm sorry, I forgot his name."

Her mother had told her the story of Majorie Dalton's elopement with a man she had an email romance with—a man whose daughter had come to the ranch in search of the newlyweds and ended up falling for Jake's widowed older brother and his three young children.

"I believe I met him shortly after we arrived. Tall, handsome, charming smile."

"That's my dad," Caroline said ruefully. Her gaze sharpened suddenly, and Maggie had the odd sensation this woman could see into her deepest secrets.

"This all must be very uncomfortable for you."

She almost equivocated, gave some polite denial, but something in the woman's expression compelled her to honesty. "Yes. A bit. I'm not really crazy about being the center of attention."

"Jake warned Viv and Marjorie you might not be ready for a big party, that they should start with something small and intimate with just close friends if they insisted on celebrating, but I'm afraid things spiraled a little out of control. I must say you're handling it all very graciously."

Maggie made a face. "Not really. Why do you think I came in here to hide out?"

Caroline laughed, and Maggie felt an instant connection with this woman with the kind eyes. The other woman's laughter slid away after a moment, and her eyes filled with a quiet concern.

"I'm sure you've had all the counseling you could stand at the Army hospital, but if you ever need to talk to someone here, I hope you know I'm always willing to listen."

Maggie suddenly remembered her mother telling her Wade Dalton's new wife was a therapist who had become an author and life coach, focused on helping people find more joy in their lives.

"Thank you. I appreciate that."

"Listen, I need to run this tray out. I'll be back for more in a moment. You are more than welcome to stay here as long as you'd like."

She suddenly remembered the ostensible reason for her escape from the party. "I actually stepped in here looking for my mother."

"That's right. Viviana was in here a few moments before you came in but then I thought I heard her go out the front door. You could try the porch out there," Caroline suggested.

"Thank you," Maggie murmured as the other woman headed back out to the party.

The band had shifted to something slow and romantic. For a few moments, she stood alone in the kitchen, listening to the music and swaying a little.

She pressed a hand to her chest, to the little ache in her heart there, for all the slow dances she would have to sit out the rest of her life.

Enough self-pity, she told herself sternly, and went off in search of her mother.

She walked through the ranch house, surprised by how warm and comfortable the place seemed. A family lived here, she thought. Not the den of vipers she'd always wanted to imagine. A family that loved each other, at least judging by the photos lining the walls of the hallway from the kitchen to the main living area of the house.

She moved slowly past the gallery, seeing Daltons in all kinds of situations.

She saw Seth in one, handsome and compelling, with

one arm slung around Marjorie and the other around Quinn Montgomery.

In another, she saw Wade and Caroline caught in a candid pose as they leaned on a fence railing overlooking some of the ranch horses. She paused at that one, struck by the tenderness in Wade's harsh features as he looked at his lovely wife.

The one that had her stop stock-still was of Jake roughhousing with three children who must be Wade's from his first marriage. He had one little boy on his shoulders, another younger one in one arm and a pretty little dark-haired girl hanging on the other arm, and he was grinning as if he would rather be right there with those children than anywhere else on earth.

She gazed at it for a long time, unable to tear her gaze away as an odd, terrifying sensation tugged at her insides.

She reached a hand out to touch that smiling face that had become so impossibly dear to her, then jerked her hand back when she realized what she was about to do.

Breathing hard, her thoughts twirling with dismay, she forced herself to move away as fast as she dared toward the front door.

Even though it was rude, she decided she would find her mother quickly, then do anything she could to escape, to deal with the wild shock of discovering she had feelings for Jake she couldn't even bear to acknowledge.

Her pulse pounding, she yanked open the door, then had her second shock in as many moments.

Her mother was there, all right.

Wrapped tightly in the arms of Guillermo, Viviana was sharing a passionate kiss with the man she had thrown off her ranch.

Chapter 12

With every single fiber of her soul, she wanted to be able to slip away and leave them to it, if only so she could start the effort of purging this image from her mind, as well as the one she had just seen of Jake finding such joy in his niece and nephews.

She started to ease back into the house, but the door squeaked as she tried to close it, and the two figures on the porch jerked apart as if spring-loaded.

Her mother—usually so perfectly groomed—looked as if her lipstick had been devoured, and her hair was as tousled and disheveled as if she'd been standing in a wind tunnel.

Tío Guillermo wasn't much better. Most of her mother's lipstick appeared to be smeared on him, and even though they were standing several feet apart now, he still couldn't seem to look away from Viviana, his eyes hot and hungry.

Her mother raised trembling hands to her cheeks and looked miserably horrified. "Lena! Oh, Lena."

"Sorry to interrupt," she mumbled. For the life of her, she couldn't think of anything else to say, and for a few seconds the three of them stood there in a painfully awkward tableau.

"We were just, um, just…" Viviana's voice trailed off.

"I think it's safe to say I can figure out what you were doing, Mama," she said quickly.

Guillermo wore a stiff kind of dignity that seemed a little out of place on a man with lipstick on his jaw and a collar that looked as though it had been twisted in a hundred different directions.

"You are not to think less of your mother for this. I alone am responsible," her beloved uncle said, his voice stern, then he bowed slightly and headed down the steps with one last heated look at Viviana.

Maggie drew a breath, feeling as if *she* were the one caught in a wind tunnel, as if one of the last few solid things she had to hang on to had just been tossed to the heavens.

In that single look, her calm, easygoing uncle appeared tormented, wretched. A man thoroughly, miserably in love.

After he left, her mother dropped her hands from her cheeks and faced Maggie, her eyes just as miserable.

"I am sorry you saw that." Her mother spoke in agitated Spanish. "I do not know what to say. It was…we were…"

"Mama, is that what you and Tío Guillermo have been fighting about?" she asked gently. She didn't want to think about how much compassion she had for her mother's turmoil or how closely it paralleled her own.

"He is so stubborn." Her mother sank down into one of the rocking chairs on the porch that overlooked the ranch.

Maggie sat in the chair next to her and waited for the words she could see forming in her mother's dark eyes.

"I did not mean for this to happen. I did *not!* I wanted things to go on as they have since Abel died. But things have changed. I did not expect it but somehow they have.

"Guillermo wants to marry me, he says he has wanted it forever. Never did he say anything until…until the last few months, when I started to see I cared for him."

She let out a breath, gazing out at the ranch. "Before you came home, he tells me I must make a decision or he will quit. I tell him it is not fair to press me on this now, and ask him to wait a while longer, but he said he tires of waiting. He does not want to go on as we have, he says. I would not bend on this just because Guillermo he tells me I must."

"So he quit."

"No, I fire him," she insisted.

"He seems miserable, Mama," she observed quietly. "So do you. What's the big conflict?"

Her mother said nothing for a long moment, gazing out at the night. "I loved your father so much. And I have grieved for him every day since his death."

"I know that, Mama. But isn't there room in your heart for another love?"

To her dismay, her mother buried her face in her hands, her shoulders trembling. "Yes. Oh yes. I have somehow made room for Guillermo, too. But I am so afraid. What if I lose him, too? I could not bear it."

"You're losing him now," Maggie pointed out. "You're pushing him away. Tío Guillermo is a proud man, just like Papa was. How long do you expect him to wait for you to make up your mind?"

Her mother dropped her hands to look at her, and Maggie pressed her point.

"It seems to me that you should consider yourself one lucky woman, Mama. How many women have been blessed to be able to say they have been loved by two such good, decent men? Instead of worrying about some distant future pain that may never come, you should take your chance for happiness now while you still can."

Viviana gave her a searching look. "You do not mind this?"

Maggie thought of her first instant of shock at finding them together then pushed it away. In the few moments she'd had to adjust to the idea, the thought of her mother and Guillermo as a couple seemed so natural she couldn't believe she hadn't picked up on it earlier.

"Why would you think I mind? I love you both and can't imagine two people better suited for each other. You've been working the ranch together for years. That certainly seems like a long enough courtship to me."

Viviana sat for another moment absorbing her words, then a bright hope leaped into her gaze, though she still looked as if she were afraid to trust in it. "You do not think people will talk if I...if I were to marry the other Cruz brother?"

"Who cares? Let them talk. You're Viviana Cruz of Rancho de la Luna. They should envy you! You have nothing to be ashamed about for loving a good, honorable man."

Her mother let out a laugh that sounded like a half sob, then she stood and rushed to Maggie, hugging her hard. "How did a foolish woman like me raise such a smart daughter?"

She almost snorted. *Wrong, Mama. If I were smart, I would have hobbled as fast as my gimpy leg would take me away from Jake Dalton that first night he showed up to change my flat tire.*

"What are you waiting for?" she asked, to distract herself from pointless thoughts of Jake. "Don't you think you should go after Guillermo and put the poor man out of his misery?"

"I will but not now, during my daughter's party. I will find him later." Her mother's gaze sharpened suddenly. "Now, why are you out here with me instead of talking to all the people who have come to see you?"

"I was looking for you. And I needed a little break."

"It is too much for you, then? I worried you would be angry. Jacob said you might not want a big crowd."

How had he possibly come to know her so well in such a short time? She wasn't sure she wanted him to have the ability of seeing so deeply into her psyche.

She shook her head. "I wasn't angry. A little uncomfortable but not mad."

"Everyone wanted to come, to show you of their concern and support, and Marjorie and I could not say no. I did not want to say no. I wanted everyone to know how proud I am of my daughter."

She shifted her leg, searching around for another topic. With the ranch spread out before them, she said the first thing that came to her mind. "It was…surprising of the Daltons to open up the Cold Creek for the party."

"Marjorie insisted and so did Wade," Viviana said. "It is a good place for a fiesta, yes?"

Maggie had no ready answer to that so she didn't even try. Instead, something about the night and the setting prompted her to ask some of the questions that had haunted her for years.

"Mama."

She chewed her lip, not sure where to start, then she blurted the rest out. "How could you…that is, why did you remain on good terms with Marjorie and her sons. Why did you never blame them?"

Her mother's lovely, serene features shifted into a frown. "Oh, Magdalena."

"Hank Dalton was a bastard! He was the one who stole our water rights. He cheated Papa out of all his hard work—he stole the ranch's future. If not for him, Papa would never have had to work that second job in Idaho Falls. Hank was to blame for that, but the rest of them…" She clenched her hands together. "After Hank died, they never tried to make things right. They're just as responsible."

Viviana shook her head, her eyes full of sorrow. "There is much you do not know, Lena. I should have explained things to you long ago. I am sorry I did not."

"Explained what?"

"I suppose I hoped you would come to see the truth on your own, that you would put aside this foolish anger. And I suppose I did not want you to ever think less of your father."

Her mother touched her arm. "And with a mother's folly, I did not want to see how strongly you have held on to your anger all these years."

"I miss him, Mama."

"As do I, *niña.* As do I. But Marjorie and her sons are not to blame for the foolishness of Abel Cruz."

She thought of her strong, beloved father. He had been gone from her life for so long, much longer than just the years since his death. He had worked so hard those last few years trying to save the ranch he loved that she had only a handful of good memories from her adolescence, a time when she had dearly needed a father.

"Why?" she asked her mother again.

Viviana gave a heavy sigh. "Your father was a good

man. A strong, honorable man. But he was stubborn and had much of pride."

She remembered a man who had loved his ranch, what he had built with his own hands, who had adored his wife and daughter, and who had always been proud of his heritage, that he was descended from Spanish nobles who had migrated to Argentina.

"Hank Dalton died when you were young, only twelve, no?" Viviana went on.

Maggie nodded.

"The week after he was buried, Marjorie and Wade came to see your father. With them, they carried all the loan papers between our two ranches and wanted to return them to Abel."

She stared, trying to comprehend what her mother was telling her. "They tried to forgive the loan?"

Viviana nodded tightly. "Marjorie wanted to tear them up right there, but Abel would not allow it. He threw them back at them. 'I will not take Dalton charity,' he said in a cold, proud voice. He said he would continue to pay as he had been until the debt was cleared."

"He insisted?"

"Marjorie, she tried to change the loan to a better, more honest rate than Hank charged. Many times she tried. But Abel and his pride would not allow it, even as he had to work harder and harder to pay the interest."

Her mother's delicate features tightened with sorrow and no small amount of anger. "He did not have to work those two jobs, *niña*. He chose the road he traveled. No one else did that. Not Hank Dalton, not Marjorie or her sons. Only your father."

Maggie's head whirled, and she couldn't seem to take it in. Everything she had believed for twenty years was evaporating like a heat mirage in front of her eyes. She was glad to be sitting down because she was fairly certain the shock would have knocked her on her rear end.

"After Abel died," Viviana went on, "Marjorie and Wade, they came to me with a check for all the money your father paid them over the years, keeping out only enough to cover the original debt."

"And you took it?"

Her mother lifted her chin. "Yes. I used it to help pay for my beautiful daughter to attend college and become the nurse she had dreamed of for many years."

She pressed a hand to her stomach, feeling shaky and almost nauseous. During all those years of hatred, the Daltons had been paying to support her. They had put her through nursing school. Everything she had, everything she had *become,* she owed to Jake and his family, a family she had treated with nothing but scorn and anger.

No, she thought. Her father had given his life to pay that debt. Perhaps she shouldn't look at it as blood money from the Daltons but as her one enduring legacy from her father.

"You should have told me, Mama."

Viviana sighed. "Perhaps. But I did not wish you to think poorly of your father. He was a good man who acted as he thought best for his family and for his conscience."

"All for nothing! He should have let them make things right."

"I think by then he was so angry he couldn't see what was right." Viviana paused. "But while he hated their father, Abel never blamed Hank Dalton's sons for their father's actions. He knew, as I know, that those three boys suffered much from growing up with a cold, harsh man. Even with a father such as that, they grew into good, decent men who love their families and this town. None of them deserves your anger, Lena."

Everything she believed, everything she thought she had known, had just been shaken and tossed into the air like a handful of dry leaves, and she didn't know what to think.

Her mother touched a warm hand to her cheek. "Jacob, he is a good man and he has much caring for you."

Maggie shook her head. "We're friends. That's all."

Viviana made a sound of dismissal in her throat. "A mother can see these things. You care for him, as well. Do not be so stubborn and foolish and full of pride as your father. And your mother, come to that."

She had been, she realized. She had let her anger for the past and her fears for the future interfere in something that could be wonderful. Perhaps it was time to live in the present for a moment.

"I should not be keeping you out here so long when many people are wanting to talk to you," Viviana said. "Come, you will return to the party while I find somewhere to fix my face again."

Do I have to? she wanted to whine, but she knew her obligations. Everyone at this party had come to see her, and she couldn't hide out on the front porch all night.

Viviana rose and held out her arm and Maggie took it. The two of them walked arm in arm back through the Cold Creek ranch house. This time when she passed the picture of Jake on the wall, she smiled, feeling a lightness of heart that hadn't been there in a long time.

At the door Viviana paused, then reached on her toes and pressed her cheek to Maggie's. "I could not ask for a better daughter. You are the joy of my life, *niña,* and I praise God every day for bringing you home safe to me."

Tears gathered in her eyes as she hugged her mama, and

for the first time in six months, she thought perhaps there was a chance her life could go forward.

When she parted with her mother and walked outside, the whole world seemed brighter, everything sharp and in focus. She stood for a moment looking at the members of this community who had opened their arms to embrace her.

They didn't see her as broken, as forever shattered by the blast that had taken part of her leg. She had seen compassion on most faces here but not pity. Instead, when the hardworking people of Pine Gulch talked to her, their eyes glowed with pride, with approval, with support.

To them she was Lieutenant Magdalena Cruz, someone willing to serve her country even at great sacrifice.

She knew she was no great heroine. But perhaps she could live with being a loyal soldier, a loving daughter and a pretty good person.

Jake wondered if anyone else noticed he hadn't taken his eyes off Maggie all night.

He had seen her leave earlier and had started to follow her, but then Caroline had come out of the kitchen and informed him Maggie had gone in search of her mother.

When she came out sometime later, she looked different somehow. He couldn't put a finger on it but her smile seemed more genuine, her eyes brighter, her shoulders held a little higher.

She had been back nearly an hour and in that time he had watched her hold babies and kiss cheeks and talk at some length with Darwin Anderson, a neighboring rancher who wore his World War II Veteran baseball cap with pride.

She was starting to sag, though. As he moved around the dance floor with his niece Natalie, he watched as she shifted positions several times during one song as if she couldn't quite get comfortable, and though she smiled with delight at something Marilyn Summers was telling her, her eyes looked tired.

His love for her was a fierce ache inside him and he didn't know what in the hell he was going to do about it.

He couldn't bear thinking about a life without her in it, but he didn't see any other choice.

"Ow! You stepped on my foot again, Uncle Jake! I'm gonna go dance with Uncle Seth. He's a lot better dancer than you."

He laughed and shifted his attention back to his pouting niece. "Yeah, well, I'm sure he's probably better at a lot of things. He spends enough time practicing."

Natalie looked remorseful, as if afraid she'd hurt his feelings. "You know, I'll practice with you anytime you want. You only stepped on my toe a few times."

He laughed again and kissed her on the top of her head. "I won't torture you anymore, sweetheart. Go find your uncle Seth. Look for the big huddle of giggling girls and you should find him."

Natalie kissed his cheek then flitted off. When he lifted his gaze, he found Maggie staring at him.

Their eyes had met occasionally throughout the evening, but somehow this time seemed different. She seemed to stop whatever she was saying and just stare at him.

He had heard people talk about time standing still, but until that moment he thought it was just hyperbole. Even from twenty feet away, something in her eyes made him forget everything else—the party, the music, the laughter.

All he could focus on was her.

Chapter 13

She smiled tentatively as he approached, then reached to tuck a lock of hair back behind her ear.

Even after he reached her side, he couldn't seem to stop looking at her, and he was aware of a deep-seated need to scoop her up and carry her off somewhere dark and private where he could kiss away that exhaustion in her eyes.

"Do I have broccoli in my teeth or something?" she asked after a moment.

"Sorry?"

"Never mind."

If there were better light out here—and if she were any other woman—he might have thought that was a blush painted across her elegant cheekbones.

"How about a dance, Lieutenant?"

She grimaced. "I don't think I'm quite ready for that."

"Make sure you let me know when you *are* and I'll be the first one in line."

"You looked like you were doing fine with your niece."

"You must have missed the part where I crushed her delicate toes with my big, clumsy feet. She went looking for Seth. Apparently, he's a much better dancer."

"Somehow that doesn't surprise me."

He laughed. "Yeah. It's not the first time a girl has deserted me for my baby brother, and it probably won't be the last."

He settled beside her, enjoying the scent of her and the warmth from her shoulder occasionally brushing his.

From here they had a view of the entire yard—the band, the dancers, the tables still bulging with food.

The fairy lights flickered in the night, lending a soft magic to the ranch. Wade had brought in several *chimineas* to set around the conversation areas, and the outdoor fireplaces provided a crackling warmth as the April night air cooled.

"Quite a party," she said after a moment, as they watched Marjorie and Quinn fox-trot across the makeshift dance floor. As usual, his mother and her second husband looked as if they were having the time of their lives, lost in their own private joy.

"It is."

"Everyone's been so kind."

He smiled. "The best people on earth live in Pine Gulch, and they're always ready for a celebration."

She shifted again, and he saw discomfort flicker in her dark eyes.

"You're hurting. Ready to call it a night?"

She blew out a breath. "I should be tougher than this."

"If you were any tougher, you'd be tempered steel, Lieutenant." He rose and held a hand out for her. "Come on, I'll take you home."

"Won't everyone be upset if I leave while the celebration is still in full swing?"

"You've given enough tonight, Maggie. I think everyone here understands that."

She rose, obvious relief in her dark eyes, and he wanted to grab her right there in front of everyone and kiss her pain away.

"I'd better find my mother and tell her goodbye," she murmured after a moment.

"Why don't I meet you back here in five minutes?"

"You don't mind leaving early?"

This time he couldn't resist. He kissed her forehead. "I don't mind. I'm yours to command, Magdalena. Haven't you figured that out yet?"

He walked away before she could respond and somehow found himself in the crowd of people—mostly female—around his younger brother.

"Hey, Jake, tell old Myron Potter and his band to stick to something a little more lively, would you? No more of this moldy-oldy stuff. It's a party—we want to move."

"You'll have to tell them yourself. I'm leaving."

"Leaving?" He hadn't noticed Wade approach, his littlest son, Cody, asleep in his arms. "Aren't you supposed to be taking Maggie home?"

To his dismay, he felt his face grow hot, for some inconceivable reason. "Yeah. She's worn out, so we're bugging out. As soon as she says goodbye to her mother, I'm taking her home so she can rest."

"Right." Seth snickered. "So she can rest."

He sliced a glare at his brother. "I'd like to see you spend all day walking around on a narrow metal rod, then get through the evening making polite conversation in the middle of phantom pain that feels like knives ripping into skin and bone and muscle. You have no idea what it took Maggie to face everyone here. She's been through enough tonight, so I'm taking her home. If you've got a problem with that, too damn bad."

His voice trailed off when he realized both of his brothers were gazing at him with odd expressions.

"What?"

Seth shook his head. "Man, you have got it bad."

Yeah, he'd had it bad for so long he couldn't remember what it felt like *not* to have it, but he couldn't quite figure out what he'd said to tip them off. "I don't know what you're talking about," he muttered.

"Maggie know how you feel about her?" Wade asked slowly, his eyes serious.

Did she? He had told her a hundred different ways, but he'd never actually put his feelings into words. "She knows I'm concerned about her physical well-being, yes."

Wade and Seth looked at each other, then treated Jake to identical smirks. He had a strong urge to punch one or both of them. Seth was the logical choice as he was the youngest—and pounding him would provide the added benefit of messing up that pretty face.

He actually caught himself flexing his fist and jerking back his forearm but then he decided he was a physician—and older besides—and it was up to him to be the mature one here.

"Thanks for lending the ranch for the party, Wade," he said instead. "It was a nice thing to do. Who knows? Maggie might actually stop thinking all Daltons should be shot on sight."

"I wouldn't put away your bulletproof vest just yet." Maggie spoke up behind him, a small smile playing around her mouth.

He wondered why her soft flowery scent hadn't tipped him off to her presence—and he wondered what his brothers would do if he grabbed her right there in front of them both, wrapped her in his arms and carried her away from here.

"Actually, let me add my thanks," she said to Wade. "It was a wonderful gesture and a great party."

After a moment she actually held out her hand. Wade slanted Jake a look, his eyebrows raised slightly, then he shifted Cody to his left arm so he could shake her hand.

"We were honored to do it," he murmured. "Welcome home, Lieutenant Cruz. We're proud to call you one of our own."

She blinked a few times, and Jake saw she was fighting back tears. He knew she would hate shedding them here in front of his brothers so he stepped forward quickly.

"Let's get you home."

With a last wave to his brothers, he took her arm and helped navigate her through the crowd.

She didn't seem to want to make conversation as they traveled the short drive to the Rancho de la Luna so he drove in silence as she leaned against the headrest and closed her eyes.

Five minutes later he pulled up to the house, and she immediately opened her door and swung her legs out.

"Just a minute, and I'll help you."

"I can do it on my own."

"I know you *can.* But you don't always *have* to."

To his gratification, she waited for him to come around the SUV. He reached to help her stand, but she stumbled a little and had to grab for him for support.

He caught his breath as her hands gripped his shirt, then he forgot to breathe entirely when she wrapped her arms around his waist and tucked her head under his chin with a soft sigh.

His heart beating hard, he froze in disbelief for just an instant, then he folded his arms around her and held on tight, bracing himself to support her weight.

They stood that way for a long time as the April night eddied around them, cool and sweet. He could have stayed that way forever, but she pulled away far too soon.

"I'd like to show you something. Will you come with me?"

Baffled but curious, he nodded, wondering at this strange mood of hers. With their way lit only by the bright full moon, she led him down a narrow gravel path that cut between the house and the barn. They were heading toward the creek, he realized.

She moved slowly on the uneven ground, and he took her arm. "Are you doing okay?"

"I can make it this far. Come on, you'll like this."

She tugged him closer to the sound of the rushing, run-off-swollen creek, to a small open-air bowery he'd noticed from a distance while he'd been working on the ranch.

Up close, he discovered it was more than just a place for picnics, it looked like a comfortable outdoor retreat with bright Spanish tiles and gauzy mosquito netting curtains tied back at the supports.

Inside was a table and several chairs as well as a padded chaise and even a porch swing and a clay fireplace in one corner.

"What is this place?"

Maggie dug through a drawer in one of the tables and pulled out some matches and candles. She set a trio of long white candles on an intricate wrought-iron holder on the table and lit them.

"Mama loves to read and her favorite place to come was always here by the creek. One year she went to Mexico City to visit my grandparents and my father and I built this for her birthday to surprise her when she returned."

"It's great! She must have been thrilled."

"She was. She still comes down here to read, even in wintertime." She drew her sweater tighter around her and he noticed the air had chilled considerably since they left the Cold Creek.

"Why don't I light a fire?"

"That would be good. There should be starters and kindling in the firebox there."

She settled on the chaise and watched him while he found the supplies and worked to coax a flame. In a short time the fire was burning merrily, warming the small space quickly.

He took a chair next to her, and they sat in a companionable silence lit only by the moonlight slanting in from outside, the trio of candles and the fire's glow. He felt as if he'd been contracting every muscle all day and finally they could begin to relax.

Though he had tried to subvert it during the party, he had been desperate for peace, he realized, as he felt the stress and anguish of his failures—of losing a friend and a patient—recede a little further.

He closed his eyes, letting the night and the place and Maggie's presence soothe his soul.

"I used to come down here a lot after my father died," she said after a moment. "You can see the Cold Creek across the river. See?"

He opened his eyes and followed the direction of her gaze. Through the trees, he could see lights flickering from the party. Over the fast, pounding creek, he thought he could hear the musicians as well, playing some kind of a waltz.

"My mother and Guillermo are in love. I caught them locking lips on the front porch tonight."

Of all the things she might have chosen to discuss with him, that particular conversational bent would never have entered his mind. "That must have been awkward for all three of you."

"You could say that." She gave him a considering look. "You don't seem very surprised."

"Should I be?" he asked, distracted by the flickering play of light on her lovely features.

"I don't know. It shocked the heck out of me. I guess I was the last to know."

Jake smiled at her disgruntled tone. "I have a home-field advantage here. You've been away since high school while I've been right here with both of them for the past three years since finishing my residency."

"Do you think something's been going on all that time?"

"I couldn't say for sure. But I can tell you that I didn't start to sense any kind of vibe between them until the last year or so. I thought I might be mistaken—and it was none of my business, anyway—but when you told me they were fighting, I started to wonder about it. What does Viviana have to say about it?"

"She didn't want me to find out. I think she was afraid of my reaction, that maybe I wouldn't understand or accept that she could have feelings for anyone but my father."

"Can you?" he asked. "How do you feel about the idea of the two of them together?"

"Branching out into psychiatry now, Dr. Dalton?"

He smiled. "Whatever works."

With exaggerated movements, she slouched down on the

chaise and folded her arms across her chest as if she were on a therapist's couch. "I'm fine with it. I *am.* I want her to be happy. Both of them, really. Tío Guillermo is a good man and I have no doubt he'll treat her well."

"When my mother ran off with Quinn, I struggled a little at the idea of her with someone new, even though I was certainly happy for her. It might take you a while to adjust."

"I don't think it will. I'm thrilled for them. My mother's still a lovely woman and only in her mid-fifties. I sometimes forget that."

She was quiet. "My father's been gone for thirteen years," she finally said, her voice low. "Perhaps it's time for all of us to let him go."

Her words seemed to hang in the air like dandelion puffs on a calm day, and he wondered if she was trying to tell him something significant. Was *she* ready to let the past go? His heart stirred but he almost didn't dare let himself hope.

"My father would want Mama to be happy. I know that."

He reached for her hand. Her fingers were cold, and he tightened his around her, wishing he could warm all the cold places inside her.

"What about you? Abel adored you."

He laughed a little as a forgotten memory fought its way to the surface. "He used to come to the bus stop after school sometimes just to greet you. I can still see the way you would fly into his arms and he would twirl you around while you shrieked and laughed."

He hadn't meant it to happen but his words sparked tears in her eyes that hovered on her thick, spiky eyelashes before spilling over. "I never doubted he loved me. Never."

He squeezed her fingers. "You said your father would want Viv to be happy. Don't you think he would want *you* to be happy, too?"

"He would have hated to see me like this." She swiped at her cheeks, at more tears sliding down. "I think it would have been harder on him than it's been on Mama."

"Oh, Maggie." He chose his words carefully, sensing this was important to her. "Like your mother, I'm sure Abel would have hated that you had to go through pain. But I know without a doubt that no father would have been more proud of his daughter than Abel would have been of you, Lieutenant Cruz. You served with honor and courage. No father could ask more than that."

She pulled her fingers away from his, shifting restlessly on the chaise. "Don't."

"Don't what?"

"I wasn't brave, Jake. I'm not some kind of hero. I was scared every single moment I served in Afghanistan. Every second. We were in a damn safe zone and I was still terrified out of my wits to walk outside. Anytime we had to leave the base, I just about soaked my Kevlar vest with flop sweat."

"But you did it."

"I didn't have a choice! When you're a soldier, you go where they send you!" The words gushed out of her like a slick, oily geyser, making him wonder how long they'd festered inside her.

"Everyone tonight went on and on about how heroic I was. 'Brave Magdalena Cruz. Our hero. She's got the medals to prove it and everything.' I hate that damn Purple Heart. I wanted to shove it down their throats when they came to Walter Reed to present it to me. I would trade every medal in the Army for the chance to have my friends back. To be myself again. To be whole."

Her voice broke on the last word, and his heart broke

right along with it. He couldn't stand it and he scooped her up, then settled back on the chaise with her in his arms.

"I hate that I feel this way," she mumbled against his chest.

Sensing she needed to talk more than listen to him spout more platitudes, he remained silent, just holding her close.

"I'm alive. I know I am. I'm alive and I should be grateful. Two of my team weren't so lucky. Every time I start to feel sorry for myself, I see their faces and I'm so ashamed."

His arms tightened around her. "Have you ever thought maybe you should cut yourself a little slack?"

"Easy to say, Dr. Dalton. Not so easy in practice."

"You didn't plant that bomb, Maggie. You were over there to help people, just doing what you signed up to do, when you were caught up in circumstances beyond your control. You're certainly not to blame for surviving when your friends didn't, for getting a second chance even if it's not exactly the life you would have chosen for yourself."

He paused and pressed a soft kiss to her hair, wondering how his heart could bleed at the same time it continued to expand to love her more deeply than he ever thought possible.

"You're not responsible for what happened to you," he went on, his voice low. "But you *are* to blame if you don't grab that second chance you were given and run with it."

"I don't know if you've noticed but I'm not doing much running these days."

"Walk, hop or crawl on your hands and knees if you have to. But move forward. That's all you can do, sweetheart. It's all any of us can do."

His words seemed to resonate deep in her heart, and she absorbed them there. He was right. Absolutely right.

She thought of her nightly climb up those steep stairs to her bedroom, of how many nights she'd wanted to give up and curl up on the couch.

But she'd gone.

She'd started walking much faster than the doctors at Walter Reed thought prudent; she'd gone on when the physical therapy exercises had left her exhausted and shaking; she'd forced herself to do things around the ranch that were probably beyond what she should have been doing.

On the physical side, she had been pushing herself from the first time they helped her out of bed at Walter Reed.

But emotionally, mentally, she had retreated from anything that posed a risk. Nursing, for instance. All this time she'd been telling herself it was the physical challenge she couldn't handle anymore. But as she sat there in her mother's hideaway, she realized her real block against returning to medicine was her own fear of failure.

She loved being a nurse practitioner. As careers go, it had been rewarding and challenging and she had never wanted to do anything else.

But because she loved it so much, she had been deeply afraid of failing at it, that she wouldn't be able to handle the physical and mental strain of it anymore.

That terrible fear of failure was holding her back, preventing her from even daring to attempt the things that used to provide her with such satisfaction.

How many other things had she avoided even trying since her injury, simply because she was afraid to fail at them?

Walk, hop or crawl on your hands and knees if you have to, he said. She would, she resolved.

Now that it seemed as if Guillermo would be returning

to the ranch, she resolved to look into going back to being a nurse, even if only for a few hours a week.

Wouldn't it be wonderful to focus on helping other people deal with their problems for a while instead of focusing wholly on her own?

"Maybe you *should* have thought about psychiatry as a specialty," she murmured. "You're very good with crazy people."

"You're not crazy," he said. "What you're dealing with seems perfectly normal to me. If you could survive the trauma you've endured without facing some of these issues, *then* I would have found you a good mental health specialist."

"Docs that mean you're not going to write me a referral?"

"Only your personal physician can do that, and I'm not your doctor, remember?" he teased.

I'd certainly like to know what you are to me, she thought, but the answer to that question was still one of those frightening puzzles she was afraid to dig into too deeply.

She settled closer to him, feeling the tension seep out of her like water from a wicker basket. She yawned a little and caught herself shivering at the same time.

"We should get you back up to the house," he murmured, his voice stirring her hair. "You're cold."

"Not yet. Please?"

"Let me throw another log on the fire, then."

"Mama usually keeps a blanket in the cupboard where I found the matches."

He rose and built up the fire a little, then returned to the chaise, pulling her close again and tucking the blanket around them both.

She felt wrapped in a warm cocoon, as if the world outside this moment, beyond this small circle, didn't exist.

He wrapped his arms around her tightly, pressing his cheek to the top of her head, and with a sigh she closed her eyes and let his heat and strength soothe her to sleep.

Chapter 14

When she woke, the fire was only glowing embers, the candles had guttered low in their holders, and through the trees she could see the Cold Creek was dark and quiet.

The band members must have put away their instruments and gone home with the rest of the crowd.

What time was it? she wondered, but she didn't have a watch on and she couldn't reach Jake's to see its face.

Jake.

She was surrounded by him. Engulfed. His scent, masculine and citrusy, filled her senses, and she could feel his slow, even breathing beneath her cheek where she nestled against his chest.

She lifted her face but couldn't see much of him in the pale moonlight. His features were shrouded in shadow but she didn't need light to make them out. She knew the curve of his lips, knew the tiny lines at the corners of his eyes and the straight plane of his nose.

One of his strong hands was tangled in her hair; the other held her close at the small of her back as if he couldn't bear to let her go. She didn't mind, she realized. She loved it here. She closed her eyes again and let her cheek settle against his shirt, careful not to wake him.

He must have been so tired after enduring such a traumatic day. The death of a patient was never easy. She knew that sense of defeat, of failure, all too well. On those kinds of days she used to want to go home, shut the door, turn on loud, raucous music and hide away from the world.

Yet Jake had come to take her to a party, then stayed to make sure she survived it.

She sighed, snuggling closer. Oh, this was a dangerous pleasure. She wanted to stay here forever, wrapped in his arms. It would be so easy to forget the world existed outside their little haven. But it did. She could hear the water rushing over rocks in the creek, smell the sage and pine in the cool spring air.

A strange and frightening tenderness seemed to take root inside her as she listened to his heart beat a comforting rhythm.

How had Jake Dalton managed to become so important to her in such a short time? So very dear. It seemed like only a moment ago she had been fixing her flat tire on a deserted stretch of road, annoyed with him for stopping to help.

A brief moment, yet a lifetime.

She couldn't seem to remember what her world had been like before he crashed his way back into it.

Cold. Empty. Gray.

She jerked her eyes open to stare at the darkened bowery, horrified and helpless as the truth seemed to pound into her brain with the relentless force of a jackhammer.

She was in love with him.

Her stomach knotted, and she pressed her hand to her mouth to hold in her instinctive moan.

What have you done now, Magdalena?

In love with Jake Dalton. How on earth had she let such a thing happen? Didn't she have better sense than to allow herself to make such a drastic miscalculation?

Her hand curled into a fist over his heart and she wanted to weep, but she screwed her eyes shut to hold in the tears.

Maybe she didn't love him, she tried to rationalize. Maybe she and her self-esteem had just been so battered and bruised by life and her ex-fiancé's rejection that she'd turned to the first male who had paid her a little attention.

She discarded that theory as soon as it popped into her mind. No. This was definitely love. It washed through her, strong and powerful and undeniable.

Now what the heck was she supposed to do about it?

Oh, this would never do. She couldn't bear another rejection. Her poor heart would crack apart. But she didn't see any way for this to end in anything but disaster.

What did she have, anymore, to offer to a man like him? He was strong and healthy and decent. And she was a mess.

She stretched out her gimpy leg as those damn phantom pains clawed at her.

Who would want to willingly take on someone with her problems? She faced a lifetime of challenges. Medical expenses, prosthesis adjustments, lingering physical and psychological issues.

Any sane man would run for the hills when confronted with all that, even if he could manage to get beyond the obvious deformity of her missing limb.

She let out a long, slow breath, her heart aching already in anticipation of the pain she knew was inevitable.

Every instinct warned her to make a clean, solid break

while she still had a chance, before she slipped further down this hazardous path. Starting now. It was foolish to indulge herself, to savor the pleasure of lying here in his arms when she knew what lay in store for her.

So move, already, her inner voice suggested tartly.

She didn't want to. She wanted to stay curled up against him, feeling his slow breaths in her hair and his heartbeat beneath her fingertips and his solid strength against her.

A few more moments, she told herself. Couldn't she treat herself, just this once?

Before she could answer that question, he stirred beneath her and she felt the tenor of his breathing change as he started to wake. She froze, trapped in his arms, cursing herself for not moving faster.

Now she couldn't break free as he tightened his hold and angled his head to give her a sleepy smile that curled her five remaining toes. She could swear she felt the missing ones clench, too.

Phantom sensation, they called that. Different from phantom pain but just as disconcerting when she could swear she felt someone tickle a foot that was probably decomposing in a garbage dump in Kabul right now.

"Hey, there."

"Hi." She tried to shield her expression so he wouldn't guess the tumult of her thoughts, the stunning revelation that had struck her while he slept. "I was just thinking I should try to wake you up so you could go home and stretch out on a decent bed."

"Why would I want to do that? My bed has nothing on this place. I haven't slept that deeply in a long time. Maybe I'll have to talk to Viv about renting her hideaway to me."

She forced a smile. "You might be a little cold out here in the middle of December."

"Not with you around," he murmured.

Something hot and bright flashed in his blue eyes like a brilliant firework exploding. Before she could brace herself against it, he dipped his head, and his mouth found hers.

The tenderness in his kiss scrambled all her defenses like a radar jammer, and she couldn't seem to remember all the many reasons she should put a stop to this. The man she loved held her in his arms and she could focus on nothing else.

He pulled her across him and tangled one hand in her hair. As he drew her close, she could feel the hard ridge of his arousal near the apex of her thighs.

Her breasts were full and achy where they pressed against his chest, and she wanted desperately to arch into him, to soak up his heat.

Her inner voice warned her to stop, that this was too dangerous to her heart. She listened to it for perhaps half a second, then he licked and nibbled at her mouth and she was lost, giving herself up to the magic of the night and of Jake.

They kissed forever, until her thoughts were a hazy blur of hunger and need. Until she couldn't think of anything but him—his mouth hard and demanding, his hands exploring her skin, his body solid and comforting beneath her.

Their hands explored each other through the frustrating layers of cloth, and she found it a relief when he shifted her beside him again on the wide chaise to work the intricacies of the buttons on her blouse.

The sight of his strong hands on her small buttons struck her as immensely erotic and she paused to watch him as he pulled her shirt open, baring the lacy bra beneath. His thumb danced across one nipple, and it strained, pebbling against the soft cup.

She couldn't hold back a shiver at the torrent of sensation pouring through her.

He paused, concern flitting across his lean, masculine features. "You're cold. Let me put another log on the fire."

"No. Please. Don't stop." If he did, she knew she feared she would never be able to find the courage again.

She reached for his face and drew him down to her, kissing him fiercely. He groaned and responded with the same hunger, his mouth tangling with hers and his hands exploring her curves.

He pulled her shirt free and worked the clasp of her bra, until her breasts were free and exposed. Moonlight slanted over her, and he watched her for several long moments, his eyes hot and aroused.

"Do you have any idea what you do to me?" His low voice plucked and strummed along her nerve endings.

"Show me," she murmured.

He groaned and lowered his mouth to take one taut, aching nipple into his mouth. She buried her fingers in his hair, holding him to her while he touched and licked and teased, until she was consumed with the similar need to touch him and taste him.

Her hands went to his shirt, and she pulled it free without bothering to work the buttons. His muscles were every bit as beautiful as they had felt through cloth, rippling and hard, and she couldn't resist tracing her fingers across his pectorals.

Even though she hadn't reached them yet, his abdominals contracted at her featherlight touch on his chest and he let out a long, ragged breath and kissed her.

She wanted to stay lost in his kiss, wanted to forget everything but the heat and wonder blooming to life inside her.

She should have been expecting it, bracing herself for

it, but before she quite realized what was happening, he reached a hand to the snap of her slacks and worked her zipper free.

Cold, cruel reality slapped her and she froze, her heart racing as panic suddenly burst through her with the speed and force of a bullet. In a moment she would be naked and there would be nowhere to hide. The ugly plastic and metal prosthesis—the hardware she despised—would be laid bare for all the world.

For Jake, anyway, and somehow that seemed far, far worse.

She couldn't do this. She *couldn't!*

Despising her cowardice but helpless to overcome it, she jerked away from him, nearly falling off the chaise in her hurry to escape. She couldn't bear the idea of him seeing her, of being open and exposed in front of him. She knew what she looked like without her clothes. Horrible. She wouldn't be able to survive if he turned away from her.

She scrambled to stand, holding on to the frame of the other chair until she could balance. Her shirt hung open and she leaned a hip against the chair for support so her fingers could work the buttons, but they fumbled as if the buttons were ten times larger than the holes they had to fit into.

"I'm sorry. I can't... I'm not..." She closed her eyes. "It's late. We should both be in bed."

She couldn't see his eyes in the moonlight but she could feel the heat of emotions vibrating off him.

"Dammit, Maggie," he growled. "What happened?"

She gave up on the last few buttons and just held her shirt closed with her fist. "Nothing. I'm sorry."

He stood. With his shirt off, his skin gleamed in the moonlight. She had to curl her other hand into a fist at her side to keep from reaching for him, and she finally had to jerk her gaze away, miserable with herself.

"Why did you stop me? You wanted that as much as I did. Don't bother to lie and pretend you didn't."

Knowing he was right, knowing she deserved his anger, she faced him without words, still breathing hard. She wanted to die, to curl up into a ball and disappear.

"What happened? What did I do? Don't you think I deserve to know that?" In the moonlight she saw his gaze narrow. "Was it because I was trying to undress you?"

She had no answer to that, either, and she couldn't bear to admit the truth, so again she said nothing.

He apparently took her silence as confirmation and accurately guessed the reason. "It was. You didn't want me to see you. What did you think I would do? Run screaming in the night if I happen to catch sight of your prosthesis? I know exactly what to expect. I've seen you with it and without it, remember?"

"In a clinical situation," she countered. "Not like this.'"

"What the hell difference does that make?" He reached for his own shirt, shoving his arms in the sleeves.

"Everything."

If he didn't understand, she couldn't explain it to him. Having him look at her ugly, deformed stump as a physician had been tough enough for her to bear. She couldn't endure this, to have him look at her in all her ugliness through a lover's eyes.

She didn't want to be perfect. Only normal.

She couldn't stay here, in this place that had provided such a fleeting sanctuary, where she had discovered love and heartache all in one convenient package.

With jerky movements she blew out the remaining candles and headed back along the gravel path toward the house, wanting only to be away from him.

He didn't give her the chance to escape quickly, as she supposed she knew he wouldn't. He followed right behind her, a solid mass of angry male at her back.

"How many reasons are you going to find to push me away, Maggie?" he growled, following while she moved as fast as she could across the uneven ground. "Haven't I proved to you yet that I don't give a damn about your missing parts?"

"This isn't about you. It's about me."

"It sure as hell is about me."

Sounding more furious than she'd ever heard him, he reached out a hand and stopped her just as they entered the glowing circle from the vapor light on the power pole near the house.

"It *is* about me," he repeated. "It's about you not daring to trust me, about you comparing me to your bastard of a fiancé and thinking I will turn away from you, too, just when you need me. I won't. I'm not like him. Can't you see that?"

Oh, yes. She couldn't imagine two men more different. She thought she had loved Clay. She had agreed to marry him, for heaven's sake. But what had seemed so powerful and real before she headed to Afghanistan so long ago seemed pale, insipid, compared to this raging storm inside her when she looked at Jake in the moonlight.

She pressed a hand to her stomach, to the ache starting to spread there, then let out a breath. "Go home, Jake," she murmured.

He ignored her. "Tell me, are you planning on giving up love and intimacy for the rest of your life just because you don't like the way you look beneath your clothes?"

He didn't need to make it sound as if she was some shallow creature who had a zit in an inconvenient place or who only wanted to lose five pounds to get down to a size four.

She'd lost a frigging leg! Didn't that give her a right to be a little self-conscious?

"I said go home. I think we'd both agree this date has dragged on long enough."

"Damn you, Maggie. Don't push me away. Your amputation does not matter to me. What do I have to do to prove that to you?"

"Nothing. There's nothing to prove."

She wanted to bury her face in her hands. She was mad and embarrassed and heartsore, and she just wanted to be away from him. Instead, she drew all her remaining resources around her and forced herself to give him one more cool look.

"You can sit out here all night if you want, but I'm going to bed. Thank you for the ride."

She headed up the porch steps. But through the hot tears in her eyes she misjudged a step about halfway up and stumbled.

Fortunately, she landed with the good leg first but her right knee jabbed into the edge of the wooden step as she fell and fiery pain shot up her kneecap. To her humiliation she found herself on her hands and knees, sprawled up the porch steps.

Eyes burning, she wanted nothing more than to curl up right there and weep hot, mortified tears.

She forced them back, swallowing her sob even though it choked her, and gripped the railing to pull herself up to stand.

Below her she heard Jake growl a string of oaths that would have earned him a good pinch if his mother had heard him, and a moment later he reached her and lifted her into his arms.

"You are the most stubborn woman who ever lived," he snarled as he carried her inside. "Where's your bedroom?"

"Put me down."

"Shut up," he bit out. "Where's your bedroom?"

She blinked at his furious tone. What happened to kind, good-natured Dr. Dalton? There seemed no point in arguing with him, not when he was in this kind of mood. "Upstairs."

He frowned. "Didn't Viv have a room on the ground floor you could take over while you're here?"

"I preferred my own bedroom, the same one I've always used," she said stiffly.

"Of course you did. Why doesn't that surprise me?"

As if she weighed nothing more than a baby kitten, he carried her up the long flight of stairs.

"Which door?" he asked at the top, not even breathing hard.

She pointed hers out, and he pushed it open, flipped on the light and set her on the bed with a gentle care that belied the tension in his frame.

She prayed he would leave as soon as she was settled, but instead he stepped back and studied her for a long moment, his features solemn, saying nothing.

"I want you more than I've ever wanted any woman in my life," he finally said in a low voice. "You're in my blood, my skin, my bones. I go to bed wanting you, I wake up wanting you, I spend most of the damn day wanting you. But I'm not going to beg."

He gazed at her for several moments more, then he sighed. "Aw hell. Yes, I am. Please, Maggie. No matter what you think about yourself, you are beautiful to me. You're the strongest person I've ever known. You always have been, from the time you were just a pigtailed brat at the school bus."

It hurt her to see the tenderness in his blue eyes but she couldn't seem to look away.

"Please. Don't lose your courage now and hide away from me, from this," he murmured.

She gazed at him, her emotions a wild raging river inside her. Desire still churned through her veins, and her love was heavy in her chest, weighed down by fear and uncertainty.

He called her courageous, but she wasn't. Yeah, she had run back into that damn firebombed clinic in Afghanistan to try to rescue her teammates and as many children as she could.

But the whole time she had been racing back and forth, she hadn't given a thought to the consequences. If she had known the cost when the building finally collapsed around her, crushing her leg, she wasn't sure she would have made the same choice.

Somehow this, opening her heart and her soul to him, seemed far more risky right now than running into all the firebombed buildings in the Middle East.

She was so tired of being afraid.

You survive but you do not live.

Her mother's words rang in her ears. What was the point of making it out of that burning hell if she stumbled through the rest of her life never taking chances, afraid to fail?

Afraid to *live*.

At her continued silence, something bleak and hopeless flickered across his features. His entire body seemed to sag with defeat, and he sighed and turned to leave.

Now. She had to move or he would walk out the door, down the stairs and out of her life. Somehow she knew he wouldn't be back. A man could only take so much rejection.

Her heart pounding, she sat up, gripped the headboard and rose on shaky legs, ignoring the pain from her stump and the lingering throb in the knee she had banged in her graceless fall. In one movement she reached for him, grabbing his arm both for support and to catch his attention.

He turned and she saw surprise flicker in his eyes for only an instant before she kissed him.

Chapter 15

For an instant Jake couldn't process such a rapid emotional shift, from the bone-deep despair of thinking he would never overcome her thorny barriers to this wild exhilaration as she kissed him, her soft, delectable mouth fiercely enthusiastic.

His head spun and he grabbed her to him. He didn't care why she had changed her mind. He only cared that she was here again in his arms, that she was kissing him, her arms tight around his neck as if she never wanted to let him go.

He absorbed her weight, the physician corner of his mind that worried about such things concerned that she must have reached the limit of her physical endurance some time ago after their long evening.

Through the questions swirling around in his mind, he still managed to think clearly enough to lower her back to the bed so she didn't have to stand unnecessarily, their mouths still fused together.

Her hands were suddenly everywhere—his hair, his shoulders, slipping up under the untucked tails of his shirt to slide across his skin. He groaned, instantly aroused again.

How did she do this to him so easily? One moment he was defeated, heartsore, the next hot and hard and ready for action.

Through the haze of need obscuring his thoughts, he managed to hang on to one important concept.

"What about Viv?" he asked.

Maggie paused, her fingers at the buttons of his shirt. "Her car's not out front. I'm guessing she's gone to Guillermo's."

He gave her a searching look. "How do you feel about that?"

"Like it's about the last thing I want to discuss right now, Doctor. Thanks all the same."

She kissed him again, and he decided if she didn't care where her mother spent the night, he certainly didn't. He gave himself up to the rare and precious wonder of having her in his arms again.

Then, just when things were really starting to simmer, she pulled away from him, untangling her mouth and her arms.

"What's wrong?" he asked, fighting an insane urge to bang his head against the wall a few dozen times in frustration. He didn't think he could bear it if she pushed him away again.

She swallowed hard, then reached for his hand, wrapping her fingers around his. "I'm not stopping again, I promise. I just… I want to take off the prosthesis first. Will you help me?"

He gazed at her, emotion burning behind his eyes. He

knew exactly what she was asking and offering, knew just how how difficult it must be for her to let him so deeply into this part of her world, and he knew he had never been so moved.

"Of course," he answered. Tenderness washing through him, he knelt beside her bed and waited for her to swing her legs over the side.

He didn't miss the way her hands trembled as she rolled her pant leg up or the little pause she took before reaching for the prosthesis. His heart burst with love and pride in her courage.

Then she was removing the appliance, and he helped her pull it free. The stump sock was next and for just an instant she closed her eyes, shuddering a little.

"Hurt?" he asked.

"No. The opposite. It feels so good to have the blasted thing off after I've worn it a long time. Imagine slipping off a pair of high heels that rub and pinch after a long day. Then magnify that about a million times and you have some idea how good it feels."

"My mind boggles," he said dryly.

She returned his smile, then reached for the cuff of her pants. He put out a hand to stop her before she could yank it down to cover the site of her amputation and shield herself from his view.

"Hold on."

"Jake…"

"Just a minute."

She watched him out of wary eyes as he reached for her leg. He tried to remember what he'd learned and used smooth, gentle strokes to try massaging the pain away.

Though she stiffened at his first touch, she didn't pull away, so he took that as tacit permission to continue.

Gradually he felt her muscles relax, felt the hard tightness of scar tissue and contracted muscles begin to ease. After a few moments her whole body seemed to sag into the bed, and she closed her eyes, the apprehension seeping out of her features.

Finally, when he almost thought she had fallen asleep, he kissed her just below her knee and sat back.

"Better?"

She opened one eye. "*Madre de Dios.* How and where did you learn to do that?"

"I had a rudimentary massage section in my alt-med class. The rest was just instinct."

"You've got one heck of an instinct, Dalton."

Guilt pinched at him, and he knew he couldn't lie. "Okay, that's not exactly the whole story."

Confession time, he thought, a little apprehensive at how she might react. "The day after you came back, I called a friend of mine who's a prosthetist in Seattle and asked him for some pain management techniques I could try with you. He suggested massage and sent me a couple articles and a video."

Both of her eyes were open wide and the stunned wonder in them left him deeply grateful he'd taken the time to study.

"Why?" she asked.

He shrugged. "I don't know. I hoped it might help, since you didn't seem all that crazy about the idea when I suggested trying some new medicine combinations."

"I meant, why would you possibly want to go to so much trouble for your surly neighbor?"

While he was confessing his sins, he might as well tell her the whole truth. The entire town had apparently clued in to his feelings—or at least his brothers had—so she was bound to figure it out, anyway.

"You've always been much more than just a neighbor to me, Maggie. In your heart, you know that."

He rose and kissed her before she could respond. She sighed his name against his mouth, and he found it the sexiest sound in the world as she wrapped her arms around him and pulled him close.

She seemed different now. Maybe it was his brief massage, maybe just the freedom of knowing they had crossed her personal Rubicon and there was no turning back now. But he sensed an openness to her kiss, a sweet and tender welcome, and he basked in it.

Again she reached for the buttons of his shirt and he helped her, shrugging out of it quickly, then helping her out of hers. The bowery down by the creek had been romantic and secluded in the moonlight, but there was a hell of a lot to be said for electricity, he decided, as he savored the sight of her dusky curves against the pale lavender of her comforter.

As much as he enjoyed the visual delight before him, he sensed she would be more comfortable without the harsh overhead lights. He spied a small lamp on a table in the corner and he left her to turn it on, then turned off the main switch.

A warm glow still filled the room, but it was softer, more gentle than the direct light from the overhead fixture. When he returned to the bed, Maggie gave him a smile of gratitude and reached for him again, her hands going to his back.

In moments he was naked, hard and hungry, and turned to help her undress the rest of the way. Anticipation thrummed through him, mingled with a healthy dose of anxiety.

He didn't think he could bear it if she stopped things now, and he only hoped he could be sensitive and perceptive enough to do and say the right things when his body was having a hard time focusing on anything but devouring her.

And then they were both naked. He ached to be inside her, to lose himself in her heat, but he reined in his unruly needs. Right now Maggie's fears were far more important, and he suspected she needed affirmation and reassurance more than he needed the sexual connection his body and soul craved.

He studied her several moments, his gaze ranging over the curve of her breasts, the flat plane of her stomach, the dark triangle between her legs, then his gaze shifted lower, to one long, shapely leg and foot and the other that ended abruptly a few inches below her knee.

Though he grieved again for her pain and he would have given anything to give her back what she had lost, he found nothing there that filled him with anything but desire.

"You take my breath away, Maggie." He kissed her tenderly, his eyes open. Hers remained open, as well, and he prayed she could read the truth in his eyes. "You have nothing to be uncomfortable about. Absolutely nothing. Every single part of you is beautiful to me."

She let out a ragged breath and he saw a tear drip out of the corner of her eye to her nose. He kissed it away, then another, then dipped his head to cover her mouth with his.

She had been so worried, so sure she could never enjoy this again for her self-consciousness and emotional angst. But as sweet, healing sensations surged to all her nerve endings, she wondered why she had ever been so concerned. Making love to Jake suddenly seemed the most natural, wonderful thing in the world.

She forgot to be uncomfortable, forgot to worry about what she looked like from the waist down. She focused completely on the magic they made together.

This was Jake, the man she loved, and she couldn't imagine anything more beautiful than sharing this intimacy with him.

He seemed to know exactly how to touch her, and they spent what felt like forever exploring each other. The world seemed to condense to right here, to this moment in his arms. Still, something flickered in the back of her mind, some shadow of concern that wouldn't quite crystallize.

At last, when she thought she would crack apart with anticipation, he poised himself above her and entered her slowly, sliding inside inch by torturous, wonderful inch.

She had worried about the mechanics of this, too, but she needn't have, she realized. Everything important still worked perfectly.

She clutched him to her and closed her eyes, wanting to burn every glorious sensation into her memory.

He held his weight off her as he moved slightly inside her. Heat cascaded through her but she still frowned.

"Everything okay?" he asked.

"No," she murmured.

He froze and moved as if to withdraw but she held him fast, her hands tight around the warm skin of his back.

"What's wrong?" he asked.

"You. You're treating me like some kind of fragile porcelain figurine, afraid you're going to drop me and shatter me. I won't break, Jake. Please. Don't hold back."

He paused for only a second, and she saw the careful control in his eyes slip, then with a groan he captured her mouth in a fierce, swift kiss as his body pounded into her, hard and fast.

Ah, yes. This was what she meant. She rose to meet him eagerly, as hungry as he for completion.

The room started to dip and spin and all she could do was hang on to him tightly as her body climbed toward fulfillment.

Suddenly he reached a hand between their bodies and touched her, the gentle caress of his thumb in wild contrast to the hard, insistent demands of his body. She gasped his name as she climaxed and he caught the sound with his mouth.

I love you, she thought, but the words caught in her throat as, muscles straining, he followed her and found his own release.

Neither of them seemed to be able to move for long moments after. She loved the feel of him against her, all hard, masculine muscles, and she thrilled to the sound of his racing heartbeat against her ear.

Eventually he slid off her and drew her against him and they lay curled together, one of his hard thighs between her legs.

He couldn't miss her stump now when it was lying against him, she thought, but she refused to let herself ruin the magic and wonder of the moment by obsessing about it.

Jake honestly didn't seem to care. She had searched his expression intently when she had first been fully exposed to his view, and she had seen nothing in his eyes but masculine appreciation and desire.

Maggie traced the muscles of his chest, wishing she could put her feelings into words. She felt as if a part of her she thought gone forever had just been handed back to her, wrapped in ribbons and bows.

She smiled a little at that, sure he wouldn't appreciate

the visual image, no matter how strategically placed the ribbons might be.

He drew a tender hand down the length of her hair. "Okay," he murmured. "In another three or four years I might start to get feeling back in my toes again."

"Lucky! You don't have to rub it in."

He laughed and kissed her forehead and, with a little spurt of shock, she realized that was the first genuine joke she'd made in five months about her amputation.

It felt good, she realized. Really good.

She smiled, content to lie there listening to his heartbeat. Words of love welled up in her throat but they tangled on her tongue, and she couldn't manage to find the courage to work them free.

She focused instead on what he had said earlier, those tantalizing words he hadn't explained.

"Jake, what did you mean before? When you said I've always been…more than a neighbor to you."

The hand idly dancing down her back froze in midstroke and he let out a long, slow breath.

She wasn't sure he would answer her, but after a moment he sat up, pulling the sheet along with him as he leaned against the headboard. His features were solemn when he faced her, and she felt a little spasm of nervousness when his silence dragged on.

"Do you remember when you helped me do CPR on my father?" he finally asked.

Of all the things she might have expected him to discuss at a time like this, his father's death wouldn't even have made the first cut. Tension tightened her shoulders at the mention of Hank Dalton but she took a couple of deep breaths to push it away.

"Of course."

With an odd premonition that she didn't want to have this conversation naked, she reached for her robe hanging on to the bedpost and shrugged into it, then moved to sit at the opposite end of her narrow bed, her back propped against the footboard.

"You hated us all by then, especially Hank," Jake went on quietly. "Remember? For a long time all you ever gave me was a drawn-up kind of look like you just walked past a nasty-smelling barrow pit. Yet when we got off that school bus and saw Hank lying in the field, you didn't hesitate for a second. You ran right over to see what you could do."

She wasn't quite sure where he was going with this, but she folded her hands in front of her and listened.

"Most adults I know wouldn't have lifted a finger to help someone they hated," he went on. "You were only twelve years old but you sat there for a quarter of an hour while we waited for the ambulance, blowing the breath of life into your enemy's mouth, willing him to survive."

Everything had happened so fast that day she didn't remember many of the details. But she did remember how she had forced her mind to focus only on the first-aid part of what she was doing, not the literal act of breathing for Hank Dalton.

She had closed her eyes and tried to pretend the man she despised was just one of those rubber dummies she had practiced on during the Red Cross CPR training.

"It was all for nothing. What I did didn't help at all. Not in the long run. We couldn't save your father and neither could the paramedics or Doc Whitaker."

"But you tried. That was the important thing to me. You hated him and deep in your heart you probably wanted him dead. But you still tried to save him."

He paused, his features unusually solemn. "And after the

paramedics came, while we stood there watching them load him into the ambulance, do you remember what you did?"

Went home? She couldn't really remember doing anything but the CPR part of it. She remembered being emotionally and physically exhausted and probably a bit in shock. "Not really."

"I do. I remember it perfectly. You stood beside me—the son of the man you hated—and you held my hand. The whole time they worked on Dad, while they loaded him up, after they drove away. For a long time you stood and held my hand. You were only a kid, just a little girl, but somehow you knew that was what I needed more than anything else in the world at that moment."

She gazed at him, not at all sure what to say. His eyes met hers and she caught her breath at the tangle of emotion in them.

"I fell in love a little with you that day," he murmured.

Her eyes widened and her heart seemed to forget how to beat.

"Jake…"

"I fell in love with you when I was fifteen years old, and I've never climbed back out. I love you, Maggie. I've been in love with you most of my life."

"You have not!"

He gave a short laugh. "You can argue with me all you want, sweetheart, but you won't change what I know is true. In a time of great trauma, somehow I fell a little in love with that girl. But only after you came back to Pine Gulch—my sad, wounded warrior—did I realize how deeply my feelings for you ran. I love you, Maggie. Your courage, your strength, your compassion. The whole beautiful package that makes up Magdalena Cruz."

She met his hot, glittering gaze and felt stunned, breathless, as if she'd just taken a hard punch to the gut.

She didn't know what to say, what to think. He couldn't love her!

She suddenly wanted distance from him, if only to give herself room to think. But with her prosthesis off, she was effectively trapped. Her crutches were still down in his SUV, she remembered. And since she didn't relish the idea of hopping across the room to the chair, she could do nothing but wrap her robe more tightly around her.

"How can you?" she finally asked. "I've been miserable to you and to everyone else since I've been back to Pine Gulch. I've been so mean and contrary and confrontational, I can't even stand to be around myself most of the time!"

His smile was rueful. "I almost hate to admit this, because you'll think I'm crazy, but I even love that about you, too. I know it's only one of your coping methods."

She gazed at him, her thoughts whirling. A bright and hopeful joy fluttered inside her like a trapped bird trying to break free, but she was afraid to let it go, terrified of her own insecurities.

She was so afraid to believe him, afraid to let herself trust.

"You could say something," he said after her silence dragged on. "You don't need to leave me hanging here, flapping in the wind."

"What do you want me to say?" she asked, vying for time.

A muscle tightened in his jaw, and she thought she saw hurt flicker in his eyes before he veiled them. "Nothing. You're right."

Expression closed and hard, he rose from the bed and

shoved on his pants with the economical motions of someone used to getting dressed in a hurry for emergency calls.

Before she realized what he was doing, he grabbed up the rest of his clothes and headed for the door. More than her next breath she wanted to go after him, but without her crutches she was helpless.

"Jake. Please don't leave."

He turned, his smile not really bitter, just inexpressibly sad. "I pushed you too hard. I should have quit while I was ahead."

"No you didn't. I'm just— You keep saying I'm brave but I'm not. Inside, I'm a quivering mass of nerves, full of self-doubt and insecurities. This is hard for me."

She let out a breath. "But I faced one fear tonight. I might as well tackle an even bigger one now."

He waited, his features solemn, hard.

Twelve years in the Army Reserves had taught her the importance of quickly condensing her options down to bare bones. Survival often depended on it.

As she saw things, she had two choices. She could surrender to her fear and insecurities, afraid to reach out and grab the wonderful gift he was offering because she worried he might snatch it away when he decided she was too much work and bother.

Or she could decide the time had come to go on living.

When it came down to it, there was really no choice at all.

"I love you," she murmured. "It's not easy for me to say, and I'm not quite sure how it happened, but there it is. I love you, Jacob Dalton."

At first he looked as if he hadn't heard her. He didn't move a single muscle, just continued to stare at her, then he released a shaky breath, and a fierce wonder sparked in the glittering blue of his eyes.

"Now is the part where I kiss you to show you I mean it. But I can't come after you, unless you want me to crawl."

"No. Never that."

In an instant he reached her and scooped her into his arms, then his mouth found hers.

He murmured words of love between kisses, and she held each one to her heart like a precious jewel.

This was good and right and wonderful. She thought of the long, agonizing journey she'd traveled the past five months. In a strange way she felt like each step was leading her back here, to this moment and this man.

"Our mothers will be over the moon," he murmured against her mouth.

"Ugh. Don't remind me. Mama has been throwing you at me since the moment I came back to town."

"I'm glad you listened to your mother and finally had the good sense to catch me," he said with a grin.

He kissed her again, and the tenderness of his arms around her brought tears to her eyes.

"Are you sure about this, Jake? You're a doctor. More than probably anybody else, you know I'm only just started on this road. There are plenty of challenges I haven't even faced yet and none of it will be easy."

"I know that. But I have great faith in your stubbornness to get through whatever comes along."

"I'm glad you have faith in me, because I've lost mine somewhere along the way."

"You'll find it. I'll help you. And in the meantime, you can just hang on to mine. I love you, Maggie. With your leg, without your leg. On your good days and on your grumpiest. Whatever comes along, I want to help you through it if you'll give me the chance."

"Are more of those massages part of the deal?"

His grin was slow and sexy. "Oh, you can count on it."

Some time later, she drew her mouth away from his and cupped his face in her hand. "I came back to Pine Gulch thinking my life was over. Everything I knew about myself was gone, destroyed in a moment. I've always considered myself pretty strong, tough enough to handle just about anything. I was a soldier and a nurse, two jobs that require the toughest of the tough. But being injured, losing my leg, this was so much harder than I ever would have imagined."

"I hate when you're so hard on yourself. Anybody would have had the same reaction, Maggie."

She let out a breath. "I told you I came home to hide out. That's what I thought I wanted, to be somewhere safe and comfortable where no one demanded anything of me. But you wouldn't let me cower there. Since the day I came back, you've been dragging me out of my narrow little comfort zone and back into the wide world."

She drew her mouth over his slowly, gently. "Thank you for that. It's much scarier out here, I have to admit. But I wouldn't miss it for anything."

His kiss was hard and fierce but so tender she wanted to cry and laugh and dance at the same time.

"Neither would I, Lieutenant Cruz," he murmured. "Neither would I."

Epilogue

It was a gorgeous evening for a wedding.

Maggie lifted her face to the cool August air, sweet and lush with the scents of summer and the hundreds of flowers that filled her mother's bowery on Rancho de la Luna.

The setting sun sent long shadows across the ranch and created a rich palette of colors. The moon was just starting to rise above the Tetons, shining on the tiny lights that twinkled in all the trees.

Her right foot tapped the rhythm of the salsa music as she shifted in her chair at a corner table and cuddled the little bundle in her arms closer.

Jorge Sanchez made a pouty little sound but didn't awaken, content for now to sleep while his parents danced to the music. She smiled at Carmela and her quiet husband Horatio, who had managed to obtain a green card and returned to Idaho just days before his son's birth.

Maggie touched the soft cheek of the sleeping infant,

remembering the precious wonder of that day. It had been incredible on several levels. She always loved the magical experience of participating in a birth and this one had seemed especially poignant, watching Jake in action and tumbling in love with him all over again as she had watched his quiet calm in the face of a young, first-time mother's anxieties.

Her own mother danced by in Guillermo's arms, where she'd been all night, and she smiled at the picture they made—Viviana, feminine and beautiful in her flowing peach dress, and Guillermo, so stiffly dignified in his suit and so deeply in love with his new wife.

It had been a lovely ceremony, quietly moving as Viv and Guillermo had married here beside the stream in this beautiful place created by a man they had both loved. She had felt her father's presence strongly today and had the oddest feeling that he rejoiced along with the rest of them.

She had felt Abel just as keenly a month earlier during her own wedding, at the little church in town. Her husband—she still wasn't used to that word—danced past with his niece Natalie in his arms. Jake looked tall and masculine and gorgeous, and she wondered if her breath would still catch just looking at him after they'd been married for fifty years.

He must have felt her watching him. Their eyes met and he smiled, that intense light in his eyes that always made her feel as breathless and overwhelmed as if she were sitting atop those majestic mountains looking down at the world.

As she sat surrounded by everyone she loved and watched Jake twirl his niece, she was bursting with so much joy she didn't know how her heart could possibly contain it all.

She couldn't believe a few short months ago she actually had been foolish enough to believe her life was over. When she limped home to Pine Gulch four months earlier, she had been certain everything good and right was gone from her world forever.

Instead of withering away as she had fully expected to do, she had blossomed here. What a miraculous gift these last months had been, full of more joy than she had ever believed possible.

Life wasn't perfect. She was still struggling to adjust to the prosthesis, still had some unresolved pain issues. But she had her own very sexy private physician on standby at all times. With Jake's help, she knew she could face whatever hurdles still waited on the road ahead.

Seth Dalton sauntered over and sprawled into the chair next to her. "Hey, gorgeous. What are you doing over here in the corner all by yourself?"

She held up the sleeping infant. "Babysitting duties."

He made a face. "The little rugrat looks asleep to me. Why don't you put him in his car seat thingy and come dance with me?"

She shook her head with regret. "Can't. I'm on doctor's orders to sit out the fast stuff."

"What's the fun in that? Sounds like your doctor's a real pain in the you-know-what."

"No question." She smiled. "But I'm keeping him anyway."

The flirtation that seemed as much a part of Seth as breathing slipped away for a moment and his entirely too handsome features turned serious. "I can't imagine two people more perfect for each other than you two. You both deserve every bit of it."

Touched and warmed, she squeezed his hand. Beneath Seth's charm and flirtatiousness was the boy she had been best friends with so long ago. She felt blessed that they were finding that friendship again.

She never would have believed this either but one of the perks of falling in love with Jake had been his family. All the Daltons had embraced her, to her shock. They had welcomed her into the family, had instantly seemed to forget her years of antipathy and anger.

The first time Jake had taken her to dinner at the ranch, Marjorie had fussed and cried and hugged her close and his niece and nephews had jumped all over her. Tanner and Cody thought the fact that she could take off her prosthesis and wave it around was just about the coolest thing in the world.

She and Caroline had bonded instantly and she was beginning to feel like Wade's wife was the sister she'd always dreamed of having. Even Jake's oldest brother seemed less intimidating these days.

The band suddenly shifted into a slow ballad and Seth stood up and reached for her hand. "Come on, Mag. No excuses now."

She would have refused if Carmela hadn't returned to the table then to take Jorge. "Thank you for watching him," Carmela said in Spanish. "But he's going to wake up hungry. We must be leaving."

She gave both Carmela and Horatio hugs as they said their goodbyes, then turned back to Seth. "All right. Let's dance. But I'll warn you in advance I'm still not very good on the dance floor. I can't blame having two left feet anymore since I don't even have one."

"Bad joke," Seth said. He had just started to lead her out to the floor when Jake appeared over his shoulder and her heart gave its usual happy sigh of welcome.

He didn't say anything, just raised one of those expressive eyebrows at his younger brother.

Seth sighed. "Yeah, yeah. I know. Get my own girl."

"That shouldn't be a problem for you," Jake said dryly. "If only you could narrow the field down to just one."

Seth grinned. "Now why would I want to do that?"

He kissed Maggie on the cheek. "Thanks anyway," he said, surrendering her to Jake.

She settled into her husband's strong arms with a sigh of contentment, wanting to be nowhere else on earth but right here with the summer breeze ruffling her hair and the moonlight gleaming through the trees.

Somehow Jake always seemed to move at just the right pace—not too fast that she had to move awkwardly to keep up with him but not so slow that she grew frustrated.

Here was another joy she thought long behind her but like so many other things, Jake had helped her through.

"It's been a good day, hasn't it?" he asked, his breath warm in her ear, and she saw they had moved out of the bowery closer to the creek, secluded in the shade of the trees.

She smiled, her arms tightening around him. "Wonderful. They're so happy together."

"What about you, Mrs. Dalton?"

In answer, she pulled his head down and pressed her mouth to his. As he pulled her closer, they stopped moving but she didn't mind. There would be time for dancing.

They had the rest of their lives.

* * * * *

ALWAYS THE BEST MAN

Michelle Major

For Stephanie.
You have the strongest, bravest spirit of
any mother I know and you inspire me every day.

Chapter 1

Some women were meant to be a bride. Emily Whitaker had been one of those women. For years she'd fantasized her walk down the aisle, imagining the lacy gown, the scent of her bouquet and the admiring eyes of family and friends as she entered the church.

When the day had finally arrived, there was no doubt she'd been beautiful, her shiny blond hair piled high on her head, perfect makeup and the dress—oh, her dress. She'd felt like a princess enveloped in so much tulle and lace, the sweetheart neckline both feminine and a little flirty.

Guests had whispered at her resemblance to Grace Kelly, and Emily had been foolish enough to believe that image was the same thing as reality. Her fairy tale had come true as her powerful white knight swooped her away from Crimson, the tiny Colorado mountain town where she'd grown up, to the sophisticated social circles of old-money Boston.

Too soon she discovered that a fantasy wedding was

not the same thing as real marriage and a beautiful dress did not equate to a wonderful life. Emily lost her taste for both daydreams and weddings, so she wasn't sure how she'd found herself outside the swanky bridal boutique in downtown Aspen seven years after her own doomed vows.

"You can't want me as your maid of honor."

Katie Garrity, Emily's soon-to-be sister-in-law smiled. "Of course I do. I asked you, Em. I'd be honored to have you stand up with me." Katie's sweet smile faltered. "I mean, if you'll do it. I know it's short notice and there's a lot to coordinate in the next few weeks so…"

"It's not that I don't want to…"

Katie was as sweet as any of the cakes and cookies sold in the bakery she owned in downtown Crimson. She'd been a steadfast best friend to Emily's brother, Noah Crawford, for years before Noah realized that his perfect match had been right in front of him all along.

Emily was happy for the two of them, really she was. But if Katie was pure sugar, Emily was saccharine. She knew she was pretty to look at but after that first bite there was an artificial sweetness that left a cloying taste on the tongue. Emily didn't want her own bitterness to corrupt Katie's happy day.

"You have a lot of girlfriends. Surely there's a better candidate than me?"

"None of them are going to be my sister-in-law." Katie pressed her fingers to the glass of the shop's display window. "I remember the photos of your wedding that ran in *Town & Country* magazine. Noah and I don't want anything fancy, but I'd like our wedding to be beautiful."

"It will be more than beautiful." Emily swallowed back the anger that now accompanied thoughts of her marriage. "You two love each other, for better or worse." She took a breath as her throat clogged with emotion she'd thought had been stripped away during her divorce. She waved her hand in front of her face and made her voice light. "Plus all the other promises you'll make in the vows. But I'm not—"

"I'm a pregnant bride," Katie said suddenly, resting a hand on her still-flat stomach. She smiled but her eyes were shining. "I love your brother, Emily, and I know we'll have a good life together. But this isn't the order I planned things to happen, you know?"

"You and Noah were meant to be," Emily assured her. "Everyone knows that."

"Crimson is a small town with a long memory. People also know that I've had a crush on him for years and until I got pregnant, he had no interest in me."

Emily shook her head. "That's not how it happened." It had taken Katie walking away for Noah to realize how much she meant to him, but Emily knew his love for his fiancée was deep and true.

"It doesn't stop the talk. If I hear one more person whisper *shotgun wedding*—"

"Who?" Emily demanded. "Give me names and I'll take care of them for you." Since Emily had returned to Colorado at the beginning of the summer, she'd spent most of her time tucked away at her mother's farm outside town. She needed a do-over on her life, yet it was easier to hide out and lick her emotional wounds. But it wouldn't be difficult to ferret out the town's biggest gossips and grown-up mean girls. After all, Emily had been their ringleader once upon a time.

"What I need is for you to help me take care of the wedding," Katie answered softly. "To stand by my side and support me as I deal with the details. You may not care about the people in Crimson anymore, but I do. I want my big day to be perfect—as perfect as it can be under the circumstances. I don't want anyone to think I tried to force Noah or rush the wedding." She smoothed her fingers over her flowery shirt. "But I've only got a few weeks. Invitations have already gone out, and I haven't even started planning. Josh and Sara had one free weekend at Crimson Ranch this fall, and I couldn't wait any longer. I don't want to be waddling down the aisle."

"None of that matters to Noah. He'd marry you tomorrow or in the delivery room or whenever and wherever you say the word."

"It matters to me." Katie grimaced. "My parents are coming for the wedding. They haven't been to Crimson in years. I need it to be..." She broke off, bit down on her lip. "You're right. It doesn't matter. I love Noah, and I should just forget the rest of this. Why is a wedding such a big deal anyway?"

But Emily understood why, and she appreciated Katie's need for validation even if she didn't agree with it. So what if Emily no longer believed in marriage? She'd picked a husband for all the wrong reasons, but Katie and Noah were the real deal. If the perfect wedding would make Katie happy, then Emily would give her a day no one would forget.

"I could be the wedding planner, and you can ask one of your friends to—"

"I want *you*," Katie interrupted. "I'm an only child and now I'll have a sister. My family's messed up, but that makes me value the one I'm marrying into even more."

"I haven't valued them in the past few years." Emily felt her face redden, embarrassment over her behavior rushing through her, sharp and hot. "Until Davey was born I didn't realize how important family was to me."

"When your dad got sick, you helped every step of the way."

That much was true. Her father died when Emily was in high school. She'd taken over the care of the farm so her mom could devote time to Dad. Meg Crawford had driven him to appointments, cooked, cleaned and sat by his bedside in the last few weeks of home hospice care when the pancreatic cancer had ravaged his body.

It had been the last unselfish thing Emily had done in her life until she'd left her marriage, her so-called friends and the security of her life in Boston. As broken as she felt, she'd endure the pain and humiliation of those last six months again in a heartbeat for her son.

"You're a better person than you give yourself credit for," Katie said and opened the door of the store. The scent of roses drifted out, mingling with the crisp mountain air.

"I know exactly who I am." Emily removed her Prada sunglasses and tipped her face to the bright blue August sky. She'd missed the dry climate of Colorado during her time on the East Coast. It was refreshing to feel the warmth of the sun without miserable humidity making it feel like she'd stepped into an oven.

"Does that include being my maid of honor?" Katie asked over her shoulder, taking a step into the boutique.

"Shouldn't it be matron of honor?" Emily followed Katie, watching as she gingerly fingered the white gowns on the racks of the small shop. The saleswoman, an older lady with a pinched face, stepped forward. Emily waved her away for now. Shopping was one thing she could do with supreme confidence. Not much of a skill but today she'd put it to good use. "What's the protocol for having a divorcée as part of the bridal party?"

"I'm sticking with maid. There's nothing matronly about

you." Katie pulled out a simple sheath dress, then frowned when Emily shook her head. "I think it's pretty."

"You have curves," Emily answered and pointed to Katie's full chest. "Especially with a baby on board. We want something that enhances them, not makes you look like a sausage."

Katie winced. "Don't sugarcoat it."

"We've got a couple of weeks to pull off the most amazing wedding Crimson has ever seen. You can be sweet. I don't have time to mess around."

"It doesn't have to be—"

Emily held up a hand, then stepped around Katie to pull a dress off the rack. "It's going to be. This is a good place to start."

Katie let out a soft gasp. "It's perfect. How did you do that?"

The dress was pale ivory, an empire waist chiffon gown with a lace overlay. It was classic but the tiny flowers stitched into the lace gave a hint of whimsy. The princess neckline would look beautiful against Katie's dark hair and creamy skin and the cut would be forgiving if she "popped" in the next few weeks. Emily smiled a little as she imagined Noah's reaction to seeing his bride for the first time.

"You're beautiful, Katie, and we're going to find the right dress." She motioned to the saleswoman. "We'll start with this one," she said, gently handing over the gown.

The woman nodded. "When is the big day?"

"Two weeks," Emily answered for Katie. "So we'll need something that doesn't have to be special ordered."

"Anything along this wall is in stock." The woman turned to Katie. "The fitting room is in the back. I'll hang the dress."

"Do I have to plan a cheesy bachelorette party, too?"

Emily selected another dress and held it up for Katie's approval.

Katie ignored the dress, focusing her gaze on Emily. "Is that your way of saying you'll be my maid of honor?"

Emily swallowed and nodded. This was not a big deal, two weeks of support and planning. So why did she feel like Katie was doing her the favor by asking instead of the other way around? "If you're sure?"

"Thank you," Katie shouted and gave Emily a huge hug.

This was why, she realized, as tears pricked the backs of her eyes. Emily hadn't had a real friend in years. The women who were part of her social circle in Boston had quickly turned on her when her marriage imploded, making her an outcast in their community. She'd burned most of her bridges with her Colorado friends when she'd dropped out of college to follow her ex-husband as he started his law career. Other than her mom and Noah, she had no one in her life she could count on. Until now.

She shrugged out of Katie's grasp and drew in a calming breath. "Who else is in the bridal party?"

"We're not having any other attendants," Katie told her. "I'll try on this one, too." She scooped up the dress and took a step toward the back of the store. "Just you and Jase. He's Noah's best man."

Emily stifled a groan and muttered, "Great." Jase Crenshaw had been her brother's best friend for years so she should have expected he'd be part of the wedding. Still, Crimson's favorite son was the last person she wanted to spend time with. He was the exact opposite of Emily— warm, friendly, easy-to-like. Around him her skin itched, her stomach clenched and she was generally made more aware of her long list of shortcomings. A real prince among men.

Katie turned suddenly and hugged Emily again. "I feel

so much better knowing you're with me on this. For the first time I believe my wedding is going to be perfect."

Emily took another breath and returned the hug. She could do this, even with Jase working alongside her. Katie and Noah deserved it. "Perfect is my specialty," she told her friend with confidence. Behind her back, she kept her fingers crossed.

"What the hell was that?" Noah Crawford held out a hand to Jason Crenshaw, who was sprawled across the Crimson High School football field, head pounding and ears ringing.

Jase hadn't seen the hit coming until he was flat on his back in the grass. He should have been paying more attention, but in the moment before the ball was snapped, Emily Whitaker appeared in the stands. Jase had done his best to ignore the tall, willowy blond with the sad eyes and acid tongue since she'd returned to town.

Easier said than done since she was his best friend's sister and...well, since he'd had a crush on her for as long as he could remember. Since the first time she'd come after Jase and Noah for ripping the head from her favorite Barbie.

Emily'd packed quite a wallop back in the day.

Just not as much as Aaron Thompson, the opposing team's player who'd sacked Jase before running the ball downfield. Jase brushed away Noah's outstretched hand and stood, rubbing his aching ribs as he did. "I thought this was flag football," he muttered as he turned to watch Aaron do an elaborate victory dance in the end zone.

"Looks like Thompson forgot," Noah said, pulling off his own flag belt, then Jase's as they walked toward the sidelines.

"We'll get 'em next time." Liam Donovan, another teammate and good friend, gave Jase's shoulder a friendly shove. "If our quarterback can stay on his feet."

"This is a preseason game anyway," Logan Travers added. "Doesn't count."

"It counts that we whipped your butts," Aaron yelled, sprinting back up the field. He launched the game ball at Jase's head before Logan stepped forward and caught it.

"Back off, Thompson," Logan said softly, but it was hard to miss the steel in his tone. Logan was as tall as Jase's own six feet three inches but had the muscled build befitting the construction work he did. Jase was in shape, he ran and rock climbed in his free time. He also spent hours in front of his computer and in the courtroom for his law practice, so he couldn't compete with Logan's bulk.

He also wasn't much for physical intimidation. Not that Aaron would be intimidated by Jase. The Thompson family held a long-standing grudge against the Crenshaws, and hotheaded Aaron hadn't missed a chance to poke at him since they'd been in high school. Aaron's father, Charles, had been the town's sheriff back when Jase's dad was doing most of his hell raising and had made it clear he was waiting for Jase to carry on his family's reputation in Crimson.

Jase took a good measure of both pride and comfort in living in his hometown, but there were times he wished for some anonymity. They weren't kids anymore, and Jase had long ago given up his identity as the studious band geek who'd let bullies push him around to keep the peace.

He stepped forward, crossing his arms over his chest as he looked down his nose at the brutish deputy. "Talk is cheap, Aaron," he said. "And so are your potshots at me. We'll see you back on the field next month."

"Can't wait," Aaron said with a smirk Jase wanted to smack right off his face.

The feeling only intensified when Aaron jogged over to talk to Emily, who was standing with Katie and the other team wives and girlfriends on the sidelines.

"Let it go." Noah hung back as their friends approached the group of women. "She wouldn't give him the time of day in high school, and now is no different."

"Nice," Jase mumbled under his breath. "Aaron and I actually have something in common."

Noah laughed. "Katie's asked Emily to be the maid of honor. You'll have plenty of excuses to moon over her in the next few weeks."

Jase stiffened. "I *don't* moon."

"You keep telling yourself that," Noah said as he gave him a shove. "It doesn't matter anyway. Emily has her hands too full with Davey and starting over even if she wanted a man." He gave Jase a pointed, big-brother look. "Which she doesn't."

"I'm no threat," Jase said, holding up his hands. "Nothing has changed from when we were twelve. Your sister can't stand me."

"I get that but you'll both have to make an effort for the wedding. Katie doesn't need any extra stress right now."

"Got it," Jase agreed and glanced at his watch. "I've got to check in at the office before I head home."

"How's the campaign going?"

"Not much to report. It seems anticlimactic to run for mayor unopposed. Not much work to do except getting out the vote."

"You're more qualified for the position than anyone else in Crimson," Noah told him, "although I'm still not sure why city council and all the other volunteer work you do isn't enough?"

"I love this town, and I think I can help it move forward."

Noah smiled. "Emily calls you Saint Jase."

Jase felt his jaw tighten. "How flattering."

"She might have a point. What are your plans for the weekend? Katie and I are going out to Mom's place for a barbecue tomorrow night. Want to join us?"

Jase rarely had plans for the weekend. Juggling both his law practice and taking care of his dad left little free time. But Emily would be there and while the rational part of him knew he shouldn't go out of his way to see her, the rest of him didn't seem to care. If he could get his father settled early tomorrow...

"Sounds good. What can I bring?"

"Really?" Noah's brows lifted. "You're venturing out on a Saturday night? Big time. We've got it covered. Come out around six."

"See you tomorrow," he said and headed over to his gym bag at the far side of the stands. He stripped off his sweaty T-shirt and pulled a clean one from the bag. As he straightened, Emily walked around the side of the metal bleachers, eyes glued to her cell phone screen as her thumbs tapped away. He didn't have time to voice a warning before she bumped into him.

As the tip of her nose brushed his bare chest, she yelped and stumbled back. The inadvertent touch lasted seconds but it reverberated through every inch of his body.

His heart lurched as he breathed her in—a mix of expensive perfume and citrus-scented shampoo. Delicate and tangy, the perfect combination for Emily. Noah had accused him of mooning but what he felt was more. He wanted her with an intensity that shook him to his core after all these years.

He'd thought he had his feelings for Emily under control, but this was emotional chaos. He was smart enough to understand it was dangerous as hell to the plans he had for his future. At this moment he'd give up every last thing to pull her close.

Instead he ignored the instinct to reach for her. When she was steady on her feet, he stepped away, clenching his T-shirt in his fists so hard his fingers went numb. "Looks like texting and walking might be as ill-advised as texting and driving."

"Thanks for the tip," she snapped, tucking her phone into the purse slung over her shoulder. Was it his imagination or was she flushed? Her breathing seemed as irregular as his felt. Then her pale blue eyes met his, cool and impassive. Of course he'd imagined Emily having any reaction to him beyond distaste. "My mom sent a photo of Davey."

"Building something?" he guessed.

"How do you know?"

"I was at the hospital the day of your mom's surgery. I made Lego sets with him while everyone was in the waiting room."

She gave the barest nod. Emily's mother, Meg, had been diagnosed with a meningioma, a type of brain tumor, at the beginning of the summer, prompting both Emily and Noah to return to Crimson to care for her. Luckily, the tumor had been benign and Meg was back to her normal, energetic self.

The Crawford family had already endured enough with the death of Emily and Noah's father over a decade ago. Having been raised by a single dad who was drunk more often than he was sober, Jase had spent many afternoons, weekends and dinners with the Crawfords. Meg was the mother he wished he'd had. Hell, he would have settled for an aunt or family friend who had a quarter of her loving nature.

But she'd been it, and lucky for Jase, Noah had been happy to share his mom and her affection. With neither of her kids living in town until recently and Meg never remarrying, Jase had become the stand-in when she had a leaky faucet that needed fixing or simply wanted company out at the family farm. He'd taken the news of her illness almost as hard as her real son.

"I remember," she whispered, not meeting his gaze.

"Every time I've been out to the farm this summer, Davey was building something. Your boy loves his Lego sets. He's—"

"Don't say obsessed," she interrupted, eyes flashing.

"I was going to say he has a great future as an engineer."

"Oh, right." She crossed her arms over her chest, her gaze dropping to the ground.

"I know five is young to commit to a profession," he added with a smile, "but Davey is pretty amazing." Something in her posture, a vulnerability he wouldn't normally associate with Emily made him add, "You're doing a great job with him."

Her rosy lips pressed together as a shudder passed through her. He'd meant the compliment and couldn't understand her reaction to his words. But she'd been different since her return to Crimson—fragile in a way she never was when they were younger.

"Emily." He touched a finger to the delicate bone of her wrist, the lightest touch but her gaze slammed into his. The emotion swirling through her eyes made him suck in a breath. "I mean it," he said, shifting so his body blocked her from view of the group of people still standing a few feet away on the sidelines. "You're a good mom."

She stared at him a moment longer, as if searching for the truth in his words. "Thanks," she whispered finally and blinked, breaking the connection between them. He should step away again, give her space to collect herself, but he didn't. He couldn't.

She did instead, backing up a few steps and tucking a lock of her thick, pale blond hair behind one ear. Her gaze dropped from his, roamed his body in a way that made him warm all over again. Finally she looked past him to their friends. "Katie told me you're the best man."

He nodded.

"I've got some ideas for the wedding weekend. I want it to be special for both of them."

"Let me know what you need from me. Happy to help in any way."

"I will." She straightened her shoulders and when she looked at him again, it was pure Emily. A mix of condescension and ice. "A good place to start would be putting on some clothes," she said, pointing to the shirt still balled in his fist. "No one needs a prolonged view of your bony bod."

It was meant as an insult and a reminder of their history. She'd nicknamed him Bones when he'd grown almost a foot the year of seventh grade. No matter what he'd eaten, he couldn't keep up with his height and had been a beanpole, all awkward adolescent arms and legs. From what he remembered, Emily hadn't experienced one ungainly moment in all of her teenage years. She'd always been perfect.

And out of his league.

He pulled the shirt over his head and grabbed his gym bag. "I'll remember that," he told her and walked past her off the field.

Chapter 2

Emily lifted the lip gloss to her mouth just as the doorbell to her mother's house rang Saturday night. She dropped the tube onto the dresser, chiding herself for making an effort with her appearance before a casual family dinner. Particularly silly when the guest was Jase Crenshaw, who meant nothing to her. Who probably didn't want to be in the same room with her.

Not when she'd been so rude to him after the football game with her reference to his body. He had to know the insult was absurd. He might have been a tall skinny teen but now he'd grown into his body in a way that made her feel weak in the knees.

That weakness accounted for her criticism. Emily had spent the last year of her marriage feeling fragile and unsettled. Jase made her feel flustered in a different way, but she couldn't allow herself be affected by any man when she was working so hard to be strong.

Of course she'd known Jase liked her when they were younger, but she hadn't been interested in her brother's best friend or anyone from small-town Crimson. Emily'd had her sights set on bigger things, like getting out of Colorado. Henry Whitaker and his powerful family had provided the perfect escape at the time.

Sometimes she wished she could ignore the changes in herself. She glanced at the mirror again. The basics were the same—blond hair flowing past her shoulders, blue eyes and symmetrical features. People would still look at her and see a beautiful woman, but she wondered if anyone saw beyond the surface.

Did they notice the shadows under her eyes, the result of months of restless nights when she woke and tiptoed to Davey's doorway to watch him sleeping? Could they tell she couldn't stop the corners of her lips from perpetually pulling down, as if the worry over her son was an actual weight tugging at their edges?

No. People saw what they wanted, like she'd wanted to see her ex-husband as the white knight that would sweep her off to the charmed life she craved. Only now did she realize perfection was a dangerous illusion.

She heard Jase's laughter drift upstairs and felt herself swaying toward the open door of the bedroom that had been hers since childhood. Her mom had taken the canopy off the four-poster bed and stripped the posters from the walls, but a fresh coat of paint and new linens couldn't change reality.

Emily was a twenty-eight year old woman reduced to crawling back to the financial and emotional safety of her mother's home. She dipped her head, her gaze catching on a tiny patch of pink nail polish staining the corner of the dresser. It must have been there for at least ten years, back when a bright coat of polish could lift her spirits. She'd had so many dreams growing up, but now all she wanted was to make things right for her son.

"Em, dinner is almost ready," her mom called from the bottom of the stairs.

"Be right there," she answered. She scraped her thumbnail against the polish, watching as it flaked and fell to the floor. Something about peeling a bit of her girlhood from the dresser made her breathe easier and she turned for the door. She took a step, then whirled back and picked up the lip gloss, dabbing a little on the center of her mouth and pressing her lips together. Maybe she couldn't erase the shadows under her eyes, but Emily wasn't totally defeated yet.

Before heading through the back of the house to the patio where Noah was grilling burgers, she turned at the bottom of the stairs toward her father's old study. Since she and Davey had returned, her mom had converted the wood-paneled room to building block headquarters. It had been strange, even ten years after her father's death, to see his beloved history books removed from the shelves to make room for the intricate building sets her son spent hours creating. Her mother had taken the change easier than Emily, having had years alone in the house to come to terms with her husband's death. That sense of peace still eluded Emily, but she liked to think her warmhearted, gregarious father would be happy that his office was now a safe place for Davey.

Tonight Davey wasn't alone on the thick Oriental rug in front of the desk. Jase sat on the floor next to her son, long legs sprawled in front of him. He looked younger than normal, carefree without the burden of taking care of the town weighing down his shoulders. Both of their heads were bent to study something Jase held, and Emily's breath caught as she noticed her son's hand resting on Jase's leg, their arms brushing as Davey leaned forward to hand Jase another Lego piece.

She must have made a sound because Jase glanced up, an almost apologetic smile flashing across his face. "You found us," he said and handed Davey the pieces before standing. Davey didn't look at her but turned toward his current model, carefully adding the new section to it.

"Dinner's ready," she said, swallowing to hide the emotion that threatened to spill over into her voice.

Jase had known her too long to be fooled. "Hope it's okay I'm in here with him." He gestured to the bookshelves that held neat rows of building sets. "He's got an impressive collection."

"He touched you," she whispered, taking a step back into the hall. Not that it mattered. Her son wasn't listening. When Davey was focused on finishing one of his creations, the house could fall down around him and he wouldn't notice.

"Is that bad?" Jase's thick brows drew down, and he ran a hand through his hair, as if it would help him understand her words. His dark hair was in need of a cut and his fingers tousled it, making her want to brush it off his forehead the way she did for Davey as he slept.

"It's not…it's remarkable. He was diagnosed with Asperger's this summer. It was early for a formal diagnosis, but I'd known something was different with him for a while." Emily couldn't help herself from reaching out to comb her fingers through the soft strands around Jase's temples. It was something to distract herself from the fresh pain she felt when talking about Davey. "Building Lego sets relaxes him. He doesn't like to be touched and will only tolerate a hug from me sometimes. To see him touching you so casually, as if it were normal…"

Jase lifted his hand and took hold of hers, pulling it away

from his head but not letting go. He cradled it in his palm, tracing his thumb along the tips of her fingers. She felt the subtle pressure reverberate through her body. Davey wasn't the only one uncomfortable being touched.

Since her son's symptoms had first started and her ex-husband's extreme reaction to them had launched the destruction of their family, Emily felt like she was made of glass.

Now as she watched Jase's tanned fingers gently squeeze hers, she wanted more. She wanted to step into this tall, strong, good man who could break through her son's walls without even realizing it and find some comfort for herself.

"I'm glad for it," he said softly, bringing her back to the present moment. "What about his dad?"

She snatched away her hand, closed her fist tight enough that her nails dug small half-moons into her palm. "My ex-husband wanted a son who could bond with him tossing a ball or sailing. The Whitakers are a competitive family, and even the grandkids are expected to demonstrate their athletic prowess. It's a point of pride and bragging rights for Henry and his brothers—whose kid can hit a ball off the tee the farthest or catch a long pass, even if it's with a Nerf football."

Jase glanced back at her son. "Davey's five, right? It seems a little young to be concerned whether or not he's athletic."

"That didn't matter to my in-laws, and it drove Henry crazy. He couldn't understand it. As Davey's symptoms became more pronounced, his father pushed him harder to be the *right* kind of boy."

She pressed her mouth into a thin line to keep from screaming the next words. "He forbade me from taking him to the doctor to be tested. His solution was to punish him, take away the toys he liked and force him into activities that ended up making us all more stressed. Davey started having tantrums and fits, which only infuriated Henry. He was getting ready to run for congress." She rolled her eyes. "The first step in the illustrious political campaign his family has planned."

"Following in his father's footsteps," Jase murmured.

It was true. Emily had married into one of the most well-known political families in the country since the Kennedys. The Whitakers had produced at least one US senator in each of the past five generations of men, and one of Henry's great-uncles had been vice president. "I didn't just marry a man, I took on a legacy. The worst part was I went in with my eyes open. I practically interviewed for the job of political wife, and I was ready to be a good one." She snapped her fingers. "I could throw a party fit for the First Lady with an hour's notice."

Jase cleared his throat. "I'm sure your husband appreciated that."

She gave a harsh laugh. "He didn't appreciate it. He expected it. There's a big difference." She shrugged. "None of it mattered once Davey was born. I knew from the time he was a baby he was different and I tried to hide…tried to protect him from Henry as long as possible. But once I couldn't anymore, there was no doubt about my loyalty." She plastered a falsely bright smile on her face. "So here I am back in Crimson."

Davey looked up from his building set. "I'm finished, Mommy."

She stepped around Jase and sat on the carpet to admire the intricate structure Davey had created. "Tell me about it, sweetie."

"It's a landing pod with a rocket launcher. It's like the

ones they have on *The Clone Wars*, only this one has an invisible force field around it so no one can destroy it."

If only she could put a force field around her son to protect him from the curiosity and potential ridicule that could come due to his differences from other kids. "I love it, Wavy-Davey."

One side of his mouth curved at the nickname before he glanced at Jase. "He helped. He's good at building. Better than Uncle Noah or Grammy."

"High praise," Jase said, moving toward the bookshelves. "If you make a bridge connecting it to this one, you'd have the start of an intergalactic space station."

Emily darted a glance at Davey as Jase moved one of the sets a few inches to make room for this new one. Her boy didn't like anyone else making decisions about the placement of his precious building sets. To her surprise, Davey only nodded. "I'll need to add a hospital and mechanic's workshop 'cause if there's a battle they'll need those."

"Maybe a cafeteria and bunk room?" Jase suggested.

"You can help me with those if you want." Leaving Emily speechless where she sat, Davey gently lifted the new addition and carried it to the bookshelf. With Jase's help, he slid it into place with a satisfied nod. "I'm hungry. Can we eat?" he asked, turning to Emily.

"Sure thing," she agreed. "Grammy, Uncle Noah and Aunt Katie are waiting." Her family was used to waiting as transitions were one of Davey's biggest challenges. Sometimes it took long minutes to disengage him from a project.

Her son stepped forward, his arms ramrod straight at his sides. "It's time, Mommy. I'm ready."

She almost laughed at the confusion clouding Jase's gaze. People went in front of a firing squad with more enthusiasm than Davey displayed right now. It would have been funny if this ritual didn't break her heart the tiniest bit. Embarrassment flooded through her at what Jase might think, but the reward was too high to worry about a little humiliation.

She rose to her knees and opened her arms. Davey stepped forward and she pulled him close, burying her nose in his neck to breathe him in as she gave him a gentle hug. A few moments were all he could handle before he squirmed in her embrace. "I love you," she whispered before letting him go.

He met her gaze. "I know," he answered simply, then turned and walked out of the room.

She stood, wiping her cheeks. Why bother to hide the tears? She'd left the lion's share of her pride, along with most of her other possessions, back in Boston.

"Sorry," she said to Jase, knowing her smile was watery at best. Emily might be considered beautiful, but she was an ugly crier. "It's a deal he and I have. Every time he finishes a set, I get a hug. A real one."

"Emily," he whispered.

"Don't say anything about it, please. I can't afford to lose it now. It's dinnertime, and I don't need to give my family one more reason to worry about me."

A muscle ticked in his jaw, but he nodded. "In case no one has said it lately," he said as she moved past, "your ex-husband may be political royalty, but he's also a royal ass. You deserve to be loved better." The deep timbre of his voice rumbled through her like a cool waterfall, both refreshing and fierce in its power.

She shivered but didn't stop walking out of the room. Reality kept her moving forward. Davey was her full reason for being now. There was no use considering what she did or didn't deserve.

Chapter 3

"Is that you, Jase?"

"Yeah, Dad." Jase slipped into the darkened trailer and flipped on the light. "I'm here. How's it going?"

"I could use a beer," Declan Crenshaw said with a raspy laugh. "Or a bottle of whiskey. Any chance you brought whiskey?"

His father was sprawled on the threadbare couch that had rested against the thin wall of the mobile home since Jase could remember. Nothing in the cramped space had changed from the time they'd first moved in. The trailer's main room was tiny, barely larger than the dorm room Jase had lived in his first year at the University of Denver. From the front door he could see back to the bedroom on one side and through the efficiency kitchen with its scratched Formica counters and grainy wood cabinets to the family room on the other.

"No alcohol." He was used to denying his dad's requests

for liquor. Declan had been two years sober and Jase was hopeful this one was going to stick. He was doing everything in his power to make sure it did. Checking on his dad every night was just part of it. "How about water or a cup of tea?"

"Do I look like the queen of England?" Declan picked up the potato chip bag resting next to him on the couch and placed it on the scuffed coffee table, then brushed off his shirt, chip crumbs flying everywhere.

"No one's going to mistake you for royalty." Jase's dad looked like a man who'd lived a hard life, the vices that had consumed him for years made him appear decades older than his sixty years. If the alcohol and smoking weren't enough, Declan had spent most of his adult life working in the active mines around Crimson, first the Smuggler silver mine outside of Aspen and then later the basalt-gypsum mine high on Crimson Mountain.

Between the dust particles, the constant heavy lifting, operating jackhammers and other heavy equipment, the work took a physical toll on the men and women employed by the mines. Jase had tried to get his father to quit for years, but it was only after a heart attack three years ago that Declan had been forced to retire. Unfortunately, having so much time on his hands had led him to a six-month drunken binge that had almost killed him. Jase needed to believe he wasn't going to have to watch his father self-destruct ever again.

"Maybe they should since you're a royal pain in my butt," Declan growled.

"Good one, Dad." Jase didn't take offense. Insults were like terms of endearment to his father. "Why are you sitting here in the dark?" He picked up the chip bag and dropped it in the trash can in the kitchenette, then started washing the dishes piled in the sink.

"Damn cable is out again. I called but they can't get here until tomorrow. If I lose my DVRed shows, there's gonna be hell to pay. *The Real Housewives* finale was on tonight. I wanted to see some rich-lady hair pulling."

Jase smiled. Since his dad stopped drinking, he'd become addicted to reality TV. Dance moms, little people, bush people, swamp people, housewives. Declan watched them all. "Maybe you should get a hobby besides television. Take a walk or volunteer."

His dad let out a colorful string of curses. "My only other hobby involves walking into a bar, so I'm safer holed up out here. And I'm not spending my golden years working for free. Hell, I barely made enough to pay the bills with my regular job. There's only room for one do-gooder in this family, and that's you."

It was true. The Crenshaws had a long history of living on the wrong side of the law in Crimson. There was even a sepia-stained photo hanging in the courthouse that showed his great-great-grandfather sitting in the old town jail. Jase had consciously set out to change his family's reputation. Most of his life decisions had been influenced by wanting to be something different...something more than the Crenshaw legacy of troublemaking.

"I read in the paper that you're sponsoring a pancake breakfast next week."

Jase placed the last mug onto the dish drainer, then turned. "It's part of my campaign."

"Campaigning against yourself?" his dad asked with a chuckle.

"It's a chance for people to get to know me."

Declan stood, brushed off his shirt again. "Name one person who doesn't know you."

"They don't know me as a candidate. I want to hear what voters think about how the town is doing, ideas for the future—where Crimson is going to be in five or ten years."

His dad yawned. "Same place it's been for the last hundred years. Right here."

"You know what I mean."

"Yeah, I know." Declan patted Jase on the back. "You're a good boy, Jason Damien Crenshaw. Better than I deserve as a son. It's got to be killing Charles Thompson and his boys that a Crenshaw is going to be running this town." His dad let out a soft chuckle. "I may give ex–Sheriff Thompson a call and see what he thinks."

"Don't, Dad. Leave the history between us and the Thompsons in the past where it belongs." Jase didn't mention the hit Aaron had put on him during the football game, which would only make his father angry.

"You're too nice for your own good. Why don't you pick me up before the breakfast?" Declan had lost his license during his last fall from the wagon and hadn't bothered to get it reinstated. Jase took him to doctor's appointments, delivered groceries and ran errands—an inconvenience, but it also helped him keep track of Declan. Something that hadn't always been easy during the heaviest periods of drinking. "I'll campaign for you. Call it volunteer work and turn my image around in town."

Jase swallowed. He'd encouraged his father to volunteer almost as a joke, knowing Declan never would. But campaigning... Jase loved his dad but he'd done his best to distance himself from the reputation that followed his family like a plague. "We'll see, Dad. Thanks for the offer. Are you heading to bed?"

"Got nothing else to do with no channels working."

"I'll call the cable company in the morning and make sure you're on the schedule," Jase promised. "Lock up behind me, okay?"

"Who's going to rob me?" Declan swept an arm around the trailer's shabby interior. "I've got nothing worth stealing."

"Just lock up. Please."

When his father eventually nodded, Jase let himself out of the trailer and headed home. Although he'd driven the route between the trailer park and his historic bungalow on the edge of downtown countless times, he forced himself to stay focused.

Three miles down the county highway leading into town. Two blocks until a right turn onto his street. Four hundred yards before he saw his mailbox. Keeping his mind on the driving was less complicated than giving the thoughts and worries crowding his head room to breathe and grow.

He parked his silver Jeep in the driveway, since his dad's ancient truck was housed in the garage. It needed transmission work that Jase didn't have time for before it would run again, and Declan had no use for it without a license. But Jase couldn't bring himself to sell it. It represented something he couldn't name...a giving in to the permanence of caring for an aging parent that he wasn't ready to acknowledge.

He locked the Jeep and lifted his head to the clear night. The stars were out in full force, making familiar designs across the sky. He hadn't used his old telescope in years, but Jase never tired of stargazing.

Something caught his eye, and when he looked around the front of his truck everything in the world fell away except the woman standing in his front yard.

Emily.

He wasn't sure where she'd come from or how he hadn't noticed her when he pulled up. Out of the corner of his eye he saw her mom's 4Runner parked across the street.

She didn't say anything as he approached, only watched him, her hands clasped tight together in front of her waist. Her fingers were long and elegant like the rest of her. As much as he would never wish her pain, the fact that she wore no wedding ring made him perversely glad.

"Hi," he said when he was in front of her, then silently cursed himself. He was an attorney and a town council member, used to giving speeches and closing arguments to courtrooms and crowded meetings. The best he could come up with now was *Hi*? Lame.

"I owe you an apology," she whispered. "And I didn't want to wait. I hate waiting."

He remembered that about her and felt one side of his mouth curve. Her mother, Meg, had been an expert baker when they were kids and Emily had forever been burning her mouth on a too-hot cookie after school.

"You don't owe me anything."

She shook her head. "No, it's true. You were good with Davey tonight. Before bed he told me he wants to invite you for a playdate."

He chuckled. "I told you we bonded over plastic bricks."

"His father never bonded with him," she said with a strangled sigh. "Despite my brother's best efforts, Noah has trouble engaging him." She shrugged, a helpless lift of her shoulders that made his heart ache. "Even I have trouble connecting with him sometimes. I understand it's the Asperger's, and I love him the way he is. But you're the first…friend he's ever had."

"He'll do fine at school."

"What if he doesn't? He's so special, but he's not like other boys his age."

"He's different in some ways, but kids manage through those things. I didn't have the greatest childhood or any real friends until I met your brother. I was too tall, too skinny and too poor. My dad was the town drunk and everyone knew it. But it made me stronger. I swear. Once I met Noah and your family took me in—"

"I didn't."

"No. You hated me being in your house."

"It wasn't about… I'm sorry, Jase. For how I treated you."

"Em, you don't have to—"

"I do." She stepped forward, so close that even in the pale streetlight he could see the brush of freckles across her nose. "I haven't been kind to you even since I've come back. It's like the nice part of my brain short-circuits when you're around."

"Good to know."

"What I said to you the other day on the football field about putting on your shirt."

He winced. "My bony bod…"

"Had nothing to do with it. You're not a skinny kid anymore. You must know…" She stopped, looked away, tugged her bottom lip between her teeth, then met his gaze again.

Something shifted between them; a current of awareness different than anything he'd experienced surged to life in the quiet night air.

"The women of this town would probably pay you to keep your shirt off." She jabbed one finger into his chest. "All. The. Time."

He laughed, because this was Emily trying to be nice and still she ended up poking him. "I'm popular at the annual car wash, but I figure it's because most of the other men on the council are so old no one wants them to have a heart attack while bending to soap up a front fender."

She didn't return his smile but eased the tiniest bit closer. "I didn't want you standing bare chested in front of me because I wanted to kiss you."

Jase sucked in a breath.

"I wanted to put my mouth on you, right there on the sidelines of the high school field with half of our friends watching." She said the words calmly, although he could see her chest rising and falling. He wasn't the only one having trouble breathing right now. "That's something different than when we were young. You make me feel things I haven't in a long time, and I don't know what to do about it. But it doesn't give me the right to be rude. I'm sorry, Jase. I can't—"

He didn't wait for her to finish. There was no way he was going to listen to the word *can't* coming from her, not when she'd basically told him she wanted him. In one quick movement, he leaned down and brushed his lips over hers.

So this was where she hid her softness, he thought. The taste of her, the feel of her mouth against his. All of it was so achingly sweet.

Then she opened her mouth to him and he deepened the kiss, threading his fingers through her hair as their tongues glided together. It was every perfect kiss he'd imagined and like nothing he'd experienced before. He wanted to stay linked with her forever, letting all of his responsibilities and the rest of the damn world melt away.

The moment was cut short when a dog barked—the sound coming from his house, and Emily pulled back. Her fingers lifted to her mouth and he wasn't sure whether it was to press his kiss closer or wipe it away. Right now it didn't matter.

"You have a dog?" she asked, glancing at his darkened front porch.

"A puppy," he said, scrubbing a hand over his jaw and trying to get a handle on the lust raging through him. "My former secretary Donna had a female Australian shepherd that got loose while in heat. They ended up with a litter of puppies, part shepherd and part who knows what?"

The barking turned into a keening howl, making him cringe. "Maybe elephant based on the size of their paws. But Ruby—my pup—was the runt. She was weaker than the rest and her brothers and sister tended to pick on her. They kept her, but it wasn't working with their other dogs. I went for dinner last week and..," The barking started again. "I need to let her out to do her business. Do you want to meet her?"

Emily shook her head and a foolish wave of disappointment surged through him.

"I need to get back to the farm. Mom thinks I was running to the store for..." She broke off, gave an embarrassed laugh, then looked at him again. "You rescue puppies, too? Unbelievable."

"It's not a big deal."

"Tell that to Ruby." She reached up on tiptoe, touched her lips to the corner of his mouth and then moved away. "You're damn near perfect, Jase Crenshaw."

"I'm not—"

"You are." She shook her head. "It's too bad for both of us that I gave up on perfect."

Before he could answer, she walked away. He waited, watching until she'd gotten in the SUV and pulled down his street. Until her taillights were swallowed in the darkness. Then the silence enveloped him once more, and he wondered if he'd dreamed the past few minutes.

An increasingly insistent bark snapped him back to the land of the wide-awake. He jogged to the front door and unlocked it, moving quickly to the crate in his family room. Her fluffy tail wagged and she greeted him with happy nips and yelps. He led her to the back door and she darted out, tumbling down the patio steps to find her perfect spot in-yard.

He sank down to the worn wood and waited for her to finish, lavishing praise when she wiggled her way back to him.

"I've got a story for you," he told the puppy as she covered him in dog slobber. "It's been quite a night, Ruby-girl."

Early Tuesday morning, Emily pasted a bright smile on her face before opening the door to Life Is Sweet, the bakery Katie owned in downtown Crimson. The soothing scent of sugar and warm dough washed over her as she automatically moved toward the large display case at the front of the shop.

The ambiance of the cozy bakery cheered her, even with the hellish morning of job interviews and application submissions she'd had. No surprise that businesses weren't lining up to hire an overqualified, single-mom college dropout who could only work part-time hours and needed to be able to take off when her son had a bad day. Yet it felt personal, as if the town she'd so easily left behind wasn't exactly opening its arms to welcome her back.

Life Is Sweet was different. With the warm yellow walls and wood beams stretching the length of the ceiling, the shop immediately welcomed customers both new and familiar. A grouping of café tables sat in one corner of the small space and the two women working the counter and coffee bar waved to her.

Katie pushed through the door to the back kitchen a moment later, carrying a large metal tray of croissants that she set on the counter.

"Should you be carrying pastries in your condition?" Emily asked with a laugh. Last weekend during dinner, Noah hadn't let Katie bring any of the serving bowls out to the table on the patio or clear the dishes. In fact, he'd all but insisted she sit the whole time they were at their mother's house. No matter what any of the women had told him about Katie and the baby remaining healthy despite normal activities, he couldn't seem to stop fawning over his wife-to-be.

Katie rolled her eyes. "I would have never guessed your brother had such an overprotective streak. He wants me to cut back even more on my hours at the bakery." She waved to one of the customers sitting at a café table, then looked at Emily. "I've hired a manager to run the front, but I'm still in charge of most of the baking. As long as my doctor says it's okay, I want to keep working."

"He'll get over it. I'll talk to him. Dad's death made him funny about keeping everyone he loves healthy." Her whole family had felt helpless when the pancreatic cancer claimed her father, and it had taken years for Noah to get over the guilt of not being around to help those last months.

When their mom had her health scare, Noah had returned to Crimson right away and remained at Meg's side for the duration of her recovery. But losing one parent and being scared for the other had taken a toll on him, and Emily understood his reasons for wanting Katie to be so careful.

"I know, and I love him for it." Katie sighed. "The morning sickness is done, so I feel great." She put all but two of the croissants in the case. "I'm just hungry all the time.

Can I interest you in a coffee-and-croissant break? They're chocolate."

"How did you know I need chocolate?"

"Everyone needs chocolate." Katie set the remaining pastries on a plate, then poured Emily a cup of coffee and handed it to her. "You look like you've been through the job search gauntlet today." She got the attention of one of the women working the counter and mouthed "Five minutes." There was a line forming at the cash register so the worker gave her a harried nod. "Let's go to the kitchen. More privacy."

"You're swamped right now. I'm fine."

"Never too swamped for a snack," Katie answered and picked up the plate. She led Emily through a heavy swinging door into the commercial kitchen. "I'm going to sit on a stool while you take my picture and text it to Noah. You're the witness that I'm not working too hard."

Emily snapped the photo, sent it to her brother and then pulled off a piece of the flaky dough. "Fresh from the oven?" she asked as she popped the bite into her mouth. She climbed onto a stool next to Katie, trailing her fingers across the cool stainless steel counter.

"The best kind."

"If my brother becomes too much of a pain, I'll marry you," Emily said when she finished chewing. The croissant melted in her mouth, buttery and soft with the perfect amount of chocolate in the middle.

"Don't distract me with flattery," Katie answered but moaned as she took a bite. "What happened today?"

"No one feels a burning desire to hire the woman who publicly ridiculed the town on her way out."

Katie made a face. "It was a well-known fact that you had no plans to stay in Crimson any longer than necessary."

"Or maybe I got drunk one night and announced to a bar full of locals that I was too good to waste away in this…"

"*Hellhole mountain slum*, I think you called it."

"Right. Classy."

"And endearing," Katie agreed, clearly having trouble keeping a straight face.

"I'm stupid." Emily pressed her forehead to the smooth stainless steel, let it soothe the massive headache she could feel starting behind her eyes.

"You can make this better," Katie said, placing a hand on Emily's back. "Crimson has a long history of forgiving mistakes."

"And an even longer one of punishing people for them." She tipped her head to the side. "Look at how hard Jase has worked to make amends for trouble he didn't even cause."

"But people love him."

"Because he's perfect."

"Why are you so hard on him, Em?"

Emily shook her head, unable to put into words her odd and tumbling emotions around Jase.

"You could work for him," Katie said with a laugh.

"For Jase?" Emily asked, lifting her head. "What do you mean?"

"I'm joking," Katie said quickly. "From what I can tell it bothers you to be in the same room with him."

"That's not exactly true." Emily had really liked Jase kissing her. It had been easy to lose herself in the gentle pressure of his mouth. His hands cradling her face made her feel cherished. She'd wanted to plaster herself against him and forget she was alone, at least for a few minutes. She was definitely bothered by Jase, but not in the way Katie believed. "Is he hiring for his campaign?"

"No," Katie answered slowly, as if reluctant to share what she knew. "His secretary retired a few months ago."

"The one with the litter of puppies?"

"How did you know about that?"

Emily ignored the question. "Why hasn't he hired someone?"

"He won't say, but as far as I know he hasn't even interviewed anyone for the position." Katie took another bite of pastry. "There are plenty of people who would love to work with him."

"Plenty of single women," Emily clarified.

"He's pretty hot," Katie said, her smile returning. "Not as handsome as Noah, of course. He makes me—"

"I'm working on being a good friend." Emily held up a hand. "But I draw the line on listening to you ruminate on the hotness of my brother." She hopped off her stool and took a final drink of coffee. "Break's over, friend. I just got a tip on a job opening." She picked up the plate and walked it over to the sink.

"Are you sure that's a good idea?"

"Clearing my plate?"

"Asking Jase for a job."

Emily straightened her suit jacket and smiled, pretending the nervous butterflies zipping through her belly didn't exist. "I'm not sure, but when has that ever stopped me?"

She gave Katie a short hug. "Thanks for listening. You're a pro at this whole supportive girlfriend thing."

Katie returned her smile. "Good luck, Em."

"I've got this," Emily answered with more confidence than she felt. But bluffing was second nature to her, so she squared her shoulders and marched out of the bakery to get herself a job.

Chapter 4

Jase reached for the file folder on the far side of his desk just as he heard Emily call his name. His hand jerked, knocking over the cup of leftover coffee that sat on another stack of papers, dark liquid spilling across the messy top of his desk.

"Damn," he muttered, grabbing the old towel he'd stuffed under the credenza behind him. This wasn't the first time most of his work papers had been dyed coffee brown. The mug had been half-empty so this cleanup wasn't the worst he'd seen. He quickly wiped up the spill, then moved the wet files to the row of cabinets shoved along the far wall.

By the time he turned around, Emily stood inside the door to his office. Her blue gaze surveyed the disorder of his office before flicking back to him. "Is it always this bad?"

He kicked the dirty towel out of sight behind his desk. "I've got things under control. It only looks like chaos."

She arched a brow. "Right."

Jase hadn't seen Emily since she'd walked away from him Saturday night. Letting her go had been one of the hardest things he'd ever done, but Emily wasn't the same proud, confident girl she'd been in high school. Whatever had happened when her marriage fell apart had left her bruised and tender. Jase had always been a patient man, and if she needed him to go slow he could force himself to honor that.

She didn't appear fragile now. This morning Emily wore a tailored skirt suit that looked like it cost more than the monthly rent on his office space. It was dark blue and the hem stopped just at her knee. Combined with low heels, a tight bun and a strand of pearls around her neck, Jase could imagine her on the stage next to her ex-husband, the perfect accessory for a successful politician.

He wanted to pull her hair loose, rip off the necklace that was more like a collar and kiss her until her skin glowed and her mouth turned pliant under his. Until he could make her believe she was more than the mask she wore like a coat of armor.

"Why haven't you hired a new secretary?"

He blinked, the question as much of a surprise as her appearance in his office. "I don't need one."

"Even you can't believe that." She nudged a precariously balanced pile of manila folders with one toe, then bent forward to right it when the stack threatened to topple.

"I haven't had time," he said, running a hand through his hair and finding it longer than he remembered. A haircut was also on his to-do list. "I did some interviewing when Donna first retired. She took a medical leave when her husband had a heart attack, and then they decided to simplify their lives and working here got cut. But she'd been with the practice when I took it over and ran this place and my life with no trouble at all. If I hire someone new, I'll have to train them and figure out if we can work together and…" He paused, not sure how to explain the rest.

"Let me guess." She arched a brow. "The women applying for the job think they're also interviewing for the role of your wife?"

"Maybe," he admitted, grabbing the empty coffee cup from his desk and walking toward her. There were plenty of single men in Crimson, so it was an irritating mystery how he'd ended up on the top of the eligible bachelor list. He didn't have time for dating, and even if he did…

"It would have been easier if Donna had helped screen the applicants."

One side of her mouth curved even as she rolled her crystal-blue eyes. "Because you have trouble hurting their feelings."

"You think you've got me all figured out."

She shrugged. "You're nice, Jase. Not complicated."

He touched the tip of one finger to her strand of pearls. "Unlike you?"

She sucked in a breath and stepped back so he could pass. There was a small utility sink in the kitchenette off the hallway, and he added the cup to the growing pile of dirty dishes. When he turned around, Emily was standing behind him, holding four more mugs by their handles.

"You forgot these."

He sighed and reached for them. Add washing dishes to the list.

"I appreciate the social call, but was there a reason you stopped by?" He turned and moved closer, into her space. "Unless you want to continue what we started Saturday night. That kind of work break I can use."

"No break and Saturday night was a mistake." She frowned. "You and I both know it."

He wanted to kiss the tension right off her face. "Then why can't I stop thinking about how you felt pressed against me?" He dropped his voice. "The way you taste…"

Color rose to her cheeks.

"I'm not the only one, am I? You walked away but you came back." His fingers itched to touch her. "You're here now."

"This isn't a social call." Emily straightened the hem of her jacket, looking almost nervous. "I think you should hire me."

Jase almost laughed, then realized she was serious. "No." He shook his head. "No way."

"Don't I at least get an interview?" Now her gaze turned mutinous. "That's not fair. I can do it." She spun on her heel and marched toward the front of his office. The space had a tiny lobby, two interior offices and a conference room. Jase loved the location just off Main Street in downtown Crimson.

The receptionist desk had become another place to stack papers since Donna'd left, and as he followed Emily toward the front door he realized how cluttered the area had become. Damn.

She picked up a thin messenger bag from one of the lobby chairs and pulled out a single sheet of paper. "My résumé," she said, handing it to him. He stared at it, but didn't take it from her. Her mouth thinned. "During college I was an academic assistant for two law school faculty members. I managed calendars, helped with grant proposals and assisted in the preparation of teaching materials. I'm organized and will work hard. I can come in two days this week, and then make my hours closer to full-time once Davey starts school. I'd like to be able to pick him up, but my mom can help out if you need me later in the afternoons."

She kept pushing the résumé toward him, the corners of the paper crumpling against his stomach, so he finally plucked it out of her fingers.

"Emily," he said softly. "I need a legal secretary."

"Right now," she shot back, "you need a warm body that can do dishes."

She had a point, but he wasn't about to admit it.

"I can do this. I can help you." She kept her hands fisted at her sides, her chin notched up. It must have cost her to come to him like this, but Emily still made it seem like she was doing him a favor by demanding he hire her.

"This isn't a job you want." He folded the resume and placed it on the desk. "You're smart and talented—"

"Talented at what?" she asked, breathing out a sad laugh. "Shopping? Planning parties? Not exactly useful skills in Crimson. Or maybe I'm good enough to kiss but not to work for you."

He pointed at the sheet of paper. "You just told me why you're qualified. If you can work for me, you can find another job."

"Don't you think I've tried? I spent this entire morning knocking on doors. I'm a single mom with a son who has special needs, which is a hard sell even if someone did want to hire me." She bit down on her lip. "By the way, they don't. Because I wasn't nice when I was younger and that's what people remember. That's what they see when they look at me."

"I don't."

"You're too nice for your own good," she said, jabbing a finger at him. "That's why I'm here begging." A strangled sound escaped her when she said the word begging. He studied her for crying, but her eyes remained dry. *Thank God*. He couldn't take it if she started crying. "I'm begging, Jase, because I need to know I can support my son. When I left Henry, I wanted out fast so I took nothing. Hell, I'm borrowing my mom's car like I'm a teenager again. I have to start somewhere, but I'm scared I won't be able to take care of Davey on my own. He's about to start kindergarten, but what if something happens? What if he—"

"He's going to be fine, Em." He could see her knuckles turning white even as color rose to her cheeks.

"This was a horrible idea," she muttered, turning her head to stare out onto Main Street as if she couldn't stand to meet his gaze another second. "I'm sorry. I'm a mess."

Jase took a step toward her. It was stupid and self-destructive and a bad idea for both of them, but the truth was he didn't care if Emily was a mess. He wanted her to be his mess.

Emily felt the tips of Jase's fingers on the back of her hand. She couldn't look at him after everything she'd said. All of the shattered pieces of herself she'd just revealed.

But her fingers loosened at his touch, and she wanted to sway into him. Somehow he grounded her and just maybe…

The front door to the office opened, a rush of fresh mountain air breezing over her heated skin. "Jase, you're late."

Emily whirled around to see a short, curvy woman in an ill-fitting silk blouse and shapeless skirt staring at her.

"Sorry," the woman said quickly, glancing between Emily and Jase as she adjusted the bulky purse on her arm. "I didn't realize you had a meeting or…"

"It's fine," Jase told her, stepping away from Emily. "I'll

grab my keys, and I'm ready. The Crimson Valley Hiker's Club today, right?"

The woman nodded. "If you're busy—"

He shook his head. "Mari, this is Emily Whitaker. She's Noah's sister and just got back to town. Em, Mari Simpson. Mari works at the library in town but has been kind enough to help keep me on track with my campaign." He gave Mari a warm smile, and Emily's throat tightened. Jase could smile at whomever he wanted. It didn't matter only...

"He'll be a great mayor," Mari chirped with a bright smile of her own. While the woman wasn't classically pretty, the smile softened her features in a way that made her beautiful. "I'm happy to do whatever I can." Her face was sweet and hopeful. The face of a woman who would make a perfect wife. Emily forced herself not to growl in response.

"Keys," Jase said again and disappeared into his office.

Mari continued to smile but it looked forced. "So you're Noah's sister?"

"I am."

"You moved back from Boston, right?"

A simple question but Emily knew it meant that although Mari Simpson wasn't a Crimson native, she'd been downloaded on Emily's past and reputation in town. "Yes," she answered, forcing herself to stay cordial. This was new Emily.

Emily 2.0. Nice Emily.

"It's good to be close to my family and friends again."

Mari tapped a finger to her cheek. "I think I saw your name on the application list for our reference desk opening."

Emily nodded. "I applied at the library."

"Too bad we filled the position already," Mari said a little too sweetly. "Lots of talented people want a chance to live in such a great little town. We only hire people with at least an undergraduate degree. I'm sure you'll find something."

Emily 2.0.

"Thanks for the vote of confidence," she said through clenched teeth. "I think—"

"Emily's going to work for me," Jase said, pocketing his phone and keys as he came back into the room. He kept his gaze trained on Mari.

Her jaw dropped and Emily was pretty sure her own re- action was the same.

"Here? But I've heard... I thought...she's—"

"Organized and hardworking," Jase said, repeating Em- ily's words from earlier. "Just what I need to get the office back on track." He patted the tiny woman on the shoulder. "It'll be easier for you, too, Mari. You won't have to keep tabs on me all the time."

She gave a small nod but muttered, "I don't mind."

Finally Jase turned to Emily. "Does tomorrow work for an official start date? I can be here by eight. We'll keep your hours flexible until Davey starts school." For once his eyes didn't reveal any of his feelings. It was as if he hadn't said no and she hadn't broken down in an emotional rant. As if he wasn't offering her this job out of pity.

He held out his hand, palm up. On it sat a shiny gold key. "Just in case you're here before me." He flashed a self-dep- recating smile. "Punctuality isn't one of my best qualities."

No, Emily thought, he didn't need to be on time. Jase had more important traits—like the ability to rescue dis- tressed women with a single key.

She should walk away. He knew too much about her now. If there was one thing Emily hated, it was appearing weak. She'd learned to be strong watching her father lose his battle with cancer. She'd married a man who valued power over everything else in his life.

During her divorce she hadn't revealed how scared she'd felt. She'd been strong for Davey. Even when she'd been nothing more than a puddle of uncertainty balled up on the cool tile of the bathroom floor. Every time she got dressed, Emily put her mask into place the same way she pulled on a T-shirt.

But she'd kissed Jase like she wanted to crawl inside his body, then pleaded for a job as if he was her only hope in the world.

When she'd left behind her life in Boston, she'd promised herself she would never depend on a man again. She'd create a life standing on her own two feet, strong and sure.

But maybe strong and sure came after the first wobbly baby step. Maybe...

Forget the self-reflection. Right now she needed a job.

Her pause had been too long, and Jase pulled back his hand, his brown eyes shuttering. She snatched the key at the last moment and squeezed her fingers around it. The metal was warm from his skin and she clutched it to her stomach. "I'll be here in the morning," she told him and with a quick nod to Mari, ducked out of the office before he could change his mind.

A job. She had a job.

She took a deep breath of the sweet pine air. The smell of the forest surrounding Crimson always made her think of her childhood. But now as she walked down the sidewalk crowded with tourists, the town seemed a little brighter than it had been when she'd first returned.

A text came through from her mother, telling her Davey had fallen asleep on the couch so Emily should take her time returning home. What would she do without her mom?

She hated asking for help when Meg had recently come through her own health scare, but her mother insisted she loved spending time with her grandson.

Baby steps. A job. Davey starting kindergarten. After things were settled, Emily could think about finding a place of her own. Jase hadn't mentioned a salary, and she didn't care. The job was enough.

The weather was perfect, brilliant blue skies, bright sun and a warm breeze blowing wisps of hair across her cheek. She shrugged out of the suit jacket and folded it over her arm. Just as she walked by a small café, her stomach grumbled.

When was the last time she'd eaten at a restaurant? Not since leaving Boston and then it was always for some law firm party or campaign event. She and Henry hadn't gone on a proper date since their honeymoon. Here in Crimson, Davey liked the quiet and routine of her mother's house.

She sent a quick text to her mom and walked into the restaurant. It was new in town, which she hoped meant unfamiliar people. This space had been a small clothing store the last time she'd been in Crimson. The inside was packed, and she wondered if she'd even get a table in the crowded dining room. It was a disappointment, but not a surprise, when the hostess told her there was nothing available. Just as she turned to leave, someone called her name.

A woman with flaming red hair was waving at her from a booth near the front window.

"You're Emily, right?" the woman asked as she stepped closer. "You must think I'm a crazy stalker, but I recognize you from the Fourth of July Festival. I'm April Sanders, a friend of Katie's."

"The yoga teacher out at Crimson Ranch?"

April nodded. "I got the last empty booth. No pressure, but you're welcome to join me."

Emily thought about declining. She knew Katie had a big group of friends. Hell, everyone in town loved her future sister-in-law. But even though she'd grown up in Crimson, Emily had no one. That's the way she'd wanted it since she got back to town. It was simpler, less mess.

But now the thought of a full meal with adult conversation actually appealed to her. So did spending time with April. The woman was a few years older than Emily but with her gorgeous copper hair and bright green eyes, she looked like she just stepped off the pages of a mountain resort catalog. "Are you sure you don't mind?"

"I'd love it," April said, gesturing to the empty banquette across from her. "It feels strange to be eating alone when there's a crowd waiting for tables."

Emily slid into the booth. "Thank you."

A waitress came by the table almost immediately with a glass of water and another menu. Thankfully, the young woman was a stranger to Emily.

"Are you interested in staying incognito?" April asked when they were alone again. "You looked terrified the waitress might recognize you."

Emily blew out a breath. "I don't have the best reputation in town."

"A sordid past?" April leaned forward and lifted her delicate brows. "Do tell."

"Nothing exciting," Emily answered with a laugh. "Simple story of me thinking I was better than I should have as a girl. Life has a way of slapping you down if you get too big for your britches." She shrugged. "People in small towns like to bear witness to it."

"Life throws out curveballs whether you're big or small," April agreed.

The waitress returned to the table and, as she took April's order, Emily studied the other woman. April wore no makeup but her fair skin was smooth, and her body fit under a soft pink T-shirt. She looked natural and fresh—perfect for Crimson. After Emily ordered, April smiled. "I met your mom a couple of times at Katie's bakery. She's lovely."

Emily nodded. "One of the most amazing women I know."

"How is she feeling?"

"She gets tired more quickly, but otherwise is back to her normal self. We were lucky the tumor was benign and they could remove it without damaging any other part of her brain."

"She was lucky to have you and Noah come back to help her."

"I wouldn't have been any other place but by her side. That's what family is for, you know?"

"I've heard," April answered softly. "My friend Sara is the closest thing I have to family."

Sara Travers, who ran the guest ranch outside town with her husband, Josh, had moved to Crimson a couple years ago from Los Angeles. Sara had been a famous child star and still acted when the right project came along. Otherwise, she and Josh—a Crimson native and one of Noah's good friends—spent their time managing Crimson Ranch. "Did you come to Crimson with Sara?"

April nodded. "We didn't plan on staying, but then she met Josh and..."

"The rest is history?"

"She had a tough couple of years and deserves this happiness."

"If my brother is any indication, Crimson is *the* place for happy endings." She smiled. "Have you found your happy-ever-after here?"

"It's a good place to build a life," April said and Emily realized the words weren't an answer to the question.

"Or rebuild a life." The waitress brought their orders, a club sandwich for Emily and a salad for April. Emily leaned across the table. "I like you and I appreciate the invitation to lunch, but after seeing what you eat I'm not sure we can be friends." She pointed to the bowl of dark greens. "Your salad is so healthy I feel guilty picking up a fry from my plate. You don't even have dressing."

The willowy redhead stared at her a long moment and Emily did a mental eye roll. She had the uncanny ability to offend without meaning to by tossing off comments before she thought about them. Her family was used to it and she'd managed to tame the impulse during her marriage but now...

April burst out laughing. "You remind me of Sara. She gives me grief about how I eat, too. I've always been healthy but became more diligent about what I put in my body when I was diagnosed with breast cancer a few years ago."

Emily thumped her palm against her forehead. "Now I feel like an even bigger jerk."

"Don't," April said, still smiling. "I've been cancer-free for over five years."

"My dad died when I was in high school. Pancreatic cancer." She took a bite of sandwich, swallowing around the emotions that always bubbled to the surface when she thought about her father. "I still miss him."

"It's difficult for you being back in Crimson."

"I thought I'd made a life beyond this little town. Returning to Colorado has been an adjustment."

April snagged a fry and popped it in her mouth. "So is divorce."

"Are you…"

"My ex-husband left me during my cancer treatments," April answered. She shrugged. "He couldn't handle me being sick."

"Jerk," Emily muttered.

"And yours?"

"Another jerk." Emily pushed her plate closer to the center of the table, a silent invitation for April to take another fry. When she did, Emily figured this friendship might stand a chance. "I was the one who did the leaving, but it was because my ex couldn't handle that our son wasn't the child he expected or wanted. Henry needed everything to appear perfect, and I bought into the lie."

"And lost yourself in the process?" April's voice was gentle, as if she'd had experience in that area.

Emily bit down on her lip, then nodded.

"I don't have the same history with this town as you, but I can tell you it's a good place to rediscover who you are." April nabbed another fry. "Also to reinvent yourself."

"Is that what you've done?"

"I'm working on it. In addition to Crimson Ranch, I also teach yoga at a studio on the south side of town. You should come in for a class." April leaned closer. "I like you, but I'm not sure I can be friends with someone whose shoulders are so stiff they look like they could crack in half."

Emily laughed, feeling lighter than she had in months. "I may," she told April. "If only to support a friend."

April held up her water glass. "Here's to new friends and new beginnings."

Chapter 5

Jase walked toward the front door of his office at 8:05 the following morning. His tie was slung over his shoulder, his hair still damp from the quick shower he'd taken, but he'd made it almost on time.

Downtown was quiet this early in the morning, one shopkeeper sweeping the sidewalk in front of his store as another arranged a rack of sale clothes. Life Is Sweet bakery would be crowded, so Jase hadn't bothered to stop for his daily dose of caffeine.

He'd been second-, third-and fourth-guessing his decision to offer Emily a job since the words had left his mouth yesterday. He wasn't sure how he was going to handle being so close to her every day, especially when she'd told him their kiss had been a mistake. But he'd also woken up with a sense of anticipation he hadn't felt in years. Not much else could ensure that he was *almost* on time.

He opened the door, then stopped short, checking his

watch to make sure he hadn't lost a full day somewhere.
The entire space had been transformed. The reception desk
was clear other than the papers stacked neatly to one side.
The wood furniture in the waiting area had been polished,
and the top of the coffee table held a selection of magazines. There was even a plant—one that was green and
healthy—on the end table next to the row of chairs where
clients waited.

He caught the faint scent of lemon mixed with the richer
smell of fresh coffee. His office hadn't looked this good
in all the years he'd been here. There was a freshness to
the space, as if it had been aired out like a favorite quilt.

He was still taking it all in when Emily appeared from
the hallway.

"I hope you don't mind," she said, almost shyly. "I
started cleaning up before we talked about how you wanted
it done."

He rubbed a hand over his jaw, realizing in his haste to
be on time he'd forgotten to shave this morning. "I didn't
even know it needed to be done. Are you some kind of a
witch who can wiggle her nose and make things happen?"
He shook his head. "Because I'm five minutes late and what
you've done here looks like it took hours." He glanced at
the closed door to his office.

"I didn't touch anything in there. Yet." She reached behind her and shook out her loose bun, blond hair falling
over her shoulders. Jase was momentarily mesmerized,
but then she gathered the strands and refastened the bun.
"I came in early," she told him, moving to stand behind the
receptionist's desk.

"How early?"

She moved the stack of papers from one side of the desk
to the other before meeting his gaze. "Around five thirty."

"In the morning?" he choked out. "Why were you awake at that time?"

"I don't sleep much," she said with a shrug. "I've gone through the filing system Donna set up and think I understand how it works. We need to talk about how you record billable hours."

He stepped close enough to the desk that his thighs brushed the dark wood. "We need to talk about you not sleeping. How often does that happen?"

"A few times a week," she said quietly. "It's no big deal."

"How many times is a few?"

Her mouth pressed into a thin line. "Why do you care, Jase?"

"How many?"

"Most nights," she answered through clenched teeth. "My doctor in Boston gave me a prescription for pills to help, but I haven't refilled it since I've been back. Davey had trouble adjusting when we first got here, and I wanted to hear him if he needed me."

"And now?"

She shrugged. "I watch him sleep. He's so peaceful, and it makes me happy. This morning my mom's schedule allowed her to watch him for me when he woke up, so I came into the office to get a few things done." She looked up at him, her gaze wary. He noticed something more now, the shadows under her eyes and the tension bracketing her mouth. It didn't lessen her beauty or her effect on him, but he kicked himself that he hadn't seen it before. This woman was exhausted.

"You didn't have to do this," he said, gesturing to the shiny clean space. "But I'm glad you did."

She rewarded him with a small smile. "It was a pit in here, Jase. It's like you don't even care."

"I do care," he argued. "I care about my clients and this town. So what if the office isn't spotless?"

"You're a business owner and you're running for mayor. People have expectations."

He choked out a laugh. "Tell me about it." He didn't mind taking grief from her because the brightness had returned to her gaze. The Emily he remembered from high school had been so sure of herself and her place in this world. She'd held on to that pretense since returning to Crimson, but the more time he spent with her the more he could see the fragile space between the cracks in her armor. A part of him wanted to rip away all of her defenses because they were guarding things that held her heart captive. But he hated seeing her troubled and knew she hated revealing any weakness.

"Thank you for this job. I know you didn't want to hire me."

No. He wanted to kiss her and hold her and take care of her. The kissing and holding weren't going to be helped by working with her, but he could take care of her and that was a start.

"You were right," he admitted. "I needed help. There are too many things on my plate right now, so I've been ignoring the office. It's starting to show in my work, and that's not going to help anyone."

"The town loves you. They'll cut you some slack."

"They love what I do for them."

"You do too much."

He shook his head. "There's no such thing. Not for someone with my history."

"The Crenshaw family history isn't yours, Jase. The weight of a generations-old reputation shouldn't rest on one man's shoulders."

If only that were true. "My dad isn't going to help carry

the load." He didn't want to talk about this. Emily was here so he could help her, not the other way around. "I have to be at the courthouse at nine, so we should talk about what else needs to be done. I'm going to get a cup of coffee first, and you're an angel for making it. For all of this. Thank you, Em."

She tapped one finger on the screen of the desktop computer. "Eight thirty."

"Already?" He glanced at his watch.

"No, you have to be at the courthouse at eight thirty." She moved around the desk, her hips swaying under the fitted cropped pants she wore. She'd paired them with a thin cotton sweater in a pale yellow along with black heels. It was more casual than yesterday but still professional. "I'll get your coffee."

"You don't have to—"

"I want to." She tipped up her chin, as if daring him to contradict her. "So you can get ready to go."

Before he could argue, she disappeared around the corner.

This place wasn't good enough for someone like Emily. His office, even though it was clean, was too shabby for her crisp elegance. He imagined that she'd fit perfectly into the upper echelons of Boston society. Emily looked like a lady who lunched, a fancy wife who could chair events and fund-raisers and never have a hair out of place. Yet as he followed her, he watched wisps of blond hair try to escape from the knot at the back of her head.

She poured coffee into a travel mug, and Jase was momentarily distracted by the fact that the clean dishes and coffee mugs were put away on the shelf above the utility sink.

Emily turned, thrusting the stainless steel mug toward him. Her fingers were pink from the water and had several paper cuts on the tips. Not as delicate as she looked, his Emily.

No. Not his. Not even for a minute.

But she was here. Although he'd done her a favor, he needed her. He wanted her. Any way he could have her.

"You're welcome in my office while I'm gone." He brushed a lock of hair behind her ear and felt a small amount of satisfaction when she sucked a breath. "I should be back by noon."

"You have a meeting with Toby Jenkins here at one thirty."

He nodded, thankful he'd set up the calendars on his cell phone and office computers to sync automatically. He was in the habit of entering meetings in his calendar, but that didn't mean he remembered to check it every day.

"I told my mom I'd be home by two today. Davey still naps in the afternoons, and I like to be there when he wakes up."

"I can pick up lunch on my way back. Any requests?"

"You don't need to—"

"It's the least I can do, Emily. The way you transformed the office went beyond anything Donna could have done. It feels good not to be surrounded by my usual mess."

One side of her mouth curved. "I'm glad to be useful."

What had her ex-husband done to beat down the spirited girl he'd known into this brittle, unsure woman? Jase wasn't a fighter, but he would have liked to punch Henry Whitaker.

Instead, he gave Emily a reassuring smile. "You're the best."

Her smile dimmed, but before he could figure out why, she tapped her watch. "You need to go or you're going to be late."

"They're used to me being late."

"Not with me running the show." She pointed to the door. "Now go. I've got your inner sanctum to tackle."

He laughed, then wished her luck and headed back out into the bright sunshine. It was the best start to a morning he'd had in ages.

By the time he parked in front of his father's trailer a few minutes before noon, Jase's mood had disintegrated into a black hole of frustration. Even though he expected it from Emily's text, seeing the Crawfords' 4Runner at the side of the mobile home only made it worse.

He didn't want Emily here. This part of his life was private, protected. Most people in town knew his father, or knew of him if they'd lived in Crimson long enough. But even as a kid, Jase had never let anyone visit the run-down home where he'd lived. Not even Noah.

He stood on the crumbling front step for a moment trying to rein in his clamoring emotions. Then he heard Emily's laughter spill out from the open window and pushed through the door.

Her back was to him as she faced the tiny counter in the kitchen. "Canned spaghetti is not real food," she said with another laugh.

"It's real food if I eat it and like it," his dad growled in response, but there was humor in his tone. His father sat in one of the rickety wooden chairs at the table. He watched Emily like she was some sort of mystical being come to life inside his tumbledown home.

"I'm not a great cook," she shot back, "but even I can make homemade meatballs. I'll teach you." He could see she was dumping the can of bright red sauce and pasta into a ceramic bowl.

"If we're having Italian night," his dad said, pronouncing Italian with a long *I*, "you'd best bring a bottle of wine with you."

Jase let the door slam shut at that moment. Emily whirled to face him, her smile fading as she took in his expression. Declan shifted in the chair, his own smile growing wider.

"Just in time for lunch," his dad said, even though he knew how much Jase hated any food that came from a can.

"How was the courthouse?" Emily covered the bowl with a paper towel and put it in the microwave shoved in the corner of the counter.

Taking a breath, he caught Emily's scent overlaid with the stale smell of the trailer. The combination was an assault on his senses. The hold he had on his emotions unleashed as he stalked forward, shouldering Emily out of the way to punch in a minute on the microwave timer. "What the hell are you doing here?" he asked, crowding her against the kitchen sink.

"My fault," his father said from behind him. "I forgot I had a doctor's appointment this morning. When you didn't answer your cell phone, I called the office. Emily explained you were unavailable but was nice enough to drive me."

Jase looked over his shoulder. "You should have rescheduled the appointment."

"It wasn't a problem," Emily said. "Your office was organized and I—"

"I offered you a job as a legal secretary," he bit out. "That's work with professional boundaries. Inserting yourself into my personal life isn't part of the job description."

Those blue eyes that had been so warm and full of life iced over in a second. He expected her to argue but instead her lips pressed together and a moment later she whispered, "My bad. Won't happen again."

"Jase, what's crawled up your butt?" his dad asked, his

voice booming in the tense silence that had descended be-tween him and Emily.

She lifted one eyebrow. "I'm not going to stick around to find out." Skirting around him, she gave Declan a quick hug. "Enjoy your spaghetti. I'm going to hold you to that cooking lesson. But grape juice, no wine."

"Thank you, darlin'." His dad's voice softened. "You're a good girl. I'm sorry about this."

"It's not on you," she whispered.

Jase didn't turn around, his hands pressed hard to the scarred Formica. He heard the creak of the door as it opened and shut, not the angry bang he expected but a soft click that tore a hole in his gut. Still he didn't move.

The chair scraped as his father stood. He moved behind Jase to take the bowl out of the microwave. For several min-utes the only sound was the spoon clinking and the rustle of a newspaper.

"She doesn't belong here," Jase said finally, rubbing his hand over his face as he turned. "Emily works for me now. That's all, Dad. She isn't part of this."

"That girl has been a part of you for years," Declan an-swered, setting down the spoon in the empty bowl.

Jase felt his eyes widen before he could stop the reaction. He'd never talked to anyone, especially his father, about his feelings for Emily. He understood Noah knew but had never spoken it aloud.

"I'm a bad drunk," Declan said with a shrug. "But I was never blind, and you're my son. I know you better than you think."

"Emily's in a rough place now. I'm helping her get back on her feet. That's all."

"You're embarrassed about me and how you grew up."

Another bit of unspoken knowledge better left in the

shadows. "You're in a better place, Dad. I'm proud of you for staying sober."

Declan choked out a laugh. "I'm the one who's proud, Jase. But you take on too much that isn't yours. My reputation and our family history. The way you were raised. You've overcome a lot, and you don't need to be ashamed of it. You don't have to make it all better."

Jase thought about his ancestor's picture in the town jail and how he wanted his family legacy to be something more than it was. "If you won't let me move you to a better house, I respect that decision. But I don't want her here. You need to respect that."

"From what I can tell, Emily Crawford is plenty capable of making her own decisions."

But she was *working* for him now. It was what she'd wanted, and it changed things. Not his need or desire, but his inclination to act on it. "Her name is Emily *Whitaker*, Dad. She was married. She has a son. Neither one of us is who we were before."

His father smiled. "I think that's the point."

Chapter 6

Emily looked up from the old rocker on her mother's front porch at the sound of a car coming down the gravel driveway. It was almost nine at night, and Davey had been asleep close to an hour.

She hadn't expected her mother to return from her date with Max Moore so soon. But when Emily recognized Jase's Jeep, her first inclination was to run to the house and shut the door.

He'd hurt her today, and she hated that anyone—any man—had the power to do that. While she understood that Jase's reaction had been about his own issues, a part of her still took the blame he'd placed on her. Her faults sometimes felt so obvious it was easy to hold herself accountable for any perceived slight. Flawed as she might be, Emily had never been a coward.

So she remained on the rocker, her legs curled under the thin blanket she'd brought out to ward off the evening chill of the high mountains. Although she couldn't concentrate on the actual words, she kept her eyes trained on the e-reader in her lap as a door slammed shut and the heavy footfall of boots sounded on the steps.

"What are you reading?"

She ran one finger over the screen of the e-reader but didn't answer.

"You can ignore me," he said as he sank into the chair next to her, "but I won't go away."

"There's always hope," she quipped, her fingers gripping the leather cover of the e-reader tighter at his soft chuckle.

They sat in silence for a minute, and Emily's grasp began to relax. As if sensing it he said, "I'm sorry, Em."

"It's fine," she lied. "Point taken. I overstepped the bounds." There she went, instinctively making his mistake her fault.

"My reaction wasn't about you. What you did for my dad today was kind. It made him happier than I've seen him in a long time to have a beautiful woman caring for him."

"No big deal."

"Don't do that." His hand was around her wrist, warmth seeping through the fleece sweatshirt she'd pulled on when the sun disappeared behind the mountain. "It was special to him, and it should have been to me, as well." He stood, releasing her, and paced to the edge of the porch. "I love my father, but I hate the man he was when I was younger. He was mean and embarrassing. Everyone knew the problems he had, but that didn't stop me from being humiliated when I'd have to get him home after a night at the bars."

She could see the tension in his shoulders as he gazed out into the darkening night. "He showed up one year for a parent-teacher conference so drunk he ended up puking all over the first-floor bathroom. I never let him come to another school function."

She flipped closed the cover of her e-reader, her heart already melting for this man's pain. "Jase—"

He turned to her, folded his arms across his chest. "It killed me to live in that trailer growing up. The only saving grace was that no one but me had to see him at his worst. Even Noah, all the times he picked me up, has never been inside. That place represents my greatest shame, and my dad refuses to move. To see you there with all of the memories that seem to seep out of the walls to choke me... I couldn't stand it. It felt like you'd be contaminated by it."

Emily stood, placed the blanket and e-reader on the chair and walked toward him.

Jase shook his head. "You're too good for that, Em. Too good for him. I'm sorry I lashed out, but I still hate that you—that anyone—has seen that piece of who I am."

"No." She stepped into his space until she could feel his breath whispering over the top of her head. "You're too good to give in to that shame. Where you came from doesn't change who you are now."

"Are you kidding?" He didn't move away from her but leaned back against the porch rail as if he needed space. "That trailer and what it represents *made* me who I am. The night in my front yard, you said I was perfect, and I know what my reputation is around town. Nice Jase. Sweet Jase. Perfect Jase. No one sees anything else because I don't let them. Everyone thinks I work so damn hard despite my family's reputation in Crimson. I work hard *because* of where I came from. Because I'm scared to death if I don't, the poison that has crushed the self-respect of so many people in my family will take me down, too."

Something dark and dangerous flashed in his eyes and

she saw who he was under the Mr. Perfect veneer he'd spent years polishing to a bright shine. He was a man at the edge of his control and a part of her wanted him to shuck off his restraint. With her. Yes. She could handle it. She would welcome whatever he had to offer.

He blinked, and the moment was gone. His chest rose and fell like he'd sprinted up Crimson Mountain. She placed her hand on it, fingers splayed, and felt his heartbeat thrumming under her touch. "You aren't your father." She said the words softly and felt his breath hitch. "I know what it's like to want to prove something so badly it makes you into someone you're not. Someone fake and false. You're real, Jase. Not perfect. Real."

"I'm sorry," he said again, lifting his palm to press it over her hand. "For what I said and how I treated you."

She let a small smile curve her lips. "I think this makes us even."

"You did good today. In my office and with my dad. Thank you."

This was the part where she should step away. If they were even, it was a fresh start. But she couldn't force herself to move. Emily might not believe in perfect, but she had learned to appreciate real. The knowledge that Jase was different than she'd assumed both humbled and excited her. Of all people, she should have known not to judge a person by who they were on the outside. She'd built an entire life on outward impressions only to watch it crumble around her.

The connection she felt with Jase, her awareness of him, suddenly flared to life stronger than it had before. She moved her hand up his chest and around to the back of his neck. At the same time she lifted onto her tiptoes so she could press her mouth to his. He tasted like night air and mint gum, and she loved how much he could communicate simply through the pressure of his mouth on hers.

He angled his head and ran his tongue across her bottom lip. His hands came to rest on her hips, pulling her closer until the front of her was plastered against him. Unlike other men she'd known, he didn't rush the kiss. It was as if learning her bit by bit was enough for him. He savored every taste, trailing kisses along her jaw before nipping at her earlobe.

"Your ears are sensitive," he whispered when she moaned softly. His breath feathered against her skin. "You touch them when you're nervous."

"I don't," she started to argue, then he bit down on the lobe again and she squirmed. "You're observant," she amended.

"I want more. I want to know everything about you," he said and claimed her mouth again.

Her brain was fuzzy but the meaning of his words penetrated the fog of desire after a few moments. "No." She lifted her head and tried to step away but he held her steady.

"Why?" A kiss against her jaw.

"I can't think when you do that."

"Then I'll do it more."

She opened her mouth to argue, and he took the opportunity to deepen the kiss. One thing she'd say for Jase Crenshaw—the man was persistent. Even though she knew she should stop it, she gave in to the need building inside her. Her body sang with desire, tremors skittering over her skin. Jase ran his fingers up under the hem of her sweatshirt and across her spine. Everywhere he touched her Emily burned. Her breasts were heavy and sensitive where they rubbed against his T-shirt and she wanted more.

So much more.

So much it scared her into action. As Jase's hands moved to the front of her waist and brushed the swell of her breasts, she wrenched away from him. With unsteady hands, she grabbed on to the front porch rail to prevent herself from moving back to the warmth she already missed.

"We've determined I'm not perfect," Jase said, his tone a mix of amusement and frustration. "So what's the problem now?"

"I work for you."

"Are you asking to be fired?"

She glanced at him and saw he was teasing. Her shoulders relaxed. "I don't want to complicate things, Jase. I know you gave me the job because you felt sorry for me and this…" She pointed between the two of them. "Would only muddy the waters more."

"I don't feel sorry for you." He came closer and she didn't resist when he cupped her face in his hands. "I respect you, and I want you. But neither of those emotions involves pity."

"Why are you running for mayor?"

His hands dropped to his sides. "I think I can help the town move forward. I've been on city council long enough to understand what needs to be done and—"

"You have a responsibility," she finished for him.

"You say that like it's a bad thing."

"It's not, but your life is filled with obligations. I don't want to be another one."

"You're—"

"I'd like to be your friend."

He stared at her for several seconds, then blew out a breath. "I'd like that, too, but it doesn't have to mean—"

"Yes, it does," she interrupted, not bothering to hide

her smile at the crushed puppy-dog look of disappointment he gave her.

With a small nod, he moved around her. "Good night, Emily."

"Good night, Jase." She watched his taillights disappear into the darkness, then turned for the house. For the first time in forever, she fell asleep within minutes of her head hitting the pillow.

Friday morning, Jase walked the three blocks from his office to the Crimson Community Center and thought about how nice it was not to be rushing through town. He was speaking to the downtown business coalition and probably would have been late for the meeting if Emily hadn't shoved him out the door.

She was a stickler for punctuality, something that had never been a strength of his. He cared about being on time, but he often got so lost in whatever he was doing that he stopped paying attention to anything else. She hadn't been in the office yesterday, and despite how organized she'd left things on Wednesday, he'd found he missed knowing she was sharing his space.

She was a distraction but the best kind possible, and now he spent the minutes going over what he planned to say to the group of business owners. Ever since Emily had asked the question, Jase had been pondering the answer to why he was running for mayor. It wasn't as if he didn't have enough to keep him busy with his law practice.

He came around the corner and noticed Mari pacing in front of the entrance to the community center. Automatically he checked his watch, since his one campaign worker tended to pace when she was anxious.

"We have a problem," she said, adjusting her heavy-rimmed glasses as she strode toward him.

He held up his hands. "I'm not scheduled to speak for another ten minutes. It's good."

"Your opponent got here first," she answered, shaking her head. "It's *really* bad, Jase."

"What opponent?"

"Charles Thompson."

Jase's stomach dropped to the pavement like a cement brick. "Charles Thompson isn't running for mayor. I'm un-opposed in the election."

"Not anymore. He has the signatures he needs to put his name on the ballot and filed as a candidate with the court-house before yesterday's deadline. I don't understand why he's doing this."

"Because it's me." Jase rubbed a hand over his eyes. "Charles has been at loose ends since he retired as sheriff. I bet my dad called and rubbed the election in his face. If there's anything the Thompsons can't stand, it's a Cren-shaw getting ahead."

"That's plain spiteful."

Spiteful and stupid and why was he doing this again? Because he owed it to the town? Because he had some-thing to prove?

"You have to get in there and prove you're a better can-didate." Mari tugged on his arm, but Jase stood his ground. He didn't want to face Charles and everything the older man knew about his childhood. If there was one person who knew where all the Crenshaw skeletons were hidden, it was Charles Thompson. "Jase, let's go."

He could walk away right now, withdraw his candidacy. Charles would be a fine mayor, maybe even better than Jase. The older man had nothing but time to devote to the job. But if Jase won, maybe he could stop trying so hard to make amends for a past he didn't own. Perhaps it would finally be enough—he would be enough—to excise the ghosts of his past.

Jase wasn't his father or any of the infamous men in his family. He'd paid more than his dues; he'd tried to atone for every sin committed by someone with the last name Crenshaw. Now was his time to bury the past for good. He couldn't walk away.

Taking a deep breath, he straightened his tie and smoothed his fingers over the hair curling at the nape of his neck. A haircut was still on the to-do list, right after fighting for his right to lead this town.

He followed Mari into the crowded meeting room where Charles Thompson stood at the podium. A ruthless light snapped in his eyes as he met Jase's gaze over the heads of the members of the coalition. Jase knew he had friends in this room, but facing Sheriff Thompson turned him into the scared, cowering boy he'd been years ago. He'd dreaded seeing the patrol car parked in front of his dad's trailer and knowing what it meant.

Those days were a distant memory for most people, De-clan Crenshaw having faded into the background of the Crimson community. But for Jase they were like a razor across an open wound—raw and painful.

"My esteemed opponent has arrived," Charles announced into the microphone, his deep voice booming through the room.

People in the audience turned to where Jase stood at the back and he forced a neutral look on his face. He made eye contact with a couple of friends, Katie Garrity, who was representing her bakery, and Josh Travers from Crimson

Ranch. Katie gave him a sympathetic smile and Josh looked almost as angry as Jase felt.

Their support bolstered his confidence but his courage took a nosedive at Thompson's next words. "Come on up here, boy," Charles said, his gaze boring in Jase's taught nerves. "I want to talk to you about the future of this town and family values."

Jase banged through the front door of his office an hour after he'd left, holding on to his temper by the thinnest thread. Emily jumped in her chair, glancing up from the computer screen.

"How did it go?"

"Fine," he bit out, not stopping. He could feel the mask he wore beginning to crumble and needed the safety of being behind a closed door when it did. "I have a meeting with Morris Anderson at eleven. Let me know when he gets here."

He dropped his briefcase on the floor, slammed his office door shut behind him and stalked to the window behind his desk, trying to get his breathing under control as he stared out to the parking lot in back of the building.

"All those slamming doors don't sound like *fine* to me."

He didn't bother turning at Emily's cool voice behind him. "Do you understand what a closed door means?" he asked.

"Better than you'd imagine," she answered with a small laugh. "But in this case, I don't care. Either you tell me what happened at the meeting, or I can call Katie. Which do you prefer?"

Jase closed his eyes and concentrated on making his lungs move air in and out. He knew there were no secrets in Crimson, at least not for long. His phone had started ringing and beeping with incoming calls and texts as soon as he walked out of the community center.

"Charles Thompson is running against me for mayor. He announced his candidacy to the downtown coalition this morning."

She didn't say anything, and Jase finally turned. Emily stood just inside the doorway to his office. After his secretary retired, Jase convinced himself that he preferred running the entire office on his own. So much of his life was filled with people and responsibility. This space had become a sanctuary of sorts, a place where he was in total control. He answered to no one.

In only a few days, Emily's presence had become the answer to a secret need he didn't know how to voice. Not only was she organized and efficient, but she breathed new life into an existence that had become so predictable Jase couldn't seem to force its path out of the familiar ruts.

This morning she wore a simple cotton dress with a light sweater thrown over her shoulders and strappy sandals. Her hair was held back with a clip but the length of it tumbled over her shoulders. The scent of her shampoo mixed with perfume tangled in the air, and Jase had noticed on Wednesday the hint of it lingered even after she left for the day.

"So what?" she asked when he finally met her gaze. "You've done more for this town than Charles Thompson. People love you."

He shook his head. "He was sheriff," he told her, as if that explained everything. The word *sheriff* captured the past Jase had worked so hard to bury under the duty and responsibility he shouldered in town.

"You've been the de facto leader on town council for several years. Noah told me you were instrumental in convincing Liam Donovan to move his company's headquarters to Crimson."

She stepped farther into the room and, like he was magnetized, Jase moved around the desk toward her. Toward the certainty of her unmistakable beauty and the sound of her voice. Maybe if he listened to her long enough, he could believe in himself the way she seemed to.

"From what I remember, Thompson was a decent sheriff, but this town has never had a big problem with crime. Business and keeping things moving forward have been a struggle for some of the older generation. Things are different now than when I left, and people say you're the reason."

If only it were that simple. "He knows everything about me."

Her delicate brows came down, as if she couldn't understand the significance of what he was saying.

"Charles ran the department when we were kids," he explained. "During the time when my grandpa died and Mom left with Sierra. My dad was still working at the mine, and he was at his lowest. It was worse than anyone knows." He paused, cleared his throat to expel the emotions threatening his airways. "Except Charles. He knows every sordid detail."

"That past has nothing to do with you."

"That past *is* me," he argued.

She shook her head. "Charles can't use anything he knows because of his position as sheriff in this election."

"He already has. Most of what he talked about at today's meeting was family values. He had his wife of thirty-four years and his two sons sitting in the front row. Hell, Miriam brought muffins to hand out."

"You want muffins? Katie will make you dozens of

them. We can hand out baked goods to every voter in this town."

"That's not the point. You know how perception plays into politics. He's sowed the seeds of doubt about me. Now people will start talking…about me and my family and our history in Crimson."

"They'll understand he's running a smear campaign."

"No, they won't." He ran his hands through his hair, squeezed shut his eyes. "He was so smooth. Charles actually talked about how much he admired me, how much I'd overcome. He claimed he'd always felt protective of me because my mother abandoned me and my dad was so messed up. Would you believe he even compared me to his own sons?"

"Aaron and Todd?" Emily snorted. "Those two caused more trouble as teens than anyone else in the school. I haven't seen Todd, but from what I can tell, Aaron hasn't changed a bit. He's still a big bully. I don't know how many times I have to say no to a date before he quits calling me."

"He's calling you?" As angry as Jase was about Charles, temper of a different sort flared to the surface of his skin, hot and prickly. It was almost a relief to channel his frustration toward something outside himself. Something he could control. Above all else, Jase understood the value of control. "I'll take care of it."

"Hold on there, Hero-man. I don't need you to handle Aaron for me. I can take care of annoying jerks all on my own."

"You can handle everything, right?"

He regretted the rude question as soon as it was out of his mouth. Emily should snap back at him because he was lashing out at her with no cause. Instead, she flashed him a saucy grin. "Takes one to know one."

The smile, so unexpected and undeserved, diffused most of his anger, leaving him with a heaping pile of steaming self-doubt. He sat on the edge of his desk and leaned forward, hands on his knees.

"I'm sorry. I know you can take care of yourself." His chin dropped to his chest and he stared at the small stain peeking out from under one of the chairs in front of the desk. "But it's a lot easier to worry about other people than think of how quickly my own life is derailing."

A moment later he felt cool fingers brush away the hair from his forehead. He wanted to lean into her touch but forced himself to remain still. "Did you ever meet Andrew Meyer who used to run this office? I took over his practice four years ago, and I haven't changed a thing." He pushed the toe of his leather loafer against the chair leg until the stain was covered. "Not one piece of furniture or painting on the wall. You can still see the frame marks from where he took down his law school diploma and I never bothered to replace it with mine. I inherited his secretary and his clients, and I haven't lifted a finger to make this place my own. Hell, I think the magazines in the lobby are probably four years old. Maybe even older."

"I switched them for current issues," she said softly.

Her fingers continued to caress him and it felt so damn good to take a small amount of comfort from her. Too good. He lifted his head, and she dropped her hand.

"Why haven't you changed anything?" She didn't move away, and it was the hardest thing Jase had ever done not to pull her closer.

"Because this place isn't mine."

"It is," she said, her tone confused. "It's your office. Your clients. Your reputation." She laughed. "Your mortgage."

"This is the oldest law practice in the town. It was

founded in the early 1900s and passed down through the Meyer family for generations. Andrew didn't have kids, so he offered a partnership position to me when I was still in law school. He wanted a Crimson native to take over the firm. This is his legacy. Not mine."

"Jase, you are the poster child for the town's favorite son. Charles Thompson can't hold a candle to the man you've become. Whether it was despite where you came from or because of it, the truth doesn't change."

"What if who people see isn't the truth? What if I've become too good at playing the part people expect of me?"

"You don't have to reflect the town's image of you back at them. You're more than a two-dimensional projection of yourself. Show everyone who you really are."

Staring into Emily's crystal-blue eyes, it was tempting. The urge to throw it all away, create the life he wanted, curled around his senses until the freedom of it was all he could see, hear and taste. Right behind the whisper of release came a pounding, driving fear that cut him off at the knees.

Who he was, who he'd been before he'd started down the path to redeeming his family name was a lost, lonely, scared boy. The memories he'd secreted away in the parts of his soul where he didn't dare look threatened to overtake him.

He stood abruptly, sending Emily stumbling back a few steps. "I'm going to win this election. I need people to see the best version of me, not the grubby kid Charles remembers."

Her eyes were soft. "Jase."

"I've worked toward this for years. It's what people expect…" He paused, took a breath. "It's what I want."

"Are you sure?"

"Charles isn't right for this. I'm going to be mayor."

She placed a light hand on his arm. "I'm going to help you."

He looked at her elegant fingers wrapped around his shirtsleeve. "Because you work for me."

"Because we're friends."

His eyes drifted shut for a moment. "Right. I forgot."

He felt a poke at his ribs. "Liar."

She had no idea. "I saw Katie at the meeting," he told her, needing to lighten the mood. He was too raw to go down that road with Emily. As much as he craved her kiss, he couldn't touch her again and not reveal the depth of his feelings. He thought he could control how much he needed her, but not when he was carrying his heart in his hands, ready to offer it to her if she asked. "She asked about plans for the bachelor and bachelorette parties."

Emily pulled a face. "No strippers."

He laughed in earnest. "I wasn't even thinking that."

"All men think that."

"You've got the whole male population figured out?"

"Like I said before, you're not complicated."

When it came to Emily, he wished it were true. His feelings for the woman standing in front of him had been simple for years. He wanted her. An unattainable crush. Unrequited love. End of story.

But a new chapter had started since she'd returned to town, and it was tangled in ways Jase couldn't take the time to unravel. Not if he was going to stay the course to his duty to Crimson.

"Then we're talking beer and poker night?"

Emily opened her mouth, then glanced over her shoulder as the door to the outer office opened. "Your appointment's here."

"Admit it, you like beer and poker."

She shook her head. "Come over for dinner tonight and

we'll brainstorm better options." Her hand flew to cover her mouth as if she was shocked she'd extended the invitation.

"Yes," he said before she could retract the offer. "What time?"

Emily blinked. "Six."

"I'll be there."

"Jason, are you here?" a frail voice yelled from the front office.

"In my office, Mr. Anderson," Jase called. "Come on back."

"I should go...um..."

"Finish editing the brief I gave you?" Jase suggested, keeping his expression solemn.

"Exactly," she agreed.

As Morris Anderson tottered into the room, Emily said hello to the older man and disappeared.

"That Meg Crawford's girl?" Morris asked after she'd gone. Morris was here to revise the terms of his will, which he did on a monthly basis just to keep his four children on their toes.

Jase nodded, taking a seat behind his desk.

"I went to school with her grandmother back in the day. Spunky little thing."

"Good to know where Emily gets it." Jase pulled out Morris's bulging file. "Who made you angry this month?"

"Who didn't make me angry?" Morris asked through a coughing fit. "My kids are ungrateful wretches, but I love them." He pointed to the door, then to Jase. "The spunky ones are trouble," he said after a moment.

"Do you think so?" Jase felt his hackles rise. His protective inclination toward Emily was a palpable force surrounding him.

"I know so," Morris answered with a nod. "Trouble of

the best kind. A man needs a little spunk to keep things interesting."

"I'd have to agree, Mr. Anderson," he said with a smile. "I'd definitely have to agree."

Chapter 7

Emily wasn't sure how long she'd been sitting on the hallway floor when a pair of jeans and cowboy boots filled her line of sight.

"Emily?" Jase crouched down in front of her, placed a gentle hand on her knee. "What's wrong, sweetheart?"

"Nothing," she whispered. "Except dinner might be a little delayed. Sorry. I didn't realize you were here."

"I could see you through the screen door. I knocked but…"

"Hi, Jase." Davey's voice was sweet. Her boy didn't seem the least concerned to see his mother having a meltdown on the hardwood floor. "I built the space station hospital. Want to see it?"

"In a minute, buddy," Jase told him. "I'm going to hang out here with your mom first."

She tried to offer her son a smile but her face felt brittle. "Are you getting hungry, Davey?"

"Not yet." Small arms wrapped around her shoulders. "It's alright, Mama." The hug lasted only a few seconds but it was enough to send her already tattered emotions into overdrive. If her son was voluntarily giving her a hug, she must be in really bad shape.

She expelled a breath as Davey went back into the office. The tremors started along her spine but quickly spread until it felt like her whole body shook.

"Let's get you off the floor." Jase didn't wait for an answer. He scooped her into his arms and carried her toward the family room. Jase was strong and steady, the ends of his hair damp like he'd showered before coming over. She breathed in the scent of his shampoo mixed with the clean, woodsy smell she now associated with him alone. How appropriate that the man who was the poster child for Crimson would smell like the forest. As much as she wanted to sink into his embrace, Emily remained stiff against him. If she let go now, she might really lose it. "Where's your mom?"

"Book club," she managed between clenched teeth. "We should probably reschedule dinner for another night."

"I'm not leaving you like this." He deposited her onto the couch. "Not until you tell me what's going on."

Emily fought to pull herself together. She was so close to the edge it was as if she could feel the tiny spikes of hysteria pricking at the backs of her eyes. The cushions of the couch were soft and worn from years of movie nights and Sundays watching football. She wanted to curl up in a ball and ignore the constant pounding life seemed determined to serve up to her.

She couldn't look at Jase and risk him seeing the humiliation she knew was reflected in her eyes. She stood, moving around the couch in the opposite direction. The kitchen opened to the family room, separated by a half wall and the dining room table. "I'd planned to make steaks," she said quickly, ignoring the trembling in her fingers. "But I didn't get them out of the freezer, so we may be stuck with hot dogs. Do you mind turning on the grill?"

He let himself out onto the flagstone patio as she opened the pantry door and scanned the contents of the cupboard. She heard him return a few minutes later but kept her attention on the cupboard. "How do you feel about boxed mac and cheese? I don't know how Mom managed to make a home-cooked meal every night when we were younger. She worked part-time, drove us around to after-school activities, and still we had family dinners most evenings. You remember, right? She loved cooking for you and Noah."

He was standing directly behind her when she turned, close enough she was afraid he might reach for her. And if he did, she might shatter into a million tiny fragments of disappointment and regret. "I know I'm babbling. It's a coping mechanism. Give me a pass on this one, Jase."

His dark eyes never wavered. "What happened?"

Her fingers tightened on the small cardboard box so hard the corners bent. "An overreaction to some news. My meltdown is over. I'm fine."

"What news?"

"Does it matter?" She shook her head. "I lost the privilege of a major freak-out when I became a mother. Moms don't have a lot of time for wallowing when dinner is late."

"Tell me anyway."

She slammed the box of mac and cheese on the counter, then bent to grab a pot out of a lower cabinet. "I liked you better when you were nice and easygoing and not all up in my business."

Elbowing him out of the way she turned on the faucet and filled the pot with water. "Apparently, my ex-husband got remarried last weekend. One of my former friends in Boston was nice enough to text me a photo from the wedding."

She set the pot of water on the stove and turned on the burner. The poof of sound as it ignited felt like the dreams she'd had for her life. There one minute and then up in flames. "It was small—nothing like the extravaganza I planned—only family and close friends."

She laughed. "My friends are now her friends. She was a campaign worker. What a cliché." She glanced over her shoulder, unable to stop speaking once she'd started. "You know the best part? She's pregnant. A shotgun wedding for Henry Whitaker III. It's like Davey and I never existed. We're gone and he's remaking our life with someone else. Our exact damn life."

"I'm sorry."

"Don't be sorry." She ripped off the top of the box with so much force that an explosion of dried macaroni noodles spilled across the counter. "I'm not."

"You don't have to pretend with me."

"I'm not sorry, Jase. I'm mad. It's mostly self-directed. I let myself be sucked into that life. I was so busy pretending I couldn't even see Henry for who he was." She scooped up the stray noodles, dropped them in the water and then dumped the rest of the box's contents in with them. "My son has to pay the price."

"Your ex-husband is an idiot."

"To put it mildly."

"There are other words going through my mind," Jase said, his tone steely. "But I'm not going to waste my energy on a man so stupid he would let you go and give up his son because of a political image."

Emily took a deep breath and released it along with much

of her tension. "I don't miss him." It had been a shock to get the text about Henry but she hadn't been lying to Jase when she told him she was most angry at herself. "How did I marry a man who I can feel nothing but revulsion for five months after leaving him?"

"He hurt you," Jase answered simply.

"I should have seen him for who he was. My parents had a good marriage. There was so much love in this house."

He reached out, traced a fingertip along her jaw. "There was also a lot of pain when your dad died."

"Yes, and it left scars on all of us. But Noah managed to fall in love with an amazing woman. Mom is now dating someone who makes her happy. I seem to be the one with horrible taste."

Jase smiled. "Did you meet any of the women your brother dated before Katie?"

"From what I've heard, *date* is a fairly formal term for Noah's pre-Katie relationships."

"Exactly."

"He's one of the lucky ones." She sighed and stepped away from Jase. Staring into his dark eyes made her forget he wasn't for her. Jase Crenshaw was all about duty and responsibility. Whether he was willing to admit it or not, his image was a big part of his identity. He wasn't motivated by the hunger for power and prestige that had influenced her ex-husband. But it didn't change the fact he would eventually want more than Emily was willing to give.

She opened the refrigerator and grabbed a pack of hot dogs from the shelf. "Man the grill, Mr. Perfect. We're eating like kids tonight."

Jase watched her for a long, heavy moment before his lips curved into a grin. "The only thing perfect about me is my grilling skills."

She smiled in return, knowing he'd given her a pass. Maybe he'd sensed her frazzled emotions couldn't take any more deep conversation. "Let's see if your hot dogs can beat my mac and cheese."

"I'm up for the challenge," he said and let himself out onto the patio.

Alone in the kitchen, Emily went to check on her son. He was still busy with his Lego structures and she watched him for a few minutes before giving him a fifteen-minute warning for dinner. Davey's difficulty with rapid transitions had driven Henry crazy. Her ex-husband had loved sponta-neity when he wasn't working or campaigning. A game of pick up football with the neighbors, a bike ride into town for dinner or an impromptu weekend at the shore. Henry had to be moving at all times, his energy overpowering and bordering on manic.

She'd kept up with him when Davey was a baby but as the boy grew into a toddler, he liked notice if things were going to change. Henry had never been willing to accept the difficulty of swooping in and changing Davey's sched-ule without warning. Davey's difficulty with change only got worse over time, and it had become a huge source of tension with Henry.

Since returning to Crimson, Emily had done her best to keep her son on a regular schedule. Her mother and Noah had quickly adapted, making her understand the issues her ex-husband had were his own and not her or Davey's fault.

She filled a plastic cup with milk for Davey, then pulled out two beers for her and Jase. As she was setting the table, Jase let himself back into the house. "Perfect dogs," he said, holding up a plate.

"Do you know Tater?"

Emily turned to find Davey standing behind her, looking at Jase.

"She's my uncle Noah's dog," the boy explained. "Her fur is really soft, but she has stinky breath and she likes to lick me."

"Tater is a great dog," Jase answered, setting the hot dogs on the kitchen table.

"Let's wash hands," she said to her son. "Mac and cheese and hot dogs for dinner."

He climbed on the stool in front of the sink, washed his hands, then went to sit next to Jase at the table. "Tater used to live here with Uncle Noah. Now they both live with Aunt Katie. Do you have a dog?"

Jase nodded. "I have a puppy. Her name is Ruby."

"Does she have soft fur?"

"She sure does and I bet she'd like you. She's six months old and has lots of energy. She loves to play."

"I could play with her," Davey offered, taking a big bite of mac and cheese.

"Would you like to meet her sometime?"

Davey nodded. "We can drive to where you live after dinner."

"If that's okay with your mom," Jase told him.

"A short visit," Emily said, trying not to make Davey's suggestion into something bigger than it was. Which was difficult, because her son never volunteered to go anywhere. She planned outings to local parks and different shops downtown, and Davey tolerated the excursions. But there was no place he'd ever asked to go. Until now. She wondered if Jase understood the significance of the request.

He tipped back his beer bottle for a drink and then smiled at her. "I love mac and cheese."

She rolled her eyes but Davey nodded. "Me, too. And hot dogs. Mommy makes good cheese quesadillas."

"I'll have to try for an invitation to quesadilla night."

"You can come to dinner again." Davey kept his gaze on his plate, the words tumbling out of his mouth with little inflection. "Right, Mommy?"

"Of course," she whispered.

Jase asked Davey a question about his latest Lego creation. Once again, her son was talking more with Jase than he normally would to his family. Henry had a habit of demanding Davey make eye contact and enunciate when he spoke, both of which were difficult for her quiet boy. The last six months of her marriage had been fraught with tension as she and her ex-husband had waged a devastating battle over how to raise their son. The arguments and tirades had made Davey shrink into himself even more, and she'd worried the damage Henry was unwittingly doing might leave permanent scars on Davey's sensitive personality.

The way he acted toward Jase was a revelation. When Jase smiled at her again, his eyes warm and tender, Emily's heart began to race. How could she resist this man who saw her at her worst—angry or in the middle of an emotional meltdown—and still remained at her side, constant and true?

The answer was she didn't want to fight the spark between them. For the first time since returning to Crimson, Emily wondered if she hadn't squandered her chance at happiness after all.

"She needs to go out and do her business, and then you can play with her." Jase unlocked the front door of his house as he spoke to Davey.

The young boy stayed behind Emily's legs but nodded.

Emily gave him an apologetic smile. "He always takes a few minutes to acclimate to new places."

"Take all the time you need, buddy." As soon as the door began to open, Ruby started yelping. "She's usually pretty excited when I first get home."

"Davey, let's go," Emily said, her voice tense.

Jase looked over his shoulder to see the boy still standing in front of the door, eyes on the floor of the porch.

She crouched down next to her son. "It's okay, sweetie. You wanted to meet the puppy. Remember?"

"Take your time," Jase called. "I'm going to bring her to the backyard because it's fenced. Come on out whenever you're ready." The yelping got more insistent, a sure sign Ruby needed to get to the grass quickly. He lifted the blanket off the crate in the corner and flipped open the door, grabbing the puppy in his arms as she tried to dart out. She wriggled in his arms and licked his chin, but as soon as he opened the back door she darted for her favorite potty spot near a tree in the corner. He followed her into the grass with a glance back to the house. Emily and Davey hadn't emerged yet.

Ruby ran back to him and head-butted his shin before circling his legs. He didn't bother to hide his smile. Even after the worst day, it was hard not to feel better as the recipient of so much unconditional love. It didn't matter how long he'd been gone. She greeted him with off-the-charts enthusiasm every time.

After a few minutes, Ruby stopped, her whole body going rigid as her focus shifted to the back of the house. Jase went to grab her but she dodged his grasp and took off for the porch. He called for her but she ignored him as a six-month-old puppy was apt to do.

To his surprise, she slowed down at the top of the patio

steps and didn't bark once at Emily or Davey. His puppy normally gave a vocal greeting at every new person or animal she encountered. She trotted toward Emily, stopping long enough to be petted before moving closer to Davey.

The boy was standing ramrod stiff against the house's brick exterior, his gaze staring straight ahead. Jase could almost feel Emily holding her breath. Ruby sniffed at Davey's legs, then nudged his fingers with her nose. When he didn't pet her, she bumped him again, then sat a few feet in front of him as if content to wait. After a moment, Davey's chin dipped and he glanced at the puppy. She rewarded him by prancing in a circle, then sitting again. He slowly eased himself away from the house and took a hesitant step toward her.

Ruby whined softly and ran to the edge of the porch and returned to Davey with a tennis ball in her mouth, dropping it at his feet. The ball rolled a few inches.

"She's learning to play fetch," Jase called. "Do you want to throw the ball for her?"

Davey didn't give any indication he'd heard the question other than picking up the ball gingerly between his fingers and tossing it down the steps. Ruby tumbled after it, and in her excitement to retrieve the ball, she lost her balance and did a somersault across the grass. With a small laugh, Davey made his way down the steps toward the grass.

Ruby returned the ball to him and the boy threw it again.

"She'll go after the ball all night long," he told the boy. "Let me know when you get tired of throwing it."

Davey walked farther into the yard.

Jase turned for the patio to find Emily standing on the top step, tears shining in her blue eyes. "What's wrong?" he asked, jogging up the stairs to her side.

She shook her head. "Davey laughed. Did you hear him laugh?"

"Puppies have that effect on people."

"I can't remember the last time he laughed out loud," she whispered, swiping under her eyes. "It's the most beautiful sound."

"I'm glad I got to hear it."

Ruby flipped over again as she dived for the ball and this time when Davey giggled, Emily let out her own quiet laugh. She clapped a hand over her mouth.

Jase wrapped an arm around her shoulder. "It's been a while since I've heard his mother laugh, too."

"I don't know whether to laugh or cry." She sank down to the top step and Jase followed, his heart expanding as she leaned against him. "He used to laugh when he was a baby. Then things went sideways... He became so disconnected."

"You're a good mom, Em. You'll get him through this."

She turned to look at him. "Do you really believe that? You don't think I messed him up by leaving Henry and moving him across the country?"

"You protected him. That's what a mom is supposed to do." He tried not to let decades-old bitterness creep into his voice but must have failed because Emily laced her fingers with his.

"How old were you when your mother left town?"

"Nine. My sister was seven. I haven't seen either of them since the day Mom packed up the car and drove away."

"Have you ever looked?"

"My mother made it clear any man with the last name Crenshaw was bound for trouble."

"She was wrong. You've changed what people in this town think of your family. She needs to know who you've become."

"It's too late."

"What about your sister?"

"I don't blame her. Who knows how my mother poisoned her against my dad and me. I'm sure Sierra has a good life. She doesn't need me."

Emily squeezed his hand. "I didn't think I needed my family when I left Crimson. I was stupid."

He glanced down at their entwined fingers and ran his thumb along the half-moons of her nails. "You used to wear polish."

"You're changing the subject." She waved to Davey with her free hand when he turned. The boy gave her a slight nod and went back to throwing the ball.

"I don't want to talk about my family tonight." He threw her a sideways glance. "My turn for a pass?"

"Fine. Let's go back to my former beauty routine, which is a fascinating topic. I had my signature nail color and perfume. I was determined to be someone people remembered."

"You were."

"For the wrong reasons," she said with a laugh. "It's pretty sad if the thing I'm recognized for is a top-notch manicure and a cloud of expensive perfume."

"Now they'll recognize you as a strong woman and an amazing mother." He leaned closer to her until his nose touched the soft skin of her neck. "Although you still smell good."

Her breath hitched. "I wish I hadn't been so mean to you when we were younger."

"I suppose you'll have to make it up to me."

She turned, and he was unnerved by her serious expression. "I'm not the right woman for you, Jase."

The certainty of her tone made his gut clench. "Shouldn't I be the one making that decision?"

"I'm doing you a favor by making it for you."

"I don't want favors from you." He narrowed his eyes. "Unless they involve your mouth on me. Isn't that what you told me you wanted?"

Color rose to her cheeks and she dropped her gaze. "Wanting and needing are two different things."

He *wanted* to haul her into his lap and kiss that lie off her mouth. It was becoming more difficult to be patient when she was sitting so close that the warmth of her thigh seeped into his skin.

"We should talk about plans for the prewedding parties." She tugged her fingers out his and inched away from him until the cool evening breeze whispered in the space between their bodies. Jase hated that space. "Since so many of Noah's and Katie's friends overlap, I think the bachelorette and bachelor parties should be combined."

"Makes sense. Party planning is not exactly my strong suit."

"You're lucky I'm here."

There were many more reasons, but she was already spooked, so he didn't mention any of them. "I can tell you have an idea."

She flashed him a superior grin. "A scavenger hunt."

"Like we did as kids?"

"Sort of. We'll put together groups and give everyone clues to search for items important to Noah and Katie. They both grew up here so there's plenty of things to choose from."

"I like it," Jase admitted.

"Because it's brilliant."

"That's the Emily I know and..." He paused, watched her eyes widen, then added, "like as a friend."

She bumped him with her shoulder. "Mr. Perfect and a comedian—quite a combination."

"We've already established I'm not perfect."

"I like you better as a real person." She nudged him again. "And a friend."

As the sun began to fade, they watched Davey throw the ball over and over to the puppy.

"I wonder who will give up first," Jase muttered. The answer came a few minutes later when Ruby dropped the ball on the grass in front of Davey, then flopped down next to it.

"Wavy-Davey, it's time to head home," Emily called to him. "Bedtime for puppies and little boys."

The boy ignored her and sat next to Ruby, buried his face in the puppy's fur and began to gently rock back and forth.

Emily sighed. "Too much stimulation," she said, a sudden weariness in her eyes. "You might want to go inside. Chances are likely he'll have a tantrum."

"How do you know?"

"The rocking is one of his tells." She pressed her hand to her forehead. "I should have monitored him more closely but..." She gave Jase a watery smile. "I was having fun."

"Me, too," he told her and lifted his fingers to the back of her neck, massaging gently. "I'm not going to leave you. He's a kid and if he has a tantrum, so be it."

"I don't want the night to end like this." She walked down the steps slowly, approaching her son the way she might a wounded animal. Jase followed a few paces behind.

"Davey, we're going back to Grandma's now."

The rocking became more vigorous.

"Do you want to walk to the car or should I carry you?"

"No."

"You can decide or I'll decide for you, sweetheart." Emily's tone was gentle but firm. "Either way we're going home. You can visit Ruby again."

Davey's movement slowed. "When?"

"Maybe this weekend."

He shook his head and Jase stepped forward. "Hey, buddy, you did an awesome job tiring out Ruby. I bet she's going to sleep the whole night through."

"She likes the ball," the boy mumbled.

"She likes you throwing the ball," Jase told him. "But even as tired as she is, I bet she'll wake up tomorrow morning with a ton of energy."

Davey gave him a short nod.

"Do you think it would be okay if I brought her out to your grandma's farm in the morning? You can puppy-sit while I go to a meeting."

The boy glanced up at him, then back at Ruby. He nodded again.

Jase crouched down next to Davey. "I'll ask your mom if it's okay with her, but you have to get a good night's sleep, too. That means heading home now and going to bed without a fuss. Do you think you can do that?"

Davey got to his feet and lifted his face to look at Emily before lowering his gaze again. "Can Ruby come over in the morning, Mommy?"

Emily reached out as if to ruffle her son's hair, then pulled her hand tight to her chest. "You'll have to eat breakfast early."

"Okay."

"Then it's fine with me. Your grammy will love to meet Ruby."

"She can walk with us." Without another word, he turned for the house. "Let's go home, Mommy."

Jase bent and scooped the sleeping puppy into his arms. Ruby snuggled against him.

Emily ran her hand through the dog's fur, then cupped Jase's cheek. "Thank you," she whispered and pressed a soft kiss to his mouth.

"A better way to end the night?" he asked against her lips.

"Much better. Good luck at the breakfast tomorrow." She kissed him again, then ran up the back steps.

Jase followed with the dog in his arms, watching as Emily buckled her son into his booster seat. He waved to Davey as they drove away.

"You did good," he whispered to the puppy sleeping in his arms and walked back to his house.

Chapter 8

"You're looking at those pancakes like they're topped with motor oil instead of syrup."

Emily smiled as Jase spun toward her, almost spilling his cup of coffee in the process.

"You came," he said.

She glanced around at the basement reception room of one of Crimson's oldest churches. The last time she'd been here was after her father's funeral, but she tried to ignore the memories that seemed to bounce from the walls. Instead she waved a hand at the display of Sunday school artwork. "Where else would I be on a beautiful Saturday morning?"

"I don't really need to answer that, do I?"

"No, but I would like to know why the candidate who sponsored this breakfast is hiding out in the corner? Are you familiar with the term *glad-handing*?"

"I'm eating breakfast," he mumbled, pointing to the paper plate stacked with pancakes that sat on the small folding table shoved against the wall. "They're actually quite good." He set down his coffee cup and picked up the plate, lifting a forkful of pancake toward her mouth.

"I had oatmeal earlier."

"Edna Sharpe is watching. You don't want her to think you're too good for her pancakes."

Emily rolled her eyes at the glint of challenge in his gaze. But she allowed him to feed her a bite. "Yum," she murmured as she chewed. Her breath caught as Jase used his thumb to wipe a drop of syrup from the corner of her mouth.

"Jase," she whispered, "why aren't you talking to everyone?"

He dropped the plate back to the table and folded his arms across his chest. "I hate how they look at me."

"Like you're Crimson's favorite son?"

"Like I'm the poor, pathetic kid with the mother who abandoned him to his drunken dad." He held up a hand when she started to speak. "I understand most people in town know my family's history. But I've worked hard to make sure they see me and not the Crenshaw legacy. Now Charles Thompson is leaking small details about my childhood—dirty laundry I don't want aired—to anyone who will listen. You know how fast those bits of information travel through the town grapevine."

"So you're going to let him have the last word? Give up on everything you've done for Crimson?"

"Of course not."

She pointed toward the crowded tables. "Then go visit with these people. Shake hands. Kiss babies."

"Kiss babies," he repeated, one side of his mouth curving. "Really?"

"You know what I mean. I understand what happens

when you let someone else's perceived image guide your actions. That's not who you are."

"They expect—"

"You're not perfect. Neither is your history. People can deal with that. But you have to put yourself out there."

"Is that what you're doing?"

"I'm supporting a friend," she said and straightened his tie.

His warm hands covered hers. "I'm glad you're here, Em. I could use a friend right now."

"What you could use is a kick in the pants."

His smile widened. "Are you offering to be the kicker?"

She nodded. "Katie and Noah are stopping by in a bit and I left a message for Natalie."

"You didn't need to. It's a Saturday morning and they have lives."

"Support goes both ways, and you've given plenty to your friends. They're happy to return the favor."

He took a deep, shuddering breath. "There wasn't supposed to be this much scrutiny."

"Welcome to the joys of a political campaign."

"And part of a life you left behind." He bent his knees until they were at eye level. "This isn't the plan for rebuilding your life." His fingers brushed a strand of hair away from her face. A flicker of longing skittered across her skin, one that was becoming all too familiar with this man.

"I can help," she said with a shrug. "It's what I know how to do."

He glanced over her shoulder and cursed. "My father is here," he said on a harsh breath.

Emily could feel the change in Jase, the walls shooting up around him. "You mingle with the voters," she said quickly. "I'll talk to your dad."

"You don't have to—"

"Too late," she called over her shoulder. She hurried to the entrance of the reception hall, where Jase's father stood by himself. A few of the groups at tables nearby threw him questioning looks. Emily knew Declan Crenshaw's history as well as anyone. The man had been on and off the wagon more times than anyone could count.

Once Jase and Noah had become friends, Emily's whole family had been pulled into the strange orbit circling Declan and his demons. Jase had slept over at her parents' farm most weekends, and she remembered several times being woken in the dead of night to Declan standing in their front yard, screaming for Jase to come home and make him something to eat.

As a stupid, spoiled teenage girl, Emily had hated being associated with the town drunk. She'd unfairly taken her resentment out on Jase, treating him like he was beneath her. Shame at the memory rose like bile in her throat. She'd been such a fool.

Now Declan's gaze flicked to her, wary and unsure behind the fake smile he'd plastered across his face. Without hesitating, Emily wrapped him in a tight hug.

"Jase is so glad you could make it," she said, loud enough so the people sitting nearby were sure to hear.

"You're a beautiful liar," Declan murmured in her ear, "and I know you hate these events as much as I do."

She pulled back, adjusted the collar on his worn dress shirt much as she'd straightened his son's tie. Declan would have been a distinguished man if the years hadn't been so hard on him. "Maybe not quite as much. I wasn't very nice, but at least I never embarrassed the people who loved me."

"Good point," he admitted with a frown, his shaggy

eyebrows pulling low. "But things are different now. I'm sober for good. Am I ever going to live down the past?"

"I'm more concerned Jase feels the need to live it down for you." She led him toward the line at the pancake table.

"I know what Charles Thompson is trying to do." Declan picked up a paper plate and stabbed a stack of pancakes with a plastic fork. "It's my fault and it's not fair."

"Life rarely is." Emily took one pancake for herself. "We both know that."

"You're good for him."

She shook her head. "I'm not. As small of a community as Crimson is, the life Jase has here is still more public than I'm willing to handle."

Declan greeted the older man standing behind the table wiping a bottle of syrup. "Morning, Phil."

The other man's eyes narrowed. "Surprised to see you out of bed so early, Crenshaw."

Emily braced herself for Declan's retort, but he only smiled. "I'm full of surprises. How are Margie and the kids?"

Phil blinked several times before clearing his throat. "They're fine."

"I heard you have a grandbaby on the way." Declan poured syrup over his pancakes.

"My daughter-in-law is due around Thanksgiving," the other man answered, his face relaxing.

"I can't wait for Jase to find the right girl," Declan said. He nudged Emily's plate with his, which she ignored. "But until then, he's giving everything he has to this town. Do you know how many times he's taken payment for his services as a lawyer with casseroles or muffins?"

"I don't," Phil admitted. Several other volunteers had gathered around him.

Declan leaned over the table and lowered his voice, as if he was imparting a great secret. "More than I can count. He shares the food with me, and while I appreciate it, blueberry muffins don't pay the bills. But Jase wants to help people. There's his work on city council and getting Liam Donovan to move his company headquarters here." Declan glanced toward the doors leading into the hall. "There's Liam now, along with Noah Crawford. My son is good for this town, you know?"

The group on the other side of the table nodded in unison. "We know," Phil said.

With a satisfied nod, Declan turned to Emily, his dark eyes sparkling. "Shall we sit down and have breakfast, darlin'?"

She nodded, stunned, and followed him to a table, waving Noah and Liam over toward them. "You were amazing."

He threw back his head and laughed. "That's the first time I've ever heard that adjective used to describe me."

"I thought you'd get angry when Phil made the comment about you getting out of bed early."

"I don't get mad about hearing the truth. Phil and I go way back. It may have taken me a whole morning to climb out of bed in my hangover days, but at least I wasn't wearing my wife's undies when I did."

Emily felt her mouth drop. "What are you talking about?" she asked in a hushed whisper.

He winked at her. "I know plenty about the people in this town. For years, there was only one bar the locals liked. My butt was glued to one of the vinyl stools more nights than I care to admit. Most folks like to talk and they figure a drunk isn't going to remember their secrets." He tapped the side of his head with one finger. "But I got a mind like a steel trap. Even three sheets to the wind, I don't forget what I hear."

"There's more to you than anyone knows," Emily murmured with a small smile. She wouldn't forget what this man had put Jase through because of his drunken antics, but she could tell Declan was sincere in his desire to support his son.

"I think we have that in common," Declan told her.

A moment later Noah put an arm around her shoulder. "Hey there, sis. Trading one politician for another?"

She shoved him away, panic slicing up her spine.

"I'm joking, Em," Noah said quickly. "Didn't mean to strike a nerve."

"You should let Katie do the talking while you stick to looking the part of a handsome forest ranger." Emily tried to play off her reaction, but the way Noah watched her said he wasn't fooled.

He smiled anyway, smoothing a hand over his uniform. "I *am* a handsome forest ranger." His expression sobered as he looked over her shoulder. "Hello, Mr. Crenshaw."

"Noah." Declan nodded. "Congratulations on your upcoming wedding."

"Thanks. I owe a debt of thanks to Jase for helping me realize the love of my life had been by my side for years." He moved back a step to include Liam in the conversation. "Have you met Liam Donovan?"

Declan stuck out his hand. "I haven't but I've heard you're rich enough to buy the whole damn mountain if you wanted it."

Noah looked mortified but Liam only smiled and shook Declan's hand. "Maybe half the mountain," he answered.

As she greeted Liam, Emily could feel her brother studying her. She and Noah hadn't been close after their father's death, especially since they'd each been wrestling with their own private grief, and neither very successfully. They'd begun to forge a new bond since returning to Crimson, but Emily wasn't ready to hear his thoughts on her being a part of Jase's life.

Pushing back from the table, she grabbed her plate and stood. "You two keep Declan company. I see an old high school friend." She leaned down to give Jase's father a quick hug. "Thanks for breakfast," she said with a wink.

"Best date I've had in years."

Noah looked like he wanted to stop her, but she ducked around him and headed for the trash can in the corner. She waved to a couple of her mother's friends, then searched for Jase amid the people mingling at the sides of the reception hall.

Of course he was in the middle of the largest group, gesturing as he spoke and making eye contact with each person. They all stood riveted by whatever he was saying, nodding and offering up encouraging smiles.

A momentary flash of jealousy stabbed at her heart. She understood what it was like to be on the receiving end of Jase's attention, sincere and unguarded. He was the only man she knew who could make his gaze feel like a caress against her skin, and this morning was proof of why that was so dangerous to her.

Even when he was living up to other peoples' expectations, Jase was comfortable in the role. He belonged in the spotlight and in the hearts of this town. Emily had left behind her willingness to trade her private life for public favor. Davey had changed her. She'd never put anyone else's needs before his. Even her own.

She slipped out the door leading to the back of the church, needing a moment away from the curious eyes of the town. The midmorning sun was warm on her skin. She closed her eyes and tipped up her face, leaning back against the building's brick wall.

A moment later the door opened and shut again.

"What happened to catching up with old friends?" Noah asked, coming to stand in front of her.

"You're blocking my sun," she told him.

"Because from what I remember of how you left this town, you don't have many friends here."

She opened her eyes to glare at him. "Don't be mean."

He sighed. "I don't understand what you're doing. For years you couldn't stand Jase—"

"That's not true." The protest sounded weak even to her own ears.

"You certainly gave him a hard time. I stopped out at the farm this morning and saw Mom and Davey with his puppy."

"Davey bonded with Ruby right away, so Jase was nice enough to bring her by so they could play."

"Of course. Jase is a nice guy."

"Too nice for someone like me?"

Noah stepped out of her line of sight, turning so he stood next to her against the wall. "You know he's had a crush on you for years."

"It's different now. I'm working for him."

"Which means you two are spending a lot of time together. He'd moved on until you came back. Jase has a lot of responsibility in this town. Between his practice, his father and now dealing with a real campaign—"

"I understand, Noah." She hated being put on the spot and the fact her brother was doing it. "Are you telling me to stay away from him?"

Noah shook his head. "You're coming off a bad divorce.

I'm saying don't use Jase as a rebound fling. Both of you could end up hurt."

Pushing off the wall, she spun toward him. "It's Jase you're worried about, not me."

"Emily—"

"No. You don't know anything about my marriage."

"Why is that?" He ran a hand through his hair. "How the hell am I supposed to understand anything about your life? You cut me out after Dad died."

"That was mutual and you know it."

"I thought we were doing better since Mom's illness?"

"We are, Noah. But it might be too soon for brotherly lectures on my private life."

"Nothing is private in Crimson. You know that. Besides, I thought you came back to here to heal?"

"Maybe Jase is a part of me healing." Until she said the words out loud, she hadn't realized how true they were. Tears sprang to the backs of her eyes and she swiped at her cheek, refusing to allow herself to break down. She'd promised herself she was finished with crying after she'd left Henry.

Noah cursed under his breath. "I'm sorry. Don't cry."

"I'm not crying," she whispered and her voice cracked.

"You really care about him."

"We're friends. It's not a fling. Not a rebound. I don't know what is going on between us, but I'm not going to hurt him. I think…" She paused, forced herself to meet Noah's worried gaze. "I think I'm good for him. It goes both ways, Noah. I know it does."

"Okay, honey." Noah pulled her in for a tight hug. She resisted at first, holding on to her anger like an old friend. But her brother didn't let go, and after a few moments she sagged against him, understanding that even if he made her crazy, Noah was far better comfort than her temper could ever be.

"I'm sorry," he whispered into her hair.

"You're a good friend to Jase."

"But I need to be a better brother to you. You're important to me. You and Davey both."

"You have to say that because I helped your bride pick out a wedding dress that will bring tears to your eyes."

"I can't wait," he said with a lopsided grin and a dopey look in his eyes that made her smile. "But I'm *choosing* to tell you the truth about supporting you more. I mean every word."

"Then will you help me find my own place to live?"

"Mom loves having you at the farm." He frowned. "She loves helping with Davey and having you close."

"I'll still be close, but I want a home of my own, even if it's a tiny apartment somewhere. After the wedding will you help me look?"

"Of course."

"Do you have any prewedding nerves?" she asked, stepping out of his embrace. "You spent a long time avoiding commitment."

"I was a master," he agreed.

"Marriage is a big deal, especially when there's a baby on the way."

"I felt the baby kick the other night."

"Oh, Noah."

"It made this whole thing feel real. I mean, I know it's real but...yes, I'm nervous." He looked over her shoulder toward the mountains in the distance. "Not about marrying Katie. I can't believe I was blind for so long, but now I've got her and I'm never letting go." He took a breath, then said, "Even if I don't deserve her."

"You do." She nudged him with her hip. "You're a pain in my butt, but you deserve happiness."

"What if I mess up? What if I can't be as good as Dad?"

"Don't compare yourself." She gave a small laugh. "Do you think I could ever hold a candle to Mom?"

"You're an amazing mother."

"You'll be an amazing dad." She held up her hand, fist closed. "We've got this, bro."

"Are you trying to be cool?"

She shrugged and lifted her hand higher. "Don't leave me hanging."

With a laugh, Noah fist-bumped her, then pulled her in for another hug. "We'd better head back inside. I have a feeling Declan and Liam together are a dangerous combination."

Jase's lungs burned as he ran the final stretch to the lookout point halfway up the main Crimson Mountain trail. At the top, he bent forward, sucking in the thin mountain air.

The late-afternoon trail run was supposed to clear his head, but his mind refused to slow down. Images of Emily and his dad swirled inside him, mixing with thoughts of the questions he'd answered at this morning's campaign breakfast.

How do you feel about Charles Thompson running against you?

Do you have too much going on to add mayor to your list of responsibilities?

When are you going to settle down and start a family?

Are you worried about not having time to take care of your dad?

What if Declan starts to drink again?

He'd answered each of the inquiries with a nod and an

understanding smile, but he'd wanted to turn and run from the crowded church hall. Those questions brought up too many emotions inside him. Too much turmoil he couldn't control. Jase's greatest fear was losing control and it seemed he had less of a grasp on it with each passing day.

He sank down to one of the rock formations and watched as Liam Donovan came over the final ridge, a few minutes behind Jase. Liam's dark hair was stuck to his forehead and his athletic T-shirt plastered to his chest. The run up to the lookout point was almost three miles of vertical switchbacks. Jase had been running this trail since high school but today even the beauty of the forest hadn't settled him.

"Are you crazy?" Liam asked, panting even harder than Jase. "You were running like a mountain lion was chasing you."

Jase wiped the back of one arm across his forehead. "A mountain lion would have caught you instead of me. I thought you wanted a challenge."

"A challenge is different than a heart attack. You'd have a tough time explaining to Natalie that you left me on the side of the mountain."

"I wouldn't have left you." Jase grinned. "I'm too afraid of your wife."

"The strange thing is she'd take that as a compliment." He sat on a rock across from Jase. "You had a good turnout at the breakfast this morning."

"I appreciate you stopping by."

"Always happy to do my part with a plate of pancakes. Your dad is a character."

Jase laughed. "That's one word for him."

"He's really proud of you." Liam used the hem of his shirt to wipe the sweat off his face. "My dad never gave a damn about anything I did. Not as long as I stayed out of his way."

Liam's father owned one of the most successful tech companies in the world. It had been big news in the technology world when Liam broke off to start his own GPS software company and chose Crimson as the headquarters for it.

"I couldn't exactly stay out of Declan's way. I was too busy cleaning up behind him."

"A fact your new opponent in the mayor's race is exploiting?"

Jase blew out a breath. "Sheriff Thompson has seen me at my lowest. He and my dad grew up together in town and the Thompsons and Crenshaws have always been rivals—sports, women, you name it." He stood and paced to the edge of the ridge, taking in the view of the town below. "Anytime a situation involved my dad, Thompson made sure he was on the scene. Didn't matter if it was the weekend or who was on duty. The sheriff always showed up to personally cuff Dad."

"Declan seems sincere about changing."

"He's always sincere." From up here, Jase could see downtown Crimson and the neighborhoods fanning out around it. The creek ran along the edge of downtown, then meandered through the valley and into the thick forest on the other side.

As a kid, he'd battled the expectations that he'd follow in his father's footsteps. People always seemed to be waiting for him to make a misstep, to become another casualty of the Crenshaw legend. He'd worked so hard to prove them wrong. When would he be released from the responsibility of making up for mistakes he hadn't made?

Liam came to stand next to him. "I know what it's like

to have to claw your way out from a father's shadow. Our backgrounds are different, but disappointment and anger don't discriminate based on how much you have in the bank."

"But you've escaped it."

"Maybe," Liam said with a shrug. "Maybe not. My dad is known all over the world. I've created a different future for myself but his legacy follows me. I choose to ignore it and live life on my terms."

Jase wasn't sure if he'd even know how to go about setting up his own life away from the restrictions of his past. "When I graduated from law school, a firm in Denver offered me a position. I turned it down to come back to Crimson and take over Andrew Meyer's family practice."

"Do you regret the choice you made?"

Jase picked up a flat stone from the trail and hurled it over the edge of the ridge. It arced out, then disappeared into the canopy of trees below. "I don't know. Back then, I was so determined to return to Crimson as a success. Part of it was feeling like I owed something to the people in this town. As much as they judged my family, they also came forward to take care of us when things were rough. After my mom left, we had food in the freezer for months."

"Nothing says love in a small town like a casserole."

"Exactly," Jase agreed with a laugh. "There were a couple of teachers who looked after me at school. Once it became clear I was determined to stay on the straight and narrow, the town was generous with its support. I was given a partial scholarship during undergrad and always had a job waiting for me in the summer. I wanted to pay back that kindness, and dedicating myself to the town seemed like the best way to do it."

"But..." Liam prompted.

"I've started to wonder what it would have been like to go to work, come home and take care of only myself. Maybe that's selfish—"

"It's not selfish." Liam lobbed a rock over the side and it followed the same trajectory as Jase's. "It's also not too late. I was going to ask if you need support with the campaign. Financial support," he clarified. "But now I'm wondering if becoming mayor is what you really want?"

"Does it matter? I've committed to it."

"You can back out. Charles Thompson isn't a bad man. He would do a decent job."

Jase cocked a brow.

"Not as good as you, of course. But the future of Crimson doesn't rest on your shoulders, Jase."

"I'll think about that." As if he could think about anything else. "We should head back down. I'll take it easy on you."

Liam barked out a laugh. "A true gentleman."

Jase started for the trail, then turned back. "Thanks for the offer, Liam. I appreciate it, but I don't want to owe you. Having you at my back is plenty of support."

"I'd think of it as an investment," Liam answered. "And the offer stands if you change your mind."

"Thank you." Jase started running, the descent more technical than climbing the switchbacks due to the loose rocks and late-afternoon shadows falling over the trail. It was just what he needed, something to concentrate on besides the emotional twists and turns of his current life.

Chapter 9

Monday morning, Emily jumped at the tap on her shoulder, spinning around in her desk chair to find Jase grinning at her.

She ripped the headphones off her ears. "You scared me half to death," she said, wheezing in a breath.

"You were singing out loud."

"You were supposed to be in court all day." She narrowed her eyes.

"What exactly are you listening to?" He reached for the headphones, but she grabbed them, then spun around to hit the mute button on her keyboard.

"Music," she mumbled. "Why are you back so early? I didn't hear the bells on the door when it opened."

"I came in through the door to the alley out back."

"You snuck up on me," she grumbled.

"What kind of music? I didn't recognize it."

"Broadway show tunes, okay?" She crossed her arms

over her chest and glared. "*Evita* to be specific. I like musicals." The words came out like a challenge. "You're a lawyer—sue me."

His grin widened. "Don't cry for me, Emily Whitaker."

"Asking for trouble, Jase Crenshaw."

He held up a brown paper bag. "Here's a peace offering. I brought lunch from the deli around the corner. That's why I came through the back. Have you eaten?"

She held up an empty granola-bar wrapper. "I'm working through lunch since I'm leaving early today." Tomorrow was Davey's first day of kindergarten so tonight they were going to the ice cream social at the elementary school. Her son didn't seem worried about the change, but Emily had been a bundle of nerves since the moment she'd woken up this morning.

She'd had a meeting at the beginning of the week with the kindergarten teacher and the school's interventionist to discuss the Asperger's and how to help Davey have a successful school year. For a small school district, Crimson Elementary School offered many special education services. This would mark the first time he'd been away from her during the day.

She'd enrolled him in preschool in their Boston neighborhood, having added Davey's name to the exclusive program's wait list when he was only a few months old. Despite the expense of the private program, the teachers had been unwilling to work with his personality quirks.

Much like her husband, they'd expected him to manage like the rest of the children, which led to several frustrated tantrums. Davey had lashed out, throwing a toy car across the room. It had hit one of the other students on the side of the head and the girl had stumbled, then fallen, knocking her head on the corner of a bookshelf. There'd been angry calls from both the teacher and the girl's mother and even a parent meeting at the school to allay other families' concerns about Davey continuing in the program.

Henry had been furious, mostly because two of his partners had kids enrolled at the school so he couldn't brush the incident under the rug. In the end, Emily had pulled Davey, opting to work with him herself on the skills he'd needed to be ready for kindergarten.

She couldn't control the way Asperger's affected his personality and his ability to socialize with both adults and other kids. Or how he was treated by people who didn't understand how special he was.

"Come to the conference room and eat a real lunch," Jase said gently, as if he could sense the anxiety tumbling through her like rocks skidding down the side of Crimson Mountain.

"I have work to do."

"Em, you are the most efficient person I've ever met. You've already organized this whole office, updated the billing system, caught up on all my outstanding correspondence and done such a great job of editing the briefs that Judge McIlwain at the courthouse actually commented on it."

Pride, unfamiliar and precious, bloomed in her chest. "He did?"

"Yes, and he's not the only one." Jase rested his hip against the corner of her desk. "Do you remember the contract you drafted for the firm I'm working with over in Aspen?"

She nodded.

"The office manager called to see if I'd used a service to hire my new assistant. She wanted to find someone just like you for their senior partner. He's a stickler for detail and notoriously hard on office staff."

"She called me, too." Emily swallowed.

"Why?" Jase's tone was suspiciously even.

"To offer me a job."

"What was the starting salary?"

She told him the number, almost double what he was paying her.

Jase cursed under his breath. "Why didn't you take it? It's one of the most prestigious firms in the state."

"I know. I researched them."

"They can offer you benefits and an actual career path. You have to consider it, even if it makes me mad as hell hearing someone tried to poach you."

She shook her head. "I don't want to work in Aspen. I like it here with you." She flashed what she hoped was a teasing smile. "You'd be lost without me."

His brown eyes were serious when he replied, "You have no idea."

"Jase…"

"At least let me feed you. I've been thinking of ideas for the prewedding scavenger hunt."

She stood at the same time he did, too shocked to protest any longer. "You have?"

He looked confused. "Wasn't that the plan?"

"Well, yes," she admitted as she followed him to the conference room at the far end of the hall. "But I wasn't sure you'd take it seriously. You have so much going on, and it's a silly party theme."

There was an ancient table in the middle of the conference room, with eight chairs surrounding it. On her second day in the office, Emily had taken wood soap and furniture wax to the dull surface, polishing it until it gleamed a rich mahogany. She liked that she could make a difference here in Jase's small law practice.

He held out a chair for her and she sat, watching as he emptied the contents of the bag. He set a wax-paper-wrapped sandwich in front of her, along with a bag of barbecue potato chips. "Noah is my best friend. Making his wedding weekend special isn't silly, and neither was your idea. You need to give yourself more credit."

She nodded but didn't meet his gaze, running one finger over the seam of the wax paper. "What kind of sandwich?"

"Turkey and avocado on wheat," he answered absently. "Do you want a soda?"

"Diet, please," she said, unable to take her hand off the sandwich.

He left the room and Emily sucked in a breath. He remembered her favorite sandwich.

The small gesture leveled her, and the barriers she'd placed around her heart collapsed. This man who was wrong for her in every way except the one that mattered. He seemed to want her just the way she was. Her ex-husband would have brought her a salad, forever concerned she might not remain a perfect size six.

Perfect.

Her life since returning to her hometown had been anything but perfect, yet she wouldn't trade the journey that had brought her here. She was a better person for her independence and the effort she'd put into protecting Davey from any more suffering and rejection.

She did her best to gather her strength as she pulled up to the elementary school parking lot later that evening. The playground and grassy field in front of the building were crowded with people, and she wished she'd gotten to the event earlier.

Instead she'd changed clothes several times before she and Davey left her mother's house. Difficult to find an outfit that conveyed all the things she needed.

I'm a good mother. Like me. Like my son. Accept us here so I can make it a true home.

Straightening her simple A-line skirt, she got out of the SUV and helped Davey hop down from his booster seat. The desire to gather him close almost overwhelmed her. She wanted to ground herself to him with touch but knew that would only make him anxious. She dropped the car keys into her purse and gave him a bright smile. "Are you ready to meet your new teacher?"

His eyes shifted to hers, then back to the front of the school. "Okay," he mumbled and emotion knitted her throat closed.

"Okay," she repeated and moved slowly toward the playground. Several women looked over as they approached, and she recognized a couple who'd been in her grade. They waved and she forced herself to breathe. If she panicked, Davey was likely to pick up on her energy. Already she could feel him dragging his feet behind her.

"We've got this," she said, glancing back at him.

He crossed his arms over his chest and stared at the ground.

Emily's heart sank but she kept the smile on her face. All she wanted was to protect her sweet boy, but so often she didn't know how to help him.

Suddenly she heard a female voice calling her name. She looked up to see a tiny woman with a wavy blond bob coming toward her.

"I hoped you'd be here," Millie Travers said as she

wrapped Emily in a tight hug. Millie was a recent addition to the community, having moved to town last year to be close to her sister Olivia. Both sisters were married to Crimson natives. Millie's husband, Jake Travers, was a doctor at the local hospital and Emily knew he had a daughter from a previous relationship who was around Davey's age.

Emily had met Millie, along with Katie's other girlfriends, at a breakfast Katie had coordinated shortly after her engagement. Her future sister-in-law was doing her best to make sure Emily felt included in her circle of friends, which she appreciated even if it was difficult for her to trust the bonds of new friendships after her experience in Boston. But she couldn't deny Millie was an easy person to like. "Katie told me to look out for you," the other woman said with a smile. "Your son is starting kindergarten this year, right?"

Emily swallowed. "Yes." She turned to where Davey stood stiff as a statue behind her. "Davey, this is Mrs. Travers, a friend of mine."

Her son stared at the crack in the sidewalk. Around the dull roar in her head, Emily heard the sound of laughter and happy shouts from the other kids on the playground. She wondered if Davey would ever be able to take part in such carefree fun.

If Millie was bothered by Davey's demeanor, she didn't show it. Instead, she sank down to her knees but kept her gaze on the edge of the sidewalk. "It's nice to meet you. My stepdaughter, Brooke, is starting first grade this year. She can answer any questions you have about kindergarten. Mrs. MacDonald, the kindergarten teacher, is really great."

"Whatcha doin', Mama-llama?" A young girl threw her arms around Millie's neck and leaned over her shoulder. Emily saw Davey's eyes widen. The girl wore a yellow polka-dot T-shirt and a ruffled turquoise skirt with bright pink cowboy boots. Her blond curls were wild around her head.

"I'm talking to my new friend, Davey," Millie said, squeezing the small hands wrapped around her neck. "He's starting kindergarten this year."

Brooke stood up and jabbed a thumb at her own chest. "I'm an expert on kindergarten." She stepped around Millie and held out a hand. "Ms. MacDonald has a gecko in her room."

"I have a question," Davey said quietly.

Brooke waited, reminding Emily a bit of Noah's puppy. Finally she asked, "What's your question?"

"Is it a crested gecko or a leopard gecko?"

"It's a leopard gecko and his name is Speedy," Brooke told him. "Come on. I'll take you to see the classroom."

Millie straightened, placing a gentle hand on Brooke's curls. "We need to make sure it's okay with Davey's mommy."

Emily was about to make an excuse for why Davey should stay with her when he slipped his hand into Brooke's. The girl didn't seem bothered by his rigid shoulders or the fact he continued to stare at the ground.

"I'll go, Mommy," Davey said softly.

Emily opened her mouth, but only a choked sob came out. Biting down hard on the inside of her cheek, she gave a jerky nod.

"We'll be right behind you," Millie said, moving to Emily's side and placing an arm around her waist. "Go slow, Brookie-cookie. Show Davey the room and we'll meet you there so both Davey and his mommy can meet Ms. Mac-Donald."

"Okeydokey," Brooke sang out and led Davey through the crowd.

"Do you need a minute?" Millie asked gently.

Emily shook her head but placed a palm to her chest, her heart beating at a furious pace. "He doesn't usually..." She broke off, not sure how to explain what an extraordinary moment that had been for her son.

"Brooke will take care of him." Millie smiled. "He's going to be fine here. I know you don't have any reason to believe me, but something in this town rises up to meet the people who need the most help."

"I've never been great at taking help," Emily said with a shaky laugh. "I'm more a 'spit in your eye' type person."

"That's not what I hear from Katie. She's a very good judge of people. We'll follow them." Millie led her along the edge of the crowd, smiling and waving to a number of people as they went. But she didn't stop so Emily was able to keep Brooke and Davey within her sight. Millie's smile widened as she looked over Emily's shoulder. "And she's not the only one."

Emily turned to see a tall, blond, built man she recognized as Dr. Jake Travers, Millie's husband, walking through the parking lot with Jase at his side. Jase was a couple inches taller than Jake and his crisp button-down shirt and tailored slacks highlighted his broad shoulders and lean waist. Her heart gave a little leap and she smiled before she could stop herself.

"My husband is the hottest guy in town," Millie said, nudging Emily in the ribs. "But soon-to-be Mayor Crenshaw holds his own in the looks department. Wouldn't you agree?"

Emily shifted her gaze to Millie's wide grin and made her expression neutral. "He's my boss," she murmured.

The other woman only laughed. "I was Brooke's nanny when I first came to Crimson. That didn't stop me from noticing my *boss*." She gently knocked into Emily again. "Don't bother to deny it. Your game face isn't that good."

"My game face is flawless," Emily countered but the corners of her mouth lifted. Maybe not flawless when it came to Jase. The two men were almost at the playground. She leaned down to Millie's ear and whispered, "I'll only admit Dr. Travers is the second-hottest guy in town."

Millie hooted with laughter, then grabbed her husband and pulled him in for a quick kiss. "Jake, do you know Noah's sister, Emily?"

Jake Travers held out his hand. "Nice to see you, Emily."

"Your daughter was really nice to my son tonight," Emily told him. "She's a special girl."

He laughed. "A one-child social committee, that's our Brooke."

"She's giving Davey a tour of the kindergarten classroom," Millie told him. "How's the campaign, Jase?"

"Pretty good." Jase inclined his head toward the mass of kids on the playground. "But it's never too early to recruit potential voters." He smiled but Emily could see it was forced. Millie and Jake didn't seem to notice.

"Speaking of recruitment," Millie said, glancing up at Jake, who'd looped an arm around her slender shoulders. "I told the classroom mom you'd help coordinate a field trip to the hospital to see the Flight For Life helicopter." She turned to Emily. "She's working the volunteer table now so I'd like to stop by for a second. We'll see you in the kindergarten room. Brooke's classroom is right next door."

Emily nodded and kept moving toward the building. She saw Davey follow Brooke Travers inside.

"Campaign stop?" she asked Jase. He'd taken up Millie's post at her side and more people waved to him as they approached the school.

"I thought you and Davey might like some moral support." He shrugged, ducked his head, looking suddenly embarrassed. "Clearly, you've got it under control. He's made a friend and you—"

"I'm glad you're here," she said, letting out an unsteady breath. "Davey left my side, which was the whole point of this, and I almost broke down in tears on the spot." She stopped and pressed her open palm to his chest. His heart beat a rapid pace under the crisp cotton of his shirt. "Thank you for coming," she whispered.

He covered her hand with his, and then interlaced their fingers. "Anytime you need me," he said, lifting her hand and placing a tender kiss on the inside of her wrist.

Emily felt color rise to her cheeks, and she glanced around to find a few people staring at them. "Jase, we're..."

"At the elementary school," he said with a husky laugh. "Right." He lowered her hand but didn't release it.

Butterflies swooped and dived around Emily's stomach, and she felt like a girl holding hands with her first boyfriend. It took her mind off the worry of fitting in with the other mothers. Between Millie's exuberant welcome and Jase's gentle support, Emily felt hopeful she could carve out a happy life in the hometown that had once seemed too small to hold all of her dreams.

But the biggest dreams couldn't hold a candle to walking into the bright classroom to see her son solemnly shaking hands with his new kindergarten teacher.

"I'm glad Davey will be joining our class this year," the teacher said to Emily as she and Jase approached. "It's great he has a friend like Brooke to introduce him to the school."

Davey darted a glance at Emily and she saw his lips

press together in a small smile when he spotted Jase next to her. "They have a Lego-building club," he mumbled, his eyes trained on Jase's shoes.

Jase crouched low in front of Davey. "That's excellent, buddy. Are you excited about school?"

Davey took several moments to answer. Emily held her breath.

Her son looked from Jase to her and whispered, "I'm excited."

Emily felt a little noise escape her lips. It was the sound of pure happiness.

Chapter 10

Jase pulled up to his house close to nine that night. He parked his SUV in the driveway, then opened its back door for Ruby to scramble out. After the ice cream social, he'd gone directly to his dad's house with dinner.

Declan had gotten his cable fixed so they watched the season finale of some show about dance competitions, the point of which Jase couldn't begin to fathom. But his dad seemed happy and more relaxed than he'd been in ages. Ruby had curled up between them on the sofa and the quiet evening was the closest thing Jase could remember to a normal visit.

As soon as her legs hit the ground, Ruby took off for the house. Jase quickly locked the car, then came around the front, calling the puppy back to him.

But Ruby ignored him, too busy wriggling at the feet of the woman sitting on the bottom step of his front porch.

Emily.

She'd changed from the outfit she wore to the ice cream social to a bulky sweatshirt and a pair of...were those pajama pants?

"Hey," he called out, moving toward her. "These after-dark visits are becoming a habit with us."

She didn't answer or smile, just stood and stared at him.

Worry edged into his brain, beating down the desire that had roared to life as soon as he'd laid eyes on her.

"What's going on?"

She walked forward, her gaze intent but unreadable. When she was a few paces away, she launched herself at him. Her arms wound around his neck and he caught her, stumbling back a step before righting them both. She kissed him, her mouth demanding and so damn sweet. All of the built-up longing he'd tried to suppress came crashing through, smothering his self-control.

He lifted her off the ground, holding her body against his as he moved them toward the house. Ruby circled around them, nipping at his ankles as if she resented being left out of the fun. Emily's legs clamped around his hips as he fumbled with the house key. She continued to trail hot, openmouthed kisses along his jaw and neck.

"Are you sure?" he managed to ask as he let them in, then slammed shut the front door. "Is this—"

"No talking," she whispered. "Bedroom." She bit down on his lip, then eased the sting by sucking it gently into her mouth. Jase's knees threatened to give way.

He moved through the house with her still wrapped around him, and then grabbed a handful of dog treats from the bag on the dining room table as he passed. He tossed them into the kitchen and Ruby darted away with a happy yip.

He felt Emily smile against his mouth. "Always taking care of business."

"You're my only business," he told her, moving his hands under the soft cotton of her sweatshirt as he made his way down the hall. He claimed her mouth again. "I want to taste every part of you." He pushed back the covers and lowered her to the bed, loving the feel of her underneath him.

"Later," she told him. "I need you, Jase. Now."

He lifted his head to meet her crystal-blue gaze but found her eyes clouded with passion and need. The same need was clawing at his insides, making him want to rip off her clothes like a madman. To think she was as overcome as he was changed something inside him. His intention of savoring this moment disappeared in an instant.

Straightening, he toed off his shoes, then pulled his fleece and T-shirt over his head in one swift move. Emily sat up, tugging at the hem of her sweatshirt and he was on the bed in an instant.

"Let me." As she lifted her arms, he pulled off the sweatshirt, leaving her in nothing but a pale pink lace bra. Lust wound around his chest, choking off his breath as he gazed at her. He felt like a fumbling teenager again, unable to form a coherent thought as he stared.

Her eyes on his, Emily reached behind her back and unclasped the bra, then let it fall off her shoulders and into her lap.

"Beautiful," Jase murmured as her breasts were exposed. He reached out to touch her and she scooted forward, running her hands over his chest.

"Right back at you," she said.

"Emily—"

"I want this," she told him. "I want you. Please don't make me wait any longer."

He wanted to laugh at her impatience. He'd been waiting for this moment for as long as he could remember. He stood again, shucked off his jeans while she shimmied out of her pajama bottoms and panties.

"Condom?" she asked on a husky breath when he bent over her again.

He started to argue, to insist they take their time but the truth was he didn't know how long he'd last if she continued to touch him. He opened the nightstand drawer and grabbed a condom.

She reached for it but he shook his head. "I better handle this part or the night will really be over before it starts."

Emily smiled and bit down on her lip, as if pleased to know she affected him so strongly. Was there really any question?

A moment later he kissed her again, fitting himself between her legs, capturing her gasp in his mouth as he entered her.

Nothing he'd imagined prepared him for the reality of being with Emily. She drew him closer, trailing her nails lightly down his back as they found a rhythm that was unique to them.

Everything except the moment and the feel of their bodies moving together fell away. All of life's complications and stress disappeared as passion built in the quiet of the room. In between kissing her, he whispered against her ear. Not the truth of his heart. Even in the heat of passion he understood it was too soon for that.

Instead he murmured small truths about her beauty, her strength and the complete perfection of being with her. She moaned against him, as if his words were driving the desire as much as the physical act. Her grasp on him tightened and he felt her tremble at the same time she cried out. She dug her nails into his shoulders and the idea that she might mark him as hers made his control shatter.

He followed her over the edge with a groan and a shudder, and she held him to her, gentling her touch as their movements slowed.

Balancing himself on his elbows, he brushed away loose strands of hair from her face. She looked up at him, the blue of her eyes so deep and her gaze painfully vulnerable. She blinked several times, her mouth thinning but her eyes remained unguarded. It was like the normal screens she used to defend herself wouldn't engage. He understood the feeling, so when she closed her eyes and turned her head to one side, he simply placed a gentle kiss on the soft underside of her jaw.

"No regrets," he murmured, then rose and walked to the bathroom. He glanced back to her from the doorway. Emily Whitaker was in his bed, the sheet tucked around her, her long blond hair fanned across his pillow like a golden sea. Tonight reality was indeed much better than his dreams.

Run, run, run.

The voice in Emily's head wouldn't shut up, and she pressed her fists against her forehead trying to press away the doubts blasting into her mind. She felt the wetness on her cheeks and couldn't stop the sobs that coursed through her body.

She wasn't sure how long she lay there before Jase returned. His fingers were cool around her wrists as he tugged them away from her face.

"No, Em." His voice was hollow. "No tears."

"I don't want to hurt you," she whispered, knowing she already had.

"If you mean hurt me with the best sex of my life, bring on more pain."

His kindness at this moment when he should hate her

only made her cry harder. All the pain and sorrow and guilt and anger she'd bottled up during her marriage and before came pouring out. It was like being with Jase had torn away all of her emotional barricades.

"So not your best experience I take it," he said with a strained laugh.

She shook her head. "The best ever."

"Look at me and say that."

After several moments, she did. "It was amazing. You were amazing, Jase. I don't regret tonight, but I'm sorry."

"Remember I'm a simple man," he told her. "You're going to need to be a little clearer."

"I'm a mess." She used the edge of the sheet to wipe the tears from her face.

He nodded. "But a beautiful mess."

She poked at him. "You're not supposed to agree with me," she said but laughed at the fact that he had.

"Then I'm sorry. And we're even."

"We're not even." She didn't know how they ever could be. "You've been nice to me when I didn't deserve it, given me a job and connected to my son in ways not even his father could. I'm so grateful to you."

Jase raised an eyebrow. "So that was thank-you sex?"

She gasped and shifted away from him.

"I'm not complaining," Jase added, pulling her back again. "Just trying to figure out where we are here."

"You make me feel things," she whispered, scooting up so her back was against the headboard. She tucked the sheet more tightly under her arms, wishing she'd put on clothes while Jase was in the bathroom. He was wearing a pair of athletic shorts low on his hips but she still had the surprisingly awesome view of his ripped chest and broad shoulders. "Things I thought I put away to concentrate on the serious business of raising a son with special needs."

"Things like?"

She swallowed, worried her fingers together, traced the empty space on her left hand where she'd worn her wedding ring. She'd been so sure of herself when she'd met Henry. Positive that force of will could make her life perfect. Keep her heart safe. Impenetrable.

"Things like...joy...hope." There were other feelings that terrified her, but she wasn't ready to admit to anything more. She drew in a breath. "I came here tonight because I needed..."

"A release?"

"You."

The silence stretched between them, heavy with all they'd both left unspoken. He turned so he was sitting next to her and stretched his long legs out over the bed. "That's the nicest word I've ever heard."

He gathered her into his arms, sheet and all, his strong arms reminding her there was another kind of safety. The type that came from allowing another person to see her true self.

"I wanted you," she told him, circling one finger through the sprinkling of dark hair across his chest. "I've wanted you since that day at the football game. Maybe since the morning of my mom's surgery when you came to the hospital."

She could feel his smile against the top of her head. "I've wanted you for as long as I can remember."

"But I'm empty, Jase. On the inside. There are a million broken pieces scattered there. I don't know how to fix them." She slid her hand up to his jaw, running her thumb over the rough stubble. "You deserve someone who is whole. I can't be that person yet, and I may never be the woman who can support you in all you do for this town. All people expect of you."

"You already have." He ran a finger along her back at the edge of the sheet. The simple touch was both soothing and strangely erotic. "You've organized my life, focused my campaign when I needed it and smoothed over the rough edges of having my dad involved. I've learned to rely on only myself, which is a difficult habit to end. But I trust you."

She shook her head. "I'll help with your message, not be part of it. I'm comfortable with a behind-the-scenes role. A friend. It's different."

"It doesn't have to be."

"I came here because you mean something to me, but I can't be the person you need." She reached up, pressed her mouth to his and repeated, "I *don't* want to hurt you." She meant the words but she couldn't admit the bigger truth— that she was terrified of her heart being the one to break. The more she cared, the harder the loss was to bear.

"There's more," Jase said softly. "Tell me why you're afraid."

"*I* don't want to be hurt," she admitted on a harsh breath. "I can't give you my heart because having it break again would kill me, Jase."

"I won't—"

"You can't know that." She tucked her head into the crook of his arm, unable to meet his gaze and say the words she needed him to hear. "My dad certainly didn't plan to die from cancer and leave my mom alone. I never thought I'd marry a man who couldn't accept his own son."

"I'm not your ex-husband." Jase's voice was pitched low. "Henry isn't a villain. He's someone who needs his life to look perfect." She gave a strangled laugh. "I have no room to judge when it's what attracted me to him in the first place. Having a baby opened my heart in ways I didn't expect. I never wanted to feel that way, to be vulnerable. Davey is everything to me. But there isn't room for anyone else. I want you, and I don't regret coming here. But we can't let it go any further." She tried to pull away, but his arms tightened around her.

"What if this is enough?"

She stilled, risked a glance up to find him smiling at her. "Is that possible?" A piece of hair fell across his forehead, and she pushed it back, loving the feel of his skin under her fingers.

"I know it's not possible that once with you is enough for me." He lowered his mouth to hers, his lips tender. Desire pooled low in Emily's belly and she moved in his arms. The evidence she wasn't the only one affected pressed against her hip. She shifted again.

"Emily," he groaned against her mouth. "You're killing me."

"In a good way, I hope. I like being in your arms, Jase. I want to feel something. I'm tired of the nothingness. I want more. With you."

He moved suddenly and she was on her back again with Jase's body pressed to hers. "Then no worries, regrets or expectations."

"Expectations?"

"Expectations most of all." He pulled the sheet down, then skimmed his teeth over the swell of her breast. "I'm drowning under them, Em. But not with you. With you I can just *be*. And I promise you the same. We can be friends and more. But only as much as feels right. No other promises. No blame. No stress."

Another layer of joy burst to the surface inside her. It felt as if her chest was filled with bubbles, fizzy and light. She felt drunk with the exhilaration of it.

Right now, every part of her life was filled with stress. It was part of being a single mother. Even with her family's support, she could never truly let go. What Jase was offering felt like a lifeline. And the best part was she could give the same thing back to him. Pleasure for the sake of pleasure. No expectations.

It felt like freedom.

She wrapped her arms around his neck. "You've got yourself a deal, counselor."

"Sealed with a kiss," he said and nipped at the edge of her mouth.

"Sealed with a thousand kisses," she whispered and set about adding them up.

Chapter 11

The following Friday morning, Emily was busy untangling a strand of tiny twinkle lights being used to decorate the wide patio at Crimson Ranch, where tomorrow's wedding would be held. Sara worked on a separate length of lights while April Sanders arranged mason jars that would be filled with wildflowers on the tables set up around the patio.

Jase had closed the office today so they could both concentrate on wedding plans. Her mother was picking up Davey after school while April led a private yoga class for Katie and her girlfriends. The group would then go for facials and massages at a spa near Aspen before joining the men for the scavenger hunt Emily and Jase had organized. Emily had worked to make sure the activities leading up to the wedding were fun, personal and helped celebrate who Katie and Noah were as a couple.

She understood why they'd selected the ranch as their wedding venue. Located on the outskirts of town, the property had been beautifully restored in the past few years to become one of the area's most popular destinations.

In addition to the rough-hewn-log main house, there was a large red barn and several smaller cabins spread around the property. Clumps of pine and aspen trees dotted the landscape, giving the buildings a sense of privacy. Each time the breeze blew Emily enjoyed the sound of aspen leaves fluttering in the wind. She could see where the property dipped as it got closer to the forest's edge and knew the creek ran along the divide.

"You had sex." Sara grinned at Emily.

Emily spit the bite of muffin she'd picked up from the basket sitting on the table. "Excuse me?" She choked on muffin crumbs.

April patted her on the back. "Don't take offense. The more outlandish Sara's comments, the more she likes you."

Sara laughed and continued to string lights. "For the record, I like you a lot, Emily Whitaker. Not as much as I like your brother. When I first came to town, Noah flirted with me every chance he got."

"Noah flirted with everything with a pulse before Katie," Emily muttered.

"But with me he was trying to make Josh jealous." Sara's smile was devious. "You have points in your favor for being related to Noah, but there are other reasons I like you."

"You barely know me." Emily wiped the back of her hand across her mouth. "You definitely don't know me well enough to comment on my sex life." She heard the pretentiousness in her voice that she'd perfected during her short marriage.

Sara only laughed again. It was a rich, musical sound that projected across the vast pasture spreading out behind the house. Sara was petite with pale blond hair and luminous blue eyes. Her bigger-than-life presence made her hard to ignore. Emily supposed the "it girl" vibe contributed to Sara's fame from the time she'd been a child actor.

"We met at the dinner to celebrate your mom's recovery," Sara told her. "You were there with your son, and it's clear you're devoted to him. Another plus in your favor."

"I remember but—"

"You looked tense and defensive, like you might snap in two at any moment." Sara waved a hand toward Emily. "Now you're relaxed and you can't control the good-sex grin on your face—"

"I can control my smile," Emily argued, then thought of Jase and felt the corners of her mouth tug upward. She pressed her fingers to her mouth and glanced at April.

"Don't look at me. I'm certainly not smiling like that."

"Which is what we're working on next," Sara said, moving to April's side. "You've been alone for too long, my friend."

April shook her head, a tangle of red curls bouncing around her face. "One marriage was quite enough, thank you. I'm perfectly content without a man in my life."

"Don't forget I was married, too." Emily wasn't sure why she felt compelled to argue this point. The idea that these women she was only beginning to know could read her was scary as hell. "I have a son and he's my priority. I don't have time for anything else."

"But you've been making time," Sara said.

April's voice was gentle. "You do seem happier, which is a good thing."

"Maybe it's the yoga." Emily pointed at April. "I've been coming to your classes. Maybe you should take credit for my newfound calm, if that's what I have."

"It's more than calm," April told her with a smile. "It's a glow. I'd love to believe it was the yoga but—"

"It's sex." Sara winked. "You don't have to admit it for it to be true."

"Don't tell Katie," Emily mumbled after a moment. "She and Noah will want there to be more to it than there is." She bit down on her lip, then grinned. "And it's great the way it is."

It had been more than great and her stomach did a slow, sweet roll at the thought of the time she'd spent with Jase. It was easy to have him come to the farm with Ruby after work under the guise of discussing wedding plans or the mayor's race, and he'd become a fixture at their dinner table. Emily's mother had even insisted he bring Declan to join them for several evening meals.

At first it amazed her how seriously he seemed to value her opinion. Whether on reception details or the more important campaign strategies, he listened to her ideas and often used them as the foundation from which to build his own.

Emily liked being someone's foundation. And she loved the private, stolen moments when Jase would wrap her in his arms and shower her with kisses. She felt the telltale goofy smile tug at her mouth again.

Sara threw an arm around April's shoulder. "Yoga classes are lovely but nothing is better than the restorative powers of great sex." She pointed at Emily. "Are you going to tell us who it is?"

"Do I have to?"

Sara thought about that for a moment. "No, but if you don't I'll be forced to ask your soon-to-be sister-in-law."

April lifted her hand to clamp it over Sara's mouth. "Forgive her. She means well. You don't have to tell us anything." April's voice was gentle, her tone so motherly it made Emily warm inside. "For the record," April added, "I think Jase is great."

"He is..." Emily narrowed her eyes. "Wait. That was sneaky." A gorgeous earth mother with a little edge.

"April's the worst," Sara said when April dropped her hand. "She's gentle and sweet, so people don't realize she's also whip smart and far too observant. The thing that makes it less annoying is she'll protect your secrets to her grave."

"Is Jase a secret?" April asked, her eyes all too perceptive.

"Yes." Emily shook her head. "I mean, no. We're friends."

"April needs a friend like that," Sara said with a laugh.

"Why don't you worry about your own love life and leave mine alone?" April crossed her arms over her chest and did her best to glare at Sara. She still looked sweet.

"No worries in my life." Sara wiggled her brows. "Josh is absolutely perfect. In fact, just last night..."

"Save it," April said quickly. "We're talking about Emily."

"Feel free to move on," Emily told them, then held up a hand to Sara. "I'm not asking for details about your private life."

Sara grabbed a muffin off the table and dropped into a chair. "You don't seem like a sell-it-to-the-tabloids type of person."

"No."

"Of course she's not," April agreed. "So you and Jase are friends." April pointed at Emily. "The kind of friends that have seen each other naked."

"That's one way to put it," Emily answered, making a face.

"You like him?"

Emily nodded.

"A lot?" Sara asked.

"Yes."

"Everyone in town loves him," April offered. "Why just friends and why the secret?"

"Because," Sara added, popping a bite of muffin in her mouth. "You understand this town can't keep a secret? People will find out."

"If they don't already know," April said.

"We want something that belongs to us."

Now Sara's face softened. "Oh, yes. I understand." She glanced at April. "We both do."

Sara stood and came to give Emily a hug. She glanced over her shoulder at April. "Come on. Group embrace."

The willowy redhead, who smelled of vanilla and cloves, wrapped them both in a tight hug. "What is between you and Jase is yours," she whispered. "But don't hold on to it too tight. Love is like a garden, Emily. It needs light and air to breathe, or it will shrivel before it has a chance to grow strong."

Emily gasped. "It's not love," she murmured. "It can't be."

Neither Sara nor April answered. They only tightened their hold on her.

By the time the last team came through the doors of the brewpub in downtown Crimson, Jase's mood was as dark as the mahogany paneling lining the walls.

Luckily his friends didn't seem to notice. Everyone had loved Emily's scavenger hunt. The teams had raced through Crimson collecting mementoes that were special to Noah and Katie.

Now they were sharing stories about the couple, laughing and toasting the impending nuptials as the bride and groom held court at one of the large tables in the center of the bar. The entire evening had been a success if he ignored the fact that Emily was doing her best to avoid him.

With so many of their friends around, it was easy to accomplish. No matter how many times Jase tried to meet her gaze or talk to her alone, she managed to slip away. He knew she'd spent the day working out at Crimson Ranch with Sara and April, but he couldn't imagine how things could have changed between them so quickly.

He watched her step away from the main group to take a call on her cell phone, her brows puckering at whatever was being said on the other line. The conversation only lasted a few minutes, and he moved behind her as she ended the call.

"Everything okay?"

She jumped, pressing a hand to her chest. "Sneak up much?"

"Avoid people much?" he countered.

Color rose to her cheeks and she looked everywhere but into his eyes. The sudden distance between them made him angry. This had been the best week of his whole damn life. Even with the campaign, work and all the other pressures of regular life, Jase had felt happier than he could remember. He wanted more from Emily. He wanted the right to give more *to* her.

Maybe it was excitement around the wedding or so many of his friends in relationships, but he was convinced Emily was meant for him. He'd always made decisions in his life based on what was smart and responsible. Duty had governed his actions for as long as he could remember. Being with Emily was about making himself happy. Making her happy. For the first time, he wanted to commit to something more than this town and restoring his family name.

He wanted something of his own.

He wanted Emily.

"It's been a hectic day," she said, her tone stiff. "I want everything to be perfect for Noah and Katie."

"I thought we agreed perfection is overrated."

She looked at him now, her eyes sad. "Not for the two of them. They deserve it."

"You deserve—"

She held up a hand. "I can't have this conversation now. My mom called. One of Davey's completed sets fell off the shelf and broke. He's having a meltdown." The sound of laughter and music carried to them and she glanced over his shoulder at their friends. She looked so alone it made his gut twist. "I've got to go, but I don't want to worry Noah. Will you cover for me?"

"Let me come with you."

"It's better if you don't," she whispered. "People will talk."

"I don't give a damn what anyone says."

She wrapped her arms tight around her middle. "I do."

Those two words killed him. He'd told her he wouldn't push her, and he had to honor that. When she turned to walk away, it took everything in him not to stop her.

Even more when Aaron Thompson slid off his bar stool as she moved past. The man put a meaty hand on Emily's arm and she flinched. Jase saw red as Aaron leaned closer and Emily's face drew into a stiff mask.

Jase was striding forward by the time she shook free and ran out the pub's front door.

"What the hell did you say to her?" He pushed Aaron's broad chest, and the man stumbled into the empty bar stool, knocking it on its side with a clatter.

Jase felt the gazes of the crowded bar on him, but for once he didn't care. He stepped into Aaron's space as the other man straightened.

Aaron leaned closer and lowered his voice so only Jase could hear. "I told her she'd have a hard enough time raising that weirdo kid of hers in this town without hitching herself to the Crenshaw wagon." His beady eyes narrowed farther. "When she's ready for a real man, she should give me a call. Your dad couldn't keep a woman satisfied, and I doubt you're any different."

It didn't matter that Emily was gone. Jase knew Aaron's words would have prodded at her fears, the same way they slithered into his. "Don't ever," he said on a growl, "speak to her again."

"Oh, yeah?" Aaron smirked. "Whatcha going to do about it?"

Jase hauled back his fist and punched Aaron, his knuckles landing against skin with an audible thud. The burly man staggered a few steps before righting himself. Noah and Liam had already grabbed hold of Jase.

"Dude," Aaron shouted into the sudden quiet of the bar. "I'm sorry. My dad wants what's best for this town. You don't have to threaten our family."

"Settle down, man," Noah said when Jase strained against him.

"He's lying." Jase felt blood pounding against his temples. He glanced around the bar to find himself the center of attention from every corner. He was so used to being universally liked, it took him a minute to recognize the emotions playing in the gazes of the friends and strangers who stared at him.

Anger. Disappointment. Pity.

"He's a liar," Jase yelled and felt a heavy hand clasp on to his shoulder.

"What's the problem?" Cole Bennett, Crimson's sheriff, stepped between Jase and Aaron.

Aaron winced. "I made an offhand comment about the election to Jase," he said, holding a hand to one eye. "You know, *may the best man win* and whatever. He went crazy on me." He looked at the sheriff all righteous indignation. "Must have hit a nerve. My dad can tell you plenty of stories about the Crenshaws going ballistic for no reason."

Anger radiated through every cell in Jase's body. He shifted, then realized Noah and Liam were still holding him. "I'm fine," he said, shrugging away.

"You sure?" Noah's voice was concerned.

"Yeah." He pointed at Aaron. "That's not what went down and you know it."

Sheriff Bennett stepped closer to him, placing one hand on his chest. "You want to tell me a different side of the story?"

Jase opened his mouth, then snapped it shut again. He caught Aaron's smug gaze over Cole's shoulder and realized tonight was no accident. He'd been set up in this scene and had fallen right into the trap. He couldn't contradict Aaron's story without revealing specifics of the truth, which would humiliate Emily.

"No." He closed his eyes and tamped down his temper. "I've got nothing to say."

Cole heaved out a sigh. "Are you sure?"

Jase met the other man's gaze. "I am."

"What if I want to press charges?" Aaron asked.

Cole gave Jase an apologetic look, then turned to the other man. "Do you?"

"I should. It was a cheap shot." The bartender handed Aaron a bag of ice and he groaned a little as he pressed it to his eye. "But I guess we can't expect anything else from a Crenshaw."

Noah took a step forward, anger blazing in his eyes. "Don't be a—"

"It's okay," Jase interrupted, grabbing hold of his friend. "If he wants to press charges—"

"I don't. My father taught me to be the better man."

"Okay, then. Let's move on. Everybody back to their regularly scheduled evening." Cole turned to Jase. "I assume you're heading out?"

Jase nodded.

"I don't know what he did to deserve that punch," Cole said, "but I can guarantee it wasn't the story he told about the election. You sure you don't want to tell me anything else?"

"Positive."

With a nod, Cole moved away. Liam and Noah took his place.

"What the hell, Jase?" Noah asked. "I don't think I've ever seen you take a swing at somebody."

"I've got to get out of here," Jase muttered. "Sorry about causing a scene during your party."

Liam placed a hand on his shoulder. "You want company?" When Jase shook his head, Liam nodded and walked back toward their group of friends.

"Come back to our table," Noah told him. "Don't let this ruin the night."

"I'm not going to," Jase answered, "but I need to go now. Give Katie a hug for me. I'll pick you up in the morning to head out to Crimson Ranch."

Noah looked like he wanted to argue but only said, "No one expects you to be perfect, Jase."

"I know." But both of them knew it was a lie. People in this town expected perfection, duty and self-sacrifice from Jase, all of it offered with a smile. He understood that in the way of small towns, the news of the punch would spread like dandelion fuzz on the wind. The news, while inconsequential in its retelling, only needed to be nurtured a bit before it took root and grew into the start of a weed that could derail everything he'd worked to create.

At this moment he couldn't bring himself to care.

He left the bar and kept his head down as he walked to his parking space in the alley behind his office building. Driving out of town, he was tempted to take the turnoff toward the Crawfords' farm. Thoughts of Emily and her reaction to Aaron's taunts consumed him, but he'd promised not to ask her for more than she was willing to give. In his current mood he might drive a wedge between them if he pushed her.

Instead he steered his SUV toward the trailer park and pulled into his father's small lot. The blue-tinted glow from the television was the only thing lighting the inside of the trailer.

Declan hit the mute button on the remote when Jase walked in. "I thought the big party for Noah was tonight?"

"It is," Jase said, lowering himself to the sofa. "What happened to our family, Dad? Why are we so messed up? Mom leaving with Sierra, you and Uncle Steve drinking, Grandpa in jail. Why does every generation of our family have a sad story to tell?"

His father leaned back against the recliner's worn cushion. "Not every generation. Not you."

"Not yet," Jase shot back. "It's like there's a curse on us, and I don't know if I'm strong enough to break it."

"You already have."

"I decked Aaron Thompson tonight."

"Hot damn," Declan muttered. "That little jerk has been giving you grief since grade school."

"You noticed?"

"I'm a drunk, not an idiot. Hitting Aaron does not make you cursed. Hell, I've taken a swing or two at Charles over the years."

"And gotten yourself cuffed for the trouble."

"Worth it every time."

"I'm not you."

Declan laughed. "Praise the Lord." He leaned forward, placed his elbows on his knees. "In a town like Crimson, people see what they want. Once a reputation is set, it's hard to change it. I don't know how the trouble with our family started, but I do know it's easier to live down to expectations than to try to change them. At least it was for me. Your grandpa went to jail for the first time when I was ten. My brother and I had our first beers when we were eleven. Working in the mine didn't help. Nothing much good comes from sticking a bunch of ornery men inside a mountain."

Jase asked the question he'd been afraid to discuss with his dad for almost twenty years. "What about Mom?"

"Your mom was right to go. I was a mess back then."

"Yeah, Dad," Jase answered, "I know. I was the one taking care of you."

"You don't remember, do you?"

"Mom leaving?" Jase shrugged. He remembered crying. He remembered being alone at night staring at the empty bed where his sister had slept next to him.

"She wanted you to go with her."

"No. She took Sierra and left me behind."

"Because you told her I needed you more." When Declan met Jase's gaze, his eyes were shining with unshed tears. "She had your little suitcase in the trunk but you refused to get in the car. It killed her but eventually she agreed to let you stay. That's how I know you're not like the rest of us. You've never done a selfish thing in your life. You take care of this town like you've taken care of me all these years. With every ounce of who you are. You're not part of the curse. You're our family's shot at breaking it."

Jase closed his eyes and tried to remember the details of the night his mom had driven away. All he could see was Sierra's face in the car window and the taillights glowing in the darkness. The days after were a blur of tears and anger and his father going on a major bender.

"One punch doesn't make you a troublemaker, Jase."

"Tell that to the people who witnessed it."

"What I should do is talk to the man who's the cause of all your recent stress. This is Charles Thompson's fault. If he—"

"It's fine." Jase stood, ran a hand over his face. "Don't go after Thompson again. You're right. The Crenshaw curse ends with me."

He started to walk past his dad, but Declan reached out with a hand on Jase's arm. "It's what you want, Jase. Right?"

"Sure, Dad." Jase didn't know how else to answer and he was too tired to sort out his muddled emotions, either to his father or himself. "I'm picking up Noah early tomorrow to drive out to the ranch. Call if you need anything, okay?"

"Save me a piece of cake," his dad said, sitting back in the recliner. Declan had been invited to the wedding but since alcohol was being served, he'd decided to forgo the celebration. Jase appreciated his dad's effort to stay sober but hated that it isolated Declan even more than he already was.

"Are you sure you don't want me to get you for the ceremony?"

"Enjoy yourself tomorrow, son. Don't worry about me."

Jase gave the smile he knew his dad wanted to see. "Call if you change your mind."

Chapter 12

"Are you nervous?" Emily paced the guest cabin where she and Katie were waiting for the wedding to start. "You don't look nervous." She turned to Katie, who was glowing in the ivory gown they'd chosen at the bridal salon in Aspen. "You look beautiful." The satin gown had a sweetheart neckline and a lace overlay that was both delicate and modern. Katie's dark hair was pulled away from her face in a half-knot, with gentle curls tumbling over her shoulders. "Noah is going to lose his mind when he sees you. But, seriously, shouldn't you be nervous?"

Katie smiled and patted the bed next to her. "I don't need to because you've taken care of everything. It's perfect, Em. My dream day." As Emily sat down on the patchwork quilt, Katie took her hand. "Thank you for everything."

"It was easy." She gave a strangled laugh. "My mother-in-law and I were at the reception hall until two in the morning the night before my wedding redoing seating arrangements. There were so many stupid details to focus on but none of them involved preparing Henry and me to make a life together." She squeezed Katie's fingers. "You and Noah are doing this right."

"Unrequited love, fear of commitment, friendship and a baby after a breakup," Katie said with a laugh. "We might have had the order a little off."

"The love is what counts," Emily answered. She stood when Katie sniffed and Emily grabbed the box of tissues from the dresser, handing Katie a wad of them. "No crying. Your makeup is perfect."

"Then don't say sweet things to me." Katie dabbed at the edge of her eyes with a tissue. "I asked you for my dream wedding, and you've given it to me."

"Not quite yet."

A knock sounded on the door. "Ladies, are you ready?" Sara called.

"Perfect timing," Emily said with a smile.

Katie stood, her eyes widening as she pressed a hand to her stomach. "Wow. Just got nervous. Major butterflies."

"You've got this." Emily opened the door and followed Katie out, smiling as Sara oohed and aahed over the dress. Katie's father was waiting at the edge of the barn, out of sight of the chairs set up in front of the copse of aspens where the ceremony would take place. It was a perfect fall day, cool and sunny with just the slightest breeze.

She knew Katie and her parents weren't close, but her father became visibly emotional at the sight of his daughter. It made Emily's heart ache missing her own dad and all the moments she'd never get to share with him.

But this wasn't a day for sorrow, and she was honored to be Katie's maid of honor. She adjusted Katie's train and then stepped away. When the processional music began, she turned the corner from the barn toward the wedding guests. All Katie's and Noah's closest family and friends were in attendance. Emily's gaze sought Davey first, her son looking so handsome in his suit, standing next to his grandma in the front row. His eyes flicked to hers and she saw the stiffness in his small shoulders ease the tiniest bit.

The knowledge that seeing her gave him some comfort made her heart squeeze. She looked up to her brother standing in front of the grapevine arbor and smiled before her eyes met those of the man standing next to him.

She had to work to control her expression as Jase looked at her, his gaze intense. Her knees went weak and she clutched the bouquet of wildflowers tighter. One foot in front of the other, she reminded herself. Breathing in the warm mountain air, she felt her heart skip as Jase's mouth curved up at one end. As much as she'd tried to avoid him the previous night, now she couldn't break eye contact, even as she took her place in front of the assembled guests.

The music changed and Katie came into view. Emily glanced at the beautiful bride but then watched her brother's face as Katie moved closer. There was so much love in Noah's eyes. It was as if the whole world went still for a moment and there was only her brother and his bride. Emily was suddenly grateful for the tissue she'd stuffed under the ribbon of her bouquet.

She continued to need the tissue as the short ceremony progressed. By the time Noah leaned down to kiss his bride, Emily swore she could hear the whole valley choking back tears. Then there were only smiles and cheers as Noah and Katie walked back down the aisle hand in hand.

Jase offered her his elbow and she tucked her hand in it, blushing as he leaned close to her ear and whispered, "You look beautiful." She sucked in another breath and smoothed one hand over the pale pink cocktail gown she wore. She felt beautiful and happy and lighter than she had in ages. As they started down the aisle together, Emily was proud to meet the approving gazes of the people she'd come to think of as her community.

But Jase paused before the first row. "You two belong with us," he said to her mother and Davey.

Emily's heart, already so full, expanded even more at her mother's watery, grateful smile. Jase tucked Meg's arm into his other elbow and nodded at Davey. "Why don't you lead us down, buddy?"

The boy looked at the ground and Emily wanted to curse her own stupidity. She knew her son didn't like people looking at him and was afraid Jase's sweet gesture would backfire.

Davey chewed on his lower lip for a few seconds and finally muttered, "I'll follow you."

Emily breathed a sigh of relief and saw her mother do the same. Jase nodded and the four of them made their way past the other guests.

Emily didn't have a chance to speak to Jase alone until the dancing started. Meg and her new beau had taken Davey home after the cake was cut. To Emily's surprise, Davey had seemed to actually enjoy himself at the wedding, running around through the field behind the tables with the other kids.

He stuck close to Brooke Travers and didn't yell or play fight the way the other boys at the reception did, but he was definitely a part of the group and she couldn't have been prouder.

As the sky darkened over the mountain, silhouetting the craggy peaks against the deep blue of evening, a three-piece bluegrass band began to play. Noah pulled Katie onto the makeshift dance floor near the edge of the patio and other couples followed. Emily was just about to head inside to see if the caterers needed help packing up when strong arms slipped around her waist.

"Dance with me?" Jase asked but was already turning her to face him.

"I should check on things," she said but didn't protest when he lifted her hands to his shoulders.

"It's fine," he said, beginning to sway with her to the lilting sound of the fiddle drifting toward them. "Better than fine. All of your hard work made this a perfect day."

"We both worked hard," she corrected and rested her head against his chest. "You and I make a pretty good team." She was starting to trust the happiness she felt, to rely on it.

One of Noah's high school friends walked by, then stopped and clapped Jase on the shoulder. "Good to see you've grown a spine, Crenshaw."

Emily felt Jase tense and lifted her head.

He said a few words to the man, then tried to turn her away.

"Makes me want to vote for you all the more," the man said with a chuckle. "I like a mayor with a strong right hook." With another laugh, he walked away.

Emily pulled back enough to look up at Jase. "What was that about?"

He shook his head. "Nothing."

"A strong right hook isn't nothing," she argued. "Did you hit someone?" She couldn't imagine a circumstance where Jase would throw a punch.

"Let's just dance."

"Tell me."

He blew out a breath. "Aaron Thompson," he muttered. "What about him?"

"I saw him talking to you at the bar last night. You were upset when you left, so I asked him about it."

The happiness filling her moments earlier evaporated like a drop of water in the desert. Shame took its place, hot and heavy, a familiar weight on her chest. She hated that anyone, especially Jase, knew the awful things Aaron had said to her. But even more...

"You hit him?" she asked and several people nearby turned to look at them. She stepped out of Jase's arms and lowered her voice. "I didn't need you to defend me."

"He was out of line. No one has the right to speak to you that way." He reached for her, but she jerked back, giving herself a mental headshake. What was between her and Jase was supposed to be casual. Emily had let it turn into something more because he made her happy. But the way Aaron had taken advantage of that was the unwelcome reminder she needed. She couldn't let this go any further.

She caught Noah's gaze and flashed her brother a small smile as she waved. "I'm going to check if the caterers need help."

"Emily," Jase whispered, "don't walk away."

But she hurried into the cabin before Jase could stop her. She told herself it was because she was angry at Jase, although it felt more like fear clawing at her stomach. Panic at the thought of depending on someone and allowing herself to be vulnerable again. Of needing Jase and then having him leave her. It was one thing when they were on equal ground, but if she began to rely on him and truly opened her heart...what was to stop him from breaking it?

April was supervising the last of the cleanup so Emily pitched in where she could. Her hands trembled as she moved vases of flowers to the kitchen's large island but she didn't stop working.

"I think we're almost finished in here," April said eventually. "I don't have a hot guy waiting to dance with me, so I can handle the rest."

"It's fine," Emily muttered. "I'm not in the mood to dance."

"Uh-oh." April stepped in front of her as she turned for the sink. "What's wrong?"

"Nothing."

"What kind of nothing?"

Emily sighed and met the redhead's gentle gaze. "Is it really possible to start over?"

April opened her mouth, then shut it again as if she didn't actually know how to answer the question.

"It seems easy in theory," Emily continued. "Cut out the bad parts from your life and move on. Let go. Tomorrow's a new day. I can spout out greeting-card sentiments until I run out of breath. But is it possible? How can I leave the past behind? Life isn't simple, you know?"

"I do know," April said with a sad smile. "Maybe it's not about a fresh start as much as it is continuing to try to do better."

"Learn from your mistakes?" Emily laughed. "Another cliché, but I have plenty to choose from."

April picked up a flower and twirled the stem between her fingers. "Play it cool as much as you want, but it's obvious you really care for Jase, and he's crazy about you."

Emily swallowed. "I wasn't looking for…"

"For love?"

"It isn't—"

April tapped Emily on the nose with the wildflower's soft petals. "I have no history in this town, Emily. No expectations of who either of you are supposed to be. You can be honest with me."

"Which may be easier than being honest with myself."

"Start with saying the words out loud."

Emily swallowed then whispered, "I love him."

"I have a feeling he feels the same."

"He can't," Emily said, shaking her head. "We want different things from life. I can't be the woman he needs."

"Maybe what he needs is the woman you are."

Emily felt tears clog the back of her throat. A tiny sliver of hope pushed its way through the dark layers of doubt she'd heaped on top of it. "Are you always this good at giving pep talks?"

"To other people," April told her, "yes."

The catering manager walked back into the kitchen with the final bill.

"I'll take care of this," April said. "You find Jase."

"I can't tell him yet." Emily fisted her hands until her nails left marks on the center of each palm. "It's too soon. I don't know—"

"You might start with showing him how you feel," April said and nudged her toward the patio door.

"Right. Show don't tell. I think I can do that." At the thought of being in Jase's arms again, her stomach buzzed and fluttered like a thousand winged creatures were taking flight inside it. "I think I'd like that very much."

As she stepped back outside, she saw that Jase and the other guests had gathered in the center of the patio to say goodbye to Noah and Katie. The newlyweds were staying in one of the guest cabins at Crimson Ranch overnight before driving to the Denver airport tomorrow to fly out for their honeymoon to a Caribbean island.

"I'm so happy to have a sister," Katie said as Emily hugged her.

"Me, too," Emily whispered, then turned to her brother. "I'd tell you to get busy making me a little niece or nephew," she said, punching him lightly on the arm, "but for once in your life, you're an overachiever."

"Always the clever one." Noah chuckled and pulled her in for a hug. "Call if you need anything."

"I absolutely won't," Emily shot back. "You've earned these two weeks in paradise. Enjoy them."

"I intend to and thanks again, Em." Noah tipped up her chin. "You made my bride very happy."

"Go." Emily made a shooing motion. "I've laid all the groundwork for you to get lucky tonight."

Noah leaned in close and kissed Emily on the cheek. "Maybe I'm not the only one," he whispered with a wink, then turned and scooped Katie off her feet.

Everyone cheered as the couple disappeared down the pathway toward the far cabins. As the music started again, guests drifted back toward the patio. Emily continued to stare into the darkness for several minutes, nerves making her skin tingle as she thought about finding Jase in the crowd.

With a fortifying breath she turned and bumped right into him. She yelped and stumbled back. Jase grabbed hold of her arms to steady her.

"Were you some kind of a cat burglar in another life?" she asked, trying to wrestle her pounding heart under control. "You're far too good at being quiet."

He let go of her, dropping his hands to his sides. "My dad wasn't much fun with a hangover. I learned to be quiet so I wouldn't wake him."

"Oh." Her comment had been meant as a joke. The way

he answered made her remember they'd each been shaped by their past. "I'm sorry."

"No need," he said quickly. "It's a fact."

"I meant for earlier. Even if it wasn't necessary, thank you for defending my honor with Aaron."

"Again, no need. You don't deserve to be dragged into the long shadow cast by my family's reputation." The music picked up tempo and Jase turned for the house. "Should we head back?"

Emily didn't move. "What do you mean your *family's reputation*? Aaron told me I might as well be campaigning for his father since I was distracting you from the usual attention you pay to Crimson and its residents. He insinuated that a relationship with a divorced mom of a kid with special needs would work against your bid for mayor."

"I'm going to kill him," Jase muttered. "I wish I would have knocked him out cold." He ran his hands through his hair, leaving it so tousled Emily couldn't resist reaching up to straighten it.

"No," she told him. "You shouldn't have hit him at all."

He pulled her hands away from his hair, clamping his fingers gently around her wrists. "Emily, what is the real problem here?"

Where to start?

Your dreams. My fears.

Falling in love with you.

Definitely don't lead with that one.

She raised up on tiptoe and slid her lips along his, the knot of tension inside her unfurling at the warmth of his mouth and the roughness of his stubble when their cheeks brushed. He smelled like the mountains and tasted of mint and sugary wedding cake. Right now, he was everything she wanted in the world.

Show don't tell.

"The only problem is we're not undressed."

Jase gave a harsh laugh. "You're trying to distract me."

"Is it working?"

"Hell, yes." He glanced over his shoulder toward the lights of the party, which was still going strong even in the absence of the bride and groom. "Think anyone will notice if we sneak away?"

"Let them notice." She would deal with the consequences of her feelings for Jase another time. When he laced his fingers with hers, Emily almost forgot her doubts. She simply let them go.

Giving in to the happiness fizzing through her made her giggle.

Jase glanced down at her but didn't stop moving toward his SUV. "What's so funny?"

She shook her head. "Nothing. I'm glad to be with you."

He opened the passenger door and she slipped in. "You just made me the second-happiest guy on this ranch." He pulled the seat belt around her, using it as an excuse to kiss her senseless.

She took out her phone and punched in a quick text to her mother as Jase came around the front of the SUV. "Everything okay?" he asked, turning the key in the ignition.

Emily waited to speak until her mother's answering text came through. Then she smiled at him. "I've got permission for a sleepover."

"The whole night?" His voice was husky.

"Yep. I mean, I'd like to be home in the morning for breakfast. Davey usually sleeps until about eight on the weekend so that gives us…"

"All night long," Jase finished, taking her hand and lifting it to his mouth. Then he cringed a little. "Unfortunately, the puppy doesn't like to sleep in so late."

"I guess you're going to have to make waking up early worth my while."

Of course, Ruby needed some attention when they got back to the house. "One of my neighbors came over a couple of times today to let her out and play with her." Emily laughed as Ruby exploded out of her crate, yipping and running circles around Jase as he struggled to clip on her leash. "Clearly, she's ready for more. I'm sorry. This isn't exactly a great start to a romantic evening. I need to take her for a short walk so she won't be so wound up."

"I'll come with you." They followed the puppy into the front yard toward the sidewalk.

As Ruby sniffed a tree, Jase shrugged out of his coat and wrapped it around Emily's shoulders. She loved being surrounded by his scent and the warmth of him. They started down the sidewalk with Ruby happily trotting next to them. She seemed in no hurry to do her business tonight, making Jase groan and Emily laugh.

"I'm sor—"

"Don't say it." She took his hand as they walked. "This is nice. I love the quiet of your neighborhood and this time of night, especially after the past week of planning the wedding. It feels normal."

"Normal is underrated," he said with a laugh. "Every birthday wish when I was a kid was for a normal family like yours."

"As I remember, a lot of those birthdays were spent at our house."

"Your mom would bake a red velvet cake and you'd refuse to come out of your room to sing."

Emily pressed her free hand to her face. "I was horrible to you."

"You were pretty mean to Noah, too, so I took it as a compliment."

"Only you, Jase."

Ruby finally found the perfect patch of grass and they turned back toward the house. They walked in silence for a few feet until Emily felt Jase's body tense.

"What is it?"

"I wanted to ask you something, a favor really," he told her. "You know city council is holding a town hall meeting in two weeks. Charles and I are both supposed to be there. People will have a chance to ask us questions about our plans as mayor."

She nodded.

"They'll want us to introduce our families as part of the meeting. I think it was Charles's idea as a way to discredit me. He can stand up there with his wife and sons as proof he's an established family man and I'll just be...alone."

"I'm sure your dad will come if you ask him."

Jase shook his head. "He doesn't like crowds. They make him anxious and that makes him want to drink." He let out a small laugh. "Well, everything makes him want to drink but so far he seems committed to his sobriety this time around. I don't want to mess that up."

"You've supported him in so many ways over the years," Emily argued. "He can do this for you."

"Honestly, I'm not sure if having my dad there would be a help." Jase stopped at the bottom of his porch steps as Ruby nosed around in the bushes in front of the house. "I was hoping you and your mom and Davey would stand up for me."

Emily felt her mouth drop open and quickly snapped it shut at the look of disappointment that flashed in Jase's eyes.

"Never mind. Stupid idea." He let go of her hand to scoop up the puppy. "When you mentioned me celebrating my birthdays at your parents' farm, it made me think the Crawfords were almost more of a family to me than my own." Ruby wriggled in his arms and licked his chin. "But you aren't my family, and I know how you feel about being in the spotlight. I'll bring Ruby." He laughed, but it sounded forced. "Puppies are always crowd pleasers."

He turned for the house, then stopped when she placed a hand on his arm.

Show don't tell.

Emily had assumed April meant those words from a physical standpoint, which was easy enough. She wanted Jase more than she could have imagined—longed to be in his arms. She thought about all the little things he'd done for her, from allowing her full control of his office to letting her take the lead on the wedding plans to showing up at the school ice cream social to check on her and Davey.

Despite her fears and doubts, she wanted to give something back to him. The town hall meeting was big, but she was coming to realize starting over was a mix of baby steps and giant leaps. Not pretending the past didn't happen but moving through the old hurts to create new happiness.

"We'll be there," she said and had the pleasure of watching gratitude and joy wash over his features. It felt so good to give this to him. It felt right.

"You don't have to," he told her. "I mean it. I'll be fine."

"You're not alone," she whispered. She leaned forward to kiss him but stopped when Ruby licked her right on the mouth.

Jase groaned as Emily laughed.

"You should still bring the dog," Emily said as she wiped her mouth. "She's your ace in the hole."

"Right now I want her out of my arms." He nudged open the front door and deposited the puppy on the hardwood floor. "And you in them." He pulled Emily against his chest.

"I take priority over Ruby?" she asked with a laugh. "I feel so important."

"You take priority over everything," he whispered against the top of her head. His words made sparks dance across her skin. "Thank you, Em. I know what I'm asking is a lot." He tipped up her head, cupping her face between his hands. "If you decide it won't work, I'll understand."

His touch was tender. "I'll make it work," she told him and somehow she would.

Ruby scampered toward her basket of toys, picked up a stuffed bunny with her, teeth then walked into her crate to curl up with it.

"She's tired," Emily said.

"Finally."

Jase went over and locked the crate, then returned to Emily. "So how about a sleepover?"

Emily giggled. "Maybe you shouldn't call it that. It reminds me of being a kid…you know, pillow fights and nail-painting parties."

"Pillow fights, yes." Jase kissed the corner of her mouth. "Nail painting, no." He moved closer and deepened the kiss. She held on to him and he lifted her as if she weighed nothing, moving down the hall toward his bedroom. "Do you want to have a pillow fight?" he asked as he set her down on the bed, then covered her body with his.

"Maybe later."

"I'll hold you to that," he told her. "After I hold you to me."

She laughed again, loving how Jase made everything

fun. She'd never thought of the bedroom as a place for laughter until the tall, sweet man watching her from chocolate-brown eyes had come into her life.

She slipped off her shoes and reached behind her back for the zipper of the cocktail gown she wore. Her fingers paused as Jase pulled his tie over his head, then undid the buttons of his tailored shirt. His broad chest made her mouth water.

He moved to the edge of the bed and slid his palms up her bare legs. He grasped the hem of her dress and she lifted up onto her elbows as he tugged it off her. His eyes darkened as they raced over her.

"The lingerie," he said in a half growl, "I like it."

Emily whispered a silent prayer of thanks to her new sister-in-law. Katie had insisted she buy the matching bra and panties during one of their prewedding shopping trips to Aspen. At the time it had seemed like a foolish expense, but now the lavender lace made her feel beautiful. Or maybe it was the way Jase was looking at her. Her whole body grew heavy with need.

She crooked a finger at him. "Come closer, Mr. Almost Mayor, and take it off me," she whispered.

He toed out of his shoes and took off his suit pants, then climbed onto the bed, lowering his weight over her as he claimed her mouth. No more joking or laughter. His kiss was intense and demanding, and she moaned as his fingers skimmed across her breast. Emily arched off the bed as his mouth followed, grazing the sensitive peak with his teeth.

Then they were a tangle of arms and legs, sighs and whispered demands. The demands came mostly from her. She was impatient for him but he insisted on moving slowly, savoring each moment and lavishing attention on every inch of her body.

This man wrote the book on show don't tell. She'd never felt so cherished or been so fully possessed. As much as she longed to say the words *I love you*, Emily still held back. But when they moved together as the pleasure built and built and finally shattered them both, all of her defenses crumbled in a shimmer of light and passion. She knew things could never go back to the way they'd been, at least not for her. Jase Crenshaw well and truly owned her heart.

Chapter 13

Jase could feel Emily's heart beating steady against his chest early the next morning. She was wrapped around him, snuggled in tight and sleeping soundly.

She'd told him sleep was often elusive for her, so he reveled in the fact that she was snoring softly as morning light peeked in between the slats of the wood shutters that covered his bedroom windows.

He'd never allowed a woman to spend the night at his house before Emily. This place was a sanctuary to him, and he hadn't been willing to share it with anyone else. The satisfaction he felt at waking up with her beside him should be terrifying. It proved he was already in far too deep when he still expected her to break his heart.

Yet his smile wouldn't fade. It felt so damn *right* to have her here. He'd put the down payment on the modest bungalow shortly after taking over the law practice. It had been a rite of passage to buy a home he could call his own. But he wasn't sure how to be a host and the women he dated invariably wanted to take over the role. Minutes in the door and they began rearranging sofa pillows and suggesting wall colors.

So he'd stopped inviting anyone over but his guy friends. They didn't care his walls were bare and he had nothing but leftover carryout and beer in the fridge. To his surprise, Emily hadn't either. He'd even solicited her opinion on what he should do to make it homier. She'd told him to keep it as it was, which had been both refreshing and disconcerting. Especially given the ruthlessness with which she'd taken over his office.

At first he'd thought she was respecting his space but over the past few weeks, when she'd stop by but never stay, he'd wondered if it was more about her keeping what was between them casual. Now she was here, and it seemed like a damn good first step.

"I can hear you thinking," she mumbled sleepily, rolling off him.

"Good morning," he said and kissed her cheek.

She yawned, her eyes still closed. "What's got the wheels turning so hard this early?"

"Paint colors."

"Is that code for kinky morning sex?"

He laughed and pulled her close again. "Would you like it to be?"

"Talk to me about paint colors."

He combed his fingers through her hair, loving its softness and the way the scent of her shampoo drifted up to him. "I need to update the house, make it more mine. I was thinking about what color to use for the family room and kitchen."

She rose onto her elbows. "While we're in bed together?

What does that say about me?" She frowned but amusement flickered in her blue eyes.

"It says you inspire me to be a better person. Painting has been on the list for years, but I've ignored it. Even though I bought the house, I couldn't quite believe I deserved it. You make me believe."

Her gaze softened. "You make the most unromantic topics into love poems."

He tapped one finger against her nose. "Again, I give credit to you for inspiring me. Can we get back to kinky morning sex?"

"Dorian Gray."

He thought about that for a moment and then shook his head. "As in *The Picture of...*? The creepy book and movie?"

"Yes and no." She flipped onto her back again. "It's also a paint color, the perfect gray. You should use it for your family room and a shade lighter in the kitchen. It faces north so needs more light."

Jase felt a smile curve his lips. "You've been thinking about colors for my house."

Clearly misunderstanding, she crossed her arms over her chest. "You asked," she said on a huff of breath.

He levered himself over her and kissed the edge of her jaw. "Paint talk as foreplay. Works for me. What do you know about the color wheel?"

"I know you're crazy," she said, rolling her eyes.

"Only for you, Em."

She suddenly turned serious. "This isn't casual anymore."

He thought about lying so he wouldn't chase her away, but he couldn't manage it. "It's not casual for me," he agreed. "It never has been. We can still take it slow and I—"

She pressed her fingers to his mouth. "I like it slow."

Her hand curled around to the back of his neck and she drew him down for a hot, demanding kiss. "I like it most ways with you."

"Emily," he said on a groan. "Tell me you're good with where this is going." He lifted his head and stared into her eyes. "I need to know."

She closed her eyes for a moment and took a deep breath. Then she looked at him again. "I'm scared of feeling too much. But I…" She paused, bit down on her lip, then whispered, "I want it to be more than casual. I want to try with you, Jase. For you."

"For us," he said. There was more he wanted to tell her, but she wasn't the only one afraid of being hurt. Jase was used to keeping the things he wanted most locked up tight. It was when he said the words out loud that his life usually went to hell.

Mommy, don't leave. Don't take Sierra.

Dad, stop drinking before it ruins you.

His requests met with disappointment so he didn't make them, and he wasn't going to now. He needed time to believe this precious thing between them wasn't going to be taken away.

He smiled and kissed her again. "We've got approximately not many minutes until the puppy starts whining," he said, glancing at the clock on the nightstand. "We've established slow is good. Now let's see how we do with fast."

The next two weeks flew by for Jase. One of his biggest cases went to trial early at the courthouse in Aspen, so he was out of the office most of the time. He'd never been as grateful for Emily, who managed his practice with so much efficiency he didn't worry about anything falling behind while he was in court.

He was even more grateful for her when he got home at the end of each long day. She'd taken over Ruby's care, picking up his energetic puppy in the morning on her way to the office and keeping her all day. She claimed both Davey and Tater, Noah's dog that was staying at the farm during Noah and Katie's honeymoon, loved having the puppy around.

When he could manage it, Jase drove directly to the farm after work. It was like he was a teenager again, showing up for dinner at Meg's big table, only now Emily greeted him with a kiss each time he arrived.

Everything in his life was exactly where he wanted it. Everything but the mayor's race. Charles was taking full advantage of Jase's busy schedule by planning campaign events all over town. Almost overnight, yard signs with the slogan Charles Thompson, A Family Man You Can Trust had popped up on every corner. Jase got calls from friends and business owners, suggesting he ramp up his efforts with the election date quickly looming.

The problem was he didn't want to take time away from the rest of his life to focus on the campaign. He couldn't stop questioning the reasons he'd decided to run for the position in the first place. Yes, he was dedicated to Crimson, but he didn't need to be mayor to prove that. Or did he?

He was getting pressure to be seen around town when all he wanted was to spend his free time with Emily and Davey. Although the boy was adjusting to school, he still preferred the quiet of home. Jase had set up a Lego construction area in the corner of his family room so Davey was becoming more comfortable at his house. That didn't solve the issue of Emily needing a quiet life with her son, while Jase's obligations to the town pulled him to be more visible with every passing day.

He checked his watch for the fifth time as he waited for the city council meeting to end late on Tuesday, one day before the big town hall event. Monthly council meetings were held in the evenings because so many of the members also had day jobs. Jase had never minded before because his life was the town. But Emily had texted that Davey wanted to show him his latest Lego structure, and he'd hoped to get out early enough to make it to the farm.

The council members continued to debate the date for the lighting of the town Christmas tree in December while Jase's mind raced from thoughts of Emily to the trial to the doctor's appointment he needed to reschedule for his father to the campaign he was pretending didn't exist.

"Jase, do you have anything to add?" One of the long-time council members lifted a thick brow.

Jase blinked and glanced around at his fellow council members, reluctant to admit he had no idea where the thread of the conversation had gone. Liam Donovan met his gaze and gave a subtle shake of his head.

"No," Jase said firmly, as if he knew what the hell they were talking about now. "I agree on this one."

Thankfully, the general comment was enough to satisfy everyone and the meeting adjourned. He checked his phone, disappointment washing through him. He'd missed a text from Emily, telling him Davey was going to bed and they'd keep Ruby overnight at the farm. She'd added an emoji face blowing a kiss at the end, which only made him want to hurl the phone across the room.

Jase didn't want emoji. He wanted Emily in his arms.

He punched in a quick text promising to stop by in the morning before heading to Aspen.

"You realize you can't speed up or slow down time by watching the clock," Liam said from behind his shoulder.

Gathering his things, Jase turned and shook his head. "It's a damn shame, too. Thanks for saving my butt just now."

Liam nodded. "You weren't exactly dialed in for this meeting. I'll walk out with you."

Jase watched a group of council members standing on the far side of the conference table, heads together as they talked. Charles Thompson was in the middle, as if holding court, and the sight made a sick pit open in Jase's gut. One of the men glanced back at Jase, guilt flashing in his gaze before he waved.

"Looks like you weren't the only one to notice." He followed Liam out into the cool autumn night. He should be sitting on his back porch with Emily right now. Instead he was heading over to his office to work a few more hours on the cross-examination he was preparing for tomorrow.

"Also looks like your campaign is in the toilet," Liam said without preamble. "Before you got to the meeting, Charles made a pretty convincing speech about you being pulled in too many directions to give your full attention to the duties of mayor."

"Which is not true—"

"He also hinted that your dad is having problems and you've got too many distractions right now."

Jase cursed under his breath and turned on his heel. The town meetings were open to the public so Charles had every right to be there. But not to spread lies about Jase's father. "My dad is fine," he ground out, moving back toward the courthouse. "I'm going to—"

"Whoa, there." Liam placed a hand on Jase's shoulder. "It's not a coincidence Charles showed up tonight, made the comment and now is hanging out after the meeting. He's playing dirty, Jase."

"Why the hell did you tell me, then?"

"Because *you* have a choice to make."

Jase shrugged away from Liam's grasp and paced several steps before turning and slamming his palm against the side of the brick building. He cursed again and shook out his hand. "I've made my choice."

"I'm new to the council," Liam said, "but from what I've heard, the choice was made for you. When the former mayor took off, Marshall Daley stepped in as mayor pro tem. He was never going to seek another term, so the town council members suggested you run."

"That's the basic gist," Jase admitted. "It wasn't supposed to be this complicated."

"Did you ever really want to be mayor?"

"Of course I did. I can do the job."

"I'm not debating that."

"I love this town."

"Again, you'll get no argument from me there. Hell, you had a major impact on my decision to make Crimson the headquarters for LifeMap. But it felt different. You were on a mission to make a name for yourself. I didn't understand it then…"

"And now you do?" Jase sagged against the building, tired at the thought of rehashing his family history one more time. "Everyone around here thinks they know me."

Liam shrugged. "It's clear you don't want it the way you once did."

"Is it so wrong to also want a life for myself, as well?"

"No."

"I won't let Charles win."

"Even if it means you lose in the long run?"

Jase straightened. "I'm going to make sure that doesn't happen."

"How?"

"Can I make a suggestion?"

Both men turned as Cole Bennett stepped out around the street corner.

"Evening, Sheriff," Jase said. "Out for a stroll downtown or is this official business?"

Cole moved closer. He wore jeans and a T-shirt and held up his hands, palms out. "Off duty tonight. I was hoping to talk to you before the town hall meeting this week." He glanced at Liam. "It's private."

Jase started to argue but Liam held up a hand. "I need to get home anyway. Let me know if I can help. No matter what you decide."

"Thanks, man." Jase shook Liam's hand, then watched him walk across the street to where his truck was parked.

"You have some advice for me?" he asked the sheriff.

"Information," Cole clarified. "Your office is on this block, right?"

Jase nodded.

The sheriff glanced over his shoulder. "Let's go there."

"Why do I have a bad feeling about this?" Jase asked as he led Cole a few storefronts down until they reached his office.

"Because you're not stupid," Cole answered bluntly.

With a sigh, Jase unlocked the door and flipped on the light in the reception area. The scent of vanilla from the candle Emily burned at her desk filled the air, and his heart shifted. The subtle changes she'd made to his life mattered and he hated that his sense of duty to the town was keeping them apart.

It wasn't only his schedule. They'd agreed their relationship wasn't casual, but he could feel Emily holding back. He assumed it was because of his increasing commitments to work and the campaign. While he wanted to tell her it would pass, how could he make that promise if he won the election?

"Since you're not on the clock, how about a drink?" Jase asked, moving toward his office. "I've got scotch or... scotch."

Cole chuckled low. "I'll have a scotch. Thanks."

Jase motioned him into the office, then went to the kitchenette area and poured two squat glasses with the amber-colored liquid. Back in the office, he handed one to Cole, then sat behind his desk.

Cole took a slow sip before placing the glass on Jase's desk. "How bad do you want to win the election?"

The question of the hour. "Not bad enough to do something illegal for it." It was the most honest answer Jase could give without exposing the doubts plaguing him.

"What about exposing something your opponent had done?" the sheriff asked. "Not exactly illegal but it's definitely borderline. Turns out Thompson had been going easy on his friends and neighbors for years. Anytime there was a problem with someone he knew personally, the issue disappeared."

Jase actually laughed. "Everyone except my father."

Cole shrugged. "There's a lot of politics involved in small-town law enforcement. I'm overhauling the department, but I do have records that certain procedures weren't exactly...aboveboard when he was in charge."

"What are you going to do with the information?"

"That's why I'm here. Charles Thompson was supposed to retire and go fishing or whatever the hell else he wanted. I didn't take his bid for mayor too seriously at first." He picked up his glass of scotch and tipped it toward Jake.

"You had the blessing of the council, so there was no question you'd be elected."

Jase didn't shy away from Cole's scrutiny. "Now there is?"

The sheriff finished off his scotch before answering. "Thompson is pushing you hard and you're letting him. I don't know if it's because the garbage he's throwing is getting to you or because you've decided you don't care about winning."

"Maybe I'm tired of my whole life revolving around Crimson."

"Fair enough, but I'm asking you to get your head back in the game. We need you, Jase. We need somebody decent in charge of this town." Cole placed his glass back on the desk and stood. "I can leak what I know about Thompson, make him go away, but it won't change how he's trash-talking you or what it means if you don't answer the accusations. You have a chance to tomorrow night. I hope you take it, but if you need something more let me know."

"Thank you," Jase said and watched the sheriff walk out the door. He threw back the rest of his scotch, welcoming the burn in his gut. Maybe he had been ignoring the campaign in the hope the decision would be taken from him. But that wasn't who he was, and Cole's visit proved it.

Why couldn't he have Emily and the mayor's position? Yes, she had doubts but he'd worked too hard to give up now. He needed to prove that she and Davey fit into his life, every part of it. The town hall meeting would be the perfect place to do just that.

Emily stopped in front of the entrance to the Crimson Community Center where the town hall meeting was about to start. She smoothed a hand over the fitted dress she hadn't worn since she'd stood next to her ex-husband when he'd made partner at his law firm.

"I should have picked something else. This is way too formal."

Her mother squeezed her hand. "You look lovely and the sweater softens the look." Meg glanced down at Davey, who stood a few steps behind Emily, his hands tightly fisted at his sides. "You are very heroic tonight."

Emily shared a look with her mom, then smiled at Davey. He'd insisted on changing into his superhero costume after school today and refused to put on a different outfit for the meeting. She understood that sitting still in a crowd of strangers was going to be a challenge, so hoped Jase understood Davey's wardrobe choice. Her purse was stocked with Davey's favorite snacks, a small bag of Lego pieces and the fail-safe iPad loaded with a few new apps. She prayed it would be enough to keep him content during the meeting.

As her mother held open the door, Emily put a hand on Davey's shoulder to guide him, then drew back as he flinched away from her touch.

Breathe, she told herself. Smile.

She'd come back to Crimson for a quiet life, and now she was putting herself on display for the entire town. Her mother led them up the side aisle to the front row of chairs marked Reserved. Emily glanced over her shoulder as she took her seat and saw several of her new friends sitting together a few rows back. April waved and Natalie Donovan gave her a thumbs-up sign. A little bit of the tension knotted in her chest eased.

A tap on her shoulder had her swinging back around.

"It's not Halloween," Miriam Thompson, Charles's wife, said in a disapproving hiss as she made her way into the seat next to Emily, with Aaron's brother, Todd, on her other side. Aaron wasn't with them, a fact for which Emily was grateful. "You should show some respect to the seriousness of this election."

Red-hot anger rushed through Emily. Anger at Miriam for making the comment, at Jase for asking her to do this but mostly at herself for still caring what people thought of her and her son. Before she could respond, her mother whipped around in her seat.

"You should shut your mouth, Miriam," Meg said. "Before I come over there and do it for you. My grandson can be a superhero every day if it makes him happy." She wagged a finger at each of the Thompsons. "We could use more heroes in this town, not people who feel like it's their right to taunt and bully others."

Miriam gasped but turned away, her cheeks coloring bright pink as she made her son shift seats so she wasn't sitting right beside Emily.

Emily tried to hide her shocked smile as she leaned over Davey toward her mother and spoke low. "'Come over there and do it for you'?"

Meg sniffed. "I never liked that woman."

A hush fell over the room as Liam Donovan walked onto the stage, along with Jase and Charles. Liam was moderating the meeting. A few general announcements were made first and then Liam formally introduced Jase and Charles, although Emily couldn't imagine there was anyone in the room who didn't know either man. Crimson had grown in the years since she'd been gone, but it seemed as though everyone in attendance tonight had some history with the town.

The thought made her encouraged for Jase, as so much of Crimson's recent boom could be attributed to work he'd done as part of the city council. No wonder he was torn between making decisions for his own happiness and his duty to the town.

Charles took the mic first, detailing his background as former sheriff. Emily gritted her teeth as he made special mention of his long marriage, and his family's history of service and philanthropy in Crimson.

Jase didn't seem bothered, though, and stepped to the podium after shaking Charles's hand. He smiled as he looked out over the audience.

"It's great to see so many friendly and familiar faces in this crowd," he began. "This town means a lot to me and no matter what our differences, we can all agree that we want the best and brightest future for Crimson." After a ripple of applause, he spoke again. "I'd like to personally thank Charles for his contributions to our town over the years. Families like the Thompsons gave us a strong foundation. As many of you know, my family's history runs in a different direction." He chuckled softly. "Which is why I'm especially grateful for this town and the people in it."

Emily didn't turn around but she could feel the energy building in the crowd as Jase spoke. He was sincere and articulate, not shying away from where he came from but taking the power of his family's troubled history away from Charles by owning it himself. She'd never been prouder. Then she felt Davey shift next to her. It was hard to tell whether he was reacting to the excitement of the crowd or Jase's voice booming through the room or one of any number of things that might disturb his equilibrium.

The reason didn't matter. Something was also building inside Davey. He fidgeted, tugging on the tights of his superhero costume and humming softly under his breath. She reached in her purse and grabbed the bag of Lego pieces.

"Here, sweetie," she said, placing them gently in his lap.

Keeping her voice calm and trying to regulate her own energy was key for keeping him from moving any closer to a meltdown.

Her mom shot her a look but Emily shook her head. It didn't matter what anyone thought at the moment. She had to keep Davey calm or everything she'd worked so hard to create would blow up in her face.

Davey opened the bag and methodically pulled out building pieces.

Emily breathed a tentative sigh of relief and focused on Jase. He was looking directly at her.

"With me tonight," he said, "is a family who have made me a part of their own over the years." His gaze left hers, but she could still feel the warmth of it across her skin. "What makes this town special is that we take care of each other. Meg and Jacob Crawford took care of me when I needed it most. As mayor, I want to make sure we continue to move Crimson forward and, more importantly, that we continue to look out for one another."

"I guess your own father isn't part of your grand plan?" The loud, slurring voice rang out in the quiet of the meeting room. Emily heard the crowd's collective gasp but kept her eyes on Jase. His expression registered shock, confusion and finally a resigned disappointment as he looked out past the audience toward the back of the room. His gaze flicked to hers for a moment. The silent plea in his chocolate-brown eyes registered deep in her heart even as he schooled his features into a carefully controlled mask once again.

"You count, Dad," he said calmly into the microphone. "But we should talk later."

Emily turned to the back of the room to see Declan making his way up the center aisle. The door to the hallway was swinging closed and she caught a glimpse of a figure moving to the side as it shut. Aaron Thompson.

She got up immediately and moved toward Jase's dad.

"Why the hell aren't I up there with your fake family?" Declan yelled. "I'm part of this town, too. Or have you forgotten why you wanted to become such a do-gooder in the first place, Jase?"

"Declan, don't do this," she said as she got closer. The smell of liquor coming off him hit her so hard she took a step back. She had to get him out of this meeting. "This isn't you talking." She tried to make her voice gentle. "It's the alcohol. Jase needs you to get it under control. Now."

His bloodshot eyes tracked to her. "Oh, yeah, sweetheart. My son loves control. He can't tolerate anything less than total perfection." He motioned a shaky finger between himself and Emily. "The two of us are bound to disappoint him."

The words struck a nerve but she smiled and reached for his hand. "Then let's get out of here."

She could see Sheriff Bennett moving around the edge of the room toward them. A glance over her shoulder showed Jase stepping out from behind the podium toward the edge of the stage. She shook her head, hoping to diffuse Declan's alcohol-filled rant before it had a chance to gather steam.

She took his arm just as she heard Davey cry out, "Mommy, my spaceship. It broke." Her son's voice was a keening cry. "It broke!"

"I won't be handled," Declan yelled and tore his hand away from her grasp.

But Emily's attention was on Davey so instead of letting go she stumbled forward, plowing into Declan's chest and sending them both into the edge of the chair at the end of the row.

Edna Sharpe occupied the chair, and as it tipped, the three of them tumbled to the floor. Emily saw stars as her head slammed into the chair.

All hell broke loose.

People from the nearby rows surrounded them. Edna screamed and flailed at the bottom of the pile. "My ankle. You broke my ankle."

Declan moaned. "I think I'm going to be sick."

Emily scrambled to get out from under him but his thigh was pinning her down.

"Mommy!" Davey screeched, his voice carrying over the din of noise to her. "I lost a piece to my spaceship."

She pushed at Declan, recognizing the mounting hysteria in Davey's tone. Cole Bennett was there a second later, but it was too late. Jase's father coughed, then threw up, the vile liquid hitting Emily's shoulder as she tried to turn away.

He was hauled off her then and she stood, the crowd surrounding them parting as she pushed her way through. One bonus to being puked on—it cleared a path quicker than anything else.

Jase was trying to shoulder his way down the aisle, yelling at people as he moved.

Davey had started shrieking now, and she knew a full-blown meltdown could last for several minutes to close to an hour. Meg met her gaze and whispered, "I'm sorry." Meg picked a screaming Davey up and carried him out the side door of the meeting room.

Emily shook her head as she followed. There was nothing her sweet mother could have done to prevent this moment. The responsibility was Emily's. And she failed. Miserably.

Jase was in front of her a second later. She expected understanding. Instead, he glared at her. "What the hell, Em? You tackled my dad. Is Edna really hurt? This is a mess."

She blinked, unable to process the accusation in his tone, let alone to respond. "I've got to get to Davey," she whispered.

His muffled screams echoed from the hall.

Jase ran a hand through his hair. "Can you get control of him? The screaming is only making this disaster worse."

She reeled back as if he'd slapped her. A disaster. That's how Jase saw her attempt at helping him. Her head was ringing from where she'd hit the corner of the chair. Her son was having a public meltdown. And she was covered in vomit.

"We've got to pull out of this," Jase said, searching her gaze as if he expected her to have a magic solution.

"I'm going to my son," she said, pushing at him. "He's not part of a disaster. He's a scared little boy who shouldn't have been put in this situation in the first place."

"The sheriff has your dad out the door," Liam called from where he stood on the stage. "I'm going to get everyone back to their seats."

Jase closed his eyes for a moment and his gaze was gentler when he opened them again. "I didn't mean it like that. Em…"

"No." She pushed away. It was too late. She knew better. Davey was all that mattered, her only priority. "I've got to get him out of here. Take care of your image or your dad. I don't care. I'm not your problem, Jase. We're not yours."

She hurried down the row, bending to pick up a stray Lego piece as she walked. She found Davey and her mother at the end of the hallway, Davey standing stiffly in front of the wooden bench where her mother sat. She crouched in front of him. "I have the missing piece," she said. He continued to scream, his eyes shut tight and his cheeks blotchy pink as he heaved breaths in and out between shrieks. "Davey, sweetie. Look at Mommy. I have the Lego piece. You can finish the spaceship."

His screaming subsided to an anxious whine as he looked at the small yellow brick she held in front of him. Emily held her breath. He hiccuped and reached for it, holding it gently between his first two fingers. "Thank you, Mommy." He wiped at his cheeks with the back of his sleeve. "Can we go home now? You're stinky."

She let out a ragged laugh. Or maybe it was a sob. Hard to tell with the emotions swirling inside her. "Yes, Wavy-Davey, we can go home now."

She straightened, meeting her mother's worried gaze. "I'm so sorry," Meg whispered.

Emily shook her head. "No kind words, Mom. I need to keep it together until we get back to the farm."

Meg's mouth thinned but she nodded. "You might want to take off the sweater."

Emily carefully pulled the nasty sweater over her head, gagging a little as the scent of vomit hit her again. It had been easy enough to ignore when adrenaline was fueling her. But now the reality of everything that had happened— in front of most of the town and everyone who mattered to her—made her want to curl up in a tiny ball. But she still had her son to take care of, which was the only thing keeping her going.

She stuffed the sweater into a nearby trash can. The memories of this horrible evening would prevent her from ever wearing it again.

"Let's go home," she said and her mother took her hand and led them toward the car.

Chapter 14

Jase had returned to the stage after Emily left and Declan had been hauled away. He'd remained calm even though he'd wanted to walk to the front of that room and rip Charles Thompson to shreds. Everything he'd worked for had been destroyed, but he'd seen Aaron Thompson slip into the hallway as the door closed to the back of the meeting room. At that moment he realized how personal the Thompsons felt about his failure and what lengths they were willing to go to make sure he wasn't elected mayor.

None of that really mattered. All he cared about was the hurt in Emily's eyes as he'd demanded she quiet Davey. It had been his shame talking. She didn't deserve the pain he'd caused her. He'd wanted to follow her to the Crawfords' farm right away, but there had been so much fallout to deal with after the scene his dad had caused.

Jase publicly apologized for his dad's behavior. He wanted to call out Charles Thompson, but he wouldn't stoop to Thompson's level or make excuses for Declan. It had been even more difficult to keep his temper in check when Charles complained as Liam officially ended the meeting and sent the crowd home.

Several of Jase's friends had offered words of encouragement and support, but he could barely hear them over the roar in his head. Jake Travers deemed Edna's ankle only a sprain but she insisted on going to the hospital for an X-ray, so Jase stayed with her until her daughter arrived to take her home. Cole offered to let Declan ride out his bender in one of the town's holding cells.

Jase didn't bother to comment on the irony of his father in jail as he was trying to make a bid to lead the town. It was his worst nightmare come to life.

At least he'd thought it was until arriving at the ranch. Meg had come to the door before he'd knocked.

"I need to see her," he said and opened the screen.

Meg crossed her arms over her chest. "No, Jase."

"I only need a minute," he pleaded, letting the emotions he'd tried to tamp down spill into his tone. "I'll wait if she's putting Davey to bed. Maybe I could—"

"No." Meg's normally warm gaze was frigid as she met his. "She was trying to support you tonight even though it wasn't what she wanted. You hurt her when things went bad." She shook her head. "My daughter has been down that road before, and she's only begun to recover from the pain of it. I won't let her be treated that way again. She deserves better."

"I know." He felt desperate in a way he hadn't in years. He could feel the person he loved slipping away from him, only this time it was his own fault. "I let the moment get the best of me. I love her, Meg."

"You want her, Jase. You have for years. I get that, but it isn't the same as love. What happened tonight wasn't love."

"I made a mistake."

"You might not be the right man for her."

"You're wrong."

"I hope I am, and if Emily decides to allow you back into her life, I won't stop her. But for now she doesn't want to see you. You have enough to deal with in your own life. Focus on that."

"I don't care about anything else." The words came out louder than he'd intended and he forced himself to take a calming breath. "At least tell her I was here. Tell her I'm sorry. Please, Meg."

After a moment she nodded. "You're a good man, Jase. You don't have anything to prove to this town but it's time you start believing it." She backed up and shut the door, leaving him alone on the porch.

This house was the one place he'd always felt safe and welcome, and now he'd messed that up along with his relationship with Emily.

It was close to midnight by the time Jase walked into the sheriff's office. He would have been there earlier, but Cole had texted that his dad was sleeping and he'd alert Jase when Declan woke up. Jase had gone home after leaving the Crawfords' and let Ruby into the yard. As the puppy chased shadows around in the porch light, Jase had sat on the top step and left messages for each of the town council members to apologize for the spectacle his father had created at the meeting.

Declan was sitting on the bench in the holding cell when Jase walked into the office.

"It isn't locked," Cole told him, getting up from his chair, "but he said he wouldn't come out until you got here." He patted Jase on the arm. "I'm going to give the two of you some time. I'll be out front. Let me know if you need anything."

Jase walked forward, wrapped his fingers around the cool iron of the holding cell's bars. "You ready, Dad?"

Declan snorted. "That's all you've got to say to me?"

"If you're looking for me to apologize," Jase ground out, his temper sparking even through the numbness of his exhaustion, "forget it. Drying out in this cell was the safest place for you tonight. After the stunt you pulled—"

"You shouldn't be here." His dad stood, paced from one end of the small cell to the other. "You don't owe me anything, least of all an apology. Why the hell aren't you with Emily?"

"Let's go home."

"I puked on her."

"Yep."

Declan rubbed a hand over his face. "I'm sorry."

"Emily is the one who's owed an apology. Maybe she'll talk to you."

"She won't speak to you?"

Jase shook his head. "Come on, Dad. I'm tired and done with this day."

His father lowered himself back down to the metal bench. "You see me here."

"I see you," Jase said quietly, hating the memories the image conjured.

"This is *me* in here, Jase. Not you. I did this to myself, like my dad and his dad before him. Our trouble is not your responsibility."

"It sure as hell felt like it when you barged into the town hall meeting drunk out of your mind."

"I slipped," Declan said. "I let people get to me and I took one drink."

"One drink ended in the bottom of the bottle. I've seen it too many times, Dad. You can't stop at one drink."

"I know, and I didn't want to. I wanted to lose myself. To forget about everything for a little while."

"Aaron Thompson brought you to the meeting."

"It wasn't his fault, even as much as I'd like it to be. I was at the bar when he found me. Yeah," Declan admitted, "he said some things that set me off more."

"They wanted me to be humiliated."

"I brought tonight's shame on you, Jase. Not the Thompsons. I'm the reason you can't have a life of your own."

"I have a life," Jase argued, but his voice sounded flat to his own ears. Because without Emily he had nothing. "I thought we agreed the town hall meeting was too much for you. If I knew—"

"It wasn't the meeting." Declan stood, reached into the back pocket of his jeans and pulled out a small envelope. "Nearly twenty years later and she can still set me off." He handed the envelope to Jase. "It's a letter from your mom, son."

Jase stared at the loopy cursive on the front of the envelope, disbelief ripping through him. "Why didn't she track down my email or cell number? No one sends letters anymore."

"Your mother was always an original." Declan moved toward the door to the cell. "I don't know what she wrote, but I hope whatever it is gives you some closure."

"Why after all this time?"

"I don't know." He stopped, cupped his rough hand around Jase's cheek. The smell of stale liquor seeped from his skin, both familiar and stomach churning. "What I hope she says is that leaving had nothing to do with you. That she regrets not taking you with her and giving you the life you deserve." His smile was sad as he ruffled Jase's hair. "That's what I hope she says, but I don't want to know. Bennett let me use the phone when I woke up. My AA sponsor is coming by the house in the morning. Whether you believe me or not, this was a one-time mistake."

Jase stood there staring at the envelope for a few more seconds, then turned. "Dad."

Declan turned back, his handle on the door to the outer office. "Yeah?"

"I don't regret staying with you."

"Are you sure you won't stay with Mom?" Noah pulled out from the farm's driveway and started toward town. He and Katie had been home from their honeymoon for a few days so Emily had asked him to go apartment hunting with her.

"I can't keep hiding out there." Emily read the address to the first building, which was in a new development on the far side of town. She watched the midday sun bounce off the snow-dusted peak at the top of Crimson Mountain. The weather was cooler now, and while there hadn't been any snow yet in town, winter would be closing in soon.

"That's not how she thinks of it."

"Doesn't make it less true." She shifted to look at her brother, still tan from his honeymoon on the beach. "I'm staying in Crimson, Noah. I need to start making a life for Davey and me."

"He still likes school?"

She smiled. "He loves it. Since I'm now working in the elementary school front office, I can check in on him during the day." The kindergarten teacher, Erin MacDonald, had made a visit to the farm when Emily kept Davey home from school the day after his public meltdown. While Davey had spent the day building Lego sets and baking cupcakes with his grandma, Emily'd barely been able to get out of bed.

The teacher's sensitivity to Davey's outburst had made its way through Emily's fragile defenses and she'd broken down with all the details of her messed-up life. Erin had immediately called the school principal. The new secretary he'd hired had quit after only two weeks. Emily had an interview the following afternoon and started work the next day. "Millie Travers told me Ms. MacDonald was a great teacher, but she's more. She's a great person." She nudged her brother. "Turns out Crimson is full of great people. Davey is getting access to the resources he needs. He's made a friend—"

"In addition to Brooke?"

"Brooke is his *best* friend," Emily clarified. "But, yes, another boy who loves Lego building. They mainly play side by side, but it's a start."

"Does Henry know how he's doing?"

"I sent him an email," Emily admitted with a shrug. "I don't know what I was hoping for, but he's Davey's father so I thought…" She sighed. "His assistant responded to it."

"The guy is a total idiot."

"Agreed. But we're doing okay without him."

Noah turned onto the road that led into town. The aspen leaves were turning brilliant yellow, shimmering in the sunlight. It gave Emily a bright and shiny glow inside her.

"What about the other idiot in your life?" Noah glanced over at her.

"Jase isn't in my life." She paused, then whispered, "and he's not an idiot."

"You haven't talked to him?"

"You know I haven't, Noah." She'd asked April to go to his office the morning after the meeting to give him Emily's resignation letter. Maybe she should have been brave enough to face him, but the humiliation she'd felt after that night had been too raw.

"Why?"

"There's nothing to say. We want different things." She kept waiting for the pain to ease, the vise around her heart to release. Every time she thought of Jase, her whole body reverberated with the deep ache of missing him. "I hear the election is going well." She'd tried not to hear, not to listen but it was difficult in a small town where people were happy to pass around gossip like it was breaking news.

Noah nodded. "Hard to believe the stunt his dad pulled at the town hall meeting actually helped him in the campaign."

"Not hard with Jase."

"Everyone is talking about how much he's overcome and how he's a self-made success."

"He deserves every bit of his success," Emily said quietly. The Thompsons' plan to discredit Jase in the eyes of voters had backfired. She wasn't the only one who'd seen Aaron as he sent Declan into the town hall meeting. Apparently, Charles had a reputation of bending the rules while he'd been sheriff and no one wanted a man with a twisted moral compass in charge of the town.

"You missed the turn." She straightened in her seat as Noah took a right toward Crimson High School.

"I have a quick stop to make."

"What stop?"

He pulled over to the curb at the edge of the football field. "I'll show you. Hop out."

There were a few teenagers throwing a ball on the field but the stands were empty.

"Do you see it?"

She climbed out of the truck, scanning the bleachers for something familiar. "See what, Noah?"

The truck's engine roared to life and she whirled around. Noah had rolled down the passenger window. "See me making you really angry."

"Have you lost your mind?"

He grimaced. "According to my new wife. I hope you'll forgive me, and I'll be back in ten minutes."

"What are you talking about?"

Noah blew her a kiss and drove off, leaving Emily standing on the sidewalk. She didn't even have her phone. "I'm going to kill him," she muttered.

"It's not his fault," a voice said behind her. She went stock-still even as her knees threatened to sag. "He owed me for something and I called in the favor. He didn't have a choice."

She turned to face Jase, letting anger rise to the top of the mountain of emotions vying for space in her heart. "Of course he had a choice," she said on a hiss of breath. "The same way I have a choice as to which one of you I'm going to murder first."

He took a step toward her and she backed up. "Don't come any closer."

"We need to talk."

She shook her head. What she needed was to get the hell out of there before she gave in to the temptation to plaster herself against him. "No. We don't."

"I need to talk," he clarified.

"Talk to someone who wants to listen to what you have to say."

He ran his hands through his hair, looking as miserable as she felt. "Don't you understand? I only ever cared about you. From the start, Emily."

She closed her eyes and stuck her fingers in her ears, repeating the words *I can't hear you* in a singsong voice.

His hands were on her arms a moment later. She flinched away but secretly wanted to melt into him. She'd missed his warmth. Missed the scent of him, pine and soap and man. Missed everything about him.

"Open your eyes," he said, his tone an irresistible mix of amusement and desperation.

She did, keeping her gaze trained on the football field. Davey would like the symmetry of the lines dissecting the green grass.

"This was where I fell in love with you the first time," Jase whispered, following her gaze. "Every weekend you were at the football games, surrounded by a group of friends. You took great pleasure in ignoring me."

"You were my older brother's best friend. I had no use for you." She glanced back at him and her heart skipped a beat. He was watching her as if it was the first time he'd seen her. As if she really was the only thing he cared about in life.

"And still I was ruined for any other girl." His fingers brushed her hair away from her face. "I remember you on those cool fall nights, bundled up in sweaters and boots, your blond hair like a calling card as you held court in the bleachers. You were the most perfect girl I'd ever seen."

She took a step back, out of his grasp and tried to get a handle on her emotions. "I was a brat."

"I didn't care." His chocolate-brown gaze never wavered as he spoke.

"Why are you telling me this now?"

"Because you need to understand it was always you, Em. You were the first and only thing I ever wanted." He flashed a wry smile and toed his boot against the gravel. "Back then it was because you embodied the perfection that was never a part of my life."

"I wasn't perfect and—"

He pressed his finger to her lips. "Then you returned and *I* got a chance to make you happy. No, you're not perfect. Neither am I. But *real* is better than perfect." He scrubbed a hand over his face and the scratch of his stubble made her melt. Just a little. "I messed up, and I'm sorry. Sorrier than you'll ever know. I let the shame I felt about my own family change me."

"I understand."

"How can you understand when I don't?" He shook his head. "There's no excuse, Emily. I love that boy. Hell, I found myself putting together a Lego town the other night with the bin of blocks you left at the house. I miss him. I miss you."

"I understand life is messy. I wanted it to be put in easy compartments. Even Davey, especially Davey."

"You came here to protect him. I get it."

She shook her head. "I came here to hide. Henry wasn't the only one who failed him. Mothers have dreams for their kids. To-the-moon whoppers like, *Will he grow up to be President?* And the dreams that really mattered. *Will he have friends? Will he be happy?* I felt like I lost control of those the first time I noticed Davey's differences."

He stared at her, patiently waiting as always.

"I want to live life celebrating who he is."

Just when she thought it couldn't get any more painful, Jase ripped open another layer of her heart. "I want that, too, Em. I love you both so much."

And another layer. "I'm pulling out of the mayor's race."

"No," she whispered. "You wouldn't."

"I have a meeting with the council later this afternoon to officially withdraw my name."

"But you're going to win. Charles Thompson—"

"The reasons Charles is running for mayor are as convoluted as mine." The half smile he gave her was weary and strained. A different type of heartache roared through her knowing his distress was her fault. Jase had helped her regain her confidence and spirit, and she'd repaid him by allowing her fears to bring both of them low.

"Your reasons aren't convoluted." She moved to him then, put a hand on his arm. "You are straightforward and selfless. You've done so much already—"

"Trust me, I know what it's like to have fear rule your life. No matter how much I do, I'm scared it isn't enough to make amends for all the mistakes. I worry I'll never be enough."

"Those mistakes weren't yours, but the choice to make a different future for yourself has been." He was standing before her, willing to give up everything he'd built in this town. His whole life. The searing thought that this was exactly what her ex-husband had expected of her almost brought her to her knees.

"My mother contacted me," he said softly. "Her letter is what made Dad drink again."

"Oh, Jase."

He ran a hand through his hair, his jaw tight. "She's sick, and she wants to see me. After so many years, she apologized for leaving."

"You deserve that."

He trailed his fingers over hers, his touch sending shivers of awareness across her skin. "I want to deserve you, Em.

We deserve happiness. Together. Give me another chance to prove how much you mean to me. How much I love you."

She pressed a hand to her chest as if she could quell the pounding of her heart. He was willing to give her exactly what she'd wanted from Henry, but it was so wrong. She loved him for his dedication and sense of duty, for the very *rightness* of who he was. She couldn't allow loving her to destroy his dream. "You can't give up the campaign, Jase."

"I will if it means a chance with you."

"It isn't... You don't..." She took a breath, trying to give her words time to catch up with her racing thoughts. "I wanted to make my life manageable again, but love isn't manageable and neither is everything that comes with it. Life is messy. If I hide from the pain, I risk never having the love. So I'm going to stop hiding. I love Davey the way he is—"

"Me, too," he whispered, his voice raw.

"I know." She reached up, cupped his face with her hands. "You must know you're already enough for the people in this town. For me. You're the one who has to believe it now. I want to support you, even when it's a struggle. We'll find a way. I may not be the perfect politician's wife but—"

"I don't want you to be perfect. I want you, all of you. Your bossiness and your skyscraper-tall defensive walls—"

"Hey." She poked him in the chest.

"I want the way you love Davey so fiercely, the way you bullied me into stepping into my own life." He lifted a hand to trail it across her jaw. "I want you when you're fragile and vulnerable, when you're strong and stubborn. I want Davey and a house full of Lego creations." He dipped his head so they were at eye level. "I want you every day for the rest of our lives."

"You're going to win this election, Jase." She felt tears

slip down her cheeks. "You are the best thing I never expected to happen in my life." She wrapped her arms around
his neck and brushed her lips across his. "How did I miss
seeing you for so long?"

"The only thing that matters is we're here now." He
lifted her into his embrace. "Tell me you'll give us another chance."

She laughed. "A thousand chances, Jase. Because if you
take me on, it's going to be for good."

"For good and forever," he agreed. "Be mine forever."

"Yes," she whispered. "Forever."

He took over the kiss, making it at once tender and fully
possessive. Emily lost herself in the moment, in the feel of
him and the happiness bubbling up inside her like a newly
unearthed spring.

A honking horn had her jerking away a moment later.

"Get a room," Noah called as he slowed the truck. He
grinned at her. "I hope this means you're not mad at me."

"I'm not mad," she called. "But you're still in trouble."

His gaze flicked to Jase. "Are you going to help me
with her?"

Emily growled as Jase laughed. "I wouldn't be dumb
enough to try."

Emily patted him on the shoulder. "Which is why you
get a thousand chances." She pointed at her brother. "You
get none."

He blew her a kiss and she couldn't stop her smile.

"Are we still going apartment hunting?" Noah asked.

"She's got a home," Jase answered. "With me."

"And I get to pick the paint colors?" Emily asked, raising a brow.

"You get to do whatever you want."

She kissed him again. "What I want is to spend the rest

of my life with you." She felt color rise to her cheeks, realizing she'd said too much too soon.

Jase only smiled. "I've only been waiting most of my life," he said, dropping to one knee and pulling a small velvet box out of his jacket pocket. "Emily, will you marry me?"

She swallowed, struggled to take a breath and nodded. He slipped the ring on her finger and stood to take her in his arms once more.

"Katie is going to be so mad she missed this moment," she heard her brother yell. "Good thing I got the whole event on video. Congratulations, you two crazy kids." Noah honked once more, then drove out of the parking lot.

"I love you, Em," Jase whispered. "Forever."

"Forever," she repeated and felt her heart fill with all the happiness it could carry.

* * * * *

SPECIAL EXCERPT FROM

◆ HARLEQUIN
SPECIAL EDITION

*Bethany Robeson already has her hands full with an inherited
house and an overweight pooch named Meatball. She doesn't
dare make room for Shane Dupree, her former high school
sweetheart, now a single dad. Bethany doesn't believe in starting
over, but Shane, baby Wyatt and Meatball could be the family she
always dreamed of...*

*Read on for a sneak peek of
the latest book in the Furever Yours continuity,*
Home is Where the Hound Is *by Melissa Senate!*

"I remember. I remember it all, Bethany."

Jeez. He hadn't meant for his voice to turn so serious, so
reverent. But there was very little chance of hiding his real feelings
when she was around.

"Me, too," she said.

For a few moments they ate in silence.

"Thanks for helping me here," she said. "You've done a lot of
that since I've been back."

"Anytime. And I mean that."

"Ditto," she said.

He reached over and squeezed her hand but didn't let go.
And suddenly he was looking—with that seriousness, with that
reverence—into those green eyes that had also kept him up those
nights when he couldn't stop thinking about her. They both leaned
in at the same time, the kiss soft, tender, then with all the pent-up
passion they'd clearly both been feeling these last days.

She pulled slightly away. "Uh-oh."

He let out a rough exhale, trying to pull himself together. "Right? You're leaving in a couple weeks. Maybe three tops. And I'm solely focused on being the best father I can be. So that's two really good reasons why we shouldn't kiss again." Except he leaned in again.

And so did she. This time there was nothing soft or tender about the kiss. Instead, it was pure passion. His hand wound in her silky brown hair, her hands on his face.

A puppy started barking, then another, then yet another. The three cockapoos.

"They're saving us from getting into trouble," Bethany said, glancing at the time on her phone. "Time for their potty break. They'll be interrupting us all night, so that should keep us in line."

He smiled. "We can get into a lot of trouble in between, though."

Don't miss
Home is Where the Hound Is *by* Melissa Senate,
available March 2022 wherever
Harlequin Special Edition books and ebooks are sold.

Harlequin.com

Love Harlequin romance?

DISCOVER.

Be the first to find out about promotions, news and exclusive content!

 Facebook.com/HarlequinBooks

 Twitter.com/HarlequinBooks

 Instagram.com/HarlequinBooks

 Pinterest.com/HarlequinBooks

 YouTube.com/HarlequinBooks

ReaderService.com

EXPLORE.

Sign up for the Harlequin e-newsletter and download a free book from any series at **TryHarlequin.com**

CONNECT.

Join our Harlequin community to share your thoughts and connect with other romance readers!
Facebook.com/groups/HarlequinConnection

HARLEQUIN

Heartfelt or thrilling, passionate or uplifting—Harlequin is more than just happily-ever-after.

With twelve different series to choose from and new books available every month, you are sure to find stories that will move you, uplift you, inspire and delight you.

SIGN UP FOR THE
HARLEQUIN NEWSLETTER
Be the first to hear about great new reads and exciting offers!

Harlequin.com/newsletters